PRAISE FOR THE NOVELS OF

ERICA HAYES

"Weaves rich, sensual imagery and dark eroticism into a breathless thriller plot . . . Hayes's characters have distinct and delightful voices, and she's developed considerable skill at blending the gritty and the supernatural."

—*Publishers Weekly* (starred review)

"A thrilling and darkly erotic tale of betrayal, passion and redemption that will ensnare the senses with lush prose and a deadly vision of the Fae that conjures fairy tales of old."

—Caitlin Kittredge, bestselling author of *Soul Trade*

"A mind-bending blast into a darkness that enfolds and ensnares you from the first page . . . Pure magic from the word go."

—*Bitten by Books*

"Steamy urban fantasy . . . Magical [and] fast-paced."

—*RT Book Reviews*

"Hayes's debut and series opener exemplifies erotic urban fantasy at its most visceral, illuminating the splendor and squalor of life on the edge. Fans of Laurell K. Hamilton's Merry Gentry novels and Caitlin Kittredge's Nocturne City books will enjoy this tale of sex, violence and the supernatural."

—*Library Journal*

"Readers will thoroughly enjoy this entertaining tale of forbidden love. Erica Hayes has a great future ahead of her as a bestselling author." —*Genre Go Round Reviews*

"Hot, spicy and well-rounded . . . Awesome . . . I'm waiting for the next round!"

—*Tynga's Reviews*

REVELATION

A NOVEL OF THE SEVEN SIGNS

ERICA HAYES

BERKLEY SENSATION, NEW YORK

THE BERKLEY PUBLISHING GROUP
Published by the Penguin Group
Penguin Group (USA) Inc.
375 Hudson Street, New York, New York 10014, USA
Penguin Group (Canada), 90 Eglinton Avenue East, Suite 700, Toronto, Ontario M4P 2Y3, Canada
(a division of Pearson Penguin Canada Inc.) • Penguin Books Ltd., 80 Strand, London WC2R 0RL,
England • Penguin Group Ireland, 25 St. Stephen's Green, Dublin 2, Ireland (a division of Penguin
Books Ltd.) • Penguin Group (Australia), 250 Camberwell Road, Camberwell, Victoria 3124, Australia
(a division of Pearson Australia Group Pty. Ltd.) • Penguin Books India Pvt. Ltd., 11 Community
Centre, Panchsheel Park, New Delhi—110 017, India • Penguin Group (NZ), 67 Apollo Drive,
Rosedale, Auckland 0632, New Zealand (a division of Pearson New Zealand Ltd.) • Penguin Books
(South Africa) (Pty.) Ltd., 24 Sturdee Avenue, Rosebank, Johannesburg 2196, South Africa

Penguin Books Ltd., Registered Offices: 80 Strand, London WC2R 0RL, England

This is a work of fiction. Names, characters, places, and incidents either are the product of the author's
imagination or are used fictitiously, and any resemblance to actual persons, living or dead, business
establishments, events, or locales is entirely coincidental. The publisher does not have any control over
and does not assume any responsibility for author or third-party websites or their content.

REVELATION

A Berkley Sensation Book / published by arrangement with the author

PUBLISHING HISTORY
Berkley Sensation mass-market edition / October 2012

ISBN: 978-0-425-25837-8

BERKLEY SENSATION®
Berkley Sensation Books are published by The Berkley Publishing Group,
a division of Penguin Group (USA) Inc.,
375 Hudson Street, New York, New York 10014.
BERKLEY SENSATION® is a registered trademark of Penguin Group (USA) Inc.
The "B" design is a trademark of Penguin Group (USA) Inc.

PRINTED IN THE UNITED STATES OF AMERICA

10 9 8 7 6 5 4 3 2 1

ALWAYS LEARNING   **PEARSON**

CHAPTER 1

And the second angel poured out his vial into the sea,
and it became as the blood of a dead man,
and every living thing in the sea died . . .

—REVELATION 16:3

Today, of all days. It was Thursday. The world couldn't end on a Thursday.

Luniel, the fallen angel, crouched on the shore of Liberty Island in a hot August sunset with blood lapping at his feet. It licked the rocks beneath his boots, clotting. All the way across the bay, to the firelit Brooklyn shore and the gleaming blue arcs of the Narrows Bridge, what used to be water gleamed sick and scarlet.

The angel sniffed the air, and tasted copper. A dead fish bobbed belly-up, pale white flesh and fins. He poked the warm liquid with his finger, and licked. Yeah. Definitely blood. And human. There were seaweeds and algae that sported the same fleshy color. But Luniel had tasted enough blood in his three thousand years to know this wasn't algae.

He straightened. No breeze flicked his long black hair back. In his human guise, he had no wings. He scanned the distant shore with sharp blue eyes, further than any human could see, and his nose twitched. Hunting. For something. Anything. A trick. A college prank. A fish slaughterhouse. Overflow from some industrial accident, one of the factories along the built-up Jersey waterfront spilling toxic chemicals.

Not a sign of the Apocalypse. Not God's wrath.

Across the bloody bay, Babylon's glittering towers razored

the red sky, the decadent sprawl of skyscrapers and spires they once called Manhattan. The sunset flashed on steel and mirrored windows, glaring in competition with neon lights and rainbow columns of virtual advertising. Even from here, Lune's preternatural ears detected buzzing electrics, the faint digital beep of comms towers, snatches of conversations, and in his magical angelsight, the city glowed, green with the living, pulsing energy of human souls.

Helicopters lasered their searchlights through smoke and heat haze, sweeping over burned-out housing projects and shining condominiums. Traffic noise hummed—the groaning subway, horns and engines and wailing sirens, police and fire and the ever-more-urgent ambulances. At the height of summer, plague had stolen into the Empire State like a homicidal houseguest, more frightening than California dengue and deadlier than arctic flu, and people were afraid.

But terror happened in Babylon, the world's richest, rottenest city of sin. You only had to look at the shining glass spire piercing the sky, one hundred and ten stories high, built back in wiser days where a pair of ill-fated twin towers once stood. The world had turned ever more rapidly to shit since then, but Luniel still remembered that day well. That day, angels dived for earth, fiery wings flashing, but it was too late. Even the fallen, like Lune, were powerless. The people screamed and died and thought the world was ending.

Horrific? Yeah. But the monkeys had no idea what they were in for.

What the end of the world would really be like.

Luniel shivered. This wasn't over yet. It couldn't be.

He dug into his jeans pocket for his phone, and speed-dialed. Trendy SIM implants in your ears were all very well for humans, but fast-healing angelflesh rejected biotech. The irony was pleasing and bitter. "Come on, Ithiel," he muttered. "Answer your rotted phone."

Ithiel was still on heaven's A-list, but he and Lune stayed in contact. If anything was going down, Ith would know. But voicemail kicked in, his brother's laid-back laughter: *I'm busy. Leave a message. If I give a shit, I'll call back.*

Luniel swore—even after centuries, defiance felt good—and

waited for the beep. "Party never stops upstairs, huh. Call me, asshole," he said, and ended the call.

A week. Ithiel hadn't answered for a week. And now this.

It could be stupid luck. Coincidence. Random events colliding like flotsam.

But after two millennia spent dealing out heaven's wrath, and going on another one walking the earth and seeing it all from the other side, Luniel was wearily certain that what goes around, comes around to kick you in the balls.

Coincidence was bullshit. Nothing was random. Everything happened for a reason, and fate was one dastardly, despicable motherfucker you just couldn't avoid.

But inexorably—inexplicably—the blood lapping at his feet made him angry.

Defiantly, recklessly, sinfully angry.

He unclenched his fingers, and called another number. Above him, Lady Liberty looked on, unmoved. "Dash, it's Lune. There's something I think you should see."

"Lune, you old dog." Dashiel's voice, rough with whiskey and centuries of shouting on the battlefield. A shuffle, his hand over the phone to block out music, clinking glass, the laughter and noise of a party. "Got my hands full here. Can it wait?"

"No. I'm on the shore at Liberty Island. Get down here."

"Okay, but I warn you . . ."

Warm breeze rippled Lune's hair, and Dashiel materialized with a white flash and a *whoomph* of displaced air. Dashiel was the leader of their fallen gang, a bunch of shunned angels called the Tainted Host, still chained in servitude to a heaven that liked to pretend they didn't exist. The Tainted had done bad things, but not bad enough to get cast into hell forever. They were one step away from damnation. Which kinda made it hard to say no to any of the dirty jobs heaven handed out.

". . . if that luscious little lady blows me off, I'll blame you," finished Dash, stuffing his phone back into his pocket. Rich brown hair tied back, sun-bronzed skin, flashing dark eyes. Lune was taller than most humans, but Dash stacked inches on that, and pounds of extra muscle to match. He wore dark jeans, a white shirt and a golden snakecharm on leather around his neck, and he had a cherry-red lipstick kiss on his cheek.

He folded his wings, ruffling shiny feathers the color of espresso flecked with gold. "What's the emergency?"

Luniel sighed, and slipped his phone away. "Jesus. Stealth it up, Dash. It's the twenty-first century, not the Dark Ages. We're not exactly top of the charts these days."

"Like anyone can see me," Dashiel scoffed, but he did cover up, sliding on his human guise. Not that it helped much. His wings vanished, and his coloring faded to a more acceptable level, so it didn't dazzle human eyes. That was all. He still looked unearthly.

They all did. Long ago, when they'd been created, they'd needed no better disguise. Getting recognized as heaven's messenger was totally okay, back when forty-day floods and burning bushes were the rage. These days, faith was a war, with every street corner the battlefield. Nothing like making yourself a target.

Dash rolled his massive shoulders, adjusting his balance. "Satisfied? What's going on, dude? And what's that stink?" He stared, and sucked in a breath. "Holy shit."

"It's holy some damn thing. Blood in the ocean. The second sign. You know anything about this?"

"Nope." Dash crouched and swiped a sword-callused hand through the gore, bringing up a clotted handful. He rubbed his fingers together, and grimaced. "The archangels don't tell me anything. You know that. They just call when they want someone's ass kicked."

Fuck. Lune had hoped it was all under control. He'd never been too good at saving people. Get too close, they depend on you, and then *splat*! Shit happens, and you're alone and guilty. "Mike didn't mention anything?"

"Very funny. Mike never mentions anything. Still, that doesn't mean it's . . . y'know." Dash wiggled his fingers in mock mystery. "The End. Could just be—"

"Ithiel's missing, Dash." Luniel's voice strained tight.

Dash scratched his head, streaking blood. "Uh-huh. 'Off on heaven's secret business' missing? Or, y'know. 'Missing' missing?"

"Hasn't answered for a week. He always answers. You know the story, Dash. Seven vials of Himself's wrath, hidden by seven guardian angels. Empty them out, spill the seven plagues and it's all over. What if . . ." Lune hesitated. "What if Ithiel's a Guardian? And something's happened to him?"

Dash frowned. "Like what? Even if you're right, which I'm not saying you are, there's this thing kicking around called God's Plan. You might have heard of it? If the big guy says it's over, it's over."

Lune shook his dark head, stubborn. "No. Ithiel would've told me. Something's not right, and it's not just the sea going O-positive."

Garbage lapped the shore in bloody clumps. Dash poked at a dead fish with his boot. "Say you're right. Been a while since I read much. The sea turning to blood is the second plague? What's number one? Something about sores and shit?"

"'The first angel poured out his vial upon the earth, and there fell a noisome and grievous sore upon men,'" Lune recited dramatically. A chill rippled his spine, and he longed to stretch his wings and fly away. "Shit. The Manhattan virus."

"Huh?"

"Don't you watch CNN? They're calling it the zombie plague. Broke out a few weeks ago in Babylon. Rots human flesh, eventually kills them. But it turns them into cunning homicidal maniacs first. It's a real beauty."

Dash stared, silent. And then he laughed, humorless, shaking his dark head. "Oh, man. Save my life from becoming a bad movie."

"Dude, your life is already a bad movie. Complete with naked girls and bow-chicka-bow-wow."

"Watch it and weep," said Dash cheerfully. "A few more naked girls in *your* life might pull that stick from up your ass. When's the last time you got some action?"

"Bite me."

"That long, huh? It's not like you're no one's type, Lune. Chicks dig that bad-boy look."

Oh, yeah. Chicks dug it, all right. Chicks digging it wasn't the problem. The problem was getting them to undig it afterwards. Lune had learned his lesson a long time ago: don't get attached. It only ever ends in disaster.

But still, his body flushed hot and hard thinking about a woman's sweet curves. A human woman, by choice. Now he was Tainted, he didn't have to worry too much about the little sins, and Dash was right about one thing: it'd been one fuck of a long time. Female angels were beautiful, but something about human women

aroused Lune most deliciously. He'd always liked their fleshy
scents, their skin's hot salty flavor, the slick honey of their sex . . .

He snorted, avoiding the issue. "The last time? Wait, let me
see. Oh, yeah. That was right before the fucking Apocalypse
started and no one told me."

"Worst damn excuse I ever heard." Dash sighed, shoving his
hands in his pockets. "Okay. This could be just coincidence. I'll
call Mike, see if I can get the latest. But only because I like you,
Lune. You know that asshole makes me want to punch him."

"So punch him. What's he gonna do, shun you again?"

Dash guffawed. "Oh, stop it, you saucy hussy. Don't tempt
me. You wanna come?"

Lune gulped. Ever since he'd fallen foul of Michael's wrath—
it didn't matter how you felt about a woman, lust was still a sin
for an angel of heaven—the saccharine scent of archangel made
him sweat. And Michael himself was . . . hard to take.

"Ah. No. I'm gonna look for Ithiel. Why don't you take
Japheth?" he suggested. Japheth was another of the Tainted, a
mighty warrior shunned for the sin of pride. "He was Mike's
favorite once."

"And I still wonder about that boy's taste in men. I'll give
him a call. Maybe he can flirt Mike into fessing up." Dash
thumped Lune on the shoulder, affectionate. "Don't worry, kid.
You'll find your brother shacked up with a lady, or on some
secret messenger-of-oh-by-the-way-you're-screwed mission. All
this Apocalypse shit will be piss and wind. Just you watch."

"Just you watch," echoed Lune faintly as Dash disappeared.

He sighed. He should get on and look for Ithiel. He knew his
brother's scent like he knew his own. He'd cruise the city, make
a few calls. Shouldn't be too hard.

But his gaze kept drawing back to the ocean of blood.

Thing was, when the world ended, humans had somewhere to
go, be it heaven or hell. They lived forever. But unless they earned
redemption—or, more likely, heaven lost patience and finally cast
them into damnation—Tainted angels were soulless. When it all
wrapped up, they'd be . . . nothing. Emptiness. Oblivion.

Luniel glanced down at the rising blood tide, and the salty
meat stink crawled into his guts and coiled there, uneasy.

All piss and wind.

For all their sakes, it'd better be.

CHAPTER 2

In the dim green-lit laboratory, Dr. Morgan Sterling sighed, defeated, and dropped her long glass eyedropper into its metal dish. Her digital microscope's screen glared smugly at her, and she switched the display off and twisted back her sweaty hair.

Another no-result. The virus-infected cells on her slide just squirmed and evaded the serum until it imploded and died. She'd been trying for two weeks to work up some kind of antibody reaction, but none of her solutions sustained the smallest effect for more than a second or two.

Damn it.

Morgan slid off her stool and peeled off her plastic gloves, dropping them in the trash. "Lights," she ordered, and the white fluorescents flickered on, illuminating her laboratory's stainless steel benches, glass-fronted refrigerators and banks of digital tissue analysis equipment. All this technology, and this damn Manhattan virus still eluded her.

She unbuttoned her white coat and laid it over a chair, fluffing out her long dark curls. To be fair to herself, this was the Babylon chief medical examiner's office, not a disease control lab, and she was no expert virologist but just a junior pathologist who did autopsies for a living. City hall had called in the WHO and the infectious diseases crew from the CDC in Atlanta, and from the daily e-mail updates, no one was making any more headway than she.

But Morgan knew enough about virology to be disappointed she couldn't do more. She'd probably get fired for using CME resources for this, even though she was doing it on her own time. Which was why she was in the office at nine on a Thursday night, instead of at home or dating her non-existent boyfriend. Morgan wasn't big on boyfriends. Sure, she liked men, and they generally found her attractive, at least to start with. She just didn't have time for relationships when lives were at stake.

And lives were always at stake.

Beyond an internal window covered with half-open venetians, the office TV blared in shimmering 3D, a newscast featuring some religious nutter raving on about God's will and the end of the world.

Morgan snorted. Yeah, right. If there really was a God, It didn't give a shit one way or the other. She'd seen religion ruin enough lives to figure that out. It was the main reason she'd become a doctor—science meant explanations, answers, truth. Religion offered only lies and maybes.

And you sure saw a lot of those on TV these days. Twenty years of a hard-line right-wing White House had spread the war on terror to a third of the globe. The United States had made a lot of enemies, foreign and domestic, and citizens under constant threat of homegrown terror turned to God and extremism to justify their paranoia. The global economy was just one more theatre in the conflict. Wall Street soared on the back of clandestine arms deals and aggressive corporate shock tactics, and the rich got richer, while uptown, urban decay ruled, and warring gangs killed each other on the streets in the name of God. The fanatical incumbents in city hall whipped up the tension with discrimination and overzealous police presence. Some called it a new age of prosperity and righteousness—the new Babylon. Others called it asking for trouble.

Morgan pushed through plastic double doors into the deserted office. The religious nutter on the TV wasn't screaming or waving his hands, she saw. He was well groomed and handsome, with short dark hair, a neat suit and calm Latino eyes. He spoke intelligently, articulately, without hyperbole.

Didn't mean he wasn't a frickin' nutter.

They shouldn't try to cure the Manhattan virus, he said, because the disease represented God's will. It was His way of exposing sinners. The Bible said only those carrying the Beast's mark would be affected. Everyone else was safe. All we need do is pray for *deliverance, amen*!

Morgan watched for a few moments, her lip curling. God's will was a city in fear? Twelve hundred fatalities in a week, the National Guard barricading the streets and a temporary morgue in Central Park overflowing with corpses?

Preachers, churchmen, evangelists. No matter what religion, they were all the same. All liars. This guy on the TV was more dangerous, because he seemed normal. People would believe him. And when he turned on them, they'd stare and sob and say, *"What the hell happened? He seemed so nice and genuine."*

Her throat tightened, angry, and she gripped the asthma inhaler in her pocket and forced herself to breathe. "TV off," she snapped, and the screen flicked silent.

The cultist who'd seduced her mother had seemed nice and genuine, too. Right up until sixteen-year-old Morgan had hopped off the Lexington Avenue subway after Spanish class at Hillary Clinton High to find her mother on the living room floor, her Bible in her hand and a shotgun beside her. Blood everywhere. Bits of her brain dripping down the walls.

The cops had found the e-mails inciting suicide on her mother's tablet, but the cult leader who sent them had long skipped town. Similar suicides were discovered throughout the city. All part of the bastard's plan.

All her family's money had gone to the cult. All their possessions. Morgan had to pay her way through college and med school on full scholarships and part-time jobs. But she'd made it, without any help. Whenever she faltered, her mother's messy death sustained her. Depending on others was deadly. Blind trust was a killer.

But Morgan Sterling, MD, junior assistant medical examiner for Babylon County, controlled her own destiny now. And she wouldn't pray for deliverance from anyone.

The door banged open, and Suhail, the lab assistant, pushed in a trolley loaded with tissue samples in yellow plastic iceboxes, the black biohazard symbol printed on the side. "Another load for you, Dr. M.," he said cheerfully, a grin on his young face.

Suhail was studying at med school, and worked at the morgue part-time, when he wasn't smoking dope and raising hell with his numerous lurid gang boyfriends. He had messy dye-blond hair and a tongue stud, and wore a t-shirt with a cartoon of a phallic-looking rocket launcher and the words STICK THIS UP YOUR JIHAD.

He also sported a cut lip and the remains of a juicy black eye. Morgan guessed that in gang-happy Babylon, full of militant Latinos and Aryan white supremacists, a mouthy gay Arab anarchist got beaten up by pretty much everyone. But like Morgan, Suhail doggedly made the best of what he had, even if it wasn't much.

"Thanks, So-so," Morgan said. "In the last fridge. I'm almost full up." Manhattan virus was virulent and so far 100 percent lethal, but not particularly infectious. It could be transmitted by blood and fluid contact, like biting or access to an open wound. Only level-two precautions were required for samples in the lab, the same as hepatitis C or HIV. But in the wild, it was another story. When it came to spreading the infection, Manhattan's victims were cunning—and determined.

"Sure thing. A few more homicide DOAs down in the morgue, too." Suhail leaned his skinny brown elbow on his cart like the top-class time-waster he was, and lowered his voice conspiratorially. "So how's it going? You finding anything on the hush-hush?"

"Nope." Morgan bit her lip. Medicine couldn't solve every problem. But neither did it promise all the answers. She'd helped the CDC track down the virus's likely zero point, which was a start. But it was far from a cure.

"The boss, has he figured you out yet?"

His delight made her smile. Suhail liked breaking the rules, and he'd covered for her enough times, hoarding samples and fiddling paperwork and making excuses to the boss. She snorted. "J.C.? Like he'd stick his head out of his office for me."

"This is not what I hear." Suhail scratched his tight-jeaned ass loftily.

"Well, you heard wrong."

He winced. "Oh. Sorry. Bad date?"

"Something like that." Morgan sighed. "I'd better go prepare those autopsies, just in case. Give me a reason to be here so late."

"Yeah. Clear out a few fridges, why doncha? We're still swamped, even with the deadhouse tent in the Park." He chuckled. "Babylon County, Stiffs 'R' Us."

She stifled a laugh. The irony of a crazy gangboy like Suhail working in the county morgue didn't escape her. Half the corpses she examined were gang-related deaths. Still, you had to keep your sense of humor, and at least Suhail didn't spout religious platitudes while he was raising hell. "Sorry, tell me again why you're studying to be a doctor?"

He grinned. "Gotta contribute to society while I'm tearing it down."

"Well, you'd better hurry, or these damn nutters on TV will get in ahead of you. What are they trying to do, scare people?" Frustration crept into her voice. She'd volunteered for duty down at the temporary morgue. Of course she had. But her boss held a lottery, and she'd lost out. Someone still had to deal with the boring old gunshot homicides, gang assassinations, honor killings and victims of impressionist serial killers. Babylon's moniker as "crime capital of the country" was well earned, and the happy-sick funmongers didn't all take a vacation just because a nightmare plague had broken out.

Suhail fiddled with his twin-pinned steel earrings. "Hell, I believe in God. Maybe it's the end of the world, just like that preacher guy's saying. God's plan, and all that?"

She smiled. "I don't think so. The world's tougher than we think. We were all going to die of arctic flu, too, remember? Global warming? We're still here."

"I thought you believed in science, Dr. M." Suhail winked slyly.

"I do, smart-ass." Morgan tossed a rolled-up ball of paper at him, and he caught it, grinning. "What I don't believe in is scaremongering, and conjecture masquerading as data. I want proof before I'll batten down the hatches. How about 2012? That turned out to be bullshit."

"My grandma said she prayed all night that night. Just in case."

"Well, good for her," said Morgan shortly. The very idea that one person's blind wishes could alter events offended her. Even the Chairman of the Joint Chiefs, who warned nightly on the news in her severe blue Air Force uniform that the Manhattan virus might be a biological attack by terrorists—or the paranoid conspiracy theorists on the internet who insisted that The Government Did It—made more sense than that.

And that made it all the more important to Morgan that a cure for Manhattan was found. If it could be cured, it was no miracle.

"Yeah," agreed Suhail cheerfully, wheeling his cart towards the fridge. "She said I'll burn in hell, too. Not sure if that was for being nice to all you lousy unbelievers or for taking it up the ass, but still." He shrugged, tolerant. "Pity the mean old tart isn't still alive. She could try her praying mojo out on this one. Can't hurt, right?"

"Guess not," Morgan lied, smiling weakly for politeness' sake. Yes, it could hurt. It could hurt very deeply. "I gotta go. See ya."

"Have a good one, Dr. M.," he called, already loading her samples onto the stainless steel shelves.

Morgan grabbed her flash memory voice recorder and hurried out, through the office doors and down a long vinyl corridor. More fluorescents gleamed, the lemony scent of anti-viral spray hanging. At this hour, no one was about—*oh, hell.*

The CME poked his dark head from his office door, tie loose around his unbuttoned collar. "Morgan? You still here?"

"Sure am, Dr. Torres. Just finishing up tomorrow's prep." She kept walking, like she had something better to do and the work was keeping her.

Juan Carlos Torres was a fine doctor and a good boss. But lately, he kinda gave her the creeps. She should've known dating him would be a mistake. Sure, he was a little older than she— mid-forties to her thirtysomething—but he was good-looking and clever, and she'd thought they might have something in common. Something they could talk about.

Turned out they did. All he wanted to talk about was work. He hadn't asked her a single question about herself. They'd discussed cases and autopsy techniques all evening, and the worst part was, she'd had a good time.

A good time. Christ. Emotional avoidance much? He hadn't even tried to kiss her. If that was her idea of a hot date, she really needed to get out more.

Dr. Torres smiled absently, already heading back to his desk. "Don't stay too late. All work and no play."

"Sure thing." She snorted under her breath. *Physician, heal thyself.* Like he didn't sleep here half the time. Although, given the influx of work lately, a bed in the office wouldn't be a bad idea . . .

Ouch. That settled it. When she was done here, she was going out for a drink. A nice modern bar had opened on Third Avenue, just around the corner from her building, where no one did drugs or started gang-related fights, at least not yet. Maybe she'd even talk to a man. One who wasn't wearing a white coat or pushing a sample trolley.

Or lying on a cold metal slab. Dead guys were low maintenance, but their conversation sucked.

She grinned, and walked down the steps to the mortuary.

Thick plastic sheets sealed in the air-conditioned atmosphere, keeping the pressure constant, and she keyed in her pass code and entered the cool sanctum. Pale vinyl floor punctured with drains, rows of steel autopsy benches and sinks under bright lights. A digital thermostat on the wall kept the temperature even, and the ventilation system hummed. Steel trolleys carried rows of stainless instruments on white paper lining.

She strode past the benches to the refrigeration area, where one wall was filled entirely with square steel doors, their handles shining. Bodies could be stored here for months awaiting court rulings, though more commonly, autopsies were completed and the bodies released to the families within a few days. Mostly, samples sufficed for long-term storage, though lately a backlog had built up.

She checked the plastic clipboard hanging on the wall. Two new arrivals, signed in with Suhail's scrawled initials. Fridges twenty-one and twenty-two. Initial autopsy prep involved checking the body for obvious trauma, making sure it correlated with the police's suspected cause of death, reading through the police notes for any factors that might mean the autopsy needed to be done urgently and noting any irregularities that might call for the CME's personal attendance to be scheduled. It was paperwork, diarizing, prioritizing. Mortuary triage. Menial work, but it required a qualified ME.

Yes. Just what any self-respecting single girl should be doing at 9:00 p.m. Hanging out with dead guys. At least, there was no chance of date rape.

Morgan shrugged into another white coat, snapped on plastic gloves, and opened fridge twenty-one.

The trolley slid out easily on greased wheels, loaded with its black rubber body bag. She slid the handwritten notes from the pocket on the front, flipping past case ID codes and serial numbers.

Caucasian male, twenty-eight to thirty-five, DOA, single stab wound to the chest plus multiple lacerations. Dumped in Battery Park, no witnesses (yeah, right, probably a dozen people standing right there and no one saw a thing) and no weapons found on the scene. Big guy, too, if the bag's shape was any guide. She set her recorder on the trolley and pulled the zipper down.

It jammed. She gripped the plastic edges and pulled harder. The bag popped open, and something white and fluffy puffed into her face.

She jumped back, waving her hands to clear the air. Shit. If that was white powder, she was going to march down to First Precinct homicide and shoot whoever wrote those notes. Once she finished dying of anthrax.

But as the fluff settled, she realized it wasn't powder.

Feathers.

The body bag was stuffed with soft white feathers. Downy little ones that drifted and curled on the air, as well as long sleek ones with thick pale cores. They smelled of sugar, or candy. Some were smeared with blood.

Morgan sneezed, and waved her hands again. Nice prank. Any evidence on the body would be contaminated. She yanked the zipper fully open, and scraped the feathered heap aside, revealing pale flesh, strong limbs, a heavily muscled torso.

Single stab wound to the chest, all right. This guy had been run through. Gingerly, she touched the puncture wound, between two ribs just to the left of his sternum. Something had pierced clean through the intercostal muscles and into his heart. Bone fragments were shoved in deep, the flesh torn, like the weapon had been twisted to make the kill. A sharp piece of metal or alloy, broader than a knife. A sword, or maybe a spear. Babylon gangs had all kinds of weapons these days.

She brushed feathers from his face, and pursed her lips. *Well, hello, gorgeous.* Even in death, this dude was hot. Long golden hair, stained with blood. Beautiful lips, fair lashes on ice-carved cheekbones purpled with bruises. Worked out, too, his chest and abs defined like an athlete's.

She tore her gaze away, flushing. *Perving on a dead guy. Wow, Morgan. That's totally normal. Set the "mortuary attendants aren't all necrophiliacs" campaign back fifty years, why don't you?*

More feathers wrapped under the body—if smart-ass Suhail did this, she'd stick something up his jihad, that's for sure—and she tugged them free.

They wouldn't come. She tugged harder, and the body's shoulder twisted, revealing . . .

She stumbled backwards, hands flying to her mouth.

Holy shit on toast. The guy had wings.

Honest to God, feathered wings. Jointed to his shoulders like an . . . well, like a guy with wings.

It can't be.

She edged closer, holding her breath, poking at his shoulder to lift it. Pale dead skin, curving over his scapula. Tiny feathers thickening over a large spheroid joint, and . . . a wing bone, long and thick like a second humerus, lined with muscle and tendon. Damn. If this was body-modification surgery, it was the best she'd seen. No scar tissue at all, and the feathers . . . well, they'd been *growing.* She could see new ones pushing through underneath. She poked harder, and the joint twisted easily, ligaments flexing beneath the skin. Just like the real thing.

It had to be the real thing.

Excitement tingled in her bones. Amazing. She'd never seen anything like it. Hell, no one had seen anything like it, apparently including the idiot CSI who'd stuffed this into a body bag without noticing a thing. *Caucasian male, my ass. It's the frickin' bird man!*

Her mind raced. *Calm down. It could be a hoax. Do some tests. Get proof.*

She should call Dr. Torres, get some corroboration . . . *No, don't call Torres yet.* If it was a body-mod, it was expensive and purpose built. It could be military. She should get pictures first, e-mail them to herself in case someone tried to cover up her discovery before she could find corroborating evidence.

Paranoia? Maybe. But this was the age of spin and secrecy, and both city hall and the feds were ruthless, even if she didn't believe they'd planted the Manhattan virus. Seekers for truth—scientists, journalists, hackers, whistle-blowers—had a habit of disappearing.

She sprinted back into the cutting room for the tiny digital camera. Battery full. Excellent. She skidded back, fearful, but the bird man was still there. Unbelievable.

She folded the body bag back neatly, and started snapping shots from every angle. The flash fired, lighting the room in glare. Sweet. She should roll the body over, get some close-ups. Just one more shot . . .

White light erupted, brighter than any flashbulb.

She gasped, dazzled. Breeze ruffled her hair. Her elbow hit the trolley, and the camera jolted from her fingers.

A hand gripped her arm, steadying her. A man's voice, deep and unfamiliar. "Sorry, lady. I didn't think anyone would be here. Are you—oh, shit."

Her vision cleared, and she scrabbled on the floor for her camera. "Jesus, you scared the hell outta . . . oh!" She looked up, and fell right back onto her ass, her nerves in disarray.

Whoa. Not just tall, or big. *More,* in every way compared to . . . well, compared to a normal man.

This guy wasn't normal.

Black hair, blacker than soot and wilder than music. Blue eyes, hotter and deeper than summer sky, luminous pale skin, long dark lashes any woman would kill for. Arms thicker than her thighs, in a dark shirt with no sleeves, strong wrists that made her weak, hands that could crush rocks. And his thighs in those jeans . . . long, powerful, rippling as he moved.

His face was familiar, she realized. Those carved cheek-bones and, umm, luscious lips. The bird man. Only Birdy was blond, and this guy was dark and . . . tasty.

His gaze lasered onto hers, relentless, and she shivered. He looked dangerous. Driven. Not a patient man.

Morgan scrambled up, struggling to keep her mind on the issues. This was Babylon, the psycho-killer capital. Well-adjusted guys didn't break into morgues after hours. But how Mr. Huge-Dark-And-Oh-By-The-Way-Totally-Hot had gotten in here was beside the point. So was how easy it'd be for a guy his size to tear her limb from limb, or worse.

He'd seen Birdy's body. She couldn't call security. Not yet. Not before she'd preserved the evidence.

She licked her lips. "Um. Hi. I was just . . ."

He strode up to the trolley, and his fingers clenched the edge, hard enough to dent the steel. On drugs. That explained the crazy swirl in his eyes. "You found my brother," he said stiffly. "I guess asking how he died is redundant."

"Umm . . . he's . . . well . . ." Morgan stuttered, unable to keep it in any longer. "He's a frickin' bird man! Who the hell are you?"

He turned, and to her surprise, he laughed.

Her guts melted, like warm honey, and she shivered again. So beautiful. So smooth and melodic. She wanted to press her thighs together, feel his tingling warmth . . .

Or not. Her indignation sparked. He hadn't answered her question. Who the hell was he?

The guy with the Rohypnol laugh shook his head. "Bird man. Christ. You people. Never believe what's right in front of you."

"Sorry, but I'm a scientist. I believe what I can see." Morgan folded her arms, defiant, and edged closer to the wall where the alarm button was. Screw collecting more evidence. This guy was seriously creeping her out, and it wasn't just because he had her thinking about sex instead of squirting him with capsicum spray.

"You do, do you?" His gaze flicked to the alarm button, and back to her, and swift as the flashbulb he dived forward and grabbed her arm. "Then believe this."

Light shimmered again, dazzling. And glossy black wings burst from his shoulders in a rain of golden glitter.

Morgan's heart catapulted, and she gulped for breath. The golden light glimmered, and dissolved.

But his lush midnight feathers didn't. And he held her, his body close in the heady scent of altar smoke. His whisper rumbled through her chest. "I'm sorry. I can't let you call your security. You never should have seen any of this, but it's too late for that now. My name is Luniel. That's Ithiel, my twin. He's an angel. And so am I."

* * *

Morgan struggled, her mind blanking. It couldn't be true. Not possible. She must be dreaming. Yet . . .

She wriggled, beating at his massive forearm. "Let me go!"

He let go.

She stumbled away, rounding on him. More fool him. Whatever this guy was, he wasn't to be trusted. "Sorry. Not possible. I don't believe in angels."

"Not my problem." The man—Luniel—shrugged, feathers ruffling. His accent was elusive, a mixture of exotic and familiar, like he came from no place in particular.

"It'll be your problem when I call the cops, you freak." The dude still wore a shirt with no sleeves, and the wings—*his* wings—fit easily into the cutaway space. Blacker than black, like soot, broader than his massive shoulders, and long, the tips of the feathers reaching to mid-calf. It looked so real.

Morgan's mind stuttered. She must be dreaming. But if this was a dream, surely he'd be wearing white robes and a halo? Instead of all dark and smoldering and . . . and sinful, like some insane Mardi Gras biker?

She sidled backwards, towards her desk in the cutting room. A girl didn't grow up in Babylon without learning some self-defense. Her pistol was in the drawer. Maybe she could get away, lock him in, call security. Calling 9-1-1 was a waste of time, despite her threat. Resources were stretched, and police response to anything short of a terrorist plot in progress just didn't happen.

Luniel stalked her, midnight wings flaring. "Freak? Wow. I'm so pleased to meet you . . . I'm sorry, what didn't you say your name was?"

"I'm Dr. Morgan Sterling. This is my mortuary. You're trespassing." Behind an autopsy bench, a few steps closer to the desk.

He circled, leaning over the bench on two hands, muscles flexing. "As they say these days, Dr. Sterling: whatever. Tell me where they found my brother."

She fumbled against the desk, feeling behind her. "Screw you."

"Is that an offer? I'm touched." His hot blue gaze drilled her, magnetic. "But not distracted. Come on, Doctor, it's important."

She ripped the drawer open and grabbed the pistol, leveling it at him two-handed and thumbing the safety off. "So's this. Back off."

"No." He vaulted the bench with ease, landing silently before her on wafting wings. Careless of her pistol. Unruffled, like a panther facing a hissing pussy cat, some small, insignificant creature who posed no threat.

His delicious scent paralyzed her, a rich toffee sweetness. Her mouth dried. He was luminous, dazzling, too perfect to be real. Certainly too perfect to be telling the truth. "Get away."

"Wait, let's see. Umm . . . no." He cocked his head, and reached for her hair, stroking it with one finger. "You're very pretty, Morgan Sterling. Pity if that got spoiled. Tell me about my brother."

Now her gun was trapped between them. Her hands quivered, her memory of defensive moves a blank. "Get away! I'll shoot!"

"No, you won't." He wrapped her hair around his fingers, and leaned closer, sniffing her. "You're a doctor. You don't hurt people."

"Don't bet on it." She inhaled, and squeezed the trigger.

The shot thundered. Blood exploded on his chest, spattering her face. She let out a shuddering breath.

But Luniel didn't fall.

He just cursed—most unangelic—and stunned her immobile with a burning blue glare. His palm flashed up, and impossible light welled from it, and her last thought before sinking into velvety black nothingness was that it was just typical that a lying bastard of an angel should be so infernally beautiful.

CHAPTER 3

Light summer breeze swirled in red twilight around Lady Liberty's torch, bringing the scent of blood. Inside the ringed iron railing, Dashiel paced in golden-edged shadow, his rich brown wings taut and eager for flight. Squawking gulls dived around him.

Below, the bay lay stagnant, stinking, dead things floating. No boats chugged through the congealed mess, and a big orange Staten Island ferry sat motionless, its engines clogged, while helicopters hovered like blowflies, winching the passengers away. On the glittering Babylon shore, a crowd shouted and pointed. Sirens howled, flashing police lights staining the purpling sky blue.

This wasn't how it was supposed to happen.

Not the blood, mind. Dash had seen enough portents in his time—made enough himself—to know that nothing in the Book was metaphor. He'd dived in sultry storm clouds above the Flood, watched Sodom burn and Egypt's crops vanish under a plague of hungry locusts. If the Book said the sea would turn to blood, that's exactly what it meant.

But there were supposed to be warnings. Meetings. Shit, he'd expected at least a text message. Even his Tainted were still part of the team.

Maybe Lune was right. Something gonzo was going down here. And hell, Ithiel could be a Vial Guardian, for all Dash knew. Those guys' identities were well-guarded secrets. Seven bottles of holy wrath weren't the kind of thing you wanted turning up on eBay.

Answers. He needed them. Only one place to go.

He flipped out his phone. It rang for a long time before anyone picked up. "Hey, it's Dashiel . . . Yeah, the lousy sinner. I'm flattered. I need to see Mike . . . What? I don't give a toss about his schedule, it's important. Just . . ." He swore, wings flaring. "Listen, you sniveling little worm. When's the last time I called? That's right. Like, never. So if I say I need to see him, I fucking well need to see him . . . Yeah, no shit. Thanks ever so. Tell him I'll be by."

He ended the call, and added, "Shithead." Mike's staff. Worse than librarians. Not that Dash ever spent much time in libraries. If you asked him, *waiting for the movie* was the twentieth century's finest achievement.

He called another number. "Japheth, my good son. Can I have a word?"

"Sure." Japheth's musical voice was low, and some kind of god-awful yowling echoed in the background. "How about, bugger off, I'm busy?"

"Hey, you answered. I'm on Liberty Island. Get down here."

A glitter of breeze, and Japheth materialized, crouched on the spiked railing. Golden hair shot through with bronze spilled over the shoulders of his tuxedo. His white shirt shone crisp and luminous, his black tie flawless. He'd tucked his gilded wings away, but now he let them reappear, and they shimmered and coalesced as they fit through his black jacket.

Just a little breath of glory, a leftover from more righteous days. It had been the easiest way to get dressed for the last eight centuries, since men started wearing clothes that covered them to the neck. Robes and togas and shit like that were easy, with loose fabric that folded where you wanted it. All this stitching was a cow.

Japheth hopped down, feathers twitching, and quirked a perfect golden eyebrow, his hot green eyes impatient. Good-looking son of a bitch, even for an angel. "What do you want, Dash? I'm in the middle of something."

"Yeah, I heard the wailing. Rocking that fetish club again?" Heh. The day Japheth indulged himself, they'd all get ice-skating lessons in hell. Japheth was too keen on redemption to ever have any fun. He thought that if he stayed sinless, one day heaven might take him back. A total waste of the lad's first-class chick-magnet action, if he ever asked Dash's opinion, which he didn't.

"Covent Garden, actually." Japheth flicked a stray bronze feather from his black sleeve, impervious. "Verdi."

"You were at the fucking opera. Jesus. Torturing yourself won't earn you fun credits with the boss."

"And giving me rubbish won't change the fact that you're an inbred redneck with no taste. You've got lipstick on your face."

Dash grinned, and wiped his cheek. "No way. How'd that get there?"

"Other side. That's it. What do you want, Dash?"

"You looked down since you got here?"

Japheth leaned over the rail, and for a long moment, he was silent. "Uh-huh. Is that, uh, what I think it is?"

"We don't know. Lune thinks it is. Says some virus is the first plague. All I know is, no one said jack shit to me about it."

Japheth twirled his golden curls absently. "Oh, lord."

"Yeah." Together, they watched the last scarlet sliver of sun-set, breeze teasing their feathers alive. Japheth's faint golden glow smelled of coffee and warm sugar, and it brought back memories. Cities leveled, demons felled with flaming swords. No coffee in those days, of course. Jae had smelled of frankin-cense and sandalwood oil. You had to move with the times. But Japheth was a mighty warrior back in the day, and they'd fought side by side on ancient battlefields soaked with blood and dying screams.

Perhaps too mighty a warrior, too eager to pour heaven's glory upon himself. Japheth's pride in his deeds brought him undone.

Inwardly, Dashiel shrugged. Whatever. If you were kick-ass, you were, and no point denying it. Pride was a harmless sin, compared to some. Like Dash's own, for starters. Better not to go there.

The memories shone rich with death and sorrow, but with comradeship, too. Dash allowed a smile. Jae was a snotty little shit sometimes, but it was kinda cool to have him around.

"So," said Japheth at length, loosening his bow tie and flicking the top button undone. "What are we doing about it?"

"You know what. We need to know who's doing this, kid. If it's all heaven's idea, and they just forgot to tell us, fine. Gotta get us an update. You coming?"

Jae flushed, looking away. "I dunno—"

"C'mon, he'll behave if you're there."

"Don't count on it. You know he gets off on tormenting me."

"Only because you let him." Michael and Japheth had been close. Like brothers, except more complicated. But Michael had shunned him without a blink. That had to hurt.

"What else can I do? He's got something I want, and he knows it."

For once, Dash chose to let the obvious tease go by. "To rejoin Club Holy?" he scoffed. "Maybe you want it a bit too much. What's so wrong with the way things are?"

"Oh, I don't know." Japheth shrugged, angry. "An eternity of crappy jobs with no reward? Oh, and oblivion at the end of time?"

"It doesn't have to be like that—"

"I want to go home, Dash." Rage and grief shone bright in Japheth's eyes. "I want to swim in the sunlight and kill demons and drink with the girls without wondering if I'm doing anything wrong. Not wallow in the dirt down here, fishing for favors and looking away every time I see something I like. Is that too much to ask?"

Dashiel clapped him on the shoulder, awkward. Jae abstained from everything, women included, in the hope that one day he'd be redeemed. But it wasn't making him happy. And as for redemption . . . well, Dash wasn't holding his breath for Mike to change his mind. "Maybe not, kid. For now, let's get this shitstorm sorted. You coming or not?"

Japheth sighed. "Of course I'm coming. Think I'd let you go without me?"

Dashiel grinned, and they vanished.

They flashed into Michael's courtyard, and hot moonlight blinded them.

Dash blinked, eyes watering. Beside him, Japheth did the same, sweat already running from his golden hair.

A high-walled garden, awash with flowers, fragrant with frangipani and musk. The moon shone fat and bright, glaring over a yellow stucco town house with blond awnings that still radiated the day's warmth. Cicadas buzzed over distant electric club music, and heat shimmered the air, hotter even than an August night in Babylon.

Michael had always liked the heat. *Cold's all very well for grinding them down,* the archangel had confided to Dash once, as they'd gazed over a victorious battlefield by the Euphrates, the scorching sand littered with the bodies of the damned. *But you want to drive the monkeys really insane? Toss out a whiff of blood feud and stick 'em in the desert for a thousand years. Then you'll see some entertainment.*

A silvery swimming pool almost filled the terra-cotta-paved courtyard. A few naked human girls and guys swam and splashed, and by the pool, more lolled and dozed and smoked crack pipes on low lounges, breasts and lithe limbs still oiled from sunbathing. On the other side, a bunch of them were having lazy sex, kissing and thrusting and moaning. Dash could see at least two dildos, a double penetration and stuff he didn't even know the names for going on in that little lot. The air rippled with grunts and sighs. Another blond girl was bent over a bench, a guy taking her from behind and spanking her with a barbed whip, while another one pleasured himself deep in her mouth. She moaned and thrust back harder as the whip drew blood.

"Charming," murmured Japheth, shifting to human shape for a moment to shrug his tux jacket off in the heat and toss it aside. "We miss all the good parties." But an undercurrent of contempt tainted his voice sharp as his golden wings shimmered back in.

"Speak for yourself," said Dash cheerfully.

"Where are we?"

"Ibiza."

"What's he doing in Ibiza?"

"Do you need to ask?" Dash gestured, and Japheth sighed. Because there, against the courtyard wall in a jasmine vine's dappled moon shadow, stood Michael.

Naked. Shining with oil and sweat. Ice-pale hair tousled and damp, glittering glacier-blue wings swept back. The broad, luminous curve of his back flexed, thigh muscles rippling as he fucked whatever it was he had trapped between him and the wall, slow and hard. Boy or girl, human or angel or monster, it didn't matter to him, and despite what some people thought, no one in heaven gave a damn either. An equal-opportunity slayer of sanity, was Michael.

Dash sauntered up, dragging Japheth with him. Jae looked overdressed in his crisp white shirt. They both did. "Mike, how's it hanging?"

No reaction. Asshole.

The girl—it was a girl—whimpered, her eyes glazed, cheek pressed to the rough plaster. Michael's hair fell on her shoulder, shining ice-bright in the moonlight, and the ends sliced fine scarlet cuts into her skin. Bite marks bled on her throat, her breasts pink and bruised.

After five millennia, the archangel knew his own strength. He just didn't care.

"Michael." Japheth's voice was soft, short.

Michael glanced around, diamond-blue eyes glowing with pleasure. His smile flashed, homicidal. "Just a sec," he murmured, and in a few more hard thrusts, he came, sighing deeply. The girl writhed and shrieked, like she'd been burned, which she possibly had. Many things about Michael were deadlier than they looked.

The archangel lighted off her, and drifted gracefully over to them. His naked body glowed in hot moonbeams, moist and magnificent. Dash was totally straight, but he knew perfection when he saw it.

"Japheth, what a lovely surprise. You look stunning." Michael pulled the golden-winged angel into a hug.

Japheth didn't hug him back, Dash noticed. Just stood there, eyes closed, until Michael stepped away.

"And Dashiel," Michael added, not so warm. "How nice. Shall we go inside?" He slipped a black silken wrap around his hips and led the way, feet barely brushing the tiles.

Inside, beyond wide glass doors, lay a dark living room, cool and scented with orange blossom. Bookshelves stuffed neatly, a television, bottles of spirits in rows. Not Michael's things. Just some place he borrowed.

But a curled-iron birdcage hung from a stand, and a fat white cherub plopped on its ass inside, plump little legs dangling outside the bars. On the floor sat another cage, and inside hunkered a pale, bruised hellcreature on an inward-spiked neck chain. His pointy head shone hairless, and finlike wings sprouted from his knobbly back. He muttered and chewed his fingers, ravenous.

Michael's pets. The cherub was new. Mike tended to kill his playthings. But the knuckle-munching demon-thing was a favorite, apparently, and Dashiel's stomach coiled as Michael wiggled affectionate fingers through the bars and dropped in a ragged-tendoned human bone. The thing scuttled over on all fours and grabbed it, gnawing with satisfaction.

A scrawny human minion in a white waiter's uniform scrambled to pour iced water, and Michael flung himself onto the black velvet couch. "What?"

Dash sat opposite, tugging an unwilling Japheth beside him. He sipped his drink, relishing the chilled liquid, and sent the minion a blistering scowl, just in case it was the one who'd answered the phone. "What do you know about blood in Babylon Bay?"

"Nothing." Michael didn't hesitate. "What do you know about it?"

Dash glanced at Jae, who sighed and answered. "Luniel called us tonight. The bay is full of human blood. All the fish are dead or dying. You can imagine what we're thinking."

Michael pursed his lips, ice-blue eyes sharp.

Dash called up a news website on his phone, flipping the screen around so Michael could see. "Strike two. Manhattan virus. Rotting skin and munchies with a taste for human flesh. It's all over Babylon County."

Michael read, and waved his elegant hand, dismissive. "This is a sign, that's a sign, my pumpkin looks like Jesus. We got up to the fifth sign back in the twenties. Turned out it was just coincidence, and some asshole in Nevada with a cloud seeder—"

"Ithiel's missing, Michael," interrupted Japheth coldly. "You and I both know what that means. His vial could be compromised. Are you seriously telling me you know nothing about this?"

Michael stared, and new ice crackled in his glass.

Dash's drink froze solid, halfway through a sip. Icicles stung his tongue, and his feathers prickled in the sudden chill. "Well, fuck you, too," he whispered in Japheth's ear. Little shit hadn't told he knew Ithiel was a Guardian.

Japheth just shrugged. He and Michael still had issues, obviously. But how deep did it go?

Michael tossed away his frozen glass, and it smashed. "Phone," he snapped, and the minion scrambled to deliver.

The archangel called a number, and listened impatiently. "Pick the fuck up, Ithiel." But after several rings, he flung the phone onto the couch and cursed. Dash's eyes stung, and a green fern in the corner withered and died. "Okay," Michael snapped. "This goes no further than this room, hear me? Find the little bastard and bring him here."

"Lune's already on it." But dismay slicked Dash's nerves cold. If Michael truly knew nothing . . . "What if Ithiel's dead, and the vial's gone? What if . . . someone did this on purpose?"

"Then find me a demon with a vial in his trash that used to be full of the boss's wrath, and gut me the son of a sinner."

Dashiel gulped. Demons, stealing God's wrath? Jesus in a fucking jam jar.

"What did you think, that it was an accident?" Michael scowled, frigid. "No, this has hell's fingerprints all over it. Find me Ithiel. And figure out why there's a zombie plague in Babylon. Find me proof, a demon sigil, anything. If those goat-fucking ashlickers are at it again, I want to know five minutes ago."

The caged hell-thing giggled and scratched his scrawny belly with his bone. "Never fucked a goat."

"Goats have higher standards." Michael glared at it, and the cage bars glowed hot. The creature yelped, hopping on blistered feet. Michael sighed. "God's warts, you're so pathetic."

"Can we please concentrate?" Japheth snapped. "Killing these demons won't stop the chain of signs, not if they've already dispersed the holy wrath. What about the other Guardians? If they're in danger, shouldn't we warn them?"

"Easier said than done." Michael gave him an eye-aching smile. "No one knows who they are. Not even I."

Dash frowned. "But Ithiel—"

"Was like his brother: a charming idiot who couldn't keep his mouth shut. The other Guardians are . . . more subtle." Michael ruffled his shining hair with one wing. "No, it can't be done. Not yet. Bring me proof that demons are doing this, and

I'll take it upstairs. Until then, we deal with what we know. Off the books. Get me?"

Dash nodded, brusque, and stood, only half-satisfied. Michael could be cruel and capricious, but he was one hell of a leader when the shitstorm hit. Still, something didn't sit right with Dash.

Like why Michael wouldn't tell the boss right away. What was in it for him to delay? Even if they were wrong, surely . . .

Chill rippled Dash's spine, a sharp threat, and Michael caught his gaze. "Don't second-guess me, Dashiel," the archangel said mildly, but his eyes glinted like icy shards, deadly. "I still own you. You'll do as I say. Are we clear?"

Dash held his stare a few seconds, then dipped his head briefly. "Sure. No problem."

"Good. Get to it. Oh, and Japheth?" Michael called as they turned to leave. Japheth looked back, and Michael grinned. "You've got my number, babe. Call me. Ibiza gets so boring this time of year."

Michael lounged on the soft black couch and watched them vanish, his feathers twitching.

Fucking demon scum. This better not be true.

Rage flashed his ice-blue wings bright, and he grabbed his phone and hurled it at the window, glass splintering in flame. He'd slaughtered so many demons, his dreams were hip deep in blood, drenched in ragged screams. And it never. Ever. Stopped.

How many times had he throttled evil down to hell? And how many times had he watched it rise again?

It was enough to fucking tire you out. And after five thousand years, Michael was over it. Let the bloody world end, for all he cared. At least he'd get some rest.

Briefly, he debated calling Gabe and washing his hands of the whole mess. *You're the Annunciator, big brother. Go fucking announce this, and let's get it over with.*

But doubt nagged, and he tugged his ice-blond hair into a thoughtful handful. He'd always told Gabriel that keeping those vials was a goddamn stupid idea. If the demon princes really were hijacking the Apocalypse—twisting Himself's wrath to their own ends—someone better call the Kid and have him resurrect St. John of Patmos, because there'd be some serious rewriting to do. Funhouse mirror Revelation. Not a pretty sight. Their eventual goal? To pervert the prophecy, of course. Satan's victory at the End of Days. Hell, quite literally, on earth.

Well, screw that for a shitty idea. Michael had tangled with too many demons in his time to think he'd get off lightly if the hellmunchers won. He'd be first on Satan's buttfuck-with-a-pitchfork list if the stinky little weasel ever broke out of prison and stayed out.

No, letting the demons have it all their own way would never do. And besides, in the good version, Michael got to hack Satan's guts out at the end. After a few plagues, and so forth, but that was immaterial. The monkeys got the trouble, Michael got the glory.

And Michael had always craved glory.

Still, that didn't mean a deal couldn't be done to smooth things over for both sides. That was what he'd invented the Tainted Host for. Damning disobedient warrior angels was a waste of good talent. So the Tainted were neither damned nor saved—he just took their souls off them for a while, as incentive. They were no longer bound by heaven's rules, and there was the added bonus of plausible deniability if they fucked up.

But Dashiel and his gang remained frustratingly honorable. Even Japheth had turned into a rebellious little snot lately. Still, the Tainted weren't Michael's only tools . . .

"Zuul," he called softly. "You can come out now."

The creature in the cage snuffled and fawned, big eyes wet. Michael cricked one finger, and the cage door lock sprang open.

The chained demon—for it was a demon, a sly middle-management hellskank he'd tricked into servitude—crawled out on skinned knees, and flattened its face into the carpet, shiny fins quivering.

"Get up," Michael snapped. "And change yourself. You make me puke."

It snorted, and changed to human form in a puff of bitter ashes. Crimson-haired boy, pale body slight in loose pants and an open shirt, spiked collar still drawing blood around his neck.

Zuul inclined his handsome head, dark eyes warm. "Master."

"You heard all that?"

"Yes, Master." Zuul bowed. Zuul always bowed. He was a demon of pain. He liked humiliating himself.

Michael tossed him a smile that made him cringe. "And what do you think of it?"

"Sounds delightful, Master."

"You think so."

Another bow, a glint of amusement. "Certainly, Master. Or . . . is Master afraid?"

Michael backhanded him, knocking him to the floor with blood spraying from his lips. Zuul groaned in a heap, his eyes glowing red with pleasure and pain.

"You enjoyed that, didn't you?" Michael laughed, indulgent. "Afraid? Of Satan? Please. I'd back myself and a sharp flaming sword over that skanky he-trollop any day of the week. It'll be the first decent fight I've had in years." His wings flexed, aroused. "Bring it on."

"Forgive me, Master." Zuul crawled forwards, neck chain dragging, his face almost scraping the floor. "I thought . . . Master and the Lord of Lies are brothers?"

"That monkeyslime is *not* my brother." Contempt soured Michael's mouth, and he spat snowflakes. He and Lucifer had loathed each other since the beginning. Too alike.

"But—"

"It's way above your pay scale, scumbag, so I don't expect you to understand, but the whole Lucifer-thrown-out-of-heaven thing?" Michael scowled. "Trust me, Zuul. I was there, and it wasn't romantic or tragic. Satan didn't get evicted because he was proud or clever or questioned Himself's will. Any angel worth his feathers does that every day."

"If you say so, Master. Then . . . why?"

Michael relapsed onto the sofa, twitching his feathers to soothe them. Just remembering that fateful night itched his wrath trigger. He'd argued with the boss until his tongue bled razors, but He wouldn't relent. "Satan got evicted, my precious hellbaby, because he's a vicious, sadistic, selfish little motherfucker with shit for a conscience who wants it all for himself. My only regret about the whole sordid episode is that I didn't get to eviscerate him on the spot."

Zuul licked bleeding lips, hopeful. "Master is most wonderfully wrathful."

"Am I? We'll see." Michael smiled, cold. "Enough chitchat. Here's what you'll do, Zuul. Take a leave pass. Get your whimpering ass to Babylon and find me whoever's doing this. On the sly, you understand. Don't tell him I want to talk to him. Just find out who it is, and report back to me."

"Yes, Master." Zuul bowed again, obedient, crimson hair nearly brushing his knees. "Your vaguest whim is my command."

Whatever. Michael knew the psychopathic little bastard would run screeching to his demon lord the moment he got free. But that was okay. If the lords of hell interfered with Dashiel and his Tainted friends on their fact-finding mission, so much the better.

What Michael needed was time. Time to analyze, figure the best way forward. And he wouldn't get it with Luniel chasing after Ithiel's killer like a jealous lover. The demons would only accelerate their plans if Lune pissed them off.

Stopping a Dark Apocalypse was probably a good idea. Then again, what was the rush? So long as the right side won in the end, and Michael got his glory. Why wait around for God to pull the plug, when a bunch of demons would do the job for him?

He'd wait and see. Bait a few demon traps, see what crawled in. And if it meant a few Tainted angels got slaughtered, so be it. Dashiel, by choice. Too clever and uppity for his own good. And Dash already suspected something wasn't right. If Dash interfered—went over Michael's head and called Gabriel, for example . . .

Michael grimaced. That'd never do. Gabe always insisted on doing everything according to the Plan. Perhaps it was time Dash met with an unlucky accident.

He fidgeted, his blood stirring. He was getting antsy again. Using that girl's body hadn't calmed his nerves one whit. That was the downside of earth-shattering power and longevity that spanned the eons—everything was old news. Nothing quite hit the spot anymore. And when nothing truly sated your appetite, you were always hungry.

Always.

By the pool, no doubt the orgy still lingered on, but he'd been there, done that with all of them. A new club had just opened by the beach. Maybe he'd go cruising, enthrall some new disciples.

Party boys and girls liked the idea of fucking an angel, especially with their veins stuffed with drugs and their eyes glazed by his glory. Whether they liked the reality so much, once they'd seen how he liked to play . . . well, that wasn't his problem.

He waved an impatient hand, and Zuul's chained collar fell away. "Get going, filth. And remember what I said."

"Yes, Master. May I humbly beg your indulgence, Master?" Zuul rushed up and knelt at his feet, glossy crimson hair falling to hide his face.

"What is it?"

The pain demon craned his bleeding neck upwards. His dark eyes flamed red with desire, and his lips shone wet. "Hit me again?"

Michael's flesh stirred, and his lips curled in a smile. Then again, maybe he'd stay in a while.

He rose, slipping his silken wrap from his hips. Already, he was hard. "Ask me nicely."

Zuul cowered in anticipation, and started to beg.

And soon, the room filled with the scent of blood and the demon's shuddering screams.

Hot summer shadows ghosted around the summit of 30 Rockefeller Plaza, and in a puff of ashen breeze, Zuul materialized in human form, perched on a concrete pillar with his legs dangling over the edge. Seventy floors below, the city glittered and burned, oblivious.

He shifted, muscles aching deliciously, and a lazy smile licked his lips. Michael had beaten him within a breath of unconsciousness, and it had felt so good he'd made more than one mess on the floor. Then they'd fucked, and the hot hard thrust of the archangel entering him made Zuul scream with miserable delight. Angel and demon flesh burned like acid on contact, and the agony was a thing of beauty. Besides, the archangel's cock was a fucking prodigy. Michael had come three times without losing his hard-on, and he'd only stopped because Zuul fainted and didn't scream anymore.

Warm breeze lifted Zuul's bloodred hair, and he bit his lip, tasting the memory. His body had already healed the damage, but his lust for pain was insatiable. He devoured it, stored it up inside him and consumed it. It sustained him, and Michael's appetite for dealing it out had yet to be sated.

Still, the handsome archangel was just a fling, a casual if scorching-hot affair. The real prize yet awaited him.

The reign of Satan. Living hell on earth. An eternity of endless, incomparable torture, dealt out by the most prodigious torturer of them all. Zuul's dick got hard again just thinking about it, and he squirmed. The Lord of Pain. Nothing Michael offered could match that. The sooner this Apocalypse got going, the better.

Chill wind licked his skin, and the scalloped metal railing iced itself to his palms.

Zuul stumbled off the fence, his spine crackling cold. Skin ripped from his hands, delicious, but he paid no attention.

"Welcome, Zuul." The deep, empty voice swirled around him like arctic wind.

Zuul's guts knotted, though he could see no one. Just shadows, dark and shifting like a living creature.

Azaroth. Lord of Emptiness. Prince of Anguish. Bringer of Unholy Misery. The Demon King had many forms, human, animal and . . . elsewhat.

He bowed, shivering, and it wasn't the flirty obeisance he gave Michael. This was pure terror. Somehow, he kept his voice steady. "My king."

The shadows eddied, frost crackling on the glass walls. "What news?"

Zuul swallowed. "Michael is suspicious, my king. He sent me to find the one in charge."

"Does he know I am responsible?"

"He said not, my king, and I believe him. His Tainted are tracking down the signs."

"The Tainted Host." Contempt cracked the glass, and fragments fell, whistled away by the wind. "Weaklings and hypocrites. I shall take pleasure in eviscerating their emotions. You have done well."

"Thank you, my king," said Zuul fervently. But his hands shook. The coming of Satan, bringer of the torment Zuul craved, was one thing. But Azaroth, Satan's would-be savior . . .

He shuddered. Azaroth knew your darkest fears, and fed them to you mercilessly. Sought your deepest need, and tore it away from you forever.

"Very well, Zuul. You shall be rewarded."

Agony spiked down Zuul's spine, straight to his balls, the pain so intense and beautiful he whimpered and let himself go, a hot rending flood of sensation that crippled him. He fell to his knees, limp. His nerves howled, muscles turning to water. He crumpled onto his face and squeezed his thighs, but it was no good. He was going to dirty himself.

The shadows flickered mildly. "You know what to do now. My plagues must be allowed to take hold, Zuul, if Satan is to rise and return. My demon princes must proceed unmolested. See that they do."

He felt Azaroth smile, cold as a corpse. "Y-y-yes, my king." Stalk the Tainted, put obstacles in their way. Hinder their feeble efforts to stop Azaroth's plan. Zuul had a posse of imps at his command that would do the job nicely.

"And Zuul?" Azaroth's voice faded to an icy whisper.

"Yes, my king?"

The shadows drifted away, but Azaroth's voice echoed deep in Zuul's bones. "Defy me, and I'll lock you in a fleshless prison for eternity, with nothing but numbness for company."

Zuul's bladder let go, and he crawled to his knees in terrified tears and stumbled away.

CHAPTER 4

The woman fell, and Luniel caught her in his arms.

His mind stumbled. That gloryflash would only stun her. Her bullet couldn't harm him. The wound had already healed, only a bloody smear left on his shirt. It didn't matter. She'd shot him, calm and determined, though she obviously feared him. At the end, she'd understood what he was. He'd seen it in her lovely honey-dark eyes: blankness, then recognition, then amazement and distrust.

And now he held her, her lithe female body warm against his chest, and her cool dark hair spilled over his arms and her scent made him drunk on forbidden memory and he didn't know what to do. Surely, someone had heard that gunshot, would come to help her. But no one had. The place was empty. They were alone.

Ithiel was dead, killed by a demon prince's sword. A fucking demon prince. Christ. If Ithiel was a Vial Guardian, and the vial was stolen . . . Lune shuddered. The Apocalypse with Michael at the helm was scary enough. If demons were emptying the vials . . .

Catastrophe. Everything prophesied would be perverted. In the Book, the seven plagues cleansed the earth and made way for heaven's victory in the final battle. If demons twisted His holy wrath to their own ends, the opposite would happen. Evil would overrun the earth, and hell would win.

But first things first.

Morgan had seen both him and Ithiel uncloaked. Recognized them for what they were. She'd remember, and even with the remnants of his holy powers, he couldn't trick that away. He should take Ithiel's body and get rid of this Dr. Morgan Sterling, before she ran screaming to the world that she'd seen an angel.

But for some reason, he didn't want to let her go. Her heartbeat raced lightly against his chest. It made his skin tingle into bumps, his feathers springing alive. Her breasts felt so soft and full. Her legs were so long and shapely in sheer smoky stockings, covered to the knee by that prim office skirt, but luscious. And she smelled so good, lab chemicals and soap, yes, but underneath, a dusting of glimmer-sweet perfume over the hot musky scent of female skin and sex.

He bent closer, sniffing, and a growl simmered in his throat. So delicious. He hadn't held a human woman like this—one who wasn't dead or screaming—in centuries. He'd forgotten how . . . tempting they were. And this one was exquisite. He'd seen her look at him, appreciation firing her gaze. Maybe he could just . . .

No. Get rid of her, Lune. Kill her while she's still going to a good place, and get out of here. You know what happens if you get involved.

But his body reacted, blood pumping hot and hard between his legs, and the ache of longing in his flesh wouldn't ease. She was beautiful. Any man would be tempted by those curving hips, her sinful dark hair, her lickable lips. But it wasn't just her beauty that made him ache. It was the fire in her eyes. The defiance. The *screw you, angel, I don't believe in you.*

Made him want to claim her. Tame her. Lick and plunge and stroke that defiance into fever. Hold her down beneath him and pleasure her until she screamed his name in submission.

His cock twitched, and hardened further, and he groaned. *Yeah. Because that turned out so well last time.*

Morgan murmured, stirring. Her lips parted as she breathed deeply. Her white coat and blouse pulled taut, revealing more of the soft curve of her breast. Her lacy black bra's edge peeked out.

He wanted to slip his finger inside. Longed to pop the buttons, reveal what lay underneath. What color would her nipples be? He imagined the springy feel of them on his tongue. By the time he finished sucking and biting them, they'd be pink and hard, so swollen . . .

Yeah. Bad idea. Once demons got wind of any attachment, even a whiff of affection passing between angel and human, that human became a target for their vicious power games. Screwing around worked okay for Dashiel, because Dash truly didn't care. He didn't get attached. Lune wasn't like that. He'd never been like that. Wherever he lay, he left a piece of his heart behind, and demons took sniggering delight in eating it up.

He'd seen enough souls spin screaming to damnation because of him. Just one, long ago. But one was enough.

Lune gritted his teeth in frustration. So what was he supposed to do, kill her? Just for being in the wrong place at the wrong time? She wasn't his enemy. He wasn't a murderer. And Christ, she smelled glorious. He could smell the soft wet flesh between her thighs. Wanted to ease his fingers inside her, stroke her, feel that moist warmth just one more time . . .

Can't make love to her. Can't kill her. What are you going to do, Lune? Walk away, now she's seen what you are? There's a word for people who've had one little glimpse of heaven. Insane. You think she deserves that, just because you blundered in here without paying attention?

Inwardly, he cursed, but the truth was inescapable. This was the twenty-first century. Modern humans were too damn reasonable, especially the science-y ones like Morgan Sterling. They couldn't just accept this shit without explanation anymore. And he'd gone too far already to wash his hands of her now. She at least deserved the choice. He'd just have to make the best of a bad situation.

Yeah. Because it's not like you just want her, or anything.

He drifted his lips over hers, letting their breath mingle, and magical glory tingled over his skin, a tiny euphoria spell he hoped would calm her down enough to talk. "Morgan," he whispered, resisting the desperate need to slant his mouth over hers, taste her lips, kiss her until they both couldn't breathe. "Don't be afraid. Wake up."

* * *

Morgan stirred, her slumber dissolving in gentle heat that wrapped her like a sparkling blanket. Cool air flowed over her skin, the mortuary's familiar chemical odor, but the arms holding her were warm. A man's arms, strong, protective, her head resting against his chest.

She inhaled, dreamy. God, he smelled fantastic, melted chocolate and whiskey and every sinful thing.

Lips brushed hers, a searing caress, his warm breath tingling her tongue. "Morgan," he whispered, and her name sounded so soft and wonderful in his mouth. "Wake up."

Warmth stole deep into her belly. The flesh between her legs tingled. Mmm. What a way to wake up.

"Don't be afraid." His whisper dizzied her, so calm and safe. "I won't hurt you."

His hair drifted over her cheek, long and silken, imbued with that powerful sweet scent, and she moaned in surrender and tilted her mouth up for his kiss.

His lips danced over hers, an intake of his breath. "Morgan . . ."

"Mmm." She pressed closer. "Kiss me."

And he did, with a soft groan. Oh, wow. So hot. So wonderful. So deeply sexy, she shuddered. His lips explored hers, tasting, tempting her to open. She parted her lips. His tongue teased inside to caress hers, and heat sparkled down her body, sinking deep into her flesh where she ached. And now he gasped, and kissed her harder, deeper. Her breasts swelled to be touched. Heat slicked between her legs, ready for him, and beneath her his body strained hard and tense. Oh, yes. She'd not been touched like this in far too long. She was so ready. How good he would feel, easing inside her . . . She sighed, and shifted her thighs apart, inviting.

A groan rumbled inside his chest. "Morgan. Don't. We have to stop."

Well, maybe so soon was unreasonable. She blinked, sleepy, and opened her eyes.

Soot-black hair tumbled on her shoulder. A massive chest, bare arms, curving male lips still shiny with her kiss. Burning eyes, deep sky blue. And behind him . . . glossy feathers, blacker than black.

She jerked backwards, her heart pounding even harder.

Shit. The lunatic bird guy.

She'd let him hold her. Let him *kiss* her. And damn it all if he hadn't felt as shiveringly, achingly good as any man she'd ever touched.

Hell, he *looked* better than any man she'd ever touched. And it was disgustingly fitting that an angel of God—or whoever—would be so gorgeous. So seductive.

All the better to screw you over with, my dear.

She tried to leap out of his embrace, but her feet found nothing. The bastard was holding her. Carrying her, effortlessly, like a bride over the threshold. She struggled, kicking. "Let me go, you brute!"

And he did, setting her gently on her feet. But his gaze didn't let her go. It blazed deep into her body, rich with desire. He had a hard-on for her. At least he was honest about that.

Morgan staggered back, wiping her mouth, her thoughts racing. Her gun. No good. He'd already picked it up. In any case, she'd already shot him, and the wound was gone. Just a blot on his dark shirt. And no one had come running to help her. Did no one hear the shot? Had everyone gone home? And then, she'd kissed him. Opened her mouth to let him in, and he'd made her ache, for things and in ways that no man had for a very long time.

But he wasn't a man. He was an angel, as mad as that sounded. And angels, no doubt, just like preachers, were all filthy liars.

She struggled to reset her mind, adapt, make it believe. Angels existed. Fine. That didn't mean there was a God who cared. And it didn't mean angels were good. On the contrary. She could never trust this . . . *creature*. No matter how good a kisser he was.

She swallowed. "Just . . . just don't touch me, okay? What's going on? Why are you here? And what's that . . ." She waved her hand, impatient. "That thing doing in my refrigerator?"

"Fair questions." He didn't release her. Didn't look away. "Do you really want the answers, or are you just giving me your tough-chick act to make a point?"

"What's that supposed to mean?"

A massive shrug. "It means you've got a choice. You can turn away, let me do what I've gotta do and pretend like this never happened. That'd be best."

"Or?"

"Or, you can open your eyes."

"I choose door number two."

The angel laughed, harsh like glass. "You won't be able to unsee what I show you. Believe me, you'll want to."

She didn't drop her gaze. "I'm a doctor. A scientist. I always want the truth. If you think you can manage that much."

He stared back at her, grim. And then he leapt backwards on a sweep of black wings, and settled his annoyingly cute butt on the autopsy bench, elbows resting on knees and fingers locked together. "Okay," he said lightly. "Your choice. Don't say I didn't warn you. You ready, or are you going to pass out again?"

"Screw you, okay? It's been kind of a rough night."

"They did that a lot in the Dark Ages, you know. Fainted whenever we came by. People falling on their faces left and right. It got tiresome. I'm like, 'This is His holy word, folks! Show a bit of class. Now's not the time to cower in the ditch like a dog. Stand up like a man and listen.'" He settled his wings, long feathers curling on the steel. "Or woman, as the case may be. Twenty-first century, and all. We do affirmative action revelations now, or so I've heard."

His sardonic tone insulted her. "Listen, mister—"

"Luniel. Lune, if you want. Do me the courtesy."

Morgan yanked out the desk chair and sat down, squeezing her thighs together. They still tingled. She crossed her ankles, defensive. "Luniel, then. There's no need to be a smart-ass. I've never seen an angel before. I'm taking a minute to adjust, if that's not too much trouble."

He stared, bemused. And then he gave a sexy smile that quickened her pulse. "Well, good for you, Doctor. I'm impressed. If they don't faint, most people only do one other thing."

"And what's that?"

"Run screaming."

She forced a smile. "I'm not afraid of you."

"I'd give that a few more minutes if I were you. You ready for this?"

Morgan took a deep breath. She was a scientist. Everything had a rational explanation. "Yes."

"You ever read the Bible, Dr. Sterling?"

"No. I mean, yes. A long time ago. But I don't, ah . . ." She grinned suddenly. She wasn't the only one who had to face the truth. "I don't believe in it. Present company excepted, on a provisional basis, of course."

"That makes it all worthwhile," he observed dryly. "You remember a book called Revelation? Seven signs of the Apocalypse?"

She laughed. "Okay. I've seen this movie, right? Demi Moore has a baby and saves the world? I'm not sure I remember the angel in that one being such a wiseass."

"Shut up and listen, human, or I'll put you over my knee."

Stupidly, she flushed. "That's not funny."

"It could be." A wicked glint fired his eyes.

"You know, I have another pistol? Just let me—"

"Okay, okay. The signs are seven plagues, caused by seven golden vials, filled with holy wrath. Empty those bad boys out, Satan pops out of the pit and it's all over. With me?"

"Sure. God kills Satan, Judgment Day comes, the world ends. Bing-bam-boom."

"That's the plan. Naturally, we don't want just any idiot splashing this stuff around whenever they feel like it. So we've got seven guardian angels, one for each vial. All secret. No one knows who or where they are. And on it goes, waiting for God to say the word. Okay?"

"Sure."

"Ready for the good part?"

"I'm holding my breath."

Luniel pointed at the fridge room with one wing's tip. "That murdered angel is my brother, Ithiel. That hole in his chest was made by a demon's sword. I'm here to find out if Ithiel was a Vial Guardian. Because if he was, we're in deep shit."

"And how's that?"

"Taken a walk by the shore lately?"

"No. Why?"

"Because the sea turned to blood tonight. That's the second plague."

Morgan stared. He had to be kidding, right? All lies. A plot to trick her into doing whatever he wanted.

Yeah, right, her inner critic scoffed. *Like he needs a plot. You'd have done whatever he wanted eagerly enough a few minutes ago . . .*

"That's not true," she covered quickly. "People would notice. I'd have heard about it."

"Only just happened. Switch on the TV, if you like."

She bit her lip. There wasn't one here. She'd check when she got upstairs. "Okay. Say I believe you. Go on."

"Well, we're all in a flap about it, aren't we? It could be just some"—Luniel waved a hand—"some random thing, y'know? But it might not. If a demon tipped out the mojo and caused the plague, we're in for some serious trouble."

"The end of the world? Please."

"Worse than that, I'm afraid."

She shook her head, exasperated. "Worse than everyone dying, angel? Astonish me."

"Don't you get it? Heaven's supposed to win. It's all meant to go just as the big guy said it would. But if demons get a hold of His wrath, everything gets twisted. And in the end, hell wins."

"Riiight. The demon Apocalypse. Bummer. Whose stupid idea was it to leave those vials lying around in the first place, eh?"

"Look, I'm just gonna pretend you're taking this seriously, okay? Ithiel is the key. I have to know if a demon stole the vial."

"And how will you find this out, again?"

"I've got a few tricks." He grinned, cheeky and handsome. Like he was just some guy flirting with her in a bar. "I can do magic. Wanna see?"

Morgan swallowed. Flyboy had all the moves, all right. Charming, funny, sexy. And disarming. You wouldn't believe he had a lying bone in his body. Far too much like her mother's killer. She wanted to punch his face in. "In a minute. I've got a few questions first."

She expected him to brush her off, shy away from scrutiny. But Luniel just shrugged. "Fire away."

Okay. Time to concentrate, catch him out. She frowned,

trying to remember what she knew about angels. "You bled when I shot you. Are all angels flesh and blood?"

"Yep. Between you and me? We were kind of a practice run for humans. Bigger, stronger, heal faster, don't age, that kind of thing. And I guess He decided the wings were too much fun. Toned the whole thing down for mark two." He frowned. "Come to think of it, you guys got a raw deal."

"Oh." She shifted, uncomfortable. "So that's why you're so, ah . . ."

"Tough? Witty? Roguishly handsome?" He winked. "Wait till you see Dashiel."

"One's enough, thanks," she replied dryly. "So gunshots won't kill you, huh? You're immortal, then?"

"Nothing's polished me off yet." A cocky grin.

"And nothing can?"

"Ithiel's dead, isn't he? Demonsteel through the heart tends to do that. Forgive me if I don't make you a list."

"Fair enough. You say this blood is the second sign. What's the first?"

"Supposed to be boils and sores. Rotting skin, the crazies, that kind of thing. Seen any of that recently, Doctor?"

Morgan laughed, uneasy. "The Manhattan virus? You can't be serious. I've been studying that. It's just a blood-borne pathogen."

"Is it?" His gaze didn't falter.

Doubt crept into her guts, and she swallowed. "Another thing. You say that guy's your brother, yet you don't seem too cut up about him being dead. Why's that?"

His gaze darkened, but he didn't let it slip. "We, uh . . . don't see too much of each other these days."

"Oh. You guys fall out, or something?"

"Heh. Yeah. You could say that. But blood's blood. We still talk occasionally. Talked. Whatever."

"But he never mentioned this guardian business?"

"Nope."

"Doesn't that seem strange?"

"So he's a tight-assed son of a bitch. What can I say? I love the guy."

"Okay." She thought hard, adding up what he'd said. The explanation requiring the fewest unusual assumptions was the most likely . . . "You say this demon could have stolen your brother's bottle thingy—"

"Vial."

"Yeah. That. Whatever. You say the demon could've taken it. But if the blood in the ocean really is one of your signs, it could've been one of your guys who did it, right? Not a demon?"

"Yeah, I suppose."

"And I'm guessing you angels and demons slaughter each other all the time, right?"

"And twice on Sundays," he said cheerfully. "Best fun you can have with your pants on."

"So Ithiel's murder probably had nothing to do with this. If the blood really is a sign, it's actually more likely that this is the real thing, isn't it? Just like in Revelation? God wins?"

"Guess so. If you put it like that."

She held her breath. "So if it is, why wouldn't you know about it?"

Luniel wrinkled his nose. "Yeah. Was afraid you'd ask that."

"Uh-huh. And why would you even care, either way? Isn't it 'meant to happen'?" She made ironic quote marks in the air. "When it's all over, won't you guys just get sucked up into heaven, or something?"

"It's complicated . . ."

"Yeah. Right." She folded her arms. "Whose side are you really on? And don't even think about lying to me."

Luniel sighed, tilting heavenblue eyes to the sky. "It's not really a matter of sides—"

"Answer me, creature. If you're really a demon, I swear to God I'll slice you up with this autopsy saw."

He leaned back, palms warding her off. "I'm not a demon, okay? Give me a break. Demons have beady little red eyes and smell bad."

"But you're not exactly in the club, are you? You curse, you flirt, you don't exactly look . . . *angelic*. Sorry, I don't buy it. What's the catch?" She held his gaze with hers, triumphant, determined not to let him get away with anything.

He grimaced. "Look, it's not as bad as it sounds. We had . . . kind of a disagreement. About . . . stuff. It's not important."

She shook her head, incredulous but satisfied. "I should've

known. You're a fallen angel, right? Did the wrong thing by Dad and got grounded for it like a sulky teenager."

He jammed his chin into his hands and pouted comically. "We're not exactly *fallen*, okay? We still play for heaven. We're just not on the first team."

"That has to be the worst rationalization I ever heard."

"We're called the Tainted, and there's a bunch of us. We're not damned, but we're not exactly heaven's favorites, either. It's kind of a halfway thing?"

"Uh-huh."

"Hey, I don't make the rules, okay? We work for an archangel called Michael. He calls us when he's made a mess and doesn't want to get his hands even dirtier than they already are."

Morgan blinked. "Michael? *The* Michael? From all those paintings? Girly long-haired guy with the armor and the big sword?"

"Girly." Luniel snickered. "I am so telling him you said *girly*. But yeah. Isn't more than one Mike, far as I know. Thank heaven."

"And so you want to stave off the Apocalypse. How come? What do you care? Won't it all be nectar and ambrosia and harp music . . . ?" She stared. "Oh, shit. Heaven doesn't want you, right?"

Luniel shrugged, sheepish. "Hey, at least you guys got somewhere to go. Heaven repossessed my soul. I'm just gonna blink out. Even hell's gotta be better than oblivion."

Her mind worked it over, incredulous. *I can't believe I'm sitting here talking about the end of the world. With an angel. A fallen angel. Who's probably lying through that killer smile with every blasted word.*

He lighted to his feet. "Okay? Done with the inquisition? Let's go see if we can't raise a few demon sigils—"

"One more thing." Morgan stood, facing him. If he was going to lie, he'd have to lie to her face. No more omissions. Just the facts.

Luniel halted, exasperated. "What?"

"What was your sin?"

"Excuse me?"

"Your sin. What did heaven throw you out for?"

His jaw tightened. "You really wanna know?"

"Yes."

"Come closer, then. Trust for trust."

Morgan took a step. She didn't trust him. Not at all. But she had to know.

"Closer." Luniel beckoned, a fiery glint in his eyes.

She edged closer. She could feel his body heat. Smell that delicious toffee scent. Feel his lips on hers in her memory, that scorching kiss, his strong arms around her . . .

She tightened her mouth, stoic. His magnetism affected her, she couldn't deny that. Didn't mean it wasn't all part of the trick.

He leaned over her. His sooty hair fell on her shoulder, fragrant, inviting. She shivered. *It's a game. Don't fall for his lies. Don't let him touch you . . .*

His lips brushed her ear. Unwillingly, she gasped, heat sparkling all the way down.

She felt him smile, his mouth curling. "I spanked too many disobedient doctors," he whispered. "Watch out, or I might fall right off the wagon. Now, you wanna see Lune's magical angel autopsy, or what?"

CHAPTER 5

Morgan gave him a playful grin, and stalked off towards the fridges, and Luniel's gaze licked the sweet curve of her ass every step of the way.

He swore, and tore his eyes away. *Nice work, Lune. Because flirting with her is such a good idea right now.*

He took a deep breath and closed his eyes, willing her scent to fade, her skin's smoothness under his fingers to disappear. Kissing her was a mistake. But fuck it if it wasn't the most pleasurable one he'd made in a long time. He still had an aching hard-on that stretched his jeans, and if she hadn't noticed she was either dead or blind.

He felt like smacking his face into the wall until it bled, just to take the pain. What was he thinking?

Hell, he wasn't thinking. He just wanted her. Wanted to have her, own her, silence those clever questions with kisses and make her stupid with sensation, pleasure her so deep and breathless that she couldn't make more than an incoherent sound.

Because she'd always come back with more. And her puzzle-riddled mind tantalized him. Almost as much as her sin-sultry body.

Unwilled, his mind lurched back centuries, to another woman who'd captivated him, body and spirit. Beautiful, too, though she'd covered herself with headscarves and long skirts as befitted the era. His lady Eleanor, a wildcat beneath her demure exterior, clever, spirited and sharp tongued. His obsession with her had chewed his heart raw. But she was a woman, God-fearing, bred in those days to be weak and helpless, and when the demons came for her, she couldn't defend herself.

They'd taken her to spite him, and he couldn't protect her from temptation. Her soul was damned forever, screaming in hell because he'd dared to love her.

Ever since then, he'd kept away from human women. For their safety, and his own sanity.

But this Dr. Morgan Sterling, with her quick questions and sexy crooked smile and that luscious lover's body hidden beneath her cool white coat, was surely teasing that sanity away.

Fuck. He could tell Morgan liked how he looked, even if she trusted him as far as a cat could spit a furball. Her pretty honey-dark gaze betrayed her, the way it caressed him when she thought he wasn't watching. How she caught her bottom lip between her teeth when she thought carefully. That drove him wild. He wanted to bite her lip himself, suck it into his mouth . . .

Telltale sparks of desire crackled golden in his feathers, and he struggled to extinguish them. Curse her. She knew she tempted him. Dr. Vixen was trying to seduce him. No other explanation. Well, he wouldn't have her. For her sake, and his own.

He adjusted himself, pretending it wasn't totally obvious he was horny as a fuckdemon, and followed her into the fridge room.

She stood by Ithiel's body, eyeing his white feathers thoughtfully. "So why didn't the CSI notice this when they loaded the body bag? Some kind of weird angel mojo, I suppose?"

"Very good." Lune strode up and folded his wings. *Don't look at her. Mind on the job.* "They thought he was human. You saw me when I first appeared. We have a human guise. If we die while we're wearing it, it takes a while to wear off."

"How long?"

"Anywhere from a few hours to a week. Depends on how powerful you are."

"And how powerful was Ithiel?"

"He had his moments."

"Must run in the family."

Lune snorted. "I'll take that as the compliment I'm sure you intended." He bent over the body, inhaling. Ithiel's flowery scent hit his nostrils, mixed with the rich, raw smell of death.

He closed his eyes, and to his surprise they burned. A long time had passed since he and his twin had anything except phone calls between them. But it still hurt, like they said an amputated limb was supposed to hurt. And it still fired anger into his veins.

Should've been me, Ith. You were always the better one. I'll get the devil-kisser who did this, heaven help me.

He straightened, stoic, clearing his throat. "How, uh, how long would you say he's been dead for, Doctor?"

"Excuse me?" Morgan waved her hand in front of his eyes. "Hello? Angel physiology? Not my strong point."

"If he was human, I mean. Take a stab. How long?"

"Well, I'd have to do the proper tests, but from the color of the skin and the hypostasis . . . I'd say twenty-four hours max."

He poked his finger into the hole in Ithiel's heart, swiping up a clot of dark angel blood. He sniffed his finger, and licked it. Faint putrefaction stung. The demon magic had faded a lot. A week since Ithiel stopped answering. It fitted.

Morgan wrinkled her nose. "Ew, gross."

"Is that the scientific term? You should try it in your autopsies. Taste is a powerful attractant."

"Tell me about it."

He grinned. "No, I mean for spells. Magic has its own distinct flavor, depending on the caster. That one has the definite stink of demon prince."

A sexy cocked eyebrow. "And what does yours taste like?"

"Breathe in and see." He flattened his palm on Ithiel's broken chest, and murmured the words for a sigil burn.

Blue light flashed, the hissing stink of burning flesh. Lune snatched his hand back, shaking it. *Ouch.*

He turned Ithiel's left palm over. Now a sigil glowed there, two circles and a cross, carved into the flesh in burning blue light.

Morgan gasped. "How did you . . . ?" She broke off. "No, don't answer that. What is it?"

"It's lettering. An angelic sigil. It's a mark given by the archangels. Should tell us what Ithiel was up to, if he was a Guardian or not." Lune took a picture with his phone and sent it to Dash, with the caption *Ithiel—show M*.

She peered over his shoulder, her own camera in hand. She'd been photographing, too, recording everything he did. Have to do something about that later. "You guys use phones? What happened to telepathy, or whatever?"

"Sorry. No longer one of my many talents."

"Who are you texting?"

"Dashiel. He's kinda the boss of the Tainted. If you ask him, anyway."

A blue glow leaked from his left hand, and he pulled it back, but too late. She grabbed his wrist and twisted his palm upwards. "You've got one, too," she accused.

He clenched his fist and yanked away. Time was, he'd tried to carve those crossed lightning bolts from his flesh. "Yeah. It's the mark of the Tainted. Got a better tatt on my butt, though. Wanna see?"

She snorted. "Not in this lifetime." But her gaze slipped to his butt, just for a second.

He grinned, and examined Ithiel's chest where the contaminated blood was. Blue smoke curled and glimmered, but that was all. Recalcitrant son of a bitch. He'd have to try again.

He forced his hand into the hole, grating past broken bone, grabbed Ithiel's heart and ripped it out. Bone cracked. Blood squelched, the flesh cold in his palm.

Morgan swatted his arm. "Excuse me? Autopsy tomorrow? Me explaining to my boss why the heart's already removed?"

"Sorry. Secret angel business." He squeezed, making the thick dead blood flow, and whispered the spell again.

Light flashed again, this time red like fire. The blood ignited, flames licking Ithiel's skin, and a glowing scarlet sigil painted itself across Ithiel's chest.

"Don't tell me. Red for demons?" Fascination lit Morgan's face like sunshine. Her eyes shone, dark gold, and her lips parted just far enough for him to see the tip of her tongue brushing her teeth.

Not helping his concentration. "Yep. Demon sigil. Mark of the hellspawn who killed him. Their weapons leave a signature." A diagonal-slashed cross, two oblique lines. It rang a distant bell. Somewhere, he'd seen it . . . He closed his eyes.

Flashes of a muddy field, pigs rooting in bloody snow, a pile of bloated corpses . . .

He put down the heart and took another pic, bending in closer to sniff the flames. Sulfur, of course. Putrefying flesh. And the cloying odor of . . . yes. Rotten passion fruit and tooth decay.

Gotcha, you god-rotting slime.

He straightened, fierce. "Quuzaat," he pronounced.

"Koo-who?"

"Qu-u-zaat," he spelled out. "Fat demon prince, beady eyes, bad breath. The Black Death, back in the fourteenth century? His idea. Same with California dengue. Kind of a pestilence junkie, to be honest. Skanky little asshole."

He murmured ancient words, planting his palms one last time on Ithiel's mangled chest. White heat rose, and the body engulfed itself in flame. In a few moments, nothing but ashes remained.

Morgan goggled. "You can't do that!" she demanded. "Did I look like I was finished? I have to account for that body. There's paperwork!"

"What'd you want me to do, leave him here where everyone can see?"

She sighed. "Fine. Whatever. I guess it would have looked a little strange on the autopsy report. White male angel, twenty-eight to immortal, cause of death: demon slaughter. Still, would've been a unique examination."

Luniel grinned. "Hey, if you want to examine someone, I'm av—"

"Don't even finish that sentence." Her lips twitched. "So that's what you're telling me we're dealing with? A demon who spreads disease?"

"Yup. I'm thinking this Manhattan virus is looking more likely, Dr. Sterling. What do you think?"

She shook her head, her eyes gleaming with stubbornness that made him want to take her right there and fuck her into oh-so-pleasurable submission. "Doesn't prove anything. Even if I believed in your magic spells—"

"Not saying you do, of course," he cut in. He enjoyed teasing her, he realized. Making her think. Watching her in action. Glorious. Dangerous.

"Not saying I do. But even if I did, all it proves is that your pal Quuzaat's weapon killed Ithiel," she pointed out reasonably. "Doesn't even mean he did it."

He faced her. She was closer than he'd expected, and he stumbled and caught his balance with a graceless wing flare. Smooth. "Well, with the end of the world at stake, I'm prepared to show a little faith. Are you?"

She bit her bottom lip. "I can't believe I'm saying this. But . . . yeah."

God fucking damn. He wanted to crush her, kiss her, lay her down and make her his own. "That's good," he murmured. "Because now I have to decide what to do with you."

"*Do* with me?" She frowned. "I'm sorry, but no one *does* anything with me in my own office."

A dozen naughty replies jumped to his lips, and he swallowed them all, along with images of bending her over the desk and taking her, hot and hard. "But you've seen everything. You know everything I know. I can't just let you go."

"Really. And what would the other options be?"

"I could kill you." He stroked her cheek with his knuckle. So soft, that fragrant human skin. "That'd probably be best."

Her eyes shone wide, but she didn't flinch. "You'd have done it already, angel," she said, her voice barely audible. "You had your chance."

"I did," he agreed. But somehow he'd pulled her closer, his hand on her shoulder. Her body heat caressed him, sweet and shivering, just a breath from touching.

"But you didn't do it." Her lips drifted apart, only a few inches under his.

He could taste her, honey and spice, and the temptation to take more prickled his feathers hot. The hellcat was teasing him, and he was far from up to resisting her. "A smart guy wouldn't make the same mistake twice," he managed.

"Neither would a smart woman." She pushed him away, with one finger on his chest and a saucy smile. "Hands off, flyboy."

And Lune wanted to smash his head into the wall until it exploded. He let go, aching.

"Anyway," she added, tossing shining hair over her shoulder, "where's the percentage for you in killing me?"

"Nowhere." Lune still struggled with his breath. "It doesn't matter to me one way or the other. But if demons get their hands on you, they'll torture it out of you without breaking a sweat. I can't risk that."

"Torture what out of me? The fact that your brother's dead, and you're pissed, even though you're too much of a tough guy to admit it? That you're hunting down this Quuzaat so you can tear him a new asshole?" She cocked that eyebrow again at his expression. "C'mon, they know that already. Isn't that the point?"

"You know more than you think," Lune said roughly. She'd cut too close. "I did warn you. You saw me casting. You saw me texting Dash. Once they get started with you, you'll drag things from your memory you never realized you witnessed, if you think it'll make them stop. Believe me. It's not pretty."

"So take me with you, then."

He choked. "What?"

"I've studied the Manhattan virus. I can help you. I *want* to help you."

"Y'know, thanks and all, but I really don't—"

"I've found Patient Zero, okay?" Excitement flushed her face, and she waved animated hands. "Well, not exactly. But we've pinpointed the neighborhood where the virus started. The info's all there in the CDC reports, but I had more samples they didn't get yet. I e-mailed them yesterday, and they concur. If this Quuzaat guy opened up a can of zombie virus whup-ass, that's where he did it, right?"

Lune stared. She could save him hours of hunting. Days, even. "O-kaay . . ."

"Please. I really want this. If you're so worried about me? You protect me, tough guy. Just take me with you, to . . ." She lifted her hands helplessly. "To wherever it is you're going."

"I'm sorry, did you just ask to come with me? I thought you didn't believe in angels and demons, *Doctor* Sterling." He loaded the title with sarcasm, but his guts churned. Protecting beautiful women from demons wasn't exactly his strong suit. Demons: 1, Luniel: 0. Better not to even try.

"I did. I don't." She stopped, flustered. "I mean, yes, I did ask. And no, I don't understand it all, and I don't know if I believe you. But I have to be part of this, can't you see? I'm a doctor. I can't just stand by and let all these people die."

Lune nodded slowly. He'd witnessed too many disasters not

to understand. He'd dragged drowning children from swirling tsunami waters on the beach in Sri Lanka, only to watch their parents smother in the mud. It was futile, that late December day, one hundred fifty thousand dead and counting. But to stand by and do nothing was worse than failure.

But if he took her with him . . . Jesus. He'd drive himself batfuck trying to keep his hands off her, and get her killed. Or screw her senseless and *then* get her killed. Either way, she'd end up in hell.

Unacceptable. "Look, I appreciate that, but I can't—"

"Listen, you don't understand, okay." Her gaze clouded, fatigue and desperation showing. "The CDC and Patient Zero? All that stuff I told you? It's just conjecture. This virus, it's . . . like nothing we've ever seen. None of our techniques are making a dent. Infection rates are skyrocketing, and the mortality, it's . . ." She coughed, and swiped a hand across her eyes, but not before he saw glimmering tears. "We can't stop it from spreading. There's no precaution we can take that works. If we can't make a breakthrough soon, this thing is going to wipe out half of Babylon. Hell, maybe you're just insane, but at this point? I'll take any insight I can get. If there's even the smallest chance that I can find something . . ."

And don't I feel like an asshole right now. Inwardly, Lune swore. She was smart. Driven. Too damn persuasive for his good.

She swallowed, and sighed. "Look, I know you probably don't care. But we're hunting the same prize here. We can help each other, whether you want to call it searching for this Quuzaat, or finding a cure for Manhattan. Different words, same ending. Everyone wins."

"I get that." He tried to keep his voice gentle. "I really do. But I still can't take you out there, Morgan. These demons are dangerous. It's not safe."

"Monsters? Are you trying to scare me?" She laughed harshly. "The city's dying, angel. Is that really the best you can do?"

In the distance, glass shattered. Lune's ears pricked, and he lifted his finger for silence. He sniffed the air, rot and ashes. Cocked his head. Looked up.

And the ceiling broke open, and a pile of screeching imps

poured down on them in a hail of ash. Talons slashing, spiked leathery wings flapping like manic-ass bats.

Morgan stumbled backwards, trying to shield her face with her hands. Lune dived for her, wings streaked back, and rolled with her under the trolley.

Bat wings slapped the metal, a cloud of sulfury stink. He covered her with his body, his feathers a protective shield, and hissed a sparking blue resistance charm that made the filthy critters screech and howl.

Her heartbeat raced against his chest, her warm body so sweet under his. He gathered her up, ready to leap, and flicked his gaze upwards. "You believe me now?"

"Right this instant? I'm prepared to give you a chance." Morgan gazed up at him, her eyes wide but her chin firm, and Lune's heart did a besotted backflip.

Keep her. Protect her. Make her his own.

Oh, heaven. Here we go again.

CHAPTER 6

Luniel whirled them both out from under the trolley, and dived through the window.

Broken glass exploded. Morgan screamed. The angel's arms tightened around her, and they crashed through the metal security mesh, hit the sticky alley pavement behind the CME building and rolled as one. Streetlights glared, the stink of hot asphalt and cigarettes. The smelly bat-things flapped and clawed at her hair, but couldn't reach her.

Not bats. Demons. And they've come for us. For me.

Luniel leapt to his feet, and pushed her behind him with a sleek black wing. "Stay back," he ordered her. Blinding blue light flashed, and a fiery sword the color of midday sky flared to life in his grip.

Morgan staggered, falling into broken glass that stung her palms. Her thoughts tumbled in free fall. *Fiery sword. Demons. O-kaay.*

The bat-things sniggered and flapped in a swirling mass, sharp teeth bared. The size of large cats, covered in ragged fur and scales. Their rotting-meat stench made her retch.

Luniel crouched, sword balanced lightly in his right hand. Blue flame dripped, liquid light. "Come get it, chuckles," he snarled, and dived in headlong.

Morgan stared, openmouthed. His flight was a thing of beauty. Surely such a heavy, muscle-bound creature couldn't swoop and dive so effortlessly. How did he even get off the ground? Let alone fight airborne with such sharp, deadly grace?

He angled his wings, driving the air to breeze as he flipped and rolled. Blue light flashed. Blood splashed, black and fetid, and decapitated bat bodies flew, heads splattering the pavement.

The creatures screeched, and speared for him, teeth gnashing, their leathery wings a blur.

One flew for Morgan's face, cackling, wicked talons outstretched. She shrieked and swatted at it, shielding her eyes.

A neon-blue bolt seared her cheek, and the bat-thing dropped in two halves at her feet with a stinking squelch.

"I said stay back, not jump in." Luniel's gaze drilled her, blazing with the heat of the fight. His sooty hair knotted wild. Clawmarks slashed his cheekbone crimson, but as Morgan stared, the skin sizzled and healed over, perfect. "I can take a scratch from this filth. You can't."

"But—"

His left hand flashed out, and he crushed a bat in his fist, inches from her ear. He threw the smoldering carcass away. "Just do as I say, Morgan. Fight me later." And he whirled, and pushed her behind him again, and spun his blade in challenge.

The remaining bats coalesced and dived as one, and he leapt over them and slashed, backhanded. Bodies flopped dead. And he grabbed the last one by the throat and slammed it against the wall.

The contact sizzled, burning his hand. He paid no notice. "Who sent you, hellshit?"

The bat-thing cackled, and spat green vitriol.

Luniel ducked, and the acid hit the sidewalk and burned a smoking hole. He squeezed harder, biceps bulging. "Tell me and I'll make this quick."

"Your ass on a pitchfork," it growled, and laughed.

"Have it your way." Luniel clunked his sword down, grabbed the thing's rubbery black wing and ripped it off.

Bone crunched, a splash of blood. The bat shrieked and writhed, and started sobbing.

Morgan's guts twisted. She wanted to cover her ears. The thing had tried to kill her. But such cruelty . . .

"Dry your eyes, shitball." Remorseless, Luniel twisted the other wing, threatening. "You've still got two arms and two legs once I've finished with this. Then I'll start in on your balls. Who sent you?"

"Luniel, stop it. Let it go." Morgan grabbed his arm, trying to drag him away.

Luniel shook her off. "Morgan, get b—motherfucker!"

His grip slipped, and abruptly, the cunning bat stopped wailing, and launched itself at Morgan's face.

Its neck elongated like a serpent's. Sharp teeth connected, ripping her cheek. Pain seared.

Luniel yanked the thing off her and punched it, hard, twice. Its nose splurted black, but it cackled in glee. "Screw you, angel," it crowed, and with a final triumphant screech dived for its own chest and chewed its own heart out.

Steaming blood gushed down Luniel's arm. The thing stopped thrashing, and Luniel cursed and tossed the mangled carcass away.

Morgan's cheek burned, sharp like a wasp sting. Her tongue ballooned. She couldn't move her jaw. Her throat was swelling closed. She gulped for air, fumbling in her pocket for her asthma inhaler. "Ugh. Mmm."

Luniel jumped for her, cradling her in his arms. "Shit. Morgan, stay with me." His voice strained raw. "I've got you. Just keep your eyes open." He murmured a charm, some bizarre hissing language she didn't understand, and pressed his palm to her cheek.

White light seared, dazzling her. Pain sizzled like fire. Her eyes burned, and she choked, the swelling receding enough to let her gulp a breath. The stink of singed hair stung her nose. She panted, aching, relief washing her lungs fresh. Air never tasted so good.

Luniel stroked her hair back. "Shh. S'okay, darling. Breathe."

Her resolve weakened, dizzy. His embrace felt good. Safe. She wanted to stay there.

But she pushed away, and sucked down two deep puffs from her inhaler. The taste embittered her tongue. Her throat muscles relaxed, but her pulse still raced. He'd saved her life, maybe. But to what end? And at what cost?

She touched her cheek. The wound was gone. Like it never

was. "What was that?" she managed, hoarse. "Did you cast a spell on me?"

He stared, his mouth tightening. The demon's teeth marks had been transferred to his own cheek, and this time they bled freely down his face instead of healing. "Sure," he retorted. "It's called 'how'd you like breathing?' Working well for you?"

She coughed, her throat raw. "I've got medicine for that."

"Your human drugs won't work on demon poison."

"That's not the point."

"No?" He strode up to her, his eyes glinting golden. "Here's one for you, then: never trust a demon. No matter how it cries its lying eyes out."

"But—"

"They play for your sympathy, Morgan. Your trust. Your compassion." His hard gaze didn't drop. "Every. Little. Weakness. Don't listen to them. Never trust them. Ever."

She folded her arms, defensive. He'd just described himself perfectly, hadn't he? "Right. I should trust you, though?"

"Have I lied to you yet?" A challenge, magnetic.

She couldn't look away. "I don't know," she admitted, after far too long a moment. Of course he'd lied. Everything about him was a lie.

No matter that he looked directly at her, and his face held no deceit, and his eyes burned always with the steady fire of truth.

He gave a humorless laugh, and turned away, but not before she saw his jaw clench in disappointment. "Clue for you, Dr. Sterling," he said harshly, ruffling his feathers in tight. "Be nice to me. Or next time a demon chews your face off? I might just let you choke."

Lune retrieved his sword, avoiding her gaze. He'd shown her too much. And now she feared him. But seeing her strangling to death because he hadn't kept her safe . . . His fingers clenched around the bloodstained grip. Curse her.

She watched him, wary. "So what now?"

"Now, we get the fuck out of here before more of them show up," he replied shortly. His wounded cheek stung and swelled, and he wiped it roughly with his wrist. And then he realized what he'd said.

We. Jesus.

Taking her with him was stupid. Trying to protect her was even stupider. But the most thickheaded stupidity of all was that he hadn't thought. Hadn't considered his options when those imps crashed through the ceiling.

He'd just grabbed her and fled.

Like protecting her came naturally. Like he hadn't spent the last eight hundred years beating that protective impulse out of himself with slaughter and fury and lithe, pretty angel girls he didn't really care for.

So just fuck her. Dashiel's imagined voice sounded in his head. *Screw your no-human-women thing. Take her to your bed and show her a good time. Your smart-ass attitude will scare her away soon enough afterwards. Don't sweat it.*

But he couldn't. Not him.

Even though he refused to take human women, abstinence wasn't an option. Heaven, he was male, and unlike Japheth, he wasn't a saint. But sex had always meant something, even with the angel girls, who sometimes got besotted and had to be avoided. Some just giggled and called him *cute* or *old-fashioned.* He preferred to think of it as *steadfast.*

Making love to a girl didn't mean he wanted her more than once. But his lovers became part of him, in some tiny way. He was there for them, even if it just meant a shoulder to cry on, or doing the menacing friend thing to chase away amorous morons in bars. *Everyone's bloody big brother,* Dash would scoff, and he was right. For better or worse, Lune was one of those rare guys who said *call me if you ever need anything* and actually meant it.

For all the fucking good it had done him. Taking Morgan Sterling anywhere near his bed—or anywhere else he could lay her down and strip her naked with his teeth—was out of the question. He was already too fascinated with her for his own good. If demons got a whiff of it, she'd be helltoast before he could blink.

Just like Eleanor.

And just like with Eleanor, the guilt would tear him apart.

"Hold on just one second, okay?" Morgan said. "Can we get a few things straight first?"

He clenched frustrated teeth. "Sure. Why not. Can we make it quick?"

"We sure can." She lifted her pretty chin, defiant. "I don't appreciate being violated. I said I wanted to come with you. That doesn't mean you can do whatever you like to me." She dusted her hands down her white coat, an unconscious move. Like she was trying to return to normality. But her breath rasped too fast, her face too pale. Lune could hear her heartbeat, racing, like he'd felt it against his chest when he thrust his hands into her hair and opened her mouth under his and . . .

Fever washed him, dizzying. He swiped his stinging cheekbone. Blood dripped, discolored dark with demon venom. *Poisoned. Great. Good thinking, Lune. You know what you'll have to do to get rid of that.*

He concentrated on cleaning his hands, deliberate. "Violated, huh? I'm sorry, did I save your life? My mistake."

She flushed, but kept her gaze steady. "I appreciate your concern. But I don't remember saying that it was okay for you to . . . flash your mojo on me, or whatever that was. In the future, I'll thank you to discuss it with me beforehand."

"Give me a break. It was for your own good!"

Her eyes flashed, furious. "Yeah. It's always 'for their own good' with people like you. You lie and seduce and take everything, and it's always 'for their own good.' Well, not me, angel. The only one who takes care of my 'good' is me. You got that?"

Luniel gritted his teeth, and vanished his sword in a flash of blue. "Sure. Whatever. You coming or not?"

"And where exactly would we be going?"

To hunt Quuzaat, of course. But he hesitated. His fingers itched where grabbing that hellspawn had scorched him. Already his wing muscles burned with venom.

He coughed, and spat stained phlegm. Awesome. He'd done more than he'd shown Morgan when he'd charmed that demon slash from her face. Healing humans was . . . well, it was kind of forbidden, unless you were Jesus Christ, which Lune most certainly wasn't.

Not that he gave a spit about the rules these days, but it meant the spell didn't work all that well, at least not for him. He'd had to take the damage himself, and because she was human, he was healing like a human. Which was to say, slowly and painfully.

His blood scorched, sick. The venom hissed and ate away

inside him. He couldn't fight like this. He needed to take care of himself or they'd both be demon fodder.

"My place," he replied shortly.

"You're kidding, right?"

"Yeah, I'm a real funny guy. Just do as you're told for once, human. I haven't forgotten about that spanking."

She folded her arms defiantly, tossing her hair over her shoulder, but her mouth quirked in tempting curiosity. "You've got a place? In Babylon?"

Blood stained her chin. He wanted to kiss it off. "Yeah," he said gruffly, sweating. "I need to get a few things. Is there a subway near here?"

"Huh?"

"Subway. Transport. Unless you want to walk all the way to Harlem."

She goggled. "Sure. It's out on Second Avenue. But can't you . . . y'know. Fly there? Beam yourself up, or something, like you did into my office?"

"So you believe in magic, now?"

"Just plumbing the depths of your delusions, flyboy."

Despite his aching limbs, he grinned. "Why, yes, Dr. Sterling. I can 'beam' myself there, if by 'beam' you mean teleport on a wish. We call it *flashing*. But I can't carry you, at least not right now. And as for flying . . ." His smile faded. The demon poison rotted his blood, weakening his powers. He couldn't flash them both. And he wasn't convinced he could defend her in the air if they were attacked. He shrugged, offhanded. "Maybe I just don't feel like it."

"Maybe I don't feel like taking the subway."

"We can get a cab, then. And on the way, you can tell me about this Patient Nothing."

"Patient Zero." Amusement flickered warm in her eyes.

"Whatever."

Along the alley, deep in demon-spelled shadow, Zuul licked trembling lips, scarlet hair falling over his eyes. He'd enjoyed watching that. All that blood and exposed flesh. And that imp's screams as the angel tortured him made Zuul shiver and sigh. Pain pornography, a cruel tease for a desperate addict like himself. He'd wanted to feel it, the exquisite pop of bone and ligament, those harsh angel fingers searing his throat.

He sweated, hard. Fuck. He needed a fix again. Babylon sported any number of fight bars and torture clubs, and a handsome boy like Zuul never had any trouble finding volunteers. Especially when they found out how far he was prepared to go . . .

He slammed his head into the brick wall at his back, trying to keep his mind on the job as the angel and his human slut walked away.

Sugary angel stink curled in the air, and a sneer twisted Zuul's lips. Luniel. One of the Tainted. Such pathetic rebellion, to defy Michael's will on a whim but still come crawling to the archangel's table for scraps. He'd enjoy watching Azaroth chew them all into bleeding shreds of holymeat.

But the blue-eyed son of a gloryworm was strong. He'd dispatched Zuul's imps without breaking a sweat. Still, that was fine. The fucker was sure as hell sweating now. That fever flushing his face and setting his hands aquiver told tales of demon poison. The healing process would distract him a while.

Just what Zuul's masters ordered. Both of them.

The feathered freak and his girl crossed the street, traffic whizzing by. The girl was sexy, in a serious, fuck-your-math-teacher-fantasy sort of way. Curving hips, luminous eyes, ripe red lips. Mmm. How blood would spurt from those lips if Zuul bit them. How she'd wail.

Zuul noted how Luniel walked a step behind her and to the side, his gaze always roving, searching for threats. He'd flashed his show-off sword away, but it lay only a half second's wish from his hand. And the smell of his blood, open to the air through his demon-slashed face, spoke of more than casual connection. Beneath the flowery heavenstink—Zuul gagged, and spat—Luniel smelled raw. On edge. Hungry.

Zuul giggled. Stupid angel, lusting after a human woman. It only gave the demons more leverage. And Zuul knew one particular demon who'd be very interested in Luniel's sordid little love affair. Yes. A pretty Prince of Poison who'd be more than happy to reward Zuul for his news.

Azaroth wouldn't mind him doing a little job on the side, after all. Hell on earth was coming. Every demon for himself.

Satisfied, Zuul snapped his fingers, and vanished.

CHAPTER 7

Morgan hugged her knees to her chest on the subway car's slick vinyl bench, her back against the warm spray-painted window. The train stank of piss and sweat, and syringes littered the floor. Her heart still thudded, unwilling to calm down. She still wore her white lab coat, smeared with blood and alley dirt, as well as stinking black grease from the demon's wings.

A demon's wings. Her arms shook, and she clutched her knees tighter. Her stay-up stockings were torn, and she tried to cover the hole. *Get a grip, Morgan. Either demons tried to kill you, or rabid bats bleed black acid and speak English. Accept the evidence and move on.*

The subway rattled and lurched along the curved tracks. Fluorescent lights gleamed. In one corner, a scruffy group of Latino kids in baggy jeans played cards. A man and a woman wore dark business suits, briefcases and SIM implants flashing behind their ears. The woman had a pistol in a holster under her short jacket. A trio of blond Aryan gangboys with razor-cut hair and shamrock tattoos loaded their guns from a take-out tub of rounds. Their studded belts and chains glinted, the telltale lumps of knives or nerve gas canisters in their pockets. One guy in a creased red leather jacket had a machete and smoked a crack pipe. Two dark-eyed boys in turbans played knife games on the seat, blades slashing the plastic as they stabbed for each other's fingers.

No one commented. Everyone watched everyone, exchanged dark whispers with their companions, avoided eye contact. In Babylon, at this hour, no one rode the subway alone.

Tense. Exhilarating. Nerve-wracking. But none of them had anything on the creature sitting at her side.

He'd slipped on his human guise, and his wings weren't visible, but he still radiated menace and strangeness. He was the wrong colors, for starters. Inhuman, his skin too luminous and smooth. His blacker-than-night hair glistened, strands sticking to his bleeding cheek, and his ridiculously blue eyes glittered fever bright.

Not to mention he was the biggest guy on the train by inches. Veins stood out on his glossy arms, his muscles twitching. He was stained with demonslime and grit, but he didn't smell like a human would, of sweat and corruption. No, he still smelled of toffee and warm, clean male skin.

She smoothed her ragged hair, self-conscious. A goth gang-boy across the aisle gave her a belligerent once-over, dyed hair gleaming in front of his eyes. He wore tight black jeans and a safety-pinned black t-shirt, and his dirty kohl-lined gaze lingered on the place where her skirt rode up on her thigh.

She flushed, and crossed her legs, tugging her skirt down over her lace-edged stockings. No profit in making a scene.

But Luniel growled—yes, he actually growled, deep in his throat like an angry beast—and glared at the goth, a hot blue threat. "Watch your eyes, kid."

The goth glanced at his watching friends, and forced a sneer, flipping Luniel a black-nailed bird. "Make me."

Luniel just sniffed. The goth gulped, and his nose exploded in blood.

He doubled over, grabbing his face. Scarlet splashed over his leather-studded wrists and plinked on the floor. "Son of a bitch," he spluttered.

Luniel arched calm eyebrows, and the goth and his friends muttered and looked elsewhere, and when the train jerked to a halt at Seventy-Second Street, they got off.

Morgan swallowed, dry. How had he done that? She wasn't sure she wanted to know. She'd seen him slaughter and torture those . . . things . . . without remorse. A man who used a sword like that was a practiced killer.

Who'd apparently appointed himself her protector.

And sure, she felt safe. From demon bats, or some guylined freak who perved up her skirt. Just not from *him*.

And there was still the question of what he'd want in return. Her body still trembled in memory of that stupid, bone-tingling kiss. But she wasn't an idiot. If flyboy had designs on her body, he could damn well think again.

"So," Lune said, as if goth blood wasn't pooling all over the opposite seat. "Tell me about this zero thing."

"Well," said Morgan, relieved to have something to talk about that wasn't *how the hell did you do that?* "It's called a disease vector. If you can isolate enough samples, get the times of death and match them with locations, you can build up a picture of where and when the virus killed. Cross-reference that with incubation time, and you get a pattern of the spread of infection, which you can trace back to the likely origin."

"Wow, this science shit really works. And that's where?"

"We narrowed it down to an area in Spanish Harlem, below 110th Street." Even as she said it, dismay filtered her guts cold.

"You mean, where the mutie gangs hang out."

Yeah, that about sums it up.

The muties were their own plague, a scourge on the face of Babylon that the city had no solution for. Too many years of poverty, rage, inbreeding and bad drugs had created an underclass of unemployed poor, their bodies deformed, their brains too addled or altered to do anything but the most menial and underpaid jobs. The city had cut off services to parts of town in an effort to shrink the worst neighborhoods by attrition, but the muties wouldn't go away that easily. Most were vagrants, living in boxes and drains, roaming the streets in gangs and attacking anything they thought might have money or food. Put a bike chain or an axe in their hands and they were deadly.

A few extremists in city hall were always angling to deploy nerve gas and scour the neighborhoods clean. Some said those same extremists had engineered the Manhattan virus to wipe out the muties.

If so, it ranked up there with carbon sequestration and

mandatory live flu vaccinations as one of the worst ideas of the century. The muties were bad enough when they were just hungry and pissed off. Splash on a dose of Manhattan virus . . .

Morgan hugged her knees again as the train swayed to a halt beside dirty white tiles at Cathedral Parkway. A trio of Mormons got on, black suits and truncheons. The train took off again. "The virus started in mutie land," she confirmed. "I guess if you're already a mindless zombie, it can't hurt too much, can it?"

It was a poor joke, and Luniel didn't smile. "But it does hurt, from what I've heard."

"Yeah." Her lips squeezed tight. She'd seen enough virus victims to know what they went though. Ravenous hunger, enough to make them chew their own bodies for food. Rotting skin, flesh turning to pulp. Blood clotting as it pumped, organs liquefying, eyeballs bursting red.

But before that was the worst. They still looked normal, no lesions or popped veins. But their minds twisted, their impulses turned homicidal and they developed a taste for raw meat.

Specifically, human flesh. More specifically, uninfected human flesh that was still alive.

Manhattan's victims liked to spread the disease. They were compelled to, so fiercely they'd die in the attempt. And they used all their still-human wits and cunning to do it.

Luniel's gaze didn't waver. "We'll put a stop to it, Morgan," he said, his voice steady and hard. Damn it if she didn't want to believe him. "We'll find Quuzaat and get rid of him."

"And will that help?" The virus was already wild. Surely killing one . . . creature couldn't stem the tide of death? Even if that creature really had started it. But she had to go along with this, even if it was just to prove this Quuzaat didn't exist and wasn't responsible.

Then again, if Quuzaat wasn't responsible . . . how to cure the virus? Killing a demon seemed easy—at least, it would be with Luniel on her side—compared to developing a cure or a vaccine, when so many people were already at risk or infected.

She could almost wish this demon was the cause. If it wouldn't mean everything she'd ever believed was misguided.

Worse than misguided. Arrogantly, perilously wrong.

She sighed. You could do your head in thinking about this.

Luniel grinned, feral and dangerous, and her pulse skipped. "Will it help? One way to find out."

They got off the subway at 116th Street, where dusty fluorescents were broken above blue-painted columns, and spray paint colored the white-tiled walls along the dim platforms. Ripped bill posters flapped in the breeze as the train rumbled on. Luniel ushered her towards the steps, avoiding sleeping vagrants. Broken concrete stuck jagged where last summer, a bungled suicide bomb had blasted a hole in one wall and no one had bothered to fix it. Someone had hung a wreath of wildflowers there, now withered and dry.

At the top of the steps, midnight breeze blew in from the river, bringing the coppery smell of blood. The moon shone, casting red shadows. Old apartment blocks loomed like skeletons, broken windows coated in dust, red neon advertising a halal deli. Garbage lined the alleyways, and security screens were pulled down tight over the sidewalk store windows. A coffee vendor's wagon hunkered in a dim pool of light on the corner, and the guy inside rested his shotgun openly on the counter.

The gang of Aryans had gotten off at their stop, and stood by the green-fenced steps, inhaling some drug from a plastic crusher and passing it around. One gave her a sloppy grin, nudging his friends.

Luniel tugged her closer as they sidled past, beneath rippling virtual advertising for cell phone plans and home security. Sirens ebbed and flowed, and the air stank of smoke. "Walk with me."

She tugged away, the broken pavement scraping beneath her shoes. She'd lived in Babylon ever since her student days, and she was used to the occasional guy bothering her, or racists calling her dirty names because her dark coloring made them think she was Latina or mixed race. "I'm okay. Let go."

"Tell me you weren't born yesterday. If you look like my girlfriend, those guys will leave you alone." And he dropped his muscled arm around her shoulder and leaned to whisper in her ear with a showy smile. "Is it such a trial?"

"I'll ask your girlfriend and let you know." She swallowed, dizzied by his scent. The top of her head barely came to his shoulder. His big body felt strong and safe. But it wasn't reassuring. It was threatening.

"Sorry. Can't help you there." A dark blue glance, close. "Relieved?"

"Just forewarned."

"Believe me, princess, if I decide to have designs on you, you'll see it coming." They hustled across a traffic-thick street towards the overgrown jungle of Morningside Park, headlights whizzing by. Smoke hung over the road, the stink of burning garbage.

"A man of subtlety, then?"

"I prefer to think of it as honesty."

"How refreshing." She spoke lightly, but her belly heated when she remembered the untamed desire that burned in his eyes after he kissed her. And what a kiss. His embrace was . . . overwhelming. She hadn't wanted so badly to be touched in a long time. She'd always been too focused, too obsessed with order to pay much attention to men. But Luniel had blown all that to splinters with his hot lips and glossy black wings and fiery, sinful blue eyes.

Pity she'd been unconscious when he started kissing her. She really needed to get out more.

He stopped in front of a dusty apartment block opposite the park, shutters pulled low over UV-filtered windows, and spun her to face him, pulling her into his arms so her body fitted against his chest. "Ready?"

Uh-huh. He felt just like she thought. Warm, hard, tempting. "Ready for what?"

"This." He snapped his feathers taut, and dived skywards.

Her breath rushed out. Breeze dragged her hair back, the ground spinning away. Her stomach plummeted. He crushed her close to his chest, effortless, and she could feel his muscles pumping as he swooped aloft.

She clutched him, exhilarated and terrified. Glass windows flashed past, concrete girders, the long dark web of a fire escape. A bird squawked and dived, startled, and suddenly they rocketed above the city skyline, with only the moon shining down.

Luniel rolled, soaring, cradling her body against his. His deep voice tingled dark shivers in her ear. "Like it?"

Morgan's breath caught. The buildings below seemed so far

away. Lights glittered, a spray of diamonds twinkling in the night, and bonfires spat scarlet in the park. Warm moonlight caressed her. She almost could taste it, shining on her tongue, the breeze riffling her hair. It was beautiful.

"Hold tight," he murmured.

She tightened her grip—somehow she'd linked her wrists around his neck, and his arms folded around her body—and he swooped, and landed on the rooftop, light and graceful, a flick of ink-dark feathers.

She let out her breath in a rush. "Whoa. That was . . . incredible. Unbelievable."

"But you do believe it." His voice sparkled in her ear, dark, his lips hot. "C'mon, Morgan. I'm here, you're here. This is real. No use pretending."

She realized he still crushed her against him. She could feel his heartbeat, strong and rapid, pounding through her like it was her own. His heat burned her, and his breath rasped, feverish.

She swallowed. "Put me down."

"Why? I like the feel of you."

That much was clear. Evidently, angels had all the same body parts as humans, because if that thing pressing into her belly wasn't . . . oh, my. Apparently, he liked the feel of her quite a lot. "Is, uh . . . is that what you call honesty?"

"Just making conversation." His wicked grin shivered all the way down her spine. "Is that your scientific curiosity showing, Dr. Sterling, or are you enjoying yourself?"

She flushed, and pushed away. Great. A horny angel. She knew she wasn't that attractive, despite her probably better-than-average looks—no matter what they all said, most guys found a smart, career-focused woman intimidating. And a ridiculously good-looking guy like Luniel would have no trouble finding pretty girls to play with. He was just teasing her. Putting her off her guard.

"Where are we?" At her feet, skylight windows pierced the gently sloping roof, moonbeams slanting onto a distant wooden floor. The iron rooftop banked sharply away at the edges.

"Told you. My place." Luniel danced across on light wings and levered the skylight up on its hinges, unhooking a battered wooden ladder that creaked down inside. "After you, Doctor."

"You live in a loft in Harlem?"

"So? It's convenient."

"Who pays your rent, anyway? Don't tell me you've got a regular job."

His eyes twinkled. "We have ways of getting stuff for free."

"I'm sure. So why not Central Park West, or something? You slumming it?"

"It's less noticeable here. You think the people in this building care about one more weird neighbor? They're just happy I don't set the place on fire too often." He gestured downwards with a glossy wingtip. "You coming in, or do I have to carry you?"

She shivered suddenly. Going to some strange guy's apartment. This was insane. *She* was insane.

All the same, seeing an angel's . . . what? House? Nest? Aerie? It'd be kinda cool. How did he live? What did he eat? Did he have . . . stuff, like normal people?

Yes, her scientific curiosity was definitely showing. She hid a smile, and stepped forward.

CHAPTER 8

Luniel took her hand and eased her down the ladder. It was a tall attic room, the white ceilings high and airy, and she had to hop the last few feet to reach the hardwood floor.

He lighted beside her, feathers fluffing. He coughed, and wiped his mouth. "Welcome to Casa de Lune. Make yourself at home."

She dusted off her hands. Moonlight slanted through the skylights, dust motes dancing in warm toffee scent. Kitchenette in one corner, white tiles and stainless steel. It looked spotless. Did he cook? Did he even eat? Bathroom in another corner, behind a frosted glass screen. A low flat sofa, a pile of fat black cushions to sit on, a TV, a cabinet overflowing with magazines and paperbacks. Above hung a mezzanine loft, too high to reach and with no ladder. Presumably where he slept.

Did he have a regular bed, she wondered? A nest? A perch, even? Did he sleep in human form, or angel? Presuming, of course, that a creature of heaven had to sleep at all. He seemed to have other human male traits. A one-track mind, for instance.

What she didn't see were any trappings of religion. No altars, icons, crucifixes, Bibles or Korans or Torahs.

Didn't mean he wasn't a nutter.

Still, in her experience, the really crazy ones plastered it all over the place. Immersed themselves in it. Her mother had papered

the walls with Bible verses and drawings of Christ. It sickened
Morgan just to think about how the evil sons of bitches who
seduced her mother used symbols of love and goodness to do it.
By all accounts, after all, the real Jesus was a pretty decent guy. It
was the twisted ones among his believers who were the problem.

Still, the whole thing didn't sit right with her scientific mind.
To accept a single, sole truth without proof or debate was insane.

"Not so scary, is it?"

"Huh?" She jerked back to the present, and swayed, dizzy.
Maybe it was the sensation of flight, but her head ached anew from
the blows she'd taken, and she felt light-headed. She'd lost some
blood. There could be infection. Maybe delayed-onset shock . . .

Luniel twirled one finger, indicating his apartment. "No
unbelievers chained to the walls?"

"And here I was thinking there'd be harps and choirs of
cherubs."

He wrinkled his nose. "You ever hear a cherub sing? It's not
pretty."

She scraped her hair back, and blood smeared. Shit. She
touched her forehead gingerly. A cut had reopened. Not the
demon slash, just a bang she'd gotten as they'd escaped. It bled
fresh and uncorrupted, but there was a lot of it. She probably
needed stitches. Not to mention a rabies shot.

Luniel's gaze clouded, and he reached for her. "You're bleeding. Here, let me—"

"No, it's okay." She shuffled away. "Can I use your
bathroom?"

"Of course." He lifted her and swooped across the room, her
feet a few inches from the floor, and set her down before the
sink. His body felt even warmer, feverish, his skin shiny with
sweat.

The vanity had a long oval sink and an illuminated mirror,
and beside it lay a claw-foot bathtub and a glass shower stall
tiled in white. All spotless. A neat freak? Maybe he hired a
housekeeper. He rummaged in the cupboard beneath the sink,
his eyes glazing. "Somewhere I've got . . ."

"It's okay." She didn't want him tending her wounds. Didn't
want him touching her.

All right, part of her did want him touching her. The sensual,
hedonistic part who loved chocolate ice cream by the tub and

toasted marshmallows by the dozen, and sometimes drank herself to sleep, alone. The part who couldn't be trusted.

"I'm a doctor," she insisted. "I can handle it. Go tend to yourself." Reflexively, she put the back of her hand to his forehead and checked the dilation of his pupils. Black, glittering, only a burning ring of blue. His face shone damp, his lips pale, dark bruises ringing his eyes. "You've got a fever. And you look like crap. Is that, uh, sweating thing normal?"

"Demon venom. I've got a cure." His words slurred, thick, like he was drunk. The gashes on his face clotted and bubbled, infected with evil green fluid. "D'you mind if I go and . . ."

"Is there anything I can do?" Her instincts had taken over, and she spoke coolly, calmly and to the point. Just like a good doctor.

A flicker of surprise. "No."

"Then go." She shoved him out, her guts twisting cold. He was injured because of her, and she couldn't fix it. Frustration and worry clamored in her chest. With the dead, she was used to feeling helpless. With the living . . .

Still, it wasn't her fault. She'd never been attacked by demon bats until he showed up. Right?

Her mouth firmed, and she examined her injuries in the mirror.

Like most scalp wounds, not as bad as the bleeding made it look. She washed the slash carefully, easing out a few dirt clumps. She could hear Luniel on the phone, his voice low and careful. Who was he calling? His friend Dashiel? The local pizza store? God?

There was no disinfectant, but below the sink among soap and toothpaste she found a pile of gauze bandages. Did he need them for himself? Or wasn't she the only female . . . uh, wounded human he'd brought back here?

His voice again, a murmured chant. What was he doing? She glanced over her shoulder in the mirror as she dabbed her face. She couldn't see. Softly she put the bandages down, and crept to the screen's edge.

He was on his knees, shirtless, his black wings swept back. The muscles of his back and chest stood out, rigid, slick with sweat. His head had fallen back, and he chanted strange words at the moon, silvery light washing down over him. Blood streaked his hair, and bright red webs of corruption crept over his cheek and down his neck like living veins of poison, grasping for his heart.

As he chanted, the Tainted's twin lightning bolt sigil on his left palm flared blue. He held something shiny in his right hand—a knife with a cruelly curved blade—and as she watched, transfixed, he folded his left hand around the blade and sliced.

Blood splurted, crimson mixed with evil green corruption. It ran down his arm and pooled in a black stone cup he'd placed before him for the purpose.

Morgan gasped. He was casting some kind of spell, or at least he thought he was. And all that blood surely didn't raise the odds of it being a nice one. Her heart clenched. Had he lied all along? Tricked her with his charm? Maybe he was really . . . twisted. Bad. Evil.

He removed the blade and squeezed his fist, halting the flow to a trickle. And then the blood-filled cup burst into flame.

Not red, angry, evil flame. Pure white. It seared and flashed, dazzling. Purifying.

Not that the color meant anything. But the air hummed alive with positive energy. Morgan's skin tingled. The lights above the mirror flickered, and all the hair on her body sprang charged. It didn't feel evil. It felt . . . alive. Soothing. Invigorating.

Her forehead stung, and she glanced back to the mirror. Her wound sizzled, and healed itself.

Morgan's stomach hollowed. She gulped, and flew her hand to her forehead. No cut. Not even a scratch.

She whirled back to Lune. He took the glowing cup in both hands, and drank it down.

Fresh blood spilled on his chin, bright scarlet, free from corruption. He swallowed deep, until the last drop was gone. His muscles convulsed, straining. White radiance flashed over him, with a thunderous crack like lightning. Ozone stung her nose. The cup fell from Luniel's hands, and he collapsed to the floor, limp.

The light faded, leaving only silvery moonlight. His skin gleamed, clean, free from poison. He lifted his head, gasping for breath. The fetid wound on his cheek was gone. Vanished. Healed.

Morgan fell back against the bathtub, dazed. Her mind stumbled. She'd seen this man—this *creature*—wish a flaming sword from empty air and slaughter monsters he said were demons. Seen him heal small injuries with impossible speed, rip the heart from a dead man's chest and set it on fire. Seen him fly, damn it, flown with him in his arms. None of those things were human.

But this was something else. He'd called down some power from outside himself.

Called down the power of God.

And it had healed him. Healed her.

Her mind reeled, choking her.

Until now, she'd gone along with it, not really believing. Just fascinated by Luniel. Curious about a man with wings. Attracted by his . . . potency. Enthralled by things new and exciting.

But now . . .

Her rational mind thrashed and protested, screaming, but in a stubborn daze, she beat it down. *Scientific method, Morgan. Weigh up the evidence. Accept your observations. You can't keep only the data that supports your pet theory and toss out what you don't like.*

What if all this was real?

And this was the guy who said the world was ending. Not in four billion years when the sun went out, but soon. Now.

What if that was real, too?

Luniel clutched at the floor, gulping air. Heaven's glory sparkled over him, warm and deadly delicious, a heady mix of pain and pleasure. It stabbed deep into his body, raking every nerve raw. And then it washed away, lost, and deep sorrow drowned his heart.

He panted, willing his heartbeat to slow. *Sweet mercy, that never gets any easier.*

Ever since he'd been shunned, healing from a hellcurse that had taken root—like Morgan's illicitly stolen injury—was no easy task. You had to ask. Beg for it on your fucking knees. There'd be that terrifying moment of emptiness, when he feared he was discarded and alone. And then the glory would hit him, hot and breathtaking and magnificent, and every time, he wanted to weep.

Every time, a harsh reminder of everything he no longer had.

He crawled to his feet, snapping his feathers tight. Already, the energy flowed through him, rich and heady. He felt no pain.

No fever. The poison was defeated. His senses glittered sharp. His blood coursed swift and strong. His muscles tingled with warmth and vigor, and his feathers crackled with static, longing for flight. Even his headache was gone.

Just exhilaration, and hunger for the fight, and black anger scratching raw in his heart.

A fucking junkie, that's what he was. Just another helpless addict, like Michael's fawning little pets. Terrified of that black day when his source would dry up, and there'd be no more.

Once, he'd vowed never to ask again. But something always kept him coming back.

Luniel's fists clenched. Something like Morgan. Letting her die wasn't an option. That didn't make begging for the scraps of heaven's deliverance any less humiliating.

He stalked to the kitchen sink and doused his head, shaking it so the water streamed through his hair and over his body. Sweat and blood sloughed away. He rinsed his mouth and ruffled his feathers, spraying angry droplets onto the floor. The glory filled him with lust for demon slaughter, his muscles throbbing, all that righteous anger he'd been so long denied.

He breathed deep, fighting to relax. *Calm the fuck down, Lune. This is no way to fight.* But the thrill was irresistible. Glory was hashish for heaven's warriors. They killed on a holy high, their blood pumping hot and relentless with divine wrath. That was heaven's way, how angels were absolved from the slaughter they wrought. Cold calculation was for murderers, a slippery slide to hell.

Whatever. Lune had already called Dash, told him about the demon sigil and Quuzaat. Soon, the Host would be here. He needed to arm himself, make ready . . .

Through the moonlit heat of his own raging pulse, he heard the faint rasp of sobbing.

Morgan.

He squeezed his eyes shut, but it didn't go away.

She was crying. Up until now, she'd taken everything on board with a quip and a thoughtful nod.

His muscles jerked tight. Had she watched what he'd just done? Seen him drink his own blood and get struck by divine lightning? Enough to freak any unbelieving human out. Hell, it freaked *him* out.

His brittle nerves itched, and he alighted and wafted on warm air towards the bathroom. Peered silently over the screen, quivering.

She curled beside the bathtub, hugging her knees. Her wet dark hair lay tangled over her shoulder. She'd peeled off her white doctor's coat, and she looked so vulnerable without her armor. So feminine in her dark skirt and plum red blouse. Her smoky stockings were torn, a tantalizing glimpse of smooth skin. Her lips shone, so delicate and soft.

His pulse quickened. So beautiful. So desirable. And her tears tore his heart, even as his spell-rich blood pounded harder, drowning out his reason.

Don't go in there, Lune. Don't comfort her. Don't touch her, for heaven's sake. Not in this state, hard, aching, thirsty for action and sensation. He'd hurt her. Fuck her. Worse. Both.

But he couldn't let this proud woman cry. Not on his bathroom floor. Not when he was the cause.

As calmly as he could, he laid his spelled knife on the sink and settled on his knees at her side. "Morgan?"

Luniel's voice vibrated through her chest, and she blinked rapidly on stupid tears. He was on his knees beside her, wrapping her in his warm shadow. She didn't want him to see her cry. He'd only think her weak and vulnerable. "Go away," she muttered.

"Please, don't cry. You're okay." He brushed her hair back with shaky fingers.

She jerked away, her pulse racing. The bathtub clanged warm against her back. She couldn't retreat any further. "Don't touch me. I watched you. I saw you drink your own blood!"

"Yes." No denial. No hesitation. "It's a blood sacrifice. The cost of healing. I wasn't supposed to take your injury. I couldn't fix it." He shrugged, edgy, his dark wings jerking. "Being Tainted . . . well, it's not all fun. I have to ask for stuff I used to do on my own. But it's not devil worship or any shit like that. In case you were wondering."

"And I'm supposed to believe you?" Her throat ached. He looked so beautiful. His skin glowed, still afire with that warm white light. His black feathers gleamed. She wanted to touch them.

"Tell me I've lied to you so far." He stroked her cheek with his knuckles. "Everything I've said is true. Trust me."

Her heart clenched. His hot blue gaze unsettled her. Too close. Too strong. Too honest.

She wanted to trust him. Wanted to let him make everything okay. His face held no deceit. His gaze didn't falter. His handsome mouth didn't twitch. Her every instinct screamed at her that he was telling the truth. Not just about the blood spell. About everything.

And that made it all the more imperative that she got away from him, right now.

She scrambled to her feet, her pulse aflame, and dived for the exit.

But he got there first on a flash of black wings, and held her. "No. Stop running from me."

"Let me go!" She struggled, but it only made him hold her tighter.

"Not until you face the truth." He grabbed her wrists, fighting her. "You're a smart woman. Don't make yourself stupid over this."

"What do you mean?" His grip hurt a little. She twisted, trying to break free, trying not to notice how her heart raced when he touched her. It was all tricks. An attractive guy, a lonely woman. Oldest con in the book.

"You are," he insisted. "The light's glaring you in the face and you're deliberately shutting your eyes. I call that pretty stupid, don't you?"

"It's not like that! I just—oh!"

Swiftly, he pinned her to the wall, thrusting his thigh against her hip to hold her. The contact tingled through her. Her breasts pressed against his chest, and sweet warmth flared there.

His blue gaze seared into hers, heated and dangerous. "You just what?" His whisper deepened to a growl that sparkled her skin hot. "Just don't believe me? Then believe this." And he leaned in and trapped her mouth with his.

CHAPTER 9

So scorching hot. So delicious. His lips captured hers, shocking, alive. He took her mouth deeply, no waiting, just a commanding swipe of his tongue across her lips that demanded she open for him. And then he slanted his lips across hers to deepen the kiss further, tasting every corner of her mouth, until her eyes slid closed and all her objections and fears dissolved in a mess of hot longing.

No angels, no demons. No end of the world. Just this man, hard and delicious and hungry for her.

He growled, deep inside his chest, and pleasure tingled straight to her core. He felt so raw, so untamed. His fingers dug into her wrists as he kissed her harder, crushing her against the wall like he'd never let her go. His body felt strong, hot, hungry, his sheer size intimidating and exciting. His tongue tangled with hers, urgent, and when she moaned into the kiss, he sighed, deep. "Morgan," he breathed into her mouth, his lips never quite leaving hers. "You taste so fucking good. Can you feel how hard I am for you?"

Oh, could she feel it. Hard and delicious, pressing hungrily into her belly. She flushed hotter. "Umm. Yeah."

"Feels real enough, doesn't it? Do you like it?"

"Mmm." She struggled in his grip, wanting to slide her

palms over his chest, score his perfect skin with her nails, hear him gasp and groan as she worked his silky hot shaft in her hands. She hadn't touched a man in so long—hadn't been touched, hadn't sighed in pleasure or elicited a sigh in return—and now she knew how much she'd missed it. Everything always about work, about data and analysis and being rational.

There was nothing rational about this. She wanted this creature inside her. She wanted to touch him, taste his beautiful skin, run her hands through that sooty-silk hair, drag him downwards and let him take her. Lie beneath him and rub her cheek against his soft angel feathers while he drove into her . . .

Angel. Her wits fluttered, lost. She wanted to be touched . . . no. She wanted to be *fucked* by an angel. This angel. And nothing had ever seemed so right.

"Good." A heated whisper, tender but full of force, demanding her surrender. "That's progress. Now stroke my feathers."

"But . . ."

"Touch them, Morgan." Another kiss, deep and melting, and he curled his wing's edge over his shoulder and pulled her fingers deep into the smooth blackness. "Do you feel that?"

Warmth tingled from her fingertips deep into her body, and she gasped. So sleek and silken, yet crisp. Strange, warm, alive.

He squeezed her hand, making her clench her fingers and pull. "How does it feel?"

The feathers crunched in her fist, springy. Hot golden sparks jumped in reaction, and he growled softly, yanking her tighter against him. He obviously enjoyed that. She wanted to do it again. She struggled to breathe, think, say anything coherent. "Umm . . . it sparkles . . . it's hot, and . . . you like it . . ."

"You noticed. That's another step forward. Now tell me you want me, too."

His insistence made her quiver in delight, her breasts aching for his palms. "Mmm. Touch me."

"Not good enough. Let go, Morgan. Believe." More scorching kisses, and this time he pressed his hard thigh between hers, easing his throbbing cock against her with a feral groan of desire that made her shiver and fumble at the wall for safety. "Say it."

He was too much for her. Too big, too strong, too demanding. Fear stroked between her legs, twinned with secret, delicious desire. She was losing control, and it struck her afire. "I do," she gasped in wonder. "I want you."

"Then tell me I'm real." He released one wrist, and brushed his knuckles along the line of her throat, down to caress the side of her breast. Daring, she grabbed his hair—at last, so crisp and silky rough, just like she'd imagined—and he spread hot kisses down her neck, nipping her collarbone with a soft snarl that made her weak. His knuckles brushed the thrumming tip of her breast through her blouse. "Tell me *this* is real."

She managed an incoherent sound. Her nipples were so hard they stung. He yanked her blouse aside and tongued her through her black lacy bra, and she cried out. Her breasts were so sensitive. Always had been. "Mmm. More. Please."

His wings glittered like black ice with desire. He slid his big hand inside her bra and cupped her breast, uncovering it so it was bare. "Heaven, you're beautiful." He thumbed the nipple lightly, making her moan. "You like that? Then say it, Morgan. Tell me I'm real."

"Confession under torture," she managed with a panting smile. "Unreliable."

He squeezed her gently, stroking openmouthed kisses around her nipple but not close enough, and with his other hand he released her wrist and teased up inside her thigh. His midnight hair brushed her chest, tempting. "Say it, witch."

She crushed his hair, desperate. Her nipples swelled even harder. "You're real. This is all real. Just touch me!"

He sucked her nipple deep into his hot mouth.

She cried out, the heat spearing all the way to her sex. Nothing had ever felt so good.

"Well done," he murmured, wicked. "Didn't hurt, did it? Wanna see how real it gets?" He suckled her, nipping softly.

Oh, God. Her thighs tingled, and he crept his fingers upwards, teasing the lacy edge of her stocking. She groaned, and parted her thighs for him. She was so close. If he pushed even one finger into her, she'd break apart . . .

No. She wanted him inside her. All of him. She reached between them, searching, gliding her fingers along his hot length over his jeans. Mmm. This would fill her nicely. He didn't feel strange or wrong. He felt like a man, big and engorged and shuddering with need.

He ground against her, urgent, reaching for her panties. Her nipple slipped from his sucking mouth with a pop. "Do you want my cock, Morgan? Want me inside you?"

The simple, brutal passion in his words throbbed deep in some secret place inside. All her life, she'd fought for control, but tonight, with this man, she wanted . . . something else. Something dangerous. "Oh, yes."

"Undo me, then. Go on."

She fumbled, and his buttons popped open, his cock straining hot into her hands. Holy shit, he was huge. Go slow, can't take it huge, so long and thick and hard . . . Beautiful. She wrapped hungry fingers around him, stroking, and he growled and dived for her other nipple, baring her breast and sucking the hard bud into his mouth.

Tension clenched hot and tight inside her. "Oh, God. Now. I'm going to . . . oh!" Frantic, she wrapped her thigh around his hips, straining to reach high enough.

He swore and pushed her skirt up, guiding himself. Her panties were soaked, and he tugged them aside. "You're so wet," he growled. "You smell delicious."

When his hot flesh rubbed against her slickness, she moaned, another spasm wracking her. "Yes. Do it."

He held back, breathing hard, his lips an inch from hers. "You going to come?"

"Uh-huh . . ."

He nipped her bottom lip, a possessive snarl. "You going to come when I fuck you, Morgan?"

"God, yes! Just do it!"

He groaned, and rolled his hips, and the head of his massive cock nudged her entrance. She panted, quivering on the brink.

And then he cursed, bitter, and pulled back.

She gasped, disbelieving. Swiftly, he covered her mouth with his, and thrust his hand between her legs. Her clit swelled under his clever fingers, so hard and sensitive, and in a few moments she exploded, shuddering, liquid fire searing her nerves, her cries stifled deep in his mouth.

She let her head fall back, dazed. Heat tingled inside her, still stroking her with delight. "What? Why did you . . . ?"

"Shh." He pressed his finger to her lips, his eyes glowing violet. His other hand still caressed her lightly, teasing out aftershocks that made her gasp and whimper. His feathers sparked, electric with desire. "Hold that thought, Dr. Sterling. We've got company."

And now she heard what his supernatural hearing had already detected.

Footsteps on the iron roof. The rush of wings.

Luniel kissed her, hard, stealing her breath, and with a night-dark flutter, he was gone.

Her legs went limp, and she braced herself against the wall on sweaty palms, panting.

So what the hell was that?

Her mind swirled, drugged with pleasure. So hot. So perfect. He'd played her like a familiar instrument, and she'd gone with him, every sigh and shiver and moan of the way. She hadn't come like that in years. Or ever. And still her flesh twitched, longing to feel him inside her.

But part of her cringed, disbelieving. He'd conquered her and left her. A man she'd met only two hours ago. She'd no idea who he was. She'd gone to his apartment, for God's sake. Alone. Without telling anyone where she was. What kind of moron was she? This was Babylon. He could be a torture rapist. A skin collector. A killer. Even if he was an angel.

And even if he'd told her the truth, how could she be so stupid? To show weakness like that. To believe he wasn't using her, even for a moment. He hadn't taken his pleasure from her—and Jesus fucking Christ, it hadn't even crossed her mind to use protection, like she *wanted* a dose of HIV or something—but it didn't matter. He was manipulating her, tuning her to his will. Using her irrational attraction to his advantage. Just like any evangelist, using her own natural willingness to trust people against her.

She shuddered, remembering how she'd wanted him inside her. How she'd begged him to take her.

How she'd admitted she believed, just so he'd touch her.

And now, his friends—his so-called Tainted Host?—had shown up, and he'd left her without a blink. Careless. Embarrassed, probably, to be caught touching her. But all her instincts had told her he was for real.

Just went to show her instincts couldn't be trusted. They'd only betray her. Just like her mother's betrayed *her*.

Woodenly, she cleaned herself with a towel and tossed it onto the sink. His scent lingered in her nostrils, his hot male flavor in her mouth. Her flesh still ached for him, to feel his weight atop her, his big length filling her . . .

She washed her flushed face, willing her heartbeat to return to normal. Her wounds were completely healed. It didn't make her feel better. It only made her stomach squirm.

She stared at her reflection, and set her jaw, determination tempering like steel in her heart. Maybe all that light was the power of God. It didn't matter. Whatever else he was, Luniel was handsome, charming and exciting—which all added up to *dangerous*. She wouldn't make the same mistake again.

On her mother's life, she'd swear it.

Luniel stalked from the bathroom, refusing to look back. Moonlight glared, and hot sparks charged his skin, the physical manifestation of his desire. He was so hard it hurt him, and the memory of her soft wet flesh on his cock made him want to scream. Her legs were so sexy in those lacy stockings, so lithe as she wrapped one around him. The way she'd gasped and writhed her gorgeous body under his . . . God, he wanted to grab his cock in his fist and jerk himself off.

Fuck it, he wanted to swoop back into that bathroom and get inside her, feel her firm, slick flesh sliding over him. She'd be so tight, so hot. He was certain of it. He'd spread her thighs apart and ride her hard and deep until they both exploded . . .

Yeah. Not happening. With difficulty he refastened his jeans, every touch a desperate agony. She was too beautiful. Too tempting. Too intoxicating. He hadn't been able to resist her, not with glory a liquid flashburn in his veins and his flesh quivering with need.

But he had to. He had to, or she'd be demon bait. Already he wanted to hold her, fold her protectively in his wings, keep her safe . . .

Unwilled, memories sprang, of the day Michael sent him away. Lying on the cold stone dungeon floor, choking blood, bruises already swelling deep in his guts. He'd scrabbled blindly to retrieve his sword, but the archangel kicked it away. Michael hovered over him in torchlight, sword blazing, those impeccable

icy wings adazzle with glory, and Lune had waited for cold
flaming steel to slice his heart and end it all, but it hadn't come.
Instead, crisp ice-blond hair tortured his flayed cheek as the
archangel leaned down.

Word of advice, Luniel of the Tainted, Michael had whispered. *Staunch that bleeding heart. It'll only get you killed.*

And then his face hit dirt, and he'd woken up like this.

A whoosh of earthy breeze dragged Lune back to the present, and Dashiel clapped him on the shoulder, grinning. He'd
changed out of his jeans, and wore his silver-armored breastplate and leather pants tucked into heavy boots. His dark wings
shone, preened, his hair tied neatly back. "Hope we're not inter-
rupting anything."

Luniel slashed a grin back, furious. He still smelled of Morgan, his fingers still damp with her essence. His shadow sparkled on the floor, and he still glowed, brimming with everything
he'd done and said and felt. Pretty fucking obvious what he'd
been up to. "Bite me, Dash. Didn't you say something about a
stick up my ass?"

"Hey, don't get shitty with me," said Dashiel cheerfully.
"Enjoy yourself. Just do it on your own time. Look, the gang's
all here."

The ladder clattered, and Jadzia vaulted down, her long
blond hair fluttering. She was armored, too, the spelled silver
curving over her slim torso. Extra knives were strapped to her
black-leather-clad thighs. She landed lightly, flaring creamy
wings. "Hey, Lune," she said coolly. "Busy night?"

Luniel flushed, and looked away. Awesome. Hell of a time
for her to show up. Jadzia was a wonderful girl. He cared about
her, enough that they hadn't yet had the *this was nice but it's
over* conversation that inevitably followed when he slept with a
woman. But Jadzia was a gritty fighter who never gave up, and
that distant look in her clear blue eyes said *mistake.*

Another swoop of reddish wings, and Trillium landed in a
cloud of smoky nightclub stink. He wore similar armor and
fighting gear, but somehow contrived to look scruffy, his flame-
orange hair artfully messed like a porcupine. Tattoos flexed on
his brutally strong arms as he lounged against the kitchen counter and lit a cigarette, wafting smoke away with a careless

green-dappled wing. "Where's the party, guys? Oh, yeah, I forgot. This is Lune's place. Obviously not here."

How Trillium managed to keep all those tattoos and piercings in fast-healing angelflesh was a mystery. If you asked him, he just winked and said nothing. "Yeah, well, my place isn't a fucking ashtray, either. You stink, Trill."

"Those things'll kill you," chimed in Jadzia, testing her knife's edge with a fingernail.

Trillium blew smoke rings. "You think? All the cool kids are doing it. I wanna look like Dirty Harry." He glared and set his mouth tight in imitation, his crazy orange hair incongruous.

"Who?" Jadzia and Lune said simultaneously.

"Dirty Harry doesn't smoke," Dash pointed out, flopping into the cushions with his wings spread. "And Clint Eastwood *died* twenty years ago, dude. The cool kids haven't been doing it since the nineties."

Trillium looked shocked. "You don't say. Damn those reruns." He took another drag and tossed the cigarette hissing into the sink. "Well, what's the rumpus, chaps? When do I get to julienne some demon balls?" He conjured his sword and pirouetted with it, slicing the air with blazing orange flame. Trill loved earthly things, money and bodies and drugs—too much, as far as heaven was concerned—but he was still fit and devilishly quick.

The soft clearing of a female throat made Luniel turn.

Morgan emerged from his bathroom, her face still pink but composed. Her dark hair curled wet, and a stray lock stuck to her cheek beside her mouth. He wanted to kiss it off. With a fresh sting of desire, he remembered crushing that hair in his fists, pulling himself down to her, parting her thighs and forcing his hard cock between them, searching . . .

Telltale sizzle heated his wings, and he flushed again and turned back. "Guys? This, uh . . . this is Dr. Morgan Sterling."

CHAPTER 10

Morgan stared, swallowing. As if the sight of Luniel, still shirt-less, his lips still tender *from her kiss* and his blacker-than-black hair tousled on his massive shoulders *by her hands*, wasn't enough.

Now there were *four* beautiful angels in the room. And three were staring at her.

She lifted her fingers, a weak wave. "Hi."

The huge dark-winged one was first to break the silence. He swooped from the cushions where he'd lounged and landed lightly before her, tossing Luniel a teasing wink. Brutally hand-some, this one, flashing hot-chocolate eyes and a face carved from rough granite. And seriously massive. He towered over her and Luniel both, silver armor flashing in the moonlight, his black-coffee wings flecked with gold.

"Lune, you crafty dog." He bent to kiss her on both cheeks and flashed a smile, as brilliant as Luniel's but somehow darker. "I'm enchanted, Dr. Sterling. Lune's told me all about you . . . Well, not yet. But he sure as hell will, if he doesn't want me to kick his ass."

Morgan stuttered. He still held her hand. She didn't know whether to pull away. "Um. Right."

Luniel sighed. "Give it a rest, Dash. She's kinda new to the whole angel thing?"

"I will, when you remember your fucking manners. What's gotten into you?"

"What? Oh. Sorry." Luniel waved his hand, exaggerating. "Morgan, this scruffy lout is Dashiel, and no matter what he says, he's not lonely and single and aching for your company."

Dashiel grinned, charming as hell. "He's just jealous. Pay him no mind. But now that he mentions it . . ."

A flutter of reddish feathers, and the second angel—who a moment ago flourished a flaming sword—shouldered Dash aside. This one had elaborately messy, fire orange hair and lip piercings, rakish like a modern-day pirate, and he, too, wore silver armor, his bulky tattooed arms glistening. His mint-green eyes twinkled as he kissed her hand with a flirty bow. "I, on the other hand, am totally single, and aching like you wouldn't believe. Just so you know."

She grinned in response, infectious. The other one, Dashiel, had rough edges, but she sensed he was a gentleman underneath. This one, she felt sure, had never been any kind of gentleman.

Luniel shoved him lightly backwards, so he let go of her hand. "You'll be aching worse if you don't back off. Dr. Sterling, this carrot-headed moron is Trillium, and as you can see, it's impossible to take my so-called friends anywhere."

Morgan managed another wary smile. They all had the same eclectic accent as Luniel. And they were ruthlessly charming, in an oh-my-God-did-an-angel-just-kiss-my-hand kind of way. *Smoke and mirrors. Don't trust them.* "Right. Do you guys always, uh, flirt like this?"

Dashiel made an innocent expression, as best he could with that supernova smile.

Trillium laughed, warm like chili chocolate. "Nah. You just lucked out, is all. You'd rather get sneered at by the ice prince? Just wait till Ariel gets here—"

"Yes, they do." A husky female voice drifted, and an exquisite pale creature glided down in front of Morgan. Flowing blond hair, wings like creamy velvet, cool jasmine perfume. Her silver armor shone, spotless, curving over her slender figure, and wicked knives were strapped to her taut thighs over black leather pants. Clear blue eyes, a few shades lighter than Luniel's, surveyed Morgan distantly. "Childish, isn't it? If only any of them were worth flirting back with," the angel added coolly, her gaze flickering to Luniel.

Morgan's courage quailed. Oops. Had she stepped on some girl-angel toes? This woman—this *lady*—looked like a goddess, strong and self-possessed. Far more beautiful than she.

Envious much? She offered her hand. "I'm Morgan."

"Jadzia." The angel shook briefly, her brow creasing. "What kind of doctor are you?"

"I'm a pathologist. An assistant medical examiner for Babylon County."

"Ah." Jadzia's face cleared. "You look at dead bodies. Nice."

"Glamorous, huh?"

A beautiful smile, a flicker of warmth. "I dunno. You should fit right in around here."

"I hope so."

Jadzia leaned closer, confidential. "Never you mind the boys," she said, her voice carelessly at a level they could all hear. "They're sweethearts once you get to know them. Dash is just a big old teddy bear under all that macho bullshit, and Trill is clearly erecting intimacy barriers, with all that ink and hot metal. As for Lune, well . . ." An amused smile. "I'm not quite sure what he's compensating for with that big pointy sword of his. But I'm sure he thinks it's important."

Luniel snorted, and Trillium mimed stabbing himself in the heart. "You wound me, Jaz. Truly."

Morgan giggled, her face heating. It was kind of a big sword. If she didn't know better . . .

Dashiel cleared his throat. "Guys? Can we get on with this?"

Trillium flung himself into the cushions, preening one green-flecked coppery wing. "Sure, Teddy Bear. Apocalypse, vials, ocean of blood, blah blah. Where *is* Ariel, anyway?"

"Mike sent him to hunt down the third Guardian." Dash flopped beside him, crossing his ankles. "Don't expect him anytime soon."

"You mean we're short a dude, dude?" Trill sighed. "Great. Who's on scowling duty, then? I vote for Lune. He's best at it after Ariel."

Luniel scowled at him, comical.

Trill just grinned, and patted the cushion beside him. "Come sit by me, Dr. Sterling, and we'll see what barriers I'm erecting."

Morgan grinned back, and sat, but on the sofa, outside his reach.

Luniel smirked, and dived overhead for his loft, black wings astretch. His voice drifted down as he hunted about on the floorboards. "We're short more than that. I don't see Iria here."

"Couldn't raise her," said Dash. "Probably off eating some unsuspecting male for breakfast. She'll catch up with us in her own time."

"Did you get my text?"

"Yeah. You found Ithiel. I'm sorry, man."

Luniel swooped to the floor, his silver breastplate hooked over his arm. He'd taken off his jeans—Morgan flushed—and now he wore boots and black leather pants that hugged his thighs and curved sweetly over his ass. "Quuzaat," he said succinctly. "Dirty demon prince, loves himself a plague."

He finished dressing while he explained what they'd discovered from Ithiel's body, but Morgan barely heard a word. Luminous skin, glistening smooth in the moonlight. Muscles rippling as he tugged his black hair into a band. Long limbs stretching as he pulled a light sleeveless shirt over his head, pecs flexing as he vanished his wings to fit his breastplate. He buckled it, shrugging massive shoulders to make sure it was loose yet firm, and sprang his wings back, ruffling sooty feathers.

Her mouth dried. He was magnificent. Even in this room full of beautiful monsters, Luniel was breathtaking.

She realized they were all looking at her. "Huh? Sorry, what?"

Luniel smiled, knowing. "I was just saying about your Patient Zero? How you can help us find the plague demon?"

"Right. Sure. Yeah. At least, I think so." She explained what she'd told Luniel on the subway, feeling like a complete loon. Teaching science to the angels.

But Dash and Trill just nodded, interested. Jadzia shrugged, from where she leaned against the kitchen bench, elegant ankles crossed. "Sounds fair. Nice work, Morgan. What about the rest of us, Dash?"

"Trillium, my good son." Dashiel poked him. "Your chance to work the crowd."

Trillium raised his hands, fielding invisible adulation. "Thank you, thank you, it was nothing. In his wisdom, our fearless leader here asked me to look into this blood-in-the-ocean business. As you know, I have friends in low places, and when I asked nicely—"

"Ripped out a few fingernails, you mean," Jadzia murmured.

"Hey, sweetie, I'm with whatever gets results, okay? These mutie gangbangers aren't exactly Mensa members. The world won't miss a few dozen. Anyway. One kindly told me about a big-ass demon soiree going on tonight downtown." He paused dramatically. "The kind where you bathe your ass in blood and pledge your soul to hell? Barrels of blood? Human sacrifices? A big old hell-filthy orgy with one ugly, soul-thirsty fucker of a demon prince in charge. The Prince of Blood, they call him. Sound like anyone we're looking for?"

"The demon who spilled vial number two," confirmed Jadzia. "Wow, Trill, I take back everything bad I said about you."

"Really?" He beamed.

"No, of course not really." Jadzia flicked shining blond hair back. "But you did good, for a greasy gluttonous sinner."

"Wow, thanks. Remind me not to buy you any more drinks, okay?"

Dashiel jumped up. "Can it, kids, and let's get on with it. Japheth's already down there checking it out. It looks bad."

"How bad?" Trill asked.

"Think Peru, 1524."

"That bad, huh."

"Yeah. We'll need all the fighter power we can muster. Trill, you're with me and Jae. Lune, talk to the good doctor here and figure out where the plague prince's most likely hide is. Then I want you to leave her here, take Jaz and check it out. Questions? Good. Let's do it."

No way. Morgan's stomach twisted. *I have to go, too. See Manhattan virus for myself.* But Luniel would dump her first chance he got. *Shit. Should never have let him touch me.* She opened her mouth to protest, knowing it would do no good.

But Luniel cut in. "No. Sorry. Morgan's coming with me."

Morgan's jaw dropped.

Dashiel cocked an eyebrow. "You serious? No offence, Dr. Sterling, but you're hardly equipped to defend yourself."

"Imps attacked us on the way here." Luniel's voice whetted harshly. "They probably know where I live. She can't stay here, and I won't leave her at her place by herself. Or anywhere else, for that matter."

"Lune—"

"We've a better chance of finding Quuzaat if Morgan's there on the ground. She comes with me. Don't argue with me on this one," he added, seeing Dashiel start to speak.

Dashiel lifted his hands, wings curling back. "Okay. Fine. But Jadzia goes with you—"

"I'd rather come with you, if it's all the same," Jadzia cut in coolly. "I can handle myself against demons, Dash." Her expression brooked no argument. Still, a desperate edge to her voice made Morgan wonder if Jadzia wasn't trying to convince herself, as well as Dashiel.

"I know you can, Jaz. But . . ." Dash sighed. "Okay, kids. Whatever. I can't make you. At least give the good doctor a memory spell."

Jadzia shrugged, and whipped out the knife strapped to her left thigh. The blade shone silvery in the moonlight. She murmured a few words, and it glowed, pure white. She sparred an invisible opponent, whirling and slashing, doing stabbing moves, cutting moves, backhanded slides, flipping it like it weighed nothing. The blade hummed, glowing hotter as it danced. Finally, she tossed it spinning into the air, caught it and flung it hard at the wall. It thunked into a wooden beam and stuck there, vibrating, perfectly in the center.

Morgan goggled. Jadzia had impressive skills. Assistant medical examiner and office Sudoku champion couldn't compete with that.

Jadzia stretched out a hand, and the knife ripped itself from the wall and thudded back into her palm, the glow fading. She flipped it and handed it grip first to Morgan. "There. Now you have a knife that can fight. Try it."

Tentatively, Morgan took the weapon. Surprisingly light, and the grip felt cool. But her skin prickled. She'd never fought with a knife. Never cut anything, except ER patients and dead people, and they didn't usually move or fight back. How was she supposed to . . . ?

Jadzia lunged suddenly for her, and quick as static the knife leapt alive in Morgan's hand and slashed, dragging her hand with it.

Jadzia dodged, and smiled. "Like I said, it can fight. Just remember that you can't." She jerked her elegant chin towards Luniel. "Stay behind that big-ass lunkhead, for what it's worth."

"I will." Morgan accepted the knife's sheath, and slipped the knife away. It glowed faintly, like a memory. "Thanks."

Trillium swooped up and mussed his orange hair, making it stick up. "Okay. Let's get on with it. It's been my pleasure, Dr. Sterling. When you get sick of Lune's shit—like, you know, five minutes from now? You know where to find me." And with a dazzling grin, he vanished.

Morgan blinked. Another trick she hadn't seen before.

Luniel glided up, moonlight dancing over silvery armor and big lean muscles. God, his every movement was mesmerizing. "Think you can handle that knife?" he said gruffly.

She licked dry lips. They still tasted of his kiss. *Awkward much?* "Um. Sure. I'll give it a go."

"Don't." His tone sharpened. "That's what I'm for. Don't be a fucking hero. Just stay close to me and do as I say. Okay?"

She swallowed, stinging. It hurt that he didn't think she could defend herself. Then again, she hadn't done a bang-up job so far. "Don't think you're the only one who can take care of themselves, okay? I grew up in a crappy neighborhood. Just because I'm a woman doesn't mean I'm useless."

"You're not just a woman." A flush stained his cheeks. "You're a *human*. Humans and demons don't mix. What part of that don't you get?"

"How about the part where you drag me into this"—she waved her arms, frustrated—"this *game* of yours, and then tell me I can't play!"

"You saw those creatures that attacked us, right? Think you've seen it all? Not by a long shot. Demons have a hierarchy, and those hellshits were right at the bottom. Hell has countless unimaginable horrors waiting for you, Morgan. This is no game."

"Oh, really? Didn't seem like that ten minutes ago when

you . . ." Her fists clenched, and she slammed them into her thighs, furious. *When you sucked my nipples into your mouth and made me come.* "Never mind. Forget it, Luniel. Whatever you say."

He just glowered at her, blue eyes burning.

"Excuse me?" Dashiel poked his head between them with a polite cough. "Lune, can I have a word?"

Luniel's stare didn't falter. But his black wings twitched, and he spun away.

Aargh! Morgan felt like screaming. The big bastard really got under her skin, with his rough gallantry and careless assumptions. And now there they were, Luniel and Dashiel, talking in low voices she couldn't hear. Bitching about her, no doubt. Her scalp itched in frustration, and she yanked her hair free and scratched it ragged.

A touch spun her around, the magic knife jerking in its sheath. Jadzia smiled coolly. "Are you ready? Do you want to change?"

"You have no idea," Morgan muttered. Damn him.

"I'd recommend against tramping around mutie land in those shoes. I can take you back to your place, if you want, so you can slip into something more comfortable."

Morgan's curiosity tingled again. "You mean I get to fly?"

"No. We can flash there. It'll only take a moment. Where did you say you lived, again?"

CHAPTER 11

Lune spun away, itching. Curse that woman. She sent him stupid with her beauty, drove him witless with her snarky tongue and made him want to strangle her and kiss her and hold her down and fuck her into breathless pleasure, all at the same time. And now she was defying him, just when he most needed her to listen.

Kissing her was a bad idea. Touching her was worse. Wanting to protect her . . . well, that ranked up there with lime cola and *Survivor: East Harlem* on the all-time scale of truly shitful ideas. He flared angry feathers. "What is it, Dash? We don't have much time."

Dashiel stared him down, unmovable. "You sure you know what you're doing, kid?"

Inwardly, Lune groaned. One of *those* conversations. Dash had an irritating talent for seeing through people. "I can handle it."

"Obviously. Jesus, I can smell her on you. What happened to your famous rule?"

"What happened to you keeping the fuck out of my face? You're not exactly renowned for leaving your dick in your pants." He spied her, vanishing in Jadzia's glowing aura, and resisted the urge to snap his teeth and growl. Awesome. They could swap how-Lune-pissed-me-off stories.

"This is different." Dashiel didn't drop his stare. "I know you, Lune. You can't hide. What is she to you?"

"Nothing," Lune forced between clenched teeth. "She's nothing. I only just met her tonight. She was there when I found Ithiel and I couldn't get rid of her. She's an AME, it's her fucking morgue."

"That doesn't mean you . . ." Dash paused, and arched an eyebrow. "Your girlfriend's got a morgue? Sweet. You crush on some classy chicks."

Dash looked genuinely impressed, and laughter cracked before Lune could swallow it. "Yeah, I guess so. But she's not my girlfriend. Nothing happened. I'm not interested."

"Will you check the look on your face? For a low-down dirty sinner, you're the worst fucking liar I ever saw."

"Screw you, okay? It's not like that. She doesn't even believe in angels."

Dash grinned, and elbowed him. "Bet she does now, eh?"

"It's not like that." Lune set his jaw, stubborn.

Dash sighed, ruffling his feathers. "Look, I get it, okay? She's a total babe. Color me gobsmacked; she's the sexiest doctor I ever saw this side of HBO. And hey, if you're looking to climb back on the horse after Eleanor, it's about fucking time." He gripped Lune's shoulder, his eyes dark. "But not now, Lune. Not tonight. We're at five minutes to shitstorm on the doomsday clock. I need you, man. Don't freak out on me."

Lune lifted his arms wide. "Do you see me freaking out?"

"Not yet. But you will, if you take her down there and the hellshits get her. You know that."

"They won't," Lune said stiffly. "I'll make sure of it."

"Will you?" Dash's gaze speared him, digging deep. "Can you?"

Fiercely, Lune squeezed his eyes shut, but treacherous memories flashed. Twelve thirteen, the beginnings of the bloody Fifth Crusade, the dank stone prison below a Provençal lord's keep. His beautiful Eleanor, the lord's eldest daughter, writhing in the foul demons' grip, her dress smeared with their dirt and her modestly braided hair ripping loose.

Three of them, the prince and two minions, slobbering over her like beasts. The minions had wild hair and red eyes, their sharp teeth gnawing at her limbs, clawed fingers with too many knuckles poking and scratching, cutting her creamy skin, twisting her nipples until they bled. One raped her, his long barbed shaft hurting her deep inside. And the prince . . .

Lune gritted his teeth. Vorvian, prince of envy and false solace, one of hell's vile aristocracy, chosen by the Demon King himself. Handsome devil, pale and slender, his long white hair smooth, his narrow face ethereal. He whispered soft temptation in Eleanor's ear, words of comfort and enlightenment, caressing her hair, his cool ruby lips brushing her cheek—while at the same time his minions tortured her.

Lune had screamed with rage and agony, thrashing against his chains. But the demon-spelled iron held him fast. They'd made him watch what happened next.

Say yes, Vorvian whispered, slicking his red tongue over her earlobe. *Just say yes, and I'll make them stop. Your angel won't help you now. He doesn't care for you. He's taken everything you have. Your virtue, your dignity, your pride. Everything you have to give in this world. How will you advance your family now, when no decent man will have you?*

Eleanor groaned and thrashed, angry tears spilling. Vorvian smiled, smoky. *When he'd finished ruining you, your angel left you alone, didn't he? Abandoned you and let me in. He doesn't love you. God doesn't love you, Eleanor. Say yes, and you'll be free of them both. You'll make a good marriage. Bear children. Make your father happy. Come with me, and nothing will ever hurt you again.*

She'd leaned over, exhausted and bleeding, and whispered something in Vorvian's ear.

Red lightning crashed, and fire ignited in her eyes. And then she'd stripped naked, her pale body gleaming golden in the torchlight, and worshipped her new demon prince right in front of Lune. Atop him, her back arched wantonly, loose blond hair slapping her buttocks as they fucked, the filthiest, most sadistic words pouring from her bleeding mouth. The demon groaned and thrust brutally, torturing her breasts with clawed hands, and when he roared and spent his evil seed inside her, she howled in abandoned lust and fell to sucking him, ravenous, licking the bloody fluid from his glistening white skin.

All three of them used her body, then, in every way imaginable. Ravaged her. Covered her in their filth. And all the while, she'd cast her beautiful glance at Luniel, filled with triumph and malice and rabid hatred.

His lovely Eleanor, a good woman and a dutiful daughter, her only misfortune to fall in love with an angel. Eleanor, who'd never even kissed a man before she met him. Whom he'd made love to so sweetly, her virgin body opening to him like the most delicate flower. She became a demon's willing disciple, and he'd been powerless to stop it.

Vorvian had lied, of course, the sly way demons twisted their promises. She'd died in childbirth a year later, her husband a cruel man who cared nothing for her. But it was too late. She'd cursed her own soul to hell, and it was lost forever.

In his aerie, Lune forced his stinging eyes open. Moonlight glared, a harsh certainty that galvanized his heart with cold determination.

The grief was dulled, after centuries. The agony muted. But the guilt never faded.

He'd loved her. She'd trusted him. And he'd let Vorvian turn her into a monster, just for spite. He'd never forgive himself. And he couldn't let it happen again. Not to Morgan. Not to anyone.

But it was too late to leave Morgan behind. And too late to pretend he felt nothing for her. He'd known her only a few hours, and already she tantalized him. Turned him on. Made him laugh, for fuck's sake.

Jesus Christ on a jelly sandwich. Lune tugged his hair, rough. Him and his bleeding heart. Michael would laugh his righteous blue ass off.

Could he protect her, when he'd so badly failed to protect Eleanor?

He'd just fucking well have to try. And Quuzaat, the dirty hellshit they hunted, would never find out how Lune felt about her. He'd be cold. Distant. Professional. Keep his eyes and his hands off.

What was it Japheth always said? *Think about clubbing baby seals?* He'd imagine enough cute-ass little seals to make himself puke, if that's what it took.

Dashiel nudged him, and Lune snapped back to reality. "Huh?"

"I said, don't flake on me, man. I need you. Go jerk off and forget about her. Or fuck her and get it over with, I honestly don't care. Just man up."

Lune shrugged, tight. Dash meant well, but he honestly didn't get it. *Fuck her and get it over with* was an oxymoron. "I'm good."

Dash eyed him a moment, then clapped his shoulder. "Good. Now tell me about these god-rotted imps. You never said anything on the phone about being attacked."

Lune shook himself, settling his wings, trying to get his mind on the job. "Right. Yeah. In the morgue. A bunch of baby hatewraiths. They came through the ceiling, right on top of us."

Dash frowned. "So how'd they find you? You were there for what, ten minutes?"

"I flashed a little glory. Maybe they smelled it."

"What kind?"

"Just a sigil burn . . . make that two sigil burns. And an immolation."

"To a hatewraith? That's like lighting a match a mile away in the sun. Doesn't seem likely. Anyone follow you there?"

Lune shrugged. "Didn't sense anyone. Hell, maybe they were passing by and got a whiff of me."

"Yeah, right. I didn't inhale, either. Who knew you were going to the good doctor's morgue?"

"No one. I was hunting for Ithiel, and that's where I tracked him. Maybe the imps were watching his body, seeing who showed up. They could belong to Quuzaat. I asked one, but the fucker died on me."

"The bastard." Dash grimaced. "Unconvinced, old boy. Let's keep an eye out, eh?"

"Sure. But it's just a bunch of imps. Suspicious much?"

Dashiel sighed. "I dunno. Something Mike said, it . . . unsettled me."

"Michael, unsettling?" repeated Lune dryly. "Well, there's a surprise. C'mon, Dash, lighten up. It's only the end of the world."

White light flashed, a fragrant breeze. He turned, and if he hadn't been so tense, his jaw would have hit the floor.

Morgan was back. And she looked . . . He swallowed. She looked fucking amazing.

She'd ditched the skirt and blouse for crisp black jeans and a black t-shirt. Those sexy lace-topped stockings were gone, but it didn't matter because those jeans licked every luscious curve. Right up to her ass, which swelled proud and gorgeous. He wanted to take a bite out of it, pop it like a juicy berry. She'd strapped the spelled knife to her right thigh, and it made the smooth lines of her muscles stand out. She wore black ankle boots with a low chunky heel, and her calves looked sensational.

As for the rest of her . . . He gulped, parched. Her shining dark hair was brushed, and curls spilled from a clip near the base of her neck. No make-up, but she didn't need it, her lips full and rosy, her dark amber eyes sparkling. Her t-shirt hem kissed her silver belt buckle and the low-rise waistband of her jeans, offering him a tantalizing glimpse of smooth creamy hip and belly, and the scooped neckline showed her delicate feminine throat and revealed stunning cleavage he wanted to slide his tongue into. The t-shirt was tight enough to stretch just a bit over those beautiful firm breasts, and tiny little peaks showed.

His dick stirred, hardening. Yeah, he was staring at her nipples. That was very uncool. But he couldn't stop. Couldn't forget how rosy pink they were. Couldn't stop remembering how they'd tasted, how she'd moaned as he sucked on them . . .

"Fuck," he muttered, and spun away, flushing. Sure, keeping his cool around her would be easy. All she had to do was turn up in jeans and a t-shirt, and he was aching for her. Heaven help him if she started flirting with him again.

Taking her with you to fight demons? Awesome idea, Lune. What could go wrong?

He gritted his teeth. Nothing would go wrong. He'd make sure of it. And if that meant he had to fight his longing to touch her—resist his burning need to hold her, consume her, lay her down and make her his own—then so be it.

Morgan gasped, lightning crackling through her body, and her feet hit the floor in Luniel's apartment once more. Her head swam, dizzy, and then it righted. Amazing.

Jadzia loosened her grip around Morgan's waist. "Okay?"

"Sure." Morgan tidied her hair, self-conscious. Luniel was staring at her again. Did she look okay? Jadzia had flashed them to Morgan's dark apartment, and once she'd gotten over the impossible shock of near-instantaneous travel—she'd never watch *Star Trek* again without recalling that warm flash of light, the hollow in her stomach, that horrifying dark instant before she reappeared—she'd hurriedly changed her clothes, not wanting to keep anyone waiting. She'd grabbed the nearest comfortable thing.

And Luniel stared at her like she'd turned up naked.

Now, he turned away, and Dashiel walked over to her. Jadzia drifted off, and Luniel fluttered to his loft and didn't come down.

Morgan managed a smile for Dashiel. "I'm ready . . . I guess."

Dash just studied her, his teasing brown eyes for once thoughtful.

She fidgeted. "What?"

"You like him, don't you?" Dash spoke softly, so no one would hear, but with an edge demanding honesty.

She clasped her hands, a shield. "I . . . I suppose so. We only just met . . ."

"You suppose so, or you know so?"

She opened her mouth, and shut it again.

Dash sighed, ruffling coffee-dark wings. "Yeah. Okay. Look, he won't ever say this, so I've gotta. Will you go easy on him?"

"What?" Luniel had come on to *her*. Like a hurricane. Well, maybe she'd flirted a little . . .

"He hasn't had the best of luck with the ladies. Things go wrong for him, and people get hurt. Now he's met you, and he's a little nervous. Cut him some slack."

"I, uh . . ." She cleared her throat. Too sudden. Too soon. Too much. "I don't understand. Did he say something to you?"

"Not exactly." Dash leaned closer, curling his wings to hide the two of them from view. His feathers smelled of fresh air and earth. "You gotta understand that Lune's a simple guy. He dives in over his head. If you mess with him, I promise you, you're messing with his heart. And I can't have that."

Morgan swallowed. Luniel seemed so self-assured. So strong. "So who are you, big brother?" She winced. She'd forgotten Ithiel.

"I'm the closest one he's got who gives a shit." Dashiel's eyes fired scarlet. "So take your games elsewhere, if that's what they are. Don't flirt with him unless you mean it. Not if you don't wanna piss me off."

She bristled, but fear tingled her guts, too. What happened in the bathroom had felt . . . intense. But had they started something? Not sure she wanted that. Not sure she didn't want it. "I'm sorry, but it's none of your—"

"Everything's my business when it concerns my people." Dash's feathers sparked angry red. "So if you don't want what he thinks you're asking for? Back off, Dr. Sterling. Now. Before he follows you over a fucking cliff into hell." He smiled, bright and charming. "Okay?"

"Lune."

In his loft, Luniel dug tense fingers into the cushion in his lap. He'd come here to get some air, and so he didn't have to listen to Dash embarrass him in front of Morgan. For a few moments' peace.

Apparently not.

He stood, tossing the cushion aside. Moonlight shafted through the open skylight onto the bed, and blood-scented breeze lifted his feathers. He had a perch, too, where sometimes he liked to sit and dream, but mostly he liked to curl up on a heap of cushions to sleep, his wings folded around him.

Not that he'd be getting much fucking sleep this week, the way things were shaping up.

He sighed, and turned. "Hey, Jaz."

Jadzia perched on the bed's edge, and involuntarily he recalled the sight of her asleep on her belly in the dark cushions, her pale hair mussed, creamy wings soft along her naked back. She'd looked pretty there, drenched in the fading silver glitter of their love. But . . . distant. Absent. Even while she slept.

She tilted her cool blue gaze up. "I see you've found a new friend."

"Jaz—"

"I really don't mind what you do, Lune. She seems nice. I'm just a little disappointed you didn't bother to tell me it was over between us before you started fucking another woman."

"I am *not* . . ." His fists clenched, and he lowered his voice. "I am *not* fucking her. I've known her for an hour. C'mon, Jaz, give me some credit." Not that he deserved it. He should have talked to her. Heaven, he hated this part.

"But it is over, isn't it?" She tried to cover it, but green sadness darkened her eyes.

He bit his lip, sick, and sat beside her. "Don't be like that. You know I worship you. We all do. But—"

"But I'm not worth keeping." She laughed, and looked away, but not before he saw shimmering tears. "It's okay, I'm not here to give you a hard time. I just . . ." She sniffled, and tugged her hair into a frustrated handful. "Fuck."

Lune took her other hand and kissed it, awkward. How many times had he made this speech? The fact that it was true didn't make it any easier. "Listen to me, Jadzia. You're an amazing woman. You're beautiful and you're clever and you sure as hell kicked my ass on the sparring field last time we had a go. And you're sexy, heaven help me. We . . . y'know, had a good time. I wouldn't unhappen it for the world." He took a careful breath. "But look me in the eye and tell me you felt anything. C'mon, be honest. It was nice, but . . ."

She folded her fingers around his, a ghostly smile haunting her lips. "Yeah. I know. Nice, but."

"So let's leave it be. You deserve better. Somewhere among all us hundreds of guys who think you're a goddess"—a brighter smile, *thank you, heaven*—"is the one who'll knock you flat, Jaz. Wait for that. It's worth it."

She wiped her nose. "I guess you know, huh."

His heart stung, sharp. Eleanor was gone. He could never replace her. Fate wasn't that kind. But did that mean he shouldn't try? Stiffly, he nodded, just once.

Jaz tried another smile, and he reached out to hug her.

But she flittered to her feet. "Thanks. I know you mean it." She wiped her face with her feathers. "But I'm no good at being alone. This Tainted thing is . . . well, I can't just grin and bear it, like you guys can. I guess I stopped expecting to be swept off my feet a long time ago."

"Jaz, I'm sorry."

"I'm lonely, Lune." Her eyes gleamed bright with sorrow. "And you're my friend. Being with you was . . . sweet. Let me mourn it." And before he could speak, she vanished.

Wow, that was fun. Lune sighed, guilty. Shoulda known better. Story of his life.

He raked his hair loose, forgetting he'd already clipped it back, and had to spend a few seconds tying it up again. He focused on his reflection, trying to center his thoughts. His dark mood had spilled over into his eyes, shadowy and dangerous. Armor, angst and attitude: check. Time to get on with it.

He swooped down from the loft. Dashiel was gone, too. Only Morgan, in that goddamned sexy black outfit, running her fingers along the marble kitchen bench top, waiting for him. Moonbeams danced in her hair, kissing her berry lips with shine.

His stomach sank. Had she heard all that? Awesome. No, seriously. This night just got better and better. "You ready?" he said gruffly.

She looked up, startled. "Oh. Sure, I guess. Where are we going?"

Be casual, Lune. Relax. Forget about it. "You tell me. How do we find this zero point?"

She swung on one foot. "I need to go back to the lab. My files. I have an after-hours key. We might have to sneak in past my boss, though. And security. I mean, we broke the window, and the ceiling fell in. They'll have found that."

"Your boss work in your lab?"

"No."

"Not a problem, then." He grinned. "Let me beam you up, Scotty."

"Thought you couldn't do two people at once." Challenge shone in her eyes. She'd already flashed with Jadzia. Did she really think he couldn't do the same, or better?

"That was then. I was incapacitated. This, my lovely doctor, is now." He offered her his arm with a flowery bow. She didn't move. "You'll, um, have to come closer."

She swallowed, and stepped nearer.

His skin prickled hot, and his mouth watered with her feminine honey-spice scent. Fuck, she smelled good.

"This okay?" She licked shining lips, her brows arching in amusement. But apprehension hovered there, too. Lune could smell it, salty. What did Dash say to her?

"Turn around," he murmured. She did, and he wrapped his

arms around her. So warm and fragrant, her breasts soft against his forearms.

He resisted the urge to press his body into her, relieve the aching pressure. *Might as well get used to it, Lune. This is as close as you're getting.*

Doesn't mean I can't enjoy it while it lasts.

He dipped his nose into her hair, inhaling, and in a flash of Tainted glory, they vanished.

CHAPTER 12

On the rooftop, Jadzia sat, her leather-clad legs dangling over the edge, gazing into the ceaseless midnight sky. Moonlight glared her eyes wet, but the sting was pale compared to the ache in her heart.

Another stupid tear rolled down her cheek. Heaven, this was so idiotic. Lune was right. They'd had nothing, just a few sweet moments in the dark. She'd known him for a hundred and fifty years. They'd never be anything but good friends.

So why did she feel like she'd torn her heart from her chest and eaten it?

Jadzia swooped off into the darkness, warm updrafts buoyant under her wings. She climbed, thrusting hard, hot breeze streaming her hair. She should flash to Dash and the others. The Prince of Blood's orgy would be starting. Time to fight. But she couldn't face them, not yet.

Midnight warmth thrummed her feathers, tingling her whole body with the exhilaration of flight. Below her, the city glittered and burned, the wind stained sour with smoke and rotting blood.

Sleeping with Lune? Mistake. She should have known.

Had known, in fact. But she'd had a crappy day and was feeling lonely and maudlin—like that was an excuse—and he, truth be told, was moody and a little drunk. Alcohol didn't affect angels the same as it did humans—an angel's metabolism was more efficient—and you had to drink a lot, and fast, to get any effect. When Lune's mood darkened, and it darkened a lot lately, he drank hard.

She'd joined him in polishing off a half case of single malt scotch, and what with the flavor and the dizzying warmth, crying on shoulders led to kissing led to . . . ahem. Going down on him on the couch. Lune pulling her off him and stripping her naked, pushing inside her and making her gasp and shudder. Delirium and sighs and tears. It was good sex. He was careful, attentive, unhurried. But yeah, something missing.

Always, something missing.

Like anything to choose from, for instance. Now that she was Tainted, most of the guys she once knew didn't want anything to do with her. She snorted. Self-righteous assholes. Like they'd never done anything they were ashamed of.

Not that it wouldn't be nice to go with one of the Tainted boys. Keep it in the family, so to speak. But—Jadzia dipped one wing, wheeling in a sweeping curve over glitzy skyscrapers and neon spires towards the East River and the streaking runway lights and anti-aircraft guns of LaGuardia—they were all flawed, somehow.

Smoke billowed from a burning building, stinging her eyes as she flew. Dashiel was hot, oh my, roughly charming and a body to break your heart, but . . . ew. He'd scraped her up when she was broken, taken care of her ever since she fell. Not boyfriend material. It'd be like sleeping with her big brother.

Japheth was a darling at heart, no matter what everyone said, but a total no-show in the romance department. And Ariel was a steadfast friend, but word was that when it came to anything more than a one-night stand, he had an icicle shoved so far up his ass it poked out the top of his head. Trillium had tried, but as Iria said dismissively at the time—and worldly sex-bomb Iria would know—*Trill tries everything and never buys, honey.*

Jadzia had thought Luniel might be different. And he was. Sweet, funny, gorgeous, a kick-ass demon killer and one of nature's true gentlemen—but he just wasn't that into her. And if that wasn't the suckiest rejection of all . . .

Jadzia dived low over the bay, wrinkling her nose in the

fleshy stink. The blood was turning foul, rotting fish carcasses clogging the beaches. Clean-up crews worked into the night, men scooping the mess into plastic bins to carry it away in trucks, but the filth was endless and kept coming.

She could feel Dash and the others, close, their excitement and urgency a throbbing echo in her veins. After so many years, they were in her blood, and she in theirs. Time to come together.

She wheeled right, streaking along the bright ribbon of the Long Island Expressway and over downtown Babylon, her hair streaming back. The jeweled scattering of lights was marred by black voids of no electricity, dotted with bonfires. Down towards the financial district, cranes gleamed among the skyscrapers. A few months ago, some politico nutters had tried to go "Oklahoma City" on One Police Plaza in the name of the New Anarchy. But they'd screwed up, flattening instead a nearby office building and cracking part of the Brooklyn Bridge flyover, and the blast site still wasn't cleaned up. These NA clowns, they spray-painted their mark on everything they destroyed—an upside-down red anarchy symbol pierced by an arrow—attacked everything that stood for order. Schools, fire departments, subway stations, hospitals, no care for lives innocent or otherwise. They called it the "War on Peace." Jadzia called it a fucking mess.

She hovered over the towers of Wall Street, following her friends' buzzing vibe, and drifted down between tall steel and glass buildings to an empty street, where cigarette butts littered the pavement under glowing streetlights, and newspapers blew against the concrete barriers designed to stop traffic from entering the inner sanctum. Broken glass glinted from a smashed window on the first floor, and inside, remnants of glory floated like glowing smoke where her friends had passed.

Jaz drifted through the jagged opening. Shadows thickened, but her angelsight allowed her to see in the dark. Everything living gave off its own vital aura in the invisible spectrum, and like a big nocturnal cat's, her eyes could gather the smallest amount of visible light, too.

This place looked like a new office fit-out had been abandoned—in a hurry. Electrical leads still hung ragged from the ceiling, waiting for their light fixtures, and silver air-conditioner ducting spilled torn from an open vent. But blood splashed the walls, and a workman's chewed corpse bled at her feet, his overalls torn by hungry teeth.

She flitted over dusty office carpet for the stairs. On the second floor, the dim shadows glimmered with glory, amid unassembled cubicle fittings and stacks of unfitted ceiling plaster, and the familiar, dear scents of her friends comforted her. Coffee for Japheth, a flash of gold. Warm earth after rain for Dashiel. Cigarette smoke and roses meant Trillium, and the musky, female scent of rich perfume could only be Iria.

She rounded the corner by the open elevator shaft, and Dash flashed a handsome grin. "Gang's all here."

Jadzia landed and strode up to them, cracking her knuckles. "Let's get to it."

But her stomach churned, green. Always the same, before every fight, no matter how much she worked out, sparred, practiced with weapons. Luniel hadn't been joking when he said she could kick his ass. Not every time, but even with her slightness and lack of height, Jadzia could hold her own against the best.

But it was always the same, before every fight.

Doubt. Terror. The deep-seated fear that this time, she'd weaken, just like she weakened that fateful day a century and a half ago, when Michael showed her what his fabled wrath was really all about.

Cowardice in the face of the enemy. No fouler sin for heaven's warrior.

She'd fought herself to exhaustion, that steamy night in Cawnpore. Eighteen fifty-seven, the last murderous days of the British East India Company, bloody and ripe with sin. With the chaos of demon-haunted rebellion screaming around them, she and her posse of warrior angels had finally burst into the hellish subterranean sanctum. Miles and miles of tunnels, crawling with hellspawn. They'd split up, killing as they went, and finally she'd come upon a bunch of the demon prince's discarded minions, trapped behind a barbed iron portcullis and howling for release. They'd screamed at her, thrashing their scrawny bodies against the bars.

But not in defiance or hatred. The demons were starving. Broken. Insane with thirst, unhinged with hunger. Doomed by their prince never to waste away. Just to live on, in unimaginable torment.

They cried and clawed their faces raw, begging her for death. Implored her on their knees. Thanked her for bringing them release.

And for a moment, she'd hesitated, strange compassion warming her heart. She'd reached between the bars to touch one, and he sobbed into her hand and kissed it, burning her.

And that's how the other angels found her. Staying her sword against a demon.

Word of advice, Jadzia of the Tainted, Michael had snarled in her ear later, as she sprawled breathless and bleeding at his feet. *Never trust a demon. It'll only get you killed.*

Demons lied, Jadzia knew that. Played on your sympathy. Told you anything you wanted to hear in order to get their way.

But Michael hadn't been there. He hadn't seen the abject despair in those creatures' eyes. In her heart, she knew they hadn't deceived her.

But it didn't matter. Fact was, she'd faltered. Let an enemy get the better of her. She'd deserved to be shunned, and was fucking lucky she still lived.

And one day, she'd fail again. She knew it with a certainty that no amount of sparring and training could erase. Her heart was weak. The business with Luniel tonight only proved it. She'd lose her nerve, and die. Worse, she'd get her friends killed, and nothing Michael could do to her would top that for torture.

"Okay, dudes and dudettes." Dashiel took a step back, and they all listened, like always. "The hellshits are lurking somewhere in this building, or within a block or two. They've got mutie allies and a bunch of poor virus-mad bastards on their side. Most of 'em are already hell-bound, but they'll also have prisoners who don't want to be here, so watch your body carving. And remember, we want the Prince of Blood alive, at least for long enough to tell us who he's working for and where his friends are before we carve his ass to mustard. Stay together. And if you get separated, get on the damn phone. Don't make me come looking for your sorry ass." He swept a dark glance around. "Questions? Good. Let's do this."

Japheth gave Jadzia a frosty golden grin, and helped her check her armor, his light fingers tugging the straps. She did for him in turn, hoping his icy resolve would rub off on her. The way he hardened his heart was enviable.

Trillium flourished his favorite sword and punched her shoulder, cheerful. His orange hair already sparkled with sweat. "Let's kick some hell-spawn ass, Lady J."

"You got it." Jadzia tried not to drop her gaze. They all pretended it wasn't an issue. That they'd forgotten what she'd done, and trusted her. *Heaven, don't let me fail them. Let me deserve them all.*

Tall, voluptuous Iria cleared her throat. She wore her long dark hair braided back, and her cheeks gleamed pale, her heart-shaped lips deep scarlet. Soft black pants hugged her curving hips, her breastplate shining. A crossbow hung over one shoulder, with a quiver of spell-silver spikes. Casually, she shielded herself and Jadzia from view with an iridescent black wing, and her husky voice dropped low. "You okay, honey?"

Jadzia nodded, envious. Iria was confident. Brazen. A kick-ass fighter and a practiced seductress, every sultry movement steaming with sex or violence or both. She'd never understand *lonely* or *sad*. If Iria wanted something—or someone—she stalked right up and took it.

But Iria's green gaze softened. "I'm sensing someone's had a bad day. You want to sit this one out?"

"No." The word rushed out. "I'm fine. Just a little tired. Kicking some demon butt will do me good."

Iria smiled, wicked. "It always does me. You want to have a bitching session afterwards, get whatever's on your mind off your chest, so to speak? You just let me know."

Jadzia worked up a smile. "Thanks. I might just do that . . ."

A flash of spindly limbs, racing past a shadowed doorway with a chill-dark cackle from the depths of hell.

Jaz's head whipped around, and she flashed her sword in, blue steel blazing. "Contact," she snapped.

Iria cracked her knuckles. Japheth whipped gilded wings back with a snap. Trillium took one more drag and tossed his cigarette away. And heavensteel sang as five glowing angels armed themselves.

"Well, hallelujah," murmured Dashiel, spinning his burning blade. And it began.

CHAPTER 13

Light flashed, and ground thudded into Morgan's feet.

Dim orange glow greeted her, dry with incense. Pale moonlight sliced the gloom from above towering gothic arches, and dust motes danced over wide stone floors and endless twin rows of wooden benches. She blinked, dizzy, and wriggled out of Luniel's warm arms.

"Where are we?" She squinted down the long aisle. They'd already been to her office, flashing in without disturbing anyone, and they'd hunched over the epidemiology maps on her computer and confirmed the truth she'd already known: the virus had originated in East Harlem. Right by the shore, where blood now thickened. They'd chosen a fire-gutted public housing development by Jefferson Park on FDR Drive as a place to start.

This didn't look like a burned-out project. It looked more like . . .

Luniel stretched his arms wide, wings aloft as he pirouetted. "It's Himself's house, Dr. Sterling. Don't you recognize it?"

"You brought me to St. Patrick's? What for?"

"Don't sound so surprised. They still let me in. They just don't talk nice to me." He ran up the smooth stone aisle between rows of old wooden pews and skidded, balancing on slicked-back wings.

"Idiot." Morgan snorted, and followed. The distant altar shone golden. Behind her, the arched door was locked, the cathedral deserted. "I'm sorry, what are we doing here?"

"Arming ourselves. They've got plenty to spare. They'll never miss it." He danced around the corner into the transept, and a chapel with an ornate stone altar covered in carved reliefs. "There we are."

She peered into the dimness. Candles and tapers flickered on a offertory, throwing eerie shadows onto the stained glass window above. In the center stood a carved stone font topped with a fancy golden turret. "Holy water? You're shitting me."

"Hey, I run with what works." Luniel vaulted over the rail, gripped the turret and effortlessly ripped it off, tossing it aside on the stones with a deafening clang. "Hand me that bag?"

Morgan gaped, and risked a glance upwards, half expecting a lightning bolt. But the dust just settled, the echo fading. The dude must be asleep or something.

She shook her head, incredulous, and tossed Luniel the rucksack he'd taken from her office. He'd filled it with empty glass specimen jars, the kind with metal pop lids.

She stepped carefully over the rail. The font water glowed when Lune put his hand on the stone, golden as if sunshine pierced the depths. Morgan squinted around for light, but there was none. "Okay, I'll bite. What's that?"

Luniel's eyes glowed, too, heavenblue. "That, my good doctor, is faith. Maybe you've heard of it?"

"You still believe in God? After what they did to you? Falling to earth, and all that?"

"Honey, if God didn't exist, I wouldn't be in this mess. Just because I fucked up doesn't mean He's not there."

"So you're not pissed at Him?"

"Loving and believing aren't the same thing." Luniel's glance pierced her, unsettling. "Your science is a cruel mistress, I'll bet. Doesn't mean you don't worship her, right?"

She fidgeted, recalling all the times she'd struggled to prove a hypothesis she knew in her heart was true, fighting evidence that wouldn't support her case. Heartbreaking. But all the more satisfying when she finally got it right—and the richer the sweetness eclipsing the bitter when she admitted she was wrong. "Then you don't think it's unjust that you should suffer for breaking His rules?"

Luniel laughed, warm and delighted, like she'd said something enchanting. "You want a world without consequences? A few folks tried that. They got thrown out of the garden, so I heard." He unzipped the bag, breaking out the squat cylindrical jars. "The world is what it is. I knew the rules when I broke them. Whining about injustice won't change anything."

Her old anger flared. "So we should just do as we're told without question, then?"

"Obedience? Shit. You're asking the wrong angel. Try Japheth, he's better at it than I am."

"You're avoiding the question. Sorry, but I prefer to make up my own mind."

"Yeah. That's what we all thought." Luniel pushed a jar towards her along the font's broad stone rim. "Fill 'em up, sister."

She popped the round lid, the glass smooth and fine in her fingers. It'd break without much of a shock. "Holy water bombs?"

"More like Molotov cocktails. You'll see." He dipped a jar in the water, and snatched his hand back with a hiss of pain.

"What is it?" She touched his arm, alarmed.

A naughty smile. "Just kidding."

She thumped him, laughing in spite of herself, and he dipped the jar again and filled it. But she couldn't help noticing he used only his right hand.

The one without the Tainted sigil.

Guess he wasn't taking any chances. And it only made what he'd been saying about God more believable.

She shrugged, uneasy, and started filling jars.

After what seemed like hours, Jadzia caught her breath, leaning against a coffee shop window for a moment's respite. The fight had led her outside, into the barricaded traffic-free zone around Wall Street. Heat shimmered over the concrete. Blood—not her own—ran stinging down her cheek, and she wiped it off with a dirty hand. Her armor was splashed with gore and rotting flesh, and her sword arm ached.

The Prince of Blood's little fan club had come downtown, all right. Dozens of the ugly motherfuckers, grinning and sharp-toothed, taunting her with insults and filthy come-ons, showing her bits of their bodies she really hadn't needed to see. Mutie minions, remorseless, their souls already damned, armed with bike chains and chainsaws and heaven knew what else. Virus victims, slobbering and raging, their teeth slick with munched flesh. She'd killed them all, one after the other, slashing and stabbing and tearing with her bare hands.

She managed a feral grin. Iria was right. Slaughter had made her feel better. Her sorrow had burned away, for the time being. Now, only anger raged in her veins. At the monsters. At the minions who willingly followed them. At the as-yet-unseen Prince of Blood who ruled them all.

And at the ones who'd done this to her. The archangels who made her into a killing machine, bereft of love or hope.

A lazy footstep scraped behind her, and she whirled and stabbed straight for the hellwraith's heart.

A lanky apelike thing, grinning at her, its wiry limbs flailing as it brandished a razor-sharp pitchfork. Clotted black blood spurted, and she yanked her sword back and slashed, sending its greasy brown head spinning to splatter the glass wall.

No, raging at the archangels didn't change things. But it sure made her feel better for now.

She flicked the mess from her sword and walked on. Sweat trickled inside her armor, the heat cloying in her nostrils and drying her mouth. In the basement, she and Iria had found a bunch of terrified humans, cowering together naked in a rusted cage, where the muties and hellshits had left them waiting to be sacrificed. A vast vat already awaited their warm living blood. They screamed when they saw Jaz and Iria coming, and when the two angels tore the metal gate from its rivets and set them free, the pitiful creatures fled. Ungrateful scum.

But that was what she was here for, Jadzia reflected as she crept across the bright-lit street and under a cantilever, sword poised, her sharp angelsight gleaming white. Saving the tortured. Rescuing the benighted. Bringing relief to the almost damned.

Pity there was no one to do the same for her.

Broken glass crunched behind her. She tensed, ready to whirl, and velvety blackness snuffed out the light.

Stifling emptiness sucked away her breath. No light. Not from her sword, not from the moon nor the office windows. Nothing. She couldn't see. She couldn't hear. Only her own heartbeat, pounding in her ears.

Demon magic.

She whirled blind, slashing with her invisible sword at throat height.

Icy breeze goosepimpled her skin, blowing her hair back, and a fierce blow rammed her face-first into a wall. Something hard slammed into her wrist, and her sword fell from nerveless fingers, making no sound on the pavement.

Hot steel whispered across the back of her neck, a searing kiss, and a hand yanked her head back by the hair.

"Pleased to meet you, angel," the demon whispered into hell-spelled silence. "Now move one muscle, and I'll carve your pretty head from your neck."

Jadzia panted, her heart racing. Solid blackness. It didn't matter whether she opened her eyes or not. She couldn't see. She could only feel the demon's hard body, burning, jamming her against the wall. His fingers curled in her hair, singeing. His razor-sharp weapon licked heat down the back of her neck.

She struggled, kicking for his shins. He jammed his knee between hers, spreading her legs. She wished for her sword, but he knocked it from her hand again. His blade stung deeper. "I said, don't move."

His sepulchral voice shivered deep inside her. He was tall. Strong. She couldn't shift him. Defeated at last, by distraction and a stupid black helltrick. Fuck.

She harbored no illusions about what he'd do to her. Torture her. Flay her alive. Chew her wings off, fuck her, invite his hell-crazy friends and gang-rape her until she whimpered for death.

No more than she deserved.

One last act of defiance. Make him kill her. She rammed her head backwards, skull connecting with a sick crunch. He grunted, pain and surprise.

"I moved, hellshit," she sneered. "So kill me and get it over with."

And she closed her eyes and waited for the end. Hot demon steel, slicing her spine in two. Exquisite numbness. Nothing.

The demon's fist tightened in her hair. His blade dug deeper, and blood trickled down inside her armor. And then he cursed, sibilant hellwords that blistered her cheek, and let go.

Light sprang bright, his demonspell dissolving. She blinked, dizzy with astonishment, and lurched around.

Her sword lay on the dirty pavement, spitting angry blue sparks. And the demon—tall, lean, a tumble of soft blue-black hair—eyed her ruefully, his crimson irises glowing. He wore black studded leather armor, sparks crackling with hellmagic, his wiry arms bare beneath curved shoulder guards. His temple trickled black where she'd clocked him. A thin curved blade hovered in his grip, steady but low.

"You got me," he admitted, with a hell-sweet smile. "Can't stab a lady in the back."

For a dangerous moment, Jadzia stared, lost.

And then a disbelieving laugh throttled her. "You've got to be kidding me," she snarled, and in mid-sentence she leapt for her sword, rolled, and came up kicking.

Her boot slammed into his chiseled chin. He tumbled onto his back, and she dived on top of him, pinning his arms down with her elbows, his thighs with her knees. The angry heat of their contact—angel on demon—seared through their clothing. Skin on skin would burn.

She cracked his skull back into the pavement, and whipped her sword coolly to his throat. His satiny hair scorched her palm. "Still feeling gallant, hellslime?"

The demon choked, and metal clanged at her side. He'd dropped his blade. "Do it," he spat through sharp teeth. "At least I'll die with honor. Where's your honor, lady?"

"In the fucking cesspit with yours," she snarled, but her voice cracked, treacherous.

He'd had his chance, and let her live. *Can't stab a lady in the back*. Not even a winged lady of heaven, snarling for his blood.

And this was how she'd repay that? Fountaining his hell-cursed life to the dirt?

She gripped her sword tighter. Black blood smeared, dripping along his throat. But deep inside her chest, a shameful ache burned raw.

Fuck.

Shaking, she climbed to her feet and let him go.

The demon snaked gracefully up. His red eyes shone, warm and wary. "We understand each other, then. Be satisfied."

Jadzia stared, dazed and trembling. Dimly, she registered that the other angels' scents were faded, distant. They couldn't see her. No one would ever know she'd let a demon live.

She'd regret this. Sure as the demonslime staining her hands, he'd come back to bite her on the ass. Kill her friends. Make her life a misery.

But she couldn't kill an unarmed man who'd spared her life. Not even one from hell.

She leveled her sword, circling. "We understand nothing, demon. And I'm not satisfied. Pick up your god-rotting sword and let's have at it."

"And if I won't?" He tossed night-blue hair over his shoulder, calm. He didn't arm himself. Just stood there, glistening with sweat and blood.

She didn't lower her sword. But her mind gibbered, confused. "What's wrong with you? What do you want from me, demon?"

"You can stop calling me 'demon,' for a start. My name's Shax. What's yours?" He smiled, disarming, moonlight glittering his narrow face silver and jeweling his hair. Luminous, that face, cheekbones carved light like ice, and a sensuous, curving mouth.

So he was beautiful. Demons were. "I don't care what your fucking name is," she growled. "Fight me and let's get it done."

"I know why you're here," Shax offered, as if she hadn't spoken. "The blood sacrifice. Vats of souls, vows to Satan, copious gluttony and lust. Sound familiar?"

"You talk too much." She struck, sword flashing.

He dodged, agile, leaping back and aside. "What if I could help you? Tell you who's responsible?"

"Cease your lies, demon. Why would you tell me that? For all I know, it's you." Another lunge, stabbing for his heart.

Another leap and dodge. "Far from it. The Prince of Blood's in charge here. I'm just a sidekick. And I'm not the demon of lies, by the way."

"No, you're the demon of full of shit. Astonish me. Why the fuck would you help me?"

"Because I'm moved." Shax's sunset gaze didn't slip. "You're kind and beautiful, lady. Even hell weeps at beauty."

She flushed, her heart beating faster. His eyes were so warm. So sincere. "Whatever. Spill your secrets, if it makes you feel better. I'll only beat 'em out of you when I catch you."

"A favor in return, my moonlight-haired queen." His hot velvety voice sparkled down her spine.

Flattery. A cheap shot. But Jadzia stammered, stupid. Iria would know what to do. Flirt back. Spit in his face. Kill him.

Sweat dripped inside her breastplate, and she shivered. She tried to think, make a decision. He might have useful information. He might be lying through his teeth. She could always kill him afterwards. She should kill him right now.

But part of her just wanted to stand there and gaze into his hypnotic scarlet eyes.

She shook herself, keeping her burning sword leveled. If this . . . Shax . . . was mesmerizing her with hellmagic, he'd be sorry.

But she didn't feel spell addled. She felt . . . noticed. Warm and shivery. Aware.

She fidgeted, flushing. "I . . . I can't give you anything. I don't have anything you want."

"But you do." He edged closer, daring, within range of her blade.

She didn't strike. "What?"

"Your name, solitary lady." Shax touched her sword's tip with one finger. It hissed, smoking. He didn't flinch. Just pushed it aside, and gave her that intoxicating smile. "Tell me your name."

Her throat dried. Time stopped. And in a black flash, she was back in that stinking tunnel, fingers wrapped around steel bars, the starving demon's tears streaking her palm.

Compassion pierced her heart, sharp like ice. She'd been touched, yes. Horrified. Moved to sympathy. But she wasn't a coward. No matter how Michael judged her. And she wouldn't back down now.

She swallowed on a rough lump in her throat. "It's Jadzia."

Shax dipped his sleek dark head, but his gaze never left hers.

"Jadzia," he repeated, and the feel of his beautiful lips wrapping around her name made her shiver and sweat. "I'm humbled, lady."

She swallowed. Temptation. That's all it was. Demon lies. Not connection. Not . . . attraction.

They stayed like that, gazes locked, for a long time.

Jadzia trembled. "You're not as I expected, de—Shax."

"Likewise. Perhaps that understanding of ours is stronger than you suppose. Now," he added with a sweet dark smile, "tell me what can *I* do for *you*." And the demon reached out, and stroked one fingertip through a loose lock of her hair.

She jerked, startled, and Shax's finger brushed her cheek.

His naked touch didn't burn. It just tingled, warm and dangerous.

Jadzia stared, trapped fast by that wit-melting smile. *Never trust a demon.* Her heart somersaulted. And she whirled on quivering hot wings, and fled.

CHAPTER 14

Morgan shivered in the hostile heat as she strode beside her angel through the darkened housing development. The setting moon slanted sinister red light through the tall buildings. The trees shivered in the threatening hot breeze, and in the spray-painted playground, a twisted iron seesaw creaked up and down, ghostly. In a few windows, flames flickered, a campfire or a cigarette lighter. People still lived here.

"You okay?" Luniel murmured. His wings threw monstrous shadows on the walls.

"Yeah." Damn it. He saw everything. Like he was watching her, making her think he was looking out for her. Just like a lying, manipulative son of a bitch would.

Sweat glued her t-shirt to her belly. She tugged it, but only made it more uncomfortable. The air stung rank with sour flesh and sickness. The darkness slithered and hissed at her like a living creature, and every sound made her pulse jerk hot.

She swallowed. This was crazy. Plague. Zombies. Homicidal muties. Demons, even. *What the hell am I doing? I'm a doctor, not a kick-ass vigilante.* She touched the sheathed weapon at her thigh, trying to take comfort from being armed with an angel's enchanted knife.

It didn't make her feel better.

And neither did Luniel, stalking dark and silent beside her, the bag of water bottles slung over his shoulder. He hadn't bothered to don human guise. Far stranger things than angels lurked in this neighborhood.

She sucked in a deep breath, trying to relax. Even though the authorities repeatedly explained on the internet and TV news that Manhattan virus wasn't airborne, some people still feared the air, and wore paper face masks. But she knew you needed fluid contact from an infected person to catch it, and she'd make sure that didn't happen.

They weren't zombies, after all. Not horror movie cannon fodder. They were sick people. Patients. And she intended to treat them like patients.

Luniel could hunt his mythical demon prince, if he liked, and good luck to him. She'd be searching for signs of how the disease started. Infectious waste. A carrier animal, if the virus was zoonotic. Some diseases lived harmlessly for years in animal hosts, before transferring to humans, usually by accident, and wreaking havoc. And exotic animal smuggling was rife in the illicit markets of Harlem, rare and endangered creatures sold for pets, or for the manufacture of silly traditional medicines that didn't work.

The source must be here somewhere. Diseases didn't materialize from thin air.

Don't they? a doubting voice whispered in her head. *What if Lune's right? What if it really is a vial of God's wrath? What will you do then?*

She wiped stray hair from her eyes, determined. Angels were real? Fine. That didn't mean everything Luniel said was true. If she could confirm he was right about the holy wrath? She'd accept the evidence, and deal with it. Until then, she'd hunt for a cure.

They rounded a corner, a narrow alley leading deeper into the project. A crow croaked, mournful. A starving stray dog skittered away as they approached. Broken window edges glinted, the glass long since torn away for weapons, and rotted plastic swung slowly in the window frames, an ominous breeze.

At the alley's end, where the next shabby apartment block loomed, a foursome of slobbering muties crouched, craning their misshapen heads to stare. They wore ripped t-shirts and jeans. One waved a saw blade, blood already splashing, and infection's rich stink crawled up Morgan's nose like a fat wet worm, making her gag.

Luniel halted her beside him. "Slice off their heads, stab 'em through the heart. They're the only reliable ways once the curse is on them. If they're infected, the holy water will burn them, slow them up a bit. I want you to take some of these . . . Morgan, look at me." He touched her chin, forcing her head up.

Her stomach prickled with anger. "That's all you know, isn't it? Killing! They're not monsters, okay, and they're not cursed. They're sick people. They can be cured!"

"No, they can't. Don't you get it? There is no cure. This isn't just a disease. It's the wrath of God, twisted to a demon prince's will—"

"I don't believe that!" She spun away, distraught.

He caught her wrist. "Morgan, stop."

"Let me go," she insisted. She didn't want him touching her. It was too distracting. His warm sweet scent was hard enough to take. "I'll find my own way."

His eyes flashed neon blue. "Don't be ridiculous. They'll kill you." His tight jaw brooked no argument.

She bristled. "And they won't kill you, is that it? Angelflesh not tasty enough?"

"Morgan, use your brain. Think! You've seen me and demons. My flesh heals."

"Not outside my morgue, it didn't. What about your crazy blood-drinking spell? You gonna do that every time?"

"That was because I took on your injury!" He dragged his hair tight with a big hand. "Jesus. For a smart woman, you don't pay very much attention."

"Well, thank you *very* much . . ." She stopped, her indignation blunted. She remembered his feverish eyes, his slurring words, his skin searing her fingertips. The demon's claw marks festering on his beautiful cheek. The blood—his own blood— dripping on his chin as he swallowed from the cup.

He'd done that to himself for her? To heal *her* injury?

Whatever. It didn't mean anything.

At the alley's end, the infected muties caroused, waving their arms in a gruesome come-hither. She shuddered. What could she do if they attacked? If they ran for her? Touched her. Bit her, scratched her skin. They looked beyond reason, beyond a calming word and a doctor's cool touch. Maybe Luniel's way was the only one . . .

She shook her head, stubborn. "We'll take another route—"

Luniel pressed his finger to her lips, shocking her to silence. "Listen to me. This can't be stopped. That vial of wrath? Its damage is done. Those things will die and go to hell, and there's nothing you or I or anyone else can do about it."

His tone shivered her bones. "But—"

"Shh," he said, deathly calm. "All we can do is put them out of their misery. Make sure they don't infect anyone else. And then hunt down the demon scumsucker who did this to them, and rip off body parts one by one, until he tells us who sent him and where his friends are."

She stared, trembling. "But . . . we can't just give up."

He caressed her cheekbone with his thumb, and his eyes darkened to indigo, anger or sorrow. "There's nothing to give up on."

"So what, we'll just kill them all?"

"As many as we must to find Quuzaat. We can't save them, Morgan. But we can maybe save the world."

Her guts coiled, and she pulled away. "Sacrifice the few for the good of the many? How original. And then we'll kill all the gay people, or all the anarchists, or some other poor suckers we decide we don't like. Screw you, angel."

He laughed, short. "Grow up, Dr. Sterling. That's how it works, okay? Salt a city, torch a civilization to ashes, drown the world and start again. Didn't you read the Book? Not everyone makes it to the End."

Her mind reeled. He'd been there. This creature really was immortal. But her nerves screwed tight. "Will you listen to yourself? You are not God!"

"No, I'm not." Lune's eyes burned, dangerously bright. "But last I heard, He wants us to work for what we've got. You wanna live your life in a safe little bubble and whine when things get tough? Fine. But someone's gotta step up and do the shitty jobs. Either we do what's necessary, or we all go down together. Now, are you in, or are you out?"

She took a breath to tell him to go to hell.

A raucous shriek ripped the air ragged, and the manic muties sprinted for them.

Luniel pushed her behind him, his sword springing aflame into his hand.

Morgan stumbled, her heart racing. The muties hurtled closer, leaping and running up the walls on all fours like huge cockroaches. Luniel darted and chopped one's head off, and its body tumbled, limp. The one brandishing the saw blade landed in a crouch and locked eyes with her.

He was young, dark, scrawny. Spit dribbled onto his stubbled chin, and he twanged his saw, his gaze alight with scarlet malice. "You got some tasty meat on you, *puta*. Gimme."

She gulped, horrified. Diseased rot clogged his voice, but he could still talk. Still think. Still decide for himself that he'd like to eat her.

The magical knife ripped from its sheath and slapped into her hand.

She didn't think. She just threw.

The glittering knife whistled a deadly arc, and the blade embedded itself in the mutie's scrawny throat.

Blood spurted, thick with dead flesh. The mutie choked and dropped his saw, clutching at the gaping hole with six-fingered hands, and Luniel sliced his head off.

The other two moaned and gnashed stained teeth, too far gone for reason. One rushed her, matted hair flying in its eyes. She shrieked, startled, and the knife whipped itself from the headless corpse and found her outstretched fingers. The mutie bore down on her. Its fevered fingers reached for her. She slashed, falling back against jagged bricks.

"Get off her, hellshit." Luniel yanked the mutie's arm. The joint popped, and the arm tore away. Rotten blood gushed. Pulled off balance, the mutie fell into the path of Luniel's burning blade. Blue light flashed as its smoking corpse hit the ground.

The last mutie howled, shoved its rotting hand deep into its mouth and bit it off. Luniel broke its neck with a stab of his elbow. The decomposing flesh tore, and the head fell off all by itself. The body crumpled.

Morgan fell against the wall, panting. The poisoned corpse stench frothed bile into her mouth. Her knife slipped, sweaty, but instead of falling, it flipped over and slotted neatly back into its sheath.

Luniel flashed to her side and lifted her chin, sharp eyes scanning for cuts. "You okay? Did it touch you?"

"That was about the grossest thing I've ever seen," she croaked.

"Yeah, it was up there." Grudging admiration fired his gaze. "You fight tough, my lady. We'll make a warrior of you yet."

Her heart fluttered, dizzying. He was flattering her. Without him, she'd be dead, and they both knew it. "I'd rather be a doctor, thanks."

"No rule says doctors can't kick ass." He smoothed her hair, tender, and then abruptly averted his eyes and let her go. Like she'd disconcerted him.

Like he'd changed his mind.

He unslung the rucksack. "Here," he said coldly, staring at some spot a few inches from her face. "Throw these instead. They'll keep the fuckers away from you a few seconds longer."

She took the sack, confused. One minute, he was so intense and intimate, his presence caressing her like warm silk. The next they felt like chilly strangers, and losing him made her feel . . . empty. Lost. Like she didn't matter.

How infuriating.

He stuffed a few jars into his pockets, leaving her with the rest. "You ready for more?"

She stuffed a couple in her own pockets, shouldered the sack and stood straight, her chin high. Maybe he was right, and the sick could only die. But she wouldn't let him shame her into giving up. "Can't wait."

"Good," he replied, brutal. "Because there'll be more. A lot more."

"Well, screw me raw," muttered Dashiel, "he's not here."

Japheth slashed the last sniggering hatewraith's head off, his sword blazing blue. The corpse splattered to the basement floor, and Jae wiped blood from his face with his bare forearm. "And a big thank you to Captain Obvious."

Dash flipped him the bird, and Japheth grinned, catching his breath. Dashiel was right. The Prince of Blood wasn't here. This half-refurbished office building reeked with wraiths and shrieking underclass imps, and the angels had killed them all, but the sacrificial vat still lay empty, the human captives dead or fled. Body parts littered the floor, and it stank of demonslime, that curious mixture of sulfur, rotting meat and shit.

Japheth licked his lips, disgusted but invigorated. Reminded him of the old days. Kicking heads and taking names. Whipping cruel demon butt for heaven, back when honor and the color of the blood on your sword still mattered more than a few careless ideas.

Before Michael shunned him, for daring to aim for better things. Or something.

Dashiel vanished his sword, flicking demon brains from his armor. "Oh, well. We got to wipe out a few zillion of his minions, and the humans got away." He clapped Japheth's shoulder, a familiar gesture that never failed to irritate. "Guess that's something, eh?"

"Yeah." Japheth forced a smile. Dash was happy enough wiping out hellscum. Give him a fight to win and a party to crash afterwards, and Dash was content.

But it wasn't enough, not for Japheth. Sure, he liked a good demon slaughter as much as the next Tainted angel of vengeance. But what mattered were results. If he could do enough—win enough, kill enough, save enough souls—he might earn his redemption.

But impressing Michael wasn't easy. Not these days. Not the way the archangel taunted him, teased him to break his vow of sinlessness.

Call me, he'd said. As if they could take up where they'd left off. His number was in Japheth's phone. He should delete it. But somehow, he never did.

Like Michael hadn't already tortured him enough. *Thou shalt have no other gods but me,* the Book said. Japheth snorted. Likely Moses never had to resist a petulant, brilliant, more-beautiful-than-sin archangel.

Thinking of Michael made Japheth's heart ache, but the pain only invigorated him, and he tried to shake off holy euphoria. Coming down after a fight was always treacherous, glory tingling through his body, his blood pumping hard and hot, all those pleasure chemicals urging him to sin. He wanted to fly, scream, howl at the moon, find himself a willing woman and pour his body into hers until they both sighed in release.

Japheth was a guy, after all. He liked women. He wanted to do the stuff guys did with them. But he couldn't afford to sin, not if he wanted redemption. No matter what Dash and the others thought, being Tainted was no excuse to act like a whore.

Dash made a call. "Trill, where are you? Get your ridiculous orange butt over here."

In a blue flash, Trillium appeared, blood-spattered and sporting a huge grin. "Oh, man. Did you see those muties? They were *rampaging.* Wherever this damn sacrifice party is, it's gonna be *huge.*"

"Bringing me to my point," said Dash dryly. "We need to know where it is. When it is. You got anything else?"

Trillium shrugged, reddish feathers ruffling. "I can ask around. Trapped me a clever-ass gangbanger who might know something—oyy!"

Demonspawn dove from the shadows on leathery wings, talons outstretched for slaughter.

Trill yanked his sword from thin air and ran one through. Dash grabbed the second one's throat and broke its long snaky neck. And Japheth dived out of the third one's path into a handspring that flung him skywards, and he flipped his sword two-handed and landed on the ground astride the monster, hard enough to crack a few of its ribs.

Japheth pulled his sword point unerringly to its throat. His breath barely hitched. "Talk to me, monster, or I'll make this hurt. Who owns you? Who's running the sacrifice show?"

The beast cackled. Human flesh hung in gobbets from its mouth. Looked like it had made itself a fine dinner. It spat at him, cursing.

Acid hit Japheth's face, sizzling. His cheek stung as the wound healed, but it only steeled him harder. He liked pain. Pain was manageable. Not like . . . other things.

He crushed the creature harder between his thighs, and delicately sliced a flap of thick skin from its face.

It wailed in agony, thrashing wiry limbs. He held it easily, jamming the heel of his hand into its forehead. It screamed, flesh hissing. Japheth smiled grimly. "Tell me, and I'll stop. You'll get a clean death. On my honor."

"Prince Quuzaat," it spluttered, blood spurting from its beak.

"Tomorrow night my prince will rip the flesh from your bones, honey sucker—ugh!"

Smoothly, Japheth sliced its throat open, and it died with a wet sigh.

He was a man of his word, after all. Lying was a sin. No false witness ever passed his lips. Not even to a demon.

Slaughter was a sin, too. *Thou shalt not kill.* But heaven made an exception for that one, and death was in Japheth's blood. In all of them. You couldn't live without your heart.

He lighted up and vanished his sword. His burned palm sizzled, and healed, and he shook it. "Ouch. That hurt."

"Of course it hurt, hero." Trill shoved him. "It's the hell-spawn that *doesn't* burn you that you should worry about. Sympathy for evil, and all . . . oh, yeah, I forgot. Your thoughts aren't sinful enough for that, are they?"

"And yours are?"

"I've had my lukewarm moments." A sly Trillium grin.

Japheth snorted. "No doubt. Did you hear what that wraith said?"

Dash nodded. "Quuzaat. Either the hellshit was lying . . ."

"No." Japheth shook his head, firm. "Did you see its eyes? It was terrified. Too low in the hierarchy to be taking one for the team."

"So," added Trillium, "he was telling the truth, and Quuzaat's our guy. The Prince of Blood. Ithiel's vial must have been blood, not plague. Which means . . ."

"Which means that Quuzaat *isn't* the plague demon." Dash frowned. "It doesn't make sense. Fat-ass Q. is a plague junkie. Why would he let something like the Manhattan virus go by for the chance to bleed a few souls?"

"Unless it's a plague of sin and slaughter," suggested Japheth. "You know how these hellcreatures' minds work. Either that, or the guy giving the orders doesn't care about employee preferences." He paused. "And we still don't know who's giving the orders, Dash. Might want to look into that one next time."

"I'll be sure to ask Quuzaat. Right before I skewer his greasy ass. Either way, Lune's demon prince isn't who he thinks. I'll give him a call. Anyone touch base with Jaz and Iria?"

Trill shrugged. "Nope."

"Then I'll call them, too. And then, my good sons, I am in

the mood for a party." Dash cracked his neck bones, wings
sparking electric.

Japheth watched, fascinated. Dash had issues with glory.
Like, junkie issues. If Jae knew him at all, the fight still glittered ruby rich in Dash's blood, his nerves screaming for death
or release, and he'd have the jitters, an aching pulse and the
hard-on from hell until he did something about it.

Dash grinned, predatory. "Wine, women and wailing. You up?"

"Very funny." Japheth would go home, naturally. Shower,
cold to keep him real. Get a bite to eat, nothing decadent of
course. Pick up his phone a dozen times and put it down again.

"Like I meant you," grumbled Dash. "Trill?"

"You sure we're done here?"

"You heard the hellgoon. Tomorrow night we'll kick your
asses, no force can stop us now, blah blah. No more action tonight.
Whaddaya say we hunt us some luscious ladies and kick on?"

"I say, hell, yeah." Trill stretched, wolfish, and Japheth suppressed a twinge of envy. Self-denial was a b—well, it wasn't
very nice.

"Good man. Jae, do me a favor and don't do anything
stupid?"

Japheth bristled. "Like what?"

"Like you know what," insisted Dash. "Leave his damn
number alone."

Dash knew him too well. And he couldn't lie. Best not to say
anything. But . . .

"Okay." That sealed it. He'd promised. He'd just go to bed,
and try not to dream of home and better days. "Have a good
time. See ya." And Japheth flashed out.

His feet touched the warm tiles of his balcony. His apartment was high in a glass-walled tower on Madison Avenue—
he figured shopping was one temptation he could resist without
trouble—and tonight the moon shone crimson over the jeweled city, the eerie blood-soaked bay colored purple. Warm
breeze ruffled his feathers, tugging his hair back. Sirens pealed,
and spotlights shone in Central Park, a ring of light where they
were keeping the corpses of virus victims in a big air-
conditioned tent. Downtown, where he'd just come from, smoke
drifted over the broken black skyline, bringing with it the smell
of ash.

But he stank of demon blood. It clotted his hair and smeared his hands, stinging. He needed a shower.

He slid the glass door aside and walked in. Cool and dim, moonlight reflecting on pale minimalist furniture, the smooth black lacquer of his piano. His golden wings reflected in the mirrored walls, his armor caked with dust and gore. Japheth didn't particularly like mirrors. But he endured them. It ensured he could look himself in the eye.

He opened the fridge and grabbed a fruit juice. The tart orange pulp sweetened his parched throat. The delicious taste dizzied him. His mouth watered, wanting more, and he allowed himself another small swallow before he put the rest back. Thank heaven for small pleasures. If they ever made fruit juice a sin, he was so screwed.

He unbuckled his bloodstained armor, stripping it off as he walked into the living room. A small dent showed, from a demon's scythe. He'd have to repair it before he showered. He grabbed a chamois and a sponge from the sink and flipped on the light.

Michael smiled, blinding him.

Japheth stumbled, and bit back a bad word.

The archangel stretched on his belly on the chaise, fluffing his ice-blue wings. He wore pale jeans and no shirt, and he'd kicked his shoes off, combing his feathers with his toes.

Japheth dropped onto the sofa opposite and scowled, trying to slow his pulse. "I hate it when you do that, Misha."

Michael dropped his chin into his hands. "I got bored. How was your evening?"

"We killed some demons. How was yours?" Japheth pulled his armor into his lap and started cleaning, edgy. Michael hadn't dropped by like this in a hundred years. It didn't bode well.

"Frightful. I went clubbing. People kept offering me sex and drugs." Michael stretched, languid, shining hair falling over his back. "What could I do?"

Japheth's gaze tracked that glorious hair, slicking over smooth skin . . . Inwardly, he gnashed his teeth. He wasn't like Trillium, who counted everything male or female as fair game. No, Japheth had only two weaknesses when it came to carnal sins: women, and Misha. And Misha knew it. He coughed, tense. "Are you high?"

"Don't be ridiculous. When was the last time their shit made you high?" An arched brow. "Oh, I forgot. Don't answer that."

Like Michael wasn't the reason he had to abstain. Japheth's fingers itched. He wanted to hit him. Wanted to brush his lips along those smooth shining feathers. "I'm tired. What do you want?"

"C'mon, don't be like that." Michael rolled onto his back, muscles rippling. "We haven't chatted in such a long time."

Japheth ripped his gaze away, flushing. "Don't, okay? Chatting with me fell off your radar a long time ago."

"Clever Jae." Michael's eyes sparkled. "Knows me too well. It's true. I do have a . . . proposition for you."

Japheth's blood tingled, urging him to say *yes* to whatever the archangel wanted. But he'd learned that lesson the hard way. "Don't tell me. The kind where I do the work and you get the glory?" Uh. Yeah. That came out wrong. Or maybe his mind was just in the gutter. Penance later, a few hundred chin-ups or something.

"Actually, the glory in this one's all for you."

Japheth studied him. Serious. Not flirting. That let's-talk-business look in his eyes. "Go on."

"I've a thorn in my flesh, Jae." Michael folded his hands behind his head. "Actually, it's more of an itch. I scratch it, and it just gets worse."

Some hapless creature had pissed Michael off? Unlucky indeed. "And?"

"I want you to get rid of it for me." Michael curled up a wing-tip and picked a dirty fleck from pristine feathers, frowning.

"And does this itch have a name?" Japheth's mind turned the problem over as he wiped his armor clean and popped out the dent with his thumb. Slaughtering some extra hellspawn shouldn't be an issue. The blood sacrifice wasn't until tomorrow night . . . well, tonight, to be exact . . .

"Its name is Dashiel." Like a sword through smoke, slicing into Japheth's thoughts.

Japheth gulped, cold. "Excuse me?"

"I'm sorry, did I say you could question me?"

"But . . ." His thoughts stumbled. He couldn't fathom it. "Dash has always done whatever you asked. We need him. Why would you . . . ?"

"Why do we do anything in heaven, Jae? Consider it fate. Call it God's will. Whatever makes you feel better." The archangel's gaze glittered, glacial. "Dash has learned nothing from his time on earth. But you have. I never said this was forever. It's time we let the past be the past."

"What are you saying?" Japheth's pulse hammered, dizzying.

"Put an end to Dashiel for me, and we can talk about you coming home."

Japheth closed his eyes, disbelieving. Of all the fucked-up . . . Of all the horrid tasks to set him. Dash was his brother, or as good as. His mentor. His confessor, in an odd way. They'd fought together tonight like old friends, anticipating each other's moves, blending into each other's shadows.

But Michael made the rules. The archangel's orders might as well be from God Himself. And Japheth longed so hard for redemption that no price seemed too high.

Or did it?

He gritted his teeth, and opened his eyes. "That's not a promise."

"Oh, it is, and you know it." A dangerously charming smile. "You melt me to marshmallow, babe. You know that. I miss you, so help me. We can . . . be friends again." A smolder lit his eyes silver. "I know you like that."

Japheth's mouth dried, and he licked rough lips. But the hypocrisy made him shudder. Since he'd been shunned, he'd done his best to live without sin. Maybe he wasn't exactly a saint, but he'd tried. Michael, on the other hand, led a life of debauchery and recklessness—and it was he who had the power to redeem Japheth?

Sinful anger burned inside. Michael was a tempter, right up there with any demon prince. Japheth shouldn't succumb. Shouldn't fall into sin for the sake of what was lost.

But if this one final transgression would mean he could go home at last . . .

Heaven, help me. He didn't know what to do. Call Dash, tell him everything. Forget about it and go to sleep. Smash his head against the wall. "I'll think about it," he said at last, his throat tight.

"About doing as I ask? Or being friends again?" Michael

vanished, a dazzling white flash, and suddenly, he was inches away. His silver-blue hair spilled over Japheth's shoulder, so crisp, bathing him in that delicious icy scent. He teased a sparking finger through Japheth's golden feathers. "We could catch up right now, if you want."

Japheth's fingers clenched, denting his armor all over again. His treacherous body shuddered and burned. "*Don't do anything stupid,*" Dash said. And Japheth promised.

Right. That was before he had a half-naked archangel practically in his lap. "Misha . . ."

"Jae." A scorching blue stare.

Japheth's voice cracked. "Just get away from me. Please."

Michael laughed, and gave that lethal, bone-crushing smile, and vanished.

And Japheth hurled his armor aside and paced, fury and doubt and desire licking his blood with the cruel fires of sin, until at last he cursed and slammed his fist into the mirrors, glass splintering.

CHAPTER 15

As Morgan and Lune moved downtown, the infected only grew more numerous. More frightening. Hungrier.

Morgan unfolded sticky fingers from her knife, flexing her aching palm. Garbage littered the darkened street from an overturned trash can, a single streetlight flickering above rotting paper, cans, crushed takeout tubs, a scuffle of glint-eyed rats. An abandoned car lay in the road, burned black, panels and wheels missing. The crumbling apartment blocks cast misshapen shadows over rusted playgrounds and empty basketball courts.

She fell back against the wall, numb. Detached. She couldn't remember how many they'd killed. Her blade glistened darkly with virus-thick blood, and she'd long since stopped worrying about infecting herself from splashes. Better to worry about clawing nails and gnashing teeth, the wicked slash of a blood-soaked saw blade or machete.

They'd seen no higher-level demons, who according to Lune would look human. A few screeching wraiths, and a pack of scythe-clawed harpies that Luniel chased into the sky and dispatched without mercy. No clue to Quuzaat, if he even existed. No signs of any animal smugglers, biohazard containment failures or any other potential disease origin point. Just . . . dead things. Over and again, and endlessly.

"Need a rest?" Luniel crouched beside her, wings balancing, big thighs flexing in tight leather. Blood streaked his armor, his arms shiny with sweat and gore. His damp black hair fell in strands from its knot and stuck to his face, and he flashed his gaze left and right, up and back, ever vigilant. He took protecting her seriously. He never rested, never dropped his guard.

Never looked her in the eye. Icy, distant, like he did an unpleasant but necessary job.

A few hours earlier, she'd melted under his fiery kisses. Trembled with desire as he held her in his arms. Gasped with breathless pleasure from his smallest touch. He'd wanted her, too. She was sure of it. But now, he treated her like business, and unwanted business at that.

She straightened, determined. If that was the way he wanted it? Fine. Two could play. "No," she replied, just as cold. "Do you?" And she pushed past him and crept around the corner.

The steps to the abandoned 110th Street subway station still had the light working, papers and rubbish blown against the green iron handrails. The subway hadn't stopped here for a long time, and the station's entrance was boarded up, though someone—mutie squatters?—had kicked a hole.

Against the fence, in piles of rotting paper, a woman huddled in a dusty black dress, clutching a child. Her hair was dusty but not tattered, her face streaked not with blood, but tears.

Morgan tapped Luniel's arm, and pointed. *Clean*, she mouthed, careful not to scare this one. Maybe the woman could give them information. If the sight of Luniel didn't freak the shit out of her first.

Luniel shrugged, keeping to the shadows.

She sheathed her buzzing knife. It didn't want to go in, and she shoved a few times before it relented. She stepped carefully into the light, keeping her distance. "Hello?"

The woman's head jerked around, and she grabbed the child close.

"Don't be afraid. I'm a doctor. I won't hurt you. Do you need help? Your child?"

The woman stared, tears welling. "Oh, thank you," she prayed, fervent. "Thank you, thank you." And she scrambled up, lifting the sleepy child. Her ponytail smeared dirt onto her shoulder. "I thought there weren't no one left. Just me. They're everywhere."

Morgan edged closer, careful not to make sudden moves. She couldn't see any wounds that needed treating. "Muties, you mean?"

"The sick ones. I hear 'em screaming, chasing each other. The street ain't safe."

"Listen, we're gonna get you out of here, I promise. Have you seen an animal warehouse around here? A place where they keep pets, or livestock?"

The woman looked blank.

"How about a hospital that's still operational? Or a biological waste station?"

"Huh? Oh, you mean like a big trash place? Where they got poison and stuff? Them yellow signs on the doors?" She hefted the child on her hip. Still it slept. "Yes, ma'am, I seen that."

Morgan's heart skipped. "Do you remember where?"

"Um. Sure. I think . . . down there." She shuffled closer, and pointed over Morgan's shoulder.

Morgan turned, and the woman laughed, an ugly, cunning sound. And her hot dry fingers fastened around Morgan's neck.

Her pulse jerked, sparking her into action, and she kicked backwards, connecting with a sick crunch.

Hot toffee breeze whisked, and Luniel whirled in on midnight wings, dragging the woman off her. The child hit the ground with a wet thud, and slumped, empty eye sockets staring.

Already dead. Part of its torso and half its face were chewed off. The woman hadn't been protecting it. She'd been eating it. Slowly. Saving some for later.

Morgan gaped, stunned. Freshly infected victims looked normal. Their brains still reasoned. And they were cunning about making new friends.

And now the poisoned thing snarled and scrambled up on all fours, and Morgan could see the fever shining in her eyes, her dark-stained teeth. The blood on her dress where she'd fed. Why had Morgan not noticed before? Too determined to stop killing and get information?

Or did she want so desperately to save just one, that she'd closed her eyes to the truth? Luniel said they couldn't be saved. Maybe he was right.

Footsteps pattered on concrete, getting louder, and Luniel leapt backwards, shielding Morgan with his wings. She shook herself. No time to analyze now. Not with a dozen other zombies—what else could she call them?—charging from the subway towards them. Dirty zombies, compared to the woman, their clothes torn, their arms and faces blackening with rot.

The crafty things had set a trap, and she'd fallen right in.

They hurtled up the steps, slavering with hunger.

Her blood burned, angry survival instincts kicking in. The knife sprung eagerly into her palm. The spelled metal buzzed hot, and it felt good.

Luniel leapt, diving over the zombies' heads. He somersaulted behind them, his sword singing a blazing blue arc. Three heads toppled.

The others didn't stop. They sprinted for her in a cloud of meaty stink. The leading one whooped with laughter, his handsome young face twisted. Morgan's heart galloped. Her fingers closed around the glass jar in her pocket, and she yanked it out and hurled it, hard as she could.

It hit the lead zombie in the skull and smashed, holy water splashing free.

But it didn't bubble. His face didn't burn. No blue glow. The water just ran down his face to soak his dirty shirt.

Her guts hollowed cold. The zombie giggled and danced, flinging his arms wildly, and kept coming.

Shit. Should have known that religious crap couldn't be trusted.

Morgan's knife vibrated, glowing, hot and sticky with eagerness for the fight, and before she could think or prepare, the weapon flashed her arm out and struck.

The blade sank into the zombie's belly. *So soft*, she thought, detached. *The flesh cuts so easily when it's alive.* Blood gushed, lumpy with clotting flesh. The stink made her gag. The zombie made a sick sound, halfway between a gurgle and a shriek. Red spit erupted from his grin, and he slammed into her, knocking her off balance, clawing with sticky thumbs for her eyeballs.

Morgan shoved the knife in harder, but it didn't stop him. She fought, evading his gnashing teeth by inches. A second zombie grabbed her arm, trying to bite. Another one clawed her hair. Morgan kicked and punched, fear setting her muscles alight. *This can't be happening,* a quiet voice whispered in her head. *Eaten by zombies. What an unscientific way to die.*

CHAPTER 16

Glass shattered, and the zombies roared in agony and tumbled away.

Water splashed Morgan's face. Glass shards stung. Dumbly, she wiped them off. The three zombies howled on the ground, clawing at their melting skin, which bubbled and spat like acid.

Holy water. Thrown by a hand more blessed than hers.

Luniel swooped low over the screaming zombies. The sigil burned into his palm glowed blue, and he hurled another bomb at the lead zombie from point-blank range. "Die, hellspawn," he growled, and it sounded not like a regular epithet, but a curse.

The glass smashed into the zombie's face, and the foul creature caught fire.

Like a petrol bomb, the fiery water licked and spread. Flames consumed the body, melting clothes and skin and flesh from bone, until the shrieking creature thrashed and lay still.

The other zombies who were still upright backed off, muttering around rotting fingers. Luniel lurched upwards and dived for them, sword slashing. One tumbled, sliced in half. The others turned and fled, their shambling legs crackling. Still lucid enough to care for their lives. But only just.

Morgan's lungs heaved, searching for air. She fumbled for her inhaler and sucked, grateful. Numb with dread, she made herself check for wounds. Nothing. She was uninfected. She wiped stinking spit from her face, trying to calm down. She didn't think any had gotten in her mouth. Too damn late now if it had.

Luniel shook blood from his sword. One of the melting zombies groaned and flopped, and Lune broke its neck with a kick. The head rolled. "You okay?"

She shrugged, impatient. "How did you do that?"

"Like this?" He demonstrated another kick on the last zombie, and its skull flopped.

"You know what I mean. How'd you do it?"

"How did I what? Set some sick guy on fire with a glass of water? Or kill a hell-cursed man with a heaven-blessed bomb?" He laughed, dark. "You tell me, Dr. Sterling." And he walked on.

Morgan's throat tightened. If he were a con man or a charlatan, she knew, he'd have found some way to make it work for her. At least once. That was how these cult shysters operated. Like a pool shark. Give you a little, make you pay for a lot.

But she'd felt nothing when she threw that water. Not even an inkling. And then Luniel had set a man alight with it. It couldn't be a trick. They'd filled those jars together. She knew they contained nothing but water from the baptistery.

Damn it. He wasn't lying. Maybe the zombies really were hell-cursed. And if he wasn't lying about that . . . what else had he done out of honesty and not deceit? Protecting her? Healing her?

Kissing her?

She shook her head to clear it. She had worse upheavals to deal with than a flash of irrational desire for a man—make that a smoldering, muscled-up demon-killing machine—whom she'd barely met. A weapon that only worked if you believed in it—*because* you believed in it—mocked everything she knew. Everything she'd based her life around.

But for a heady moment, she found herself wishing it were true.

A world where following your heart worked. Where trust paid off to the good, and what you wanted actually meant something.

How wonderful. How beautiful. And how stupidly cruel.

Luniel believed, and could call down the power of his convictions. She couldn't deny that any longer. But for such a brave, faithful creature still to be headed for oblivion when the world ended . . . well, that just made her want to curse God all over again.

Maybe she just wasn't cut out for faith. Did that make her damned?

Morgan sighed, and shouldered her rucksack, and followed Luniel into the shadows. It was a good sign, at least, that the holy water hadn't burned *her*.

On the 108th Street corner, a screeching hell-thing hung from cruel talons on a streetlight, swinging its rotting moth wings and spitting vitriol. Across the street, the public school glared behind a tall iron fence under security lights. Garbage piled up against broken apartment buildings with the stink of rotting food, and in the gutter, demons like deformed children with shiny black skin and wire-brush hair played catch with a zombie corpse.

Luniel pushed Morgan back against a shadowy wall, and dimmed his sword's light, hiding them. "Bonecrushers," he whispered. "Evil little fuckers. Watch the teeth."

One cackled, its beady red eyes shining with glee, and hurled the naked corpse by one of its arms. It spun, flailing, and the arm tore off. To Morgan's horror, it moaned. Still alive.

Another bonecrusher scuttled forward to catch it. The skull smacked into the pavement, and the bonecrusher munched into its torso with long saber teeth, ripping off a meaty chunk. The zombie groaned, and stopped moving. The demon dug in with delight, flesh smearing its ugly black face, and the other two bonecrushers scuttled up and beat their friend over the head with their fists before chewing the corpse limb from limb.

Morgan shuddered at the crunch of bone. "Won't they be infected? I mean, doesn't the curse affect them?"

Lune shook his head. "A hellcurse is of their essence. Feeding on it strengthens them. Why do you think the place is crawling with hellspawn? It's dinnertime. And besides, they all want in good with the big man."

"Quuzaat." The name felt different in her mouth, now. Not

just a delusion. A real, living enemy. And deep inside her, loathing stirred, warm like a slug. Hating a disease was pointless. Hating a demon felt . . . necessary, and powerful. Like meeting the enemy on his own turf.

"Yeah." Luniel's blue gaze warmed. "You a believer yet?"

Wordlessly, she unshouldered the sack of water bombs and handed it to him.

He took it, dark.

She sighed. "I'm trying, Luniel. I really am. I just—"

"I know. For what it's worth, you're doing great." He coughed, that gruff line he always took when he'd said something nice and was trying to restore his tough-guy aura. "Plenty of people fall apart. I've seen angels hit the dirt with poorer grace than you."

Her eyes burned, and she blinked cruelly. No, she wouldn't accept sympathy. He wasn't the only one with a tough shell. "Maybe this is me falling apart," she joked.

"Yeah? Heaven keep me from you on a good day, then."

She flushed, and it maddened her. When had she started caring what he thought of her? Impressing him shouldn't be high on her list of motivations for getting on with it.

But the smoldering embers in his gaze felt good.

She snorted, covering her awkwardness. "Yeah, well. I'm no Virgin Mary, okay, so don't expect me to take it lying down."

"No lying down involved with her. That was kind of the point."

She giggled, tension easing. "You allowed to make jokes about that kind of stuff?"

"What they gonna do, ground me again? Anyway, all Gabriel told Maria was 'your kid's gonna be a star.' He left out all the gory parts. She had nothing to complain about."

Morgan paused. Maybe it was a fairy tale. Maybe not. Tonight, she was open to anything. "That was kind of mean, wasn't it? Keeping the truth from her?"

"Company policy. Need-to-know basis. Only the boss has all the answers."

"Sounds like a dictatorship."

He looked at her like she'd spoken gibberish. "This is God we're talking about. It's not a whim. It's the price of free will. Would you fight on, if you knew how it all ended?"

"I . . ." She bit her lip. Wasn't that what this was all about? To think that the two of them—or even the Tainted Host, with all their power and glory—could somehow stave off the end of the world . . . She hugged herself, chilled despite the heat. Lune's warm embrace seemed a lifetime ago, but she'd be glad of it now. "I'd like to think I'd fight on. Would you?"

He shrugged, feathers twitching. "You can't change fate," he stated flatly, and nodded at the bonecrushers, who were groaning in the gutter clutching their swollen bellies. "Looks like the three stooges have finished their supper. Let's go." He adjusted his sword grip, and ghosted into the street.

Morgan sighed, checking her knife. He hadn't answered her question. Still holding back from her. Seemed she wasn't the only one with trust issues. And his fatalism chilled her blood. If they couldn't alter their fate, then why bother fighting at all? Why not just ride the wave to its inevitable end?

But Luniel halted, looking back. His hair sifted over his armor, black and crisp like raw silk on silver, and his eyes shone, so deep a blue, it hurt to look at them. "For what it's worth, Dr. Sterling: yeah, I do believe in fate. But the answer to your question is still hell, yes. I can't sit and watch the world crumble. I'll fight until the last star burns out. It's what I was made for."

"And what about your precious obedience?"

His gaze shadowed dark with some unknowable pain. "Fuck obedience. It isn't over till it's over."

And he slipped from the shadows into the streetlight's flickering glare, and as three ugly black bonecrushers shrieked and died in slashes of holy blue flame, unwilled warmth stole into Morgan's heart like a thief.

The bonecrushers died too easily.

Their shiny black flesh sliced under Lune's sword like slime. The stink of their guts sickened him, ripe with sour human fear. Shaking gore from his sword, Luniel stole a glance at Morgan from a shaft of moonlit shadow, and his heart skipped.

She looked so alive. Her honeyed eyes shone, her chin set strong, her rosy lips gleaming. Her muscles trembled taut with adrenaline and fear, and her breasts looked so beautiful in that tight t-shirt, the fabric stuck to her skin with sweat and blood and spilled water. Her fingers curled around the skill-spelled knife, determined. If he listened, he could hear her heartbeat, swift and light, her elevated blood pressure spilling her delicious woman scent like a tempting aura.

She was wonderful.

Together, they crept down the dark alley between buildings to the next corner, beside a rust-stained brick wall. She stepped carefully, her boot soles scraping softly on the concrete. His own step was almost silent, but he had the benefit of wings and a few thousand years of practice. She had only guts and self-preservation.

Overhead, a security light buzzed, and she jumped, tense. A few seconds later he heard her breathe, and laugh softly at herself, and he couldn't help a secret smile of his own.

She was afraid, yes, bewildered, overcome with strangeness and wonder. But she wasn't broken. Not his brave doctor, whose vitality stung the air electric in his magical senses, tingling his feathers taut. Who walked like a goddess, statuesque and precious, but smelled like a woman, warm rose petals and spice and sultry feminine skin.

And he was leading her ever closer to a malevolent demon prince, who'd flay her soul alive if he ever found out that Lune . . .

His wings sparked hot. That he thought about her. Couldn't get her out of his mind. Stole glances at her, over and over, when he thought she wouldn't see, admiring the moonlight dancing over her hair. Imagined her firm skin shivering under his kiss, her soft gasp as he caressed those amazing breasts. He got hard just thinking about how she'd shuddered and sighed when he touched her oh-so-responsive nipples. She'd nearly come from that alone, and her climax was something he definitely longed to taste again. Next time, he'd tease those little buds until she lost it, flicking them with his tongue, pulling them into his mouth and suckling their ripe sweetness . . .

Lune gritted his teeth, flexing tight fingers around his sword's grip. *Mind on the job, dickhead.* Lucky some stupid hellspawn hadn't jumped his distracted ass a dozen times already.

Hell, the prince would flay her soul anyway. That's what demons did.

But that didn't make it okay to put her in danger. No matter how luscious she was.

A wet rustle around the corner made him halt, and Morgan touched his arm, her thigh brushing his. "What?" she whispered.

Lune liked how she stayed close. Almost as if she trusted him to protect her. It was a heady feeling. He'd missed it.

He sniffed the air for ashen hellspawn, and the curse's noisome stench slimed his nose. He was more careful now, after the last one. "Zombie," he whispered back. "Fresh. Not that far gone."

"How many?"

"Just the one."

Her eyes shone. "I want to try something. Give me one of those bombs."

He frowned. "But the water doesn't work for you."

"They don't know that, do they? Just give it to me. And don't kill the zombie, okay? Not until I say."

He shrugged, and handed over a jar.

She flashed him a smile, maddeningly alluring. "Ever see *The Exorcist*?"

"No." He wanted to taste that smile. Kiss it. Teach her what else she could do with those ripe red lips.

"You're about to become one. Just shut up and play along, angel," she whispered, and winked, and he wanted her so hard, his vision flashed red.

Desire forged his conviction bright like spelled steel. *Sweet sin, woman. In another lifetime, I would own you.*

She licked her bottom lip, staring as if she'd heard him. He swallowed, and vanished his sword with a soft word. And together, they leapt around the corner.

CHAPTER 17

The zombie shambled right into them, muttering, and Lune couldn't help sweeping Morgan behind him. The guy wore a cheap dark suit, maybe a young accountant or a stockbroker's minion, and his cinnamon-brown hair curled tight on his scalp. Not a mutie. Perhaps he'd come here for drugs, fights, illicit thrills. But now the demon's curse fouled his breath, and spun his eyes like pinwheels with crazy delight. He wasn't rotting, not yet.

"What the fuck?" he grumbled, stumbling over his own feet. "White people. Shit. Knew this neighborhood was going to hell."

"Not yet." Lune grabbed his shoulder, immovable. Evil heat seared his palm through the suit. Together, he and Morgan forced the zombie up against the rust-stained wall.

The guy struggled, sweating. "Hey. Cut it out. I've got nothing you want . . . fuck me, man, you've got wings—ugh!"

Lune kneed him in the guts to shut him up. He glanced down at Morgan while holding the wriggling zombie against the wall one-handed. "Your turn."

Morgan flipped the top off her water jar and thrust it before the zombie's eyes. "Know what this is, freak?"

Her face was cold, her voice hard. The zombie shook his head, bewildered. "It's just water, lady. What the h—aargh!"

She thrust it closer, and fear lit his diseased eyes scarlet. He jerked backwards, thrashing, his skull cracking the wall hard enough to bleed. "Get it away from me. Get it away! Ahh!" He flailed in panic, sick and bewildered. He was terrified, and he didn't know why.

The poor bastard was still lucid. Still human. For a few minutes more, maybe.

Lune bit back foolish sympathy, and forced the guy still, slamming him harder into the wall. Once they were damned, they were damned. They couldn't be saved. Eleanor taught him that.

Morgan dipped her fingers in the holy water and shook them in the guy's face. "You like that, huh? Want some?"

His voice trembled. "No! Please. I don't know what that shit is, lady, but I'll do anything. Take my wallet, I've got cash—"

"I don't want your money," Morgan snapped. "Where's your master?" She sounded tough, no-nonsense, Lune thought. Willing to do whatever it took. Did that make him the good cop?

"Master? What master?" His young face paled. "I don't know what the fuck you're talking about."

Morgan jerked her chin at Luniel. "Hurt him, baby. I don't have time for this."

In a flash, Lune saw where she was headed. His heart swelled with pride. *She's clever, my lady.* He dipped a fingertip in the holy water and flicked a few sizzling drops onto the zombie's face.

The zombie howled, and his eyes sprang scarlet, the curse provoked alight. His teeth gnashed wet. "Get away from me, angel, before I munch your bitch to meat."

"That's more like it," said Morgan smoothly, though her face paled a little. "You hungry? Huh? Who feeds you? Where's your master?"

The zombie just screamed, throwing his head back and shaking it like a howling wolf.

The curse made the little shit strong. Lune murmured a swift appeal to glory and raised his palm, the Tainted's lightning sigil glowing blue. "Show me, hellspawn."

The zombie thrashed, blue flames licking his skin, but the sigil burn spell shuddered and drifted loose. The curse was still in its infancy, and the demon's sigil wouldn't show. Frustrated, Lune jammed the heel of his hand into the thing's forehead.

Flesh sizzled. It screeched foul words, the demon's curse retreating inside him, and the holy flames snapped out.

The zombie panted, sweating. Its pupils shone black with shock. Terrified. Only a faint twirl of scarlet, the curse licking its wounds deep inside.

Morgan gasped. "He's cured!"

But the zombie wasn't cured, Lune knew. Just lucid, for the moment, the curse not yet rooted deeply enough to brush off Lune's spell immediately. And the abject horror in the guy's eyes as he gasped for air said it all. He remembered. Knew what he was, what he would become.

Morgan gripped Lune's arm, tense. "Do that again! It's working!"

"No, it isn't." He cracked a fist across the guy's jaw. The head flung to the side, mouth bleeding.

"Lune! Jeez." Morgan glared at him, fiery. "Chill out, will you?"

"Watch," said Lune coldly. "You started this. Just watch."

Helplessly, the guy licked his bleeding lips. Sucked them. Swallowed the blood. Groaned in disgust, but in desperate hunger, too. "Oh, God. No. Please. Help me. I can't—"

"You like that? Huh?" Lune pressed his palm over the guy's lips, forcing more blood into his mouth. Sympathy was pointless. Only killing the demon prince could stop the curse. And soon this guy would be rabid and useless. Lune didn't have time for niceties. "Eating your own blood? You want to go there? Just keep on lying to us."

The zombie spluttered red. "I'm not lying to you, man! I don't know what the fuck you're—"

"Yes, you do. Think. What happened after they bit you? Who cursed you?"

The guy's eyes widened. His bleeding lips quivered. "I . . . I thought I was having a nightmare. Zombies everywhere, all the screaming and shit . . . Some thin white dude with white hair. The Prince of Poison, they called him. He laughed at me, and this . . . thing . . . crawled down my throat. Like a . . . a hot worm, or something. I choked, I couldn't stop it. And then . . ."

"Where, kid? Tell me where."

Tears streaked his cheeks. "Oh, God. I've got it. I've got the virus, haven't I?"

"Where?" Lune and Morgan demanded at the same time.

The zombie waved his arm, at first in some general direction, and then his mouth tightened and he pointed, unwavering. "That way. By the river, where the housing project's all burned up. Not far. That's where they all are. That white-haired motherfucker and his crazy-ass gang." Sobs broke his voice. "I can feel him, laughing at me! I'm a dead man, aren't I?"

Lune gulped. Memories of Eleanor swamped him. Laughing at him as she made love to her demon master. Taunting him . . .

"No." He cut off Morgan's reluctant affirmation. "No, you're not. You'll live forever." *Probably in hell,* he added silently. But he didn't have the heart to say it. "You just have to believe."

The zombie nodded, trembling. "God is great, man. I believe in his prophet. You're an angel, right? A holy guy? Pray for me."

Lune swallowed. Like that'd do any good. "Close your eyes, kid," he said softly, and the shivering zombie obeyed.

Morgan tugged Lune's arm, eyes flashing. *Don't,* she mouthed, frowning.

I have to, he replied, and before she could say more, he called down his flaming blue sword and slit the zombie's throat.

The zombie gurgled, and fell, dead.

Morgan whirled, flinging the holy water away in fury. "You killed him! With the curse still inside!"

"Better than letting him live through it." Lune shrugged, tight. "You think I did it for fun?"

"But it was working! We could've cured him!"

"Jesus, you're not on about cures again? What part of it don't you get?" He swiped his fingers through the zombie gore on his sword, and it sizzled dry on contact. He held up his crusted fingers for her to see. "He was hell-cursed! I can't cure that! All the holy water does is react to the evil."

She stared, plucking frantically at the hem of her t-shirt. "But . . . but you cured yourself. I saw you. In your apartment. Why can't you do the same for him?"

Luniel flushed. Even after so many years, shame still burned like hellfire. "That wasn't me, Morgan," he admitted softly. "I have to call down glory for that."

"So? Why don't you?"

"Do you know how much that bloodspell hurts?" The evasion stung his tongue like a lie. "Every time I do it, I wipe myself out. I can't risk that on the battlefield. And even if it worked, who's going to decide which two or three we pick before I can't do it anymore? You?"

She shook her head, frustrated. "That's no excuse. Surely you can take a little pain to save a life!"

His stomach folded, sick. She knew he was avoiding the real answer. She deserved the truth, even if it made her despise him. "Because heaven'll say no, okay? Do I have to fucking spell it out for you?"

She stared, and shrank back. "But—"

"Believe me. I've tried. I have to beg them on my fucking knees and they don't give me much. They keep me alive, but that's all they care about."

Morgan swallowed, but her eyes blazed. "So you're more important to them than some poor human, are you?"

"Yeah, Morgan, I guess so." He didn't look away. Didn't give her the satisfaction of his shame. "At least when you pray for deliverance, they've got the grace not to tell you to your face that you can fuck off."

"Yeah?" Fury twisted her pretty mouth, but tears shimmered her eyes silver. She wasn't angry with him. He could smell it. Just with everything. She stabbed her finger at the dead zombie, who bled in a heap at their feet. "Then what do you call *that*?"

Sympathy brushed cool fingers over his temper. Hesitantly, he touched her shoulder. She didn't pull away, not exactly, but she didn't warm to him, either. He settled for a quiet caress of her hair. "I call it damnation."

"But that's not fair." She gulped, helpless. "He didn't ask for this. He just got bitten. It wasn't his fault!"

"No, but damnation is a curse now. A disease you can catch. The world's under siege. Nothing's fair anymore, if it ever was. That's why they call it the Apocalypse." His fingers trembled on her cheek. She was so soft and bruiseable. So hard to protect.

For a moment, she closed her eyes and let him touch her.

Lune's pulse burned. He wanted to take her in his arms, give her comfort. But it wouldn't fix her broken world. Wouldn't make everything okay, or put it back like it was before she knew.

He didn't have that power. No one did.

He swallowed, aching. "Do you get it now? This is the End.

We can't waste the last days trying to redeem the damned. Their journey is over. Better we fight for the ones who can still be saved."

"Is that so?" Morgan pushed away, wiping her face. "Doesn't stop you from enjoying yourself, does it?"

He drew back. "What's that supposed to mean?"

"I've seen you fight, Luniel," she accused, fiery. "You *like* it. Killing."

He shrugged, unwilling. How to explain what glory felt like, thrumming through his body, burning electric in every muscle and vein and sinew. Like sex, the breathless delight of tension and explosive release. Like agony, every nerve hacked ragged and alive. Might as well explain what it felt like to breathe. "So what? It's my job."

"It's not your job to get off on slaughtering innocent people."

"What did you fucking say?"

"You heard me." Defiance burned in her eyes. She cocked her hand on her hip, daring him to challenge her. So sexy, he wanted to bruise her lips with his, wrap his wings around her and make her his own. So infuriating, he wanted to knock her flat.

His fists clenched, and he restrained from either. But the heat in his anger shocked him hard. "Yeah. And that shows how much you know, human. Hiding in your safe little world full of corpses."

Her eyes darkened. "I bring justice to the dead. That's not hiding."

"Give me a break. Any dumb animal can rage against death. You know what takes real courage? To believe you'll live forever, and to act like it."

"Oh, really?"

"Is that why you're a dead-people doctor? To avoid taking responsibility for the living?"

Morgan's chin tightened, furious. "Maybe. You should know, angel. Because letting all these people die is really stepping up, isn't it?"

Lune's blood burned. He knew he should keep quiet. But that only made him madder, and he couldn't stop the words spilling out. "You know what? Screw excuses. Yes, I enjoy slaughtering demons. It feels fucking fantastic. I'm supposed to enjoy it, it's what I was made for. And demons are like me: they made their choice. They don't deserve sympathy. But if you think I enjoyed *that*"—he stabbed his finger to the dead zombie, mocking her gesture—"then fuck you, Morgan Sterling, because you don't know me as well as you think."

His feathers prickled, and he sucked in a shuddering breath, appalled. *Nice work, Lune. Very calm. Perfect choice of words.*

But Morgan's lip trembled, and she bit it. "Look, I didn't mean it that way. I just . . ." She thudded frustrated fists into her thighs. "Shit. Don't you ever get sick of it? Accepting your lot, I mean. Sucking it up and moving on."

Luniel closed his eyes for a moment. *Calm. She's just realized the world's ending. Don't say what can't be unsaid.* "Look, I'm . . . I shouldn't have said that. But there are things that can't be changed. Some roads are one-way."

"I guess you know that, huh." She gave a little smile, trying to lighten up. "Getting grounded, and all."

"More than I can explain." The last syllable cracked. Glitter burned his wings with shame, and he turned away. *Fuck. Not now, Morgan. Please.*

But too late. She'd seen. She touched his arm, and that tender, compassionate brush of fingers was more arresting than a tight grip could ever have been.

He halted, shaking. "Just forget it, okay—"

"Something happened to you, didn't it?" Her bottomless honey gaze held him fast. "Not just banishment. You're so full of hope, Luniel. I can feel it. They haven't broken you by casting you down. Yet you're so lost. So . . . alone." She swallowed. "But you're not alone tonight. I'm here, angel. Tell me."

Heaven, help me.

For a long moment, words wouldn't come. "It was a long time ago. I . . . loved someone, and a demon prince took her. He tortured her. Tricked her soul from her, Morgan. She was damned and I didn't . . . I couldn't stop it. I tried, but I couldn't bring her back. And Vorvian . . . the demon, he got away. I let my need for her get in the way of business, and it cost me everything."

A tiny feather of his drifted between them, and she caught it, fingering the soft black curl thoughtfully. "So that's why heaven shunned you? Because you loved her?"

"No. Because by trying to save her, I let Vorvian escape. I wanted her more than I wanted victory." He swallowed, painful, the memory piercing his heart like demonsteel, but somehow the pain tasted sweeter for Morgan's presence. "You know what they call that in heaven? Lust. There's nothing noble about it. If I ever forget my place like that again, they won't have mercy on me. And if I can't even bring *her* back, what hope for these poor fools here? No, I've learned my lesson. Damnation is forever. It can't be undone. Not by me."

"And what about me?" Morgan asked. Her gaze challenged him, but her chin trembled. "If I get the curse, will you kill me, too?"

CHAPTER 18

Lune just looked at her, dark with sorrow, and didn't answer.

Morgan sucked in a breath, her heart stinging. Disappointment tingled bitter on her tongue. She wanted so badly to help him, it hurt her deep inside. To ease his grief, make his heart well again.

But there was nothing she could say.

And he hadn't answered her question, and in the darkest recesses of her soul, she knew why.

He'd abandon her. He'd have to. Leave her to the mercy of the zombie plague, if it meant he could save the world. If he couldn't save his lover—the pain in his eyes as he spoke of her tore Morgan's heart, part sympathy, part acid anguish, part screaming green envy that shamed her—why would he pause for an instant to save Morgan, whom he'd only met tonight and had spent most of the last hour trading insults with?

The few and the many. Sensible from an ethical point of view. But it sucked the big one, if you were one of the few.

The injustice maddened her. She sighed angrily and turned away. His feather still twined her fingers, and slowly she undid it, studying. So soft, blacker than night. Only her finger's length. Not like his larger feathers, which were crisp and strong, as broad as her forearm and longer. A strange contrast, soft with steely, not unlike Luniel himself.

Frustration itched her guts. Damn him. Sometimes so gentle and forgiving. Other times, diamonds couldn't crush his icy will. He made her feel safe and threatened at the same time. And when desire moved him . . . She shivered, thinking of his remorseless fighting skills, wings slicing the air like sharp black blades, muscles bunching, cruel and invincible as he wrought demon slaughter.

And how effortlessly he stroked her to feverish need, the intensity of his passion thieving her breath away. His groan as he whispered her name into her mouth. His powerful shudder as he slid himself into her hot wetness . . .

Her flesh tingled in memory, but reluctantly, she let the feather drift away.

Best that hadn't happened, after all. This way, neither of them owed the other anything. But still, regret twinged warm, and unwilled she pictured herself lying beside him in silvery moonlight. Trailing her fingertips along his smooth back, dipping her face into warm fragrant feathers, her naked breasts sliding in his rough silken hair . . .

Yeah. Snap out of it, Morgan. Inconvenient enough that she kept daydreaming about sex with him. Imagining cuddling afterwards was a bad idea.

She stifled cynical laughter. Cuddling with an angel. How quickly one got used to strange new worlds. Twenty-four hours ago, if someone had told her she'd be hunting plague demons through Babylon with an angel fallen from heaven, she'd have prescribed Prozac and a week's rest.

Now, she'd accepted it, with the same detachment she'd accepted her mother's unfair suicide. *Mom's dead, and her faith killed her. Chin up, move on. Medical school costs how much? Get a job, study harder, move on. Angels are real? The world's ending? Fine. Accept the evidence. Move on.*

But still, her soul screamed with injustice and childish denial. *Not me. I'm special, not like all the others. When the earthquake hits, I'll survive. I won't get old, won't get wrinkles or lose my eyesight. Cancer won't find me. I'm not going to die.*

Even her angel, it seemed, couldn't save her now. But that didn't stop her hoping.

Best we fight for the ones who can still be saved, he'd said.

To imagine she'd be one of the lucky ones seemed the height of human hubris. But to accept fate, and give up?

Not Morgan Sterling. She hadn't given up when her mother died. Not when cramming for exams and working double shifts at the diner starved her of sleep. Not even in the residency from hell, when wave after wave of New Anarchist bombs rocked the city and she wept from exhaustion and helplessness, amid bleeding bodies spilling from the ER and a week without rest or respite.

And she wouldn't give up now.

Not until the last star burns out. And if that meant she had to fight on alone? Try to save them, when Luniel just wanted to kill them all? She would.

She tugged stray tangles from her face, beating back exhaustion. She'd been up all night. But thanks to the zombie, they knew where to look. For Quuzaat. The Prince of Poison. No point waiting.

Luniel watched her turn away, and wanted to slam his head against the ground until his brains bled out.

Curse her for calling him out. And curse his weak, unworthy heart.

Fuck. Lune, you could at least have said something.

But he didn't have the heart to tell her the truth. And he didn't have the strength to lie.

He couldn't promise to keep her safe. A demon prince had defeated him before. No guarantee one wouldn't again. And if Morgan got the curse, there was no saving her. Eleanor was proof of that.

Eleanor said she loved him, and he'd trusted her. But she'd believed Vorvian when he said Lune had betrayed her. She'd broken so easily. And nothing Lune could say had changed her mind.

He gritted his teeth on acid self-disgust. He didn't blame Eleanor. It wasn't fair to blame her. Demons were crafty, and knew all the right buttons to push. But still, after so many centuries, it rubbed a raw salty ache in his heart that she hadn't loved him enough to hold on a little longer.

That he wasn't worth the effort. And in the end, he'd proved her right.

But somehow, right now, he still burned to take Morgan in his arms and make her his own. Draw his flaming sword and protect her with slaughter, rip skin and rend bones and drink the stinking blood of any foul hellslime who dared glance in her direction.

Morgan. A woman he'd known for one night. Who made his skin burn and his pulse race and his heart ache for days long lost, a time when he was strong and virtuous and might have deserved her.

Staunch that bleeding heart, whispered Michael's voice in his head. *It'll only get you killed.*

Rotten frustration bubbled in Lune's chest. He wanted to scream, let his torment ring out until glass shattered in heaven.

Instead, he switched on his phone and called Dash, keeping one eye on Morgan in case of trouble.

No answer. There was a missed call, Dash's number. So why wasn't the shithead answering?

Frustrated, Lune ended the call, and made another, his sharp gaze fixed on Morgan.

"Yeah, Lune. What?" Japheth's voice, low, like he whispered with his hand over the phone.

"I can't raise Dash. He with you?"

A cool sigh. "The battle's over and it's party hour. Dash will be working off the glory rush with some besotted female. Did you really think he'd answer?"

Lune chuckled. "Guess not. Just checking in. How'd you guys fare?"

"We did okay. Look, I've gotta go—"

"Listen, we hit the jackpot down here." Quickly, Luniel told him about the Prince of Poison's burned housing project. "We're heading there now for a look-see."

"Uh-huh. Is that doctor still with you, perchance? Dash told me."

Lune bristled. "Of course. Why wouldn't she be?"

"No reason. Don't burr up. But it's five in the morning, Lune. She's probably tired?"

"Oh." He gulped. Sure enough, a pale tinge of dawn filtered the eastern sky. "Right. Thanks."

"You're welcome."

* * *

Japheth's fingers clenched, and he jammed his phone away lest he crush it. He hadn't lied, not exactly. But he knew precisely where Dashiel was.

He hovered, high on currents of warm breeze, and before him, moonshine streaked red on the apartment window. But it didn't stop Japheth seeing inside. Dark wooden furniture, rich carpets on timber, shelves of antique weapons. And Dashiel, in human guise on white silken sheets, making love to his latest conquest.

Japheth stared, mesmerized. Naked, shining with sweat, wet dark hair plastered to his shoulders. The girl was blond and tiny—Dash always chose the tiny ones—and her throaty sighs set Japheth's blood alight.

He didn't like to watch. It felt dirty and sinful. But watching was what he had instead of doing, and *not* doing it—the anticipation, the imagining, the frustration that he'd never know release—was secretly more compelling than the handful of times he'd ever tried it before he fell.

Back then, he'd always had better things to do. His liaisons were harsh, loveless, violent. But watching Dashiel make this lovely girl cry out with pleasure—over, and over, like Dash was searching for something and not finding it—filled Japheth with longing for a delirious passion he'd never known.

He ached, his feathers quivering hot. He wanted to touch himself. Hurt himself, carve slow welts in his skin, grip his aching shaft in his fist and make the need go away.

But even that was too dangerous. He should go home, take a cold shower. But he couldn't tear his gaze away, and now Dashiel flipped her over and pushed her thighs apart to taste her sweet pink folds.

Japheth bit his lip savagely. He'd never asked Dash if he minded. Dash wasn't shy, and would probably like the idea. But Japheth already felt dirty enough. And tonight, he'd extra reason to hide.

Put an end to Dashiel for me, and we can talk about you coming home. Michael's words still caressed him, dangerous like a silk-covered blade.

Dashiel was Japheth's friend. Dash picked him up when he

was broken, held him through nights of shuddering withdrawal from glory. Taught him it was okay to drown his longing in blood and slaughter, so long as he still did heaven's work.

Japheth sweated and shivered, the breeze flitting through his feathers. None of that mattered, did it? Michael's orders were simple, and the rules were whatever the archangel said they were. That was what being Tainted meant. Japheth could dive in there right now and end it. Slash the angel's throat open with his holy sword. Spill Dash's Tainted blood to the sky, and Michael would take Japheth back.

Redemption. Just like that. His soul restored. No more oblivion. And then, Michael would . . . what? Love him again? Say sorry for shunning him? Explain what in heaven he'd done to deserve it?

But the lost bliss of home tugged at Japheth's ice-coated heart, deeper than any hold the archangel once had over him. Misha loved nothing, and no one. Japheth just wanted his soul back. His happiness. An end to frustration and loneliness and empty despair.

But at what cost to his heart?

Dashiel's girl climaxed again, shuddering. Japheth's flesh twitched harder. Heaven, it was beautiful, the way she surrendered to her pleasure. The way Dash's massive body moved, climbing up to glide his glistening shaft inside her again, pinning her hands above her head and thrusting deep and hard.

Pleasure tingled over Dash's dusky skin, and Japheth shivered in electric empathy. The echo of shared glory resonated between them, a relentless link he couldn't break. Unwilling, Japheth felt Dash's pleasure with him, the sweat sliding on his skin, the girl's teeth on his nipple, the ghostly sensation of her hot wet flesh, gliding over him . . .

Japheth spun away, but too late.

Dashiel growled, and climaxed, spilling his seed deep inside her, and the feeling hit Japheth in the guts. Horrid sensation without pleasure, pain without passion. Empty. He didn't enjoy it. He just hurt, like a dead thing, unable to feel anything but echoes of what he once had.

Kill Dashiel, and he'd come alive.

Gulping down a cry of raw frustration, Japheth tumbled into uncaring air.

CHAPTER 19

Luniel slipped his phone away, mortified. How could he have forgotten? Angels could stay awake and fight for days on end if need be, especially with a dazzling gloryhit surging through their veins. That was what heaven made them for. Sustenance was essential, but not urgent. But Morgan would need rest. Food. Care.

Shit. He wasn't used to caring for anyone but himself. Least of all a human woman, so precious and vulnerable.

She was watching him, a smile tinting her lips. Her face shone pale, her eyes bright with dark rings beneath them. "Finished chatting with your friends? Can we go now?"

He fidgeted. How had he not noticed her exhaustion? "Listen. Um . . . why don't we leave it until morning?"

"It is morning." She indicated the brightening sky.

"Yeah. I mean, I think I should take you home for a while."

"I don't want to go home." She frowned, irritable. "Demons, plagues, curses. Stuff to do. Remember?"

"You've been up all night, Morgan. You need food, and sleep, and . . . y'know." He gestured vaguely. "All that human stuff." He held up his hand to stave off her protests. "The Prince of Poison will still be there tonight. Demons thrive on darkness. Now we know where to look, we'll come back when the party's started. And you're useless to me half-asleep. Let me . . ." He flushed. "You need to take care of yourself," he amended lamely.

She sighed, frustrated, but he could tell she knew he was right. "Okay. But you're not coming back here without me, hear?"

"Wouldn't dream of it. Flash or fly?"

"Huh?"

"Your place. No subway here, and I'm not walking. Wanna flash or fly?"

Her beautiful eyes glinted eagerly. "Can we fly? Please?"

Her excitement tingled his skin. He grinned, and vanished his sword—but only a tiny wish's breadth away. He could still feel it, vibrating the ether, ready to snap back into his hand. No way was he losing her now. He held out his arm, beckoning. "Madam."

She came to him, holding on tight to his breastplate. Her arms barely reached around him. She tucked her head under his chin, dark hair spilling over silver. Her scent thrilled him, sweet sweat and smoke and woman.

He'd held her before—flown with her, touched her body, felt her slick wet flesh on his fingers and tasted her pleasure's hot sigh—but somehow this was different. Closer. More real.

His heart swelled, and deep inside, for the first time in centuries, something hard and cold melted like ice in the sun.

And he folded his arms around her—so warm—and dived for the brightening sky.

Morgan hung on tightly, and let her angel make her fly.

Breeze tugged her hair, the ground falling dizzily away. His armor glistened, warm and smooth under her cheek. His scent enveloped her, toffee and hot male skin and the crisp freshness of sunrise. She gripped his hair, enjoying the wind thrumming in his thick silken locks.

He held her effortlessly, and the feel of his strong embrace filled her with a safety she'd rarely known. The pressure on her breasts as he breathed felt good. She breathed, too, slow and deep, invigorated.

His wings beat the air hard, feathers zinging. He felt warm and supple, muscles working in perfect concert. This quiet flight seemed a simple marvel, not ugly and heaving like a fuel-powered aircraft struggling against physics to get off the ground. Their weight seemed reduced to zero, gravity meaningless, yet here he was, hot and hard and real. On the ground, he was strong, graceful like a snarling panther. In the air, he was . . . magical. Like a new creature, transformed, a sleek spearing weapon.

Night breeze tugged her t-shirt tight, caressing her bare belly. Her hair tickled her face, mingling with his. Lights jeweled the city, gems on a fading black velvet sea, proud gold-flashed towers mingling with colored lanterns and bonfires. Virtual neon advertising scrolled like rainbows below her, meaningless from a vantage point never intended. Skyscrapers gleamed in a sliver of rising sun, and beyond the coast, the eastern horizon gleamed like a golden thread.

He dipped, and the skyline tilted, crazy. Pleasure tingled at the pressure of his big thighs, muscles jumping as he instinctively adjusted trim and balance.

"You okay?" His big hand gripped the curve of her ass. Warm strings of desire plucked in her belly when she felt his hot hardness press against her. He liked holding her.

"Mmm." She liked it, too. Liked him wanting her. She wanted to do the same to him with her own hand, run her palm over those taut muscles. Wrap her leg around him, enjoy the pulsing evidence of his desire, with the wind in her face and his luscious scent washing over her. It didn't seem sordid or strange. It seemed . . . worthy. Satisfying. Like tonight they'd earned the pleasure, somehow.

Desire kindled in her belly, warm and dangerous. She hadn't really wanted a man—beyond the natural itch for sex when you weren't getting any—for a long time. Not like this. Passion had been missing from her life, replaced by cold hard determination to succeed alone, and with this glorious, sensual creature in her arms, she knew it was no substitute. Only this—only he—would do.

And for the first time since her mother's death—through years of poverty and sleeplessness and harsh reality—real fear slithered warm into her guts.

God, no. She couldn't fall for him. Not an angel, this frightening creature of faith and terror. Her mind was too set, her heart too full of distrust. After this was over, she'd probably never see him again. Surely, he had more important things to do than pay attention to her.

Assuming she didn't get the virus and die at his hand.

But that didn't mean this wasn't the freshest, most liberating night of her life.

His eyes glowed, bluer than blue, scanning the horizon for threat. He had the most beautiful mouth. "Lune," she murmured.

He surveyed the airspace, but his gaze kept slipping back to hers, like he couldn't stop it. "Mmm?"

"Thank you."

"For what?" His gaze tracked to her mouth, and stayed there. His lips mesmerized her. She wanted to taste them. She wanted closeness, safety, the strange warmth of his understanding. But this was like a dream of flying, impossible and wonderful as well as terrifying. She didn't want to wake disappointed.

"For showing me a new world," she said simply, and hid her face against his chest.

His laugh rumbled, delightful. "Sorry it had to be one that's ending. But you're welcome. Where'd you say you lived?"

She risked letting go to point. "East Thirty-Seventh, near Lexington . . . Look, there's my building. The gray one. Fourth floor, on the corner. Nothing so hip as yours, naturally—ugh!"

Poisonous darkness whooshed. Reflexively, she jerked backwards against Luniel's grip. A cackle ripped her ears, the air ripe with rotting leather. Luniel rolled, dizzying her, and blue light dazzled as he flashed out his sword. His feathers thrummed tight with a sound like harp strings, and they jerked to an impossible, hanging halt.

Claws slashed inches from her face. A horrible hellcreature somersaulted away from Lune's sword. It hung on rotted black-feathered wings, snarling, reminiscent of the bats that attacked them in the mortuary, but worse.

Much worse.

These things—three of them—looked like huge rabid vultures, long scrawny necks and meat-hook talons. Sick yellow eyes gleamed with hunger in rheumy sockets, and their flesh was decomposing, their starved bodies like two-week-old corpses, bones and sinews visible. The nearest one laughed, its stinking breath wetting her face, and a wave of ghastly hunger rocked her.

Her stomach groaned. The creatures' stench coated her tongue, and her famished mouth watered. So hungry, she'd eat anything. She shuddered. What kind of curse monsters were these?

"Die, godshit." The hellvulture's snarl grated, nails on glass. "You and your doctor slut."

"Hold on!" Luniel gave her no time to react. He somersaulted, backwards, kicking the thing in the face, and flipped around with his sword spitting blue flame.

She shook herself, dizzy and ravenous, and blinked. The creature wasn't there.

And something slammed into Luniel's back. His wing bones popped, and he grunted in pain, and the thing's jagged beak crunched onto his forearm. Blood hissed. His body jolted, shaking her loose, and she fell.

CHAPTER 20

Morgan's stomach plummeted. Gravity lashed out at her with evil intent. She grabbed at the sky, useless, grasping at nothing. Air rushed up to beat her back and scream in her ears. Friction blistered her skin. Hair whipped her face. Stars and sky and ground tumbled. Her breath tore away, and terror clawed her gibbering heart. She couldn't see. Couldn't breathe. Couldn't think.

White light cracked, a stinging lash of thunder. And strong arms caught her waist and dragged her upwards.

Her neck whiplashed. Sickness lurched in her guts. Luniel cradled her against his chest, tucking her knees up. Momentum speared them into a somersault, and he drove them higher on strong wings. "You're okay, I've got you. Shh."

She clutched him, quivering. Her nerves were ripped ragged. She was safe, the foul hunger obliterated, but her heart still hammered. She couldn't calm it. She sucked in air, her throat rough like broken glass, and realized she'd been screaming.

She tried to swallow, panting. "Where are . . . those . . ."

"Starvewraiths. Dead. Gone. Never mind them. I'm so sorry, Morgan. Forgive me." He stroked her hair, crushing her to his chest, holding on like he'd make up for dropping her by never letting go.

"I'm okay." She cleared her throat, embarrassed. At least, she noted clinically, she hadn't wet herself. "I'm okay. Let me breathe."

"Sorry," he said again, and loosened his grip, but only a little.

She laughed, shaking, crazy tension ebbing. "Stop saying that. We're still here. I know you didn't mean it . . ." Her voice trailed off. Had she truly believed he'd catch her? Or assumed he'd let her fall, rather than let his enemy escape?

For a woman who hadn't believed with all her soul she was about to die, her terror had felt sickeningly real.

Guilt burned her lungs, and she coughed it away. Stupid. She didn't owe him her trust. He hadn't earned it. Had he?

His feathers whipped the wind, and she closed her eyes. It was still magical. But even enchantment could kill, if you made a mistake.

She didn't open her eyes again until she felt him land.

He eased gracefully to a halt, folding his wings. She blinked as he set her gently on her feet. Black metal railing, tiny concrete balcony, just big enough for them both to stand.

"This the one?" He still held her against his chest, like he wouldn't risk letting her go even now. His arms around her felt safe. They felt stifling, too.

"Yeah. We're kinda locked out." She tugged the curled iron door handle, feeling foolish. She always bolted from the inside, even on fourth. Babylon sickos had imagination. But until tonight, she'd never met anything that could fly.

She shuddered, cold. Would she ever feel safe alone again?

Luniel slid his hand beneath hers, gripping the handle. The bolts slid out as if by magic. He twisted the handle, and the door opened.

She forced a laugh, trying to keep it light. "So I can't lock you guys out, then? Great."

Lune shrugged against her back. "I could just flash in there. No point in the lock working against me, so it doesn't."

Her scientific mind boggled. "O-kaay. So how come I can shoot you, then, if bullets won't harm you?"

"I can only open the bolts, Morgan. I can't stop you locking the door." Reluctantly, he released her. "Go on."

She sidled inside. Just as she'd left it with Jadzia, dim and cool, the faint musk of scented candles lingering. Still tidy from her last effort at cleaning a few weeks ago. Since the virus broke out, she'd barely been here except to eat and sleep, and journals were still piled neatly on the low glass table by her desk, the scarlet cushions unmolested on the creamy sofa.

"Lights, low." The table lamp welled bright, along with a few iron-bracketed wall lamps that reflected golden on the hardwood floors. Her legs still shook, and now that she was home, exhaustion rippled over her, draining her energy. She'd been up all night, and what a night it had been.

She walked unsteadily to the kitchenette, and she'd filled a glass with iced water and microwaved some Chinese takeout before she realized her angel hadn't followed.

She craned her neck. There he stood, still on the balcony, a hulking dark silhouette in the rising light. "Luniel? You waiting for an invitation?"

"Actually . . . yeah." He fidgeted, fingers flexing.

Her belly warmed. Awkward, him? She munched a forkful of rice, ravenous. "What are you, a vampire or something?"

"No. Just old-fashioned, I guess." His blue gaze caught hers, dark like a midnight ocean. "I don't expect anything from you, Morgan. Just so you know."

She flushed. Apparently awkwardness was catching tonight. "Okay. Um . . . won't you come in?"

He dipped his head and shoulders in a bow, a courtly gesture she'd never actually seen outside a movie, and came in, locking the door behind him. He had to tuck his wings tight to squeeze through the narrow doorway. He looked feral and strange in her tiny living room, such a big wild creature, stained in blood and dirt. She glanced down, and realized she looked the same, her t-shirt ripped, her pants sticky with stains. Jadzia's knife rested cool and safe in its sheath, like it was dozing.

Her gritty eyes itched. She could really use a shower. She took a swallow from her glass, then another, the cool water steadying. "Um. Would you like a drink? Or some takeout? I don't cook, I'm afraid."

"No, thanks." He stood, uncomfortable, like he didn't know where to look or what to do. Undomesticated. His dirty wingtip brushed the sofa, leaving a dark stain, and he bent to wipe it off, hitching his wings in tighter. "Sorry."

"No problem. At least have a seat, you're wearing me out."

"I'll stand, if that's all right."

"Look, I don't blame you for dropping me, okay? I'm fine. You can relax—"

"No, I can't. It's not safe, Morgan. The hellspawn know where we are."

She shivered in memory. "What were those . . . starve things?"

"Starvewraiths. Imps of hunger. They spread gluttony." His gaze smoldered. "They knew who you were, Morgan. Someone's sending them after us. Just . . . do what you need to, and I'll watch over you."

Her heart shimmered, strangely warm. An odd feeling, being protected. She wasn't used to it. She wanted to relax, let him care for her. She wanted to shake off the shackles and run. "Don't you need to sleep, or eat anything?"

"No. You go ahead." He glanced around the room. "Your front door locked?"

"Yeah. But wouldn't they just magic it, like you?"

"Maybe, but at least I'll hear them coming." He strode over, midnight feathers gleaming, and checked the door locks anyway, making sure the chain was in place. He did the windows, too, tugging them to make them fast, and pulled the folded paper shades down.

She watched, uselessness squirming in her stomach. She was used to being in control. Her place was just that—hers. One bedroom and a living space, which she mostly used as a study. It'd save on rent to find a roommate, but she needed her own space, and rarely had anyone over. Didn't have that many friends, really, though sometimes the two women next door popped over for pretzels and a movie, mostly because they felt sorry for her. And she'd never invited a man here.

Tonight, suddenly, the room felt full of man. Dangerous, dominant, overwhelming man. And it made her shiver.

She coughed. "I'm going to take a shower. Is, uh, is that okay?"

"Sure." He concentrated on the window shades. Was that a flush, staining his cheek?

"You don't need to, um, watch or anything?" Shit. That sounded like an invitation. She just didn't want him bursting in on her. Right?

He didn't answer. But the golden sparks that fired his wings bright told her all she needed to know.

She headed down the short corridor, nerves still itching. Her bedroom lamp shone, the wooden table piled in books. She emptied her pockets onto the soft chocolate quilt, and the sight of her phone reminded her she was supposed to be at work in a few hours.

Sorry, not happening. She made a quick call to the machine, calling in sick, and switched her phone off with a twinge of guilt. They needed her. And no doubt the discovery of the mortuary's broken window and ceiling would soon be evidenced by the length of her missed call list.

But the end of the world was bigger than a few gunshot homicides. She entered the bathroom and shut the door, faint dawn light gleaming through glass bricks and over the cinnamon-brown tiles.

"Lights. Shower, hot." She kicked her boots off, unclipped the knife and peeled off her stained t-shirt and jeans. She crawled out of her sweaty underwear and under the spray.

The hot water slid through her hair, over her bruised skin, down her legs. She sighed, dousing her raised arms, her face, rinsing her mouth. God, it felt great. Her thighs ached from fighting and running, and she bent to massage them, running strong thumbs down the muscles.

Water trickled over her breasts, dripping from her nipples, and lazily she imagined how good *his* big hands would feel, kneading the tension from her thighs. He was so strong. He'd stand behind her and bend over her like this, rubbing her thigh muscles, his wet hair sliding over her shoulder. His body would brush her back, naked, so warm and smooth in the water. She'd lean back into him, pushing her butt into his lap where he'd be so deliciously hard for her, just like before . . .

Her body tingled, and she flushed at the memory. That such a man would be so hot for her made her ache. He'd groan, that deep sound that turned her on so, and wrap his hands between her thighs. Pull them apart, open her for him. And she'd tilt her hips and he'd slide into her. Fill her with his heat. Stroke her deep. It'd feel so good.

Morgan sighed, shivering, easing her fingers between her legs, caressing herself. She was wet. She ached. She hadn't wanted like this in forever, and her blood stung bright with all the idiot neurotransmitters of fight-or-flight. She could call him to her, make him finish what he started at his aerie. Surely it couldn't hurt to indulge. She was a woman, not an inexperienced girl. And he was however many thousand years old. It wasn't like she could hurt his feelings.

And she'd already experienced the raw edge on his desire. He wouldn't treat her gently. He'd give her what she needed, rough caresses, hard unforgiving flesh, thrusts that slammed her breath away . . .

She gasped, pressing harder, imagining him taking her up against the wall. Wings glittering wet, fiery sky-blue eyes fixed on hers, powerful muscles flexing. He'd take her so deep and hard, she'd never want another. He wouldn't be satisfied with merely fucking her. He'd possess her. Make her beg to be possessed. Make her his . . .

No. Insane with frustration, she yanked her hand away, and let the water rinse her aching body clean.

Yes, she wanted him. The fierceness of her desire astonished her. But all her adult life, she'd fought for control, trusted no one, taken charge. She wasn't ready to surrender, in bed or in life, and Luniel was the kind of man who wanted it all—and she didn't doubt for a moment he had the power to make her burn to give it to him.

To trust someone so completely was foolish. Suicidal, even. Her mother was proof of that.

But still, Morgan ached, fierce and weary.

"Shower off," she whispered, and the water lapsed into silence.

She dried herself, and slipped on panties and a clean t-shirt that reached to the tops of her thighs. Combing out her hair, she examined her reflection. Face pale, dark red lips a contrast, her eyes bruised with fatigue. All-nighters didn't get easier with practice, and she wasn't a young student anymore. She needed sleep. Whether she'd get any with her fire-eyed angel lurking about was another story.

Morgan tiptoed into the living room, awareness a hot stone in her belly. Luniel had removed his silver breastplate. It lay neatly on the floor by the window, and his feet were bare. The light shirt he wore glistened from within, his skin luminous, but he was still spattered with blood and dirt. He stood, gazing out the window, seemingly at ease, but his fist clenched at her footstep and he let the rippled paper blind fall.

Shit. Had he heard her, in the shower? His hearing was spectacular, and she'd breathed hard, maybe even moaned. Her face heated. God, she hoped she hadn't said his name.

She swallowed. "Luniel?"

He turned, and his gaze raked up and down her body. "Feel better?"

She flushed hotter. Did he mean after a shower? Or the fantasy almost orgasm he'd stroked her to? Her nipples tingled, warm. She wasn't wearing a bra. Surely he could see them, stiff and eager. He'd nuzzle them, hot breath teasing, tongue circling, lips closing over the tip, sucking deep . . . "I'm going to bed. You sure you don't want to sleep on the couch?"

"I'll watch you, if that's okay."

"You mean . . . in my room?"

"It'd be safer." He smiled, a hint of his former cheekiness. "It's okay, Morgan, I won't steal the covers or anything. I'll sit in the corner like a good boy. I just . . . want to be able to see you, that's all. Just in case."

"Okay." She licked her lips, and led the way.

Climbing under the covers was sweet relief. The smooth cotton sheets soothed her bruised skin. So cool and soft, a welcome antidote to her current hypersensitivity. Luniel watched her from the doorway, and she tried not to think about his gaze, caressing her body . . .

She expected him to take the chair in the corner, but when she laid her head on the pillow he lighted on the dark wooden bed end, wings flaring. He crouched there on his toes, perfectly balanced, wrists crossed on his knees. His black hair tangled, windswept. His feathers twitched, black and silky, a golden spark or two dancing, and his deep blue gaze settled on her.

She shivered. Such a dark, strange, magnificent creature. He'd protect her, all right. Until her will wore away, and she surrendered.

Still, as she closed her eyes, she imagined snuggling into his embrace, his body close and strong against her back, and warmth stole over her heart.

She slept, and dreamed of falling. Wind whipped her hair, and her eyes blistered raw with the glittering lights of Babylon. Strong arms caught her, and she sobbed with relief, only it wasn't her angel but a demon, and as the evil creature sank its poisoned teeth into her throat, she threw her head back with her own hot blood splashing her face and screamed Luniel's name like a curse.

Luniel watched her, mesmerized by the rise and fall of her chest, the play of her muscles as she sleepily brushed hair from her cheek. Soon, her breathing deepened, and he could tell by her warm contented scent that she slept. Finally, he squeezed his eyes shut and tilted his face to uncaring heaven.

God, he wanted to hold her. Slide into bed and wrap himself around her, smell her luscious damp hair. Peel off her shirt, stroke her shower-softened skin and ease her back into that gasping desire.

He wasn't deaf. He'd heard her in the shower, her sighs as she touched herself in the streaming water. The sexiest fucking thing he'd ever heard. For all he knew, she did it every day and twice on Sundays, but he hoped she was thinking of him when she stroked herself. He knew what she felt like, the smooth slick heat of her secret flesh under his fingers, the hard little pulse where her pleasure centered, and he'd wanted to join her. Taste her essence, suck that pretty bud into his mouth and feel her shudder.

But he'd nearly killed her, only a few minutes ago. Imagining himself worthy to make love to her was the worst, most sinful kind of denial.

He opened his eyes, willing his hands not to shake. There she lay, fresh and beautiful, only a few thin cloth layers covering her nakedness. The sight of her hard nipples under that t-shirt when she walked out of the bathroom nearly undid him. He'd wanted those in his mouth, too.

Temptation licked his skin aflame. He could touch her right now, at least pretend to. Hover inches away, turn her skin to bumps under soft wing breeze. Make her beautiful nipples harden again. Ease the sheet from her thighs, breathe softly on the sensitive skin there until she parted her legs, and inhale, imagining he was sliding his tongue between her luscious folds and into her heat . . .

Yeah. You know who does that, Lune? Stalkers. Crazy people. Sickos who can't get laid.

But sweet heaven, he was hard for her again. He'd have a fucking bruise if he didn't relax. His balls already ached from ill temptation, and he hopped off the bed and stretched to ease the cramp. Morgan slept on, her rose-dark lips parting on a sigh, and the image of her lowering that mouth onto him, taking his cock between her lips, wrapping her tongue around his shaft and sucking him deep, only made his pants stretch tighter.

He adjusted himself, wincing. Once this was over, he'd do something about it, find himself one of those cute giggling angel girls Trillium knew, who thought it was hot to play games with the bad boys.

But the idea didn't interest him. Other girls didn't have her brave, self-flagellating intelligence, her wit, her iron strength. They didn't make him burn to shelter and possess and consume them. Other girls didn't make him long to be better so he could deserve them. Only Morgan would do.

As if he should have expected anything else. Fate was fate. If Morgan was the one, then she was, and not a fucking thing he could do about it.

He tugged his sweaty hair hard in frustration. But he couldn't drag his eyes away from her. She was too much. In a moment, he'd forget his manners and jump on her while she was sleeping. He couldn't stay here alone.

He pulled out his phone, unease rippling his feathers. Twice, they'd been attacked by imps who seemed to know exactly where to look. The starvewraiths had even known who Morgan was. It could be coincidence, but Lune knew that coincidence was bullshit. The imps could've followed him and Morgan all along, watching them. But imps were mere helldirt, not fit to challenge a full-blood angel, even a Tainted one. Someone must have put them on his trail.

The first time, at the morgue, only Dashiel knew Lune's whereabouts. The second time, Lune called Japheth. Hard to believe either would pass information to hellspawn. But the world was going to hell. Anything was possible.

Lune gritted his teeth, bitterness scorching sick. It couldn't be true. But he couldn't take any chances, not with Morgan. Who else knew about her? Trillium and Jadzia were at his aerie, too, and might've heard where they were going. Count them out for helpers. Ariel was out of town, and in any case didn't exactly approve of humans. That left only one.

Luniel turned away, keeping Morgan just visible. He hid the glowing screen so as not to wake her, and called.

Outside the window, Zuul beetled over the brick wall, claws digging into the cracks, and peered through a gap in the blinds.

Ah, the angel's human slut, her pretty face relaxed in sleep, those ripe lips easing apart as she breathed. Her thickheaded honey licker hunkered in the corner, obviously paying more attention to his hard-on than the task at hand. The candy-rich scent of Lune's desire made Zuul gag. He could have crept right in and dived down her throat, and the stupid hunk of heaven-meat wouldn't have noticed.

To be fair, Zuul was invisible, a transparent shadow bathed in warm dawn, his telltale hellscent sloughed away with the sunlight. He was good at hiding.

His unseen hair tumbled over his forehead as he licked hate-bitter lips. He'd floated like stardust as his starvewraiths attacked Lune in flight, and his blood had burned in anticipation when the woman fell. To taste her anguish as she plummeted to her doom, the sick agony of her bowels releasing, the stabbing pain in her heart as it exploded, the lovely wet crunch of living meat slamming into earth . . . He'd nearly snapped to flesh himself and fallen with her, just so he could be there.

But the Tainted slime had ruined it. Saved her. Dragged her from the air and brought her here, and now he didn't even have the courtesy to grind her face into the floor and fuck her until she bled so Zuul could get off.

But there'd be time for that, oh, yes. The pretty Prince of Poison had spoken truly, and Zuul laughed, scattering ash. Luniel's obsession made this human more intriguing by the minute. Imagine the pain when Zuul took her. Raped her, tore her skin, cracked her bones, taught her what it meant to hurt—and made all the better by the angel's anguish. He might even let Lune thrash him a bit, just to give it a real edge.

The poison prince had promised him pain. Zuul's mouth watered just thinking about it. Azaroth would be pleased, also. Anything that tortured an angel made Azaroth smile, and when Azaroth smiled, the world suffered.

Softly, he tossed a handful of ash, a poisoned dream. It shimmered through the glass like fine snow, drifting over Morgan's face. The specks glistened on her skin, and dissolved, and she whimpered, curling up for comfort in the chilly clutches of a nightmare.

Zuul grinned, hungry. *Not long, my pretty. Soon, you'll be ours. Your blood will wash my skin, and I'll taste your salty screams. And will your Tainted angel chase you to hell, in a doomed attempt to rescue your soul?*

I think he might.

Satisfied, Zuul drifted away into hot sunlight.

CHAPTER 21

When Morgan awoke, the clock showed 6:35 p.m., and the remnants of some fevered dream itched at memory's edge. Dark clouds, thunder, sultry storms clogging her breath. Caresses she didn't want, warm twisted flesh forcing inside her, horrid unwanted pleasure, a raw scream thrashing up her throat. She'd cried for help, but got only silence and darkness . . .

She shivered, and climbed out of bed, blinking the dream away.

Her bedroom was empty, sweet with her angel's lingering scent. All was quiet. Her mouth twisted. If he'd left without her, she'd kick his holy ass.

She padded out into the living room, rubbing her eyes. Someone had opened her blinds, and evening sun streamed in. The rich scent of coffee tempted her. "Luniel, are you—oh."

An angel perched on the kitchenette bench, legs crossed, dark eyes sweeping a magazine's pages. But it wasn't Luniel.

The woman looked up, and smiled. Her sleek black wings shimmered, iridescent with a gorgeous patina of emerald and rose. Her shining hair was the same magical color, cut long and sharp with a saucy flick at the ends. Her long legs stretched taut and muscled in tight black pants and boots. Tiny waist, flaring hips, full breasts under her curved silver plating. Her beautiful face shone, pale and flawless, luminous like Morgan had come to expect. Dark, slanted green eyes, warm with tempting secrets. Her heart-shaped lips tweaked into an artful smile.

Morgan fidgeted. She wanted to fix her hair, tidy her face. She'd thought Jadzia, the blond one, was cool and beautiful. This woman was . . . sultry. Sexy. Effortlessly gorgeous. The bitch at the party who all the guys couldn't take their eyes off.

Shit. Don't tell me Lune lied about that girlfriend, because you just got outclassed, Morgan old thing.

Not that she cared, of course. Lune could do what he liked. Right?

She straightened, determined not to be bitchy. "Um. Hi."

"Hi," Ms. Gorgeous said, jumping down and laying her magazine aside. She'd helped herself to coffee, the espresso machine still gurgling. A silver crossbow lay on the bench, with a quiver of wicked-looking spikes. "I'm Iria. Lune called, said he needed a hand. He flashed home for a shower." Her eyes glinted golden. "Boys. They're so vain. And you are more than pretty, Morgan Sterling. I can see why he's so uptight."

Awesome. *Pretty* was right up there with *nice.* She offered her hand. "Uh, thanks for coming, I guess."

Iria shook it. She smelled of perfume, a spicy cocktail of patchouli and Chanel No. 5, and her voice was a husky contralto. "You're a doctor, right? You cut up dead people?"

They were all so fascinated with that. "Yeah. Assistant medical examiner. Autopsies 'R' Us."

"Cool. Smart, and skillful, too. I approve. I cut 'em up, too, you know," Iria confided, leaning closer. "I just do it before they're dead."

Morgan laughed, uneasy. "Someone's gotta do the dirty jobs, right?"

But Iria sniffed at her, and frowned. "You have any bad dreams last night?"

"Huh?" Fragmented images flashed. Icy fingers shackling her wrists, holding her down. Cruel laughter, burning hands caressing her naked skin, teasing her, torturing her, opening her. Someone—some*thing*—fucking her. Raping her. She'd fought and screamed, alone.

Iria sniffed Morgan's hair, wrinkling her lovely straight

nose. "I can smell ash. Demon mind poison. You sure you didn't dream?"

"Um. Maybe. I don't really remember." Morgan swallowed. "It was dark, I was . . . lying down. Someone . . . touched me, and I tried to get away, but . . ."

"Demons can visit you in dreams. It's one way they seed temptation."

Morgan squirmed. "Yeah? Well, this guy's planting the wrong seeds, let me tell you."

"Don't be so sure. You feel all right now?"

"I guess so. I just woke up."

"Come here." Iria touched two fingers to Morgan's forehead.

Light sparkled down her body, power scintillating in her flesh. Hot, tingling, like pleasure, only . . . alien. The flesh between her legs throbbed, not altogether nice.

Iria frowned, oblivious. "Hmm. Don't see anything left—"

"Don't see what?"

Morgan jumped back. She hadn't heard Luniel come in.

He'd showered, just as Iria said. Dressed the same, silver armor and black leather, his skin shining. His damp midnight hair tangled, tiny droplets shining on his wings like he'd returned in a hurry. He'd look gorgeous in the shower, water like quicksilver through his hair, down his back, over his muscled chest, feathers glossy and wet . . .

"I see you two have met. What's up?" Lune gazed at her, smoldering.

With a warm shiver, she remembered she wasn't wearing anything but a t-shirt and panties. "Umm . . ."

"Nothing," cut in Iria brusquely. She glided to face him, hips swaying. "Just chatting. Listen, are you sure about this imp business? I mean, I can check it out, but do you really think Dash and Jae are ratting you out?"

Lune's wings arched. "You tell me."

Iria sliced the air with her hand, an angry but graceful denial. "I don't believe it. Not Dash. And Japheth's an ice-hearted monster, we all know that, but I can't believe he'd spit on us like that."

Morgan squirmed. She hadn't met Japheth. But Dashiel seemed . . . genuine. Truthful. Like he gave a shit.

"Neither can I." Lune folded his arms, brutal muscles swelling. "But I don't know what else to think. Jaz and Trill were there, too. You're the only one I can trust."

"Trillium's heart is golden," Iria insisted, eyes gleaming. "He'd never betray us. And Jaz is just a kid. She worships you—"

"Someone told them where to look for us, Iria." Luniel's expression darkened, stormy. "I know it wasn't you, and that's all I know."

Morgan bit her lip. Lune obviously trusted Iria. But Iria hadn't told Lune about the dream. Was she hiding something? Why?

But Iria just nodded. "Okay. I'll check it out, but you might not like what I find."

Luniel shrugged. "Fate's a bitch." He turned to Morgan, and everything about him . . . eased up. Not *softened*, exactly. But calm silver light rippled his feathers, and vanished, and she sensed his temper cooling, like he didn't want to scare her.

"You ready?" he asked. Calm, soft, reassuring. But his gaze still stormed, dark, and she remembered his shattered reaction last night when she'd fallen. Was he guilty? Embarrassed? Afraid she hadn't forgiven him? He didn't need to worry. She was fine.

She forced a smile. He deserved that much, even if she still didn't trust him. "Yep. Zombies to hunt, demon ass to kick. Give me five minutes."

She hurried to the bathroom, and swiftly she showered, dried, and dressed in clean jeans (pale this time) and a black t-shirt. Emotions stirred a cocktail in her guts, tension with a dash of fear, but lashings of excitement, too. She wanted to fight this plague demon, she realized. Put an end to the horror once and for all. And if the disease was a person, not a mindless virus? All the sweeter.

She brushed her teeth and clipped her hair at the nape, studying herself in the full-length mirror. Her eyes shone, their honey color unusual enough to be striking. They were her best feature. Nice face, even if she wasn't exactly a supermodel. She was fit. Strong. Trim waist. Big butt, but not *too* big. And her boobs looked mighty good in this t-shirt. She thought he liked them. Perhaps she should put on some makeup, a swish of lipstick and something sultry around her eyes . . .

She laughed. *Nice one, Morgan. Very modern. About to get eaten by zombies, and all you care about is what some guy you've known for one day thinks of your look.*

Some guy. Right. A hot-blooded, beautiful, shockingly unhuman guy. Who spent his life surrounded by sexy, tough-as-iron warrior women like Iria. And Morgan was just a talentless human doctor, who didn't even have the guts to believe in a God who'd scorned her.

She smoothed her t-shirt, determined. She was who she was. And if Luniel thought himself above her, that was his problem.

She strapped on the silver knife in its sheath—it sighed, wriggling in her hand as if it, too, was just waking up—and walked into the living room.

Luniel and Iria were talking, close, in low voices. His hand lay on her shoulder, and her blue-green wingtip curled around his. At Morgan's footstep, they looked up and fell silent.

She swallowed, cheeks afire. "Oh. Sorry."

Iria murmured something, gave a little smile. Lune nodded, and they embraced. Kissed, the corners of their mouths touching. Maybe more than the corners. Morgan squirmed, itching. Damn it. Why was she itching?

Iria flipped her a wave, and vanished in a white flash. Another thing Morgan couldn't do.

Jealous much? She yanked open the fridge and grabbed a bottle of sliced peaches. She shoved in a spoon and munched, not trusting herself to speak. This was ridiculous. If she didn't care for Luniel's opinion, why did seeing him with Iria make her want to hide under the bed?

Luniel's sooty feathers twitched. "What? What's wrong?"

She shrugged, stuffing in another slice. "Dunno what you mean," she managed, muffled.

"C'mon, Morgan. You smell angry. It's all warm and prickly like sherbet."

"No, I'm not." Juice dripped on her chin. "And who said you were allowed to smell me?"

He stalked closer, sniffing, a teasing flare in his wings. "Yes, you are. Most definitely Sherbet Girl. But . . . wait. No." His eyes glinted, a flash of green surprise. "Morgan . . . are you jealous? Of Iria?"

Her guts wrenched tight. "No, of course not. Why would I be?"

He laughed. "Hell, I don't know. Because she's smart and gorgeous and kick-ass and perfect in about eight million other ways? C'mon. You are. Admit it."

Morgan flushed, scorching. *Gee, thanks, that really helped.* "So what if I am? What do you care?"

"Maybe it's male vanity." She could believe that, his amused grin, that smug ruffle of feathers. "Maybe I like it that I kiss her and you go all . . . prickly."

Abruptly, she was tired of the game. Tired of circling, evading, pretending she wasn't affected by him. "Don't play with me, okay?"

"Look, she's an old friend. I was just—"

"Stop it." She plonked the peaches on the counter and tossed the spoon in with a wet thunk, her appetite lost. "I don't appreciate being lied to."

His amusement faded. "I've never lied to you."

"Haven't you?" She flipped on the kitchen tap, plunging her hands under stinging water. She was being unfair. He'd given her no reason to imagine he'd lied about anything.

Except that they all lied. The tastier the bait, the bigger the lie. And Luniel was very tasty bait.

He slapped the tap off, hard, and didn't back off. He towered over her, too close, too deliciously fragrant and male to be good. "Why won't you trust me? I've done you no wrong. I've done my best to keep you safe. I grant I was . . ." He grimaced. "I was forward with you, yesterday, at my place. I'm sorry if it made you uncomfortable—"

"Uncomfortable?" She laughed, bitter. "You just don't get it, do you? You're all wrong! Everything you stand for is bullshit. The fact that I . . . Whether I like you or not has nothing to do with it. I just can't." And she strode to the window, the sunset-bright city stinging her eyes.

She couldn't stop him following her. She didn't care. She just clung with all her strength to the freedom to walk away.

He flashed to her side, light shimmering. The air crackled stormy with his frustration, and scarlet static sparked his feathers. "This isn't just about you and me, is it?"

She folded her arms, defiant.

"Tell me." His voice undid her, warm and aching. Not demanding. Just bewildered. "Please. I'm causing you pain just by standing here and it's breaking my heart. Tell me what to do. Anything."

Morgan's stomach lurched, sick. Below, traffic rumbled, careless, the neon signs and streetlights shedding rainbows in the sunset. She leaned her forehead against the warm glass. *What am I supposed to do now?* Sneer at him and walk away, let the mess she'd made between them carry on? This festering anger and helplessness and frustrated want?

Or, take one last chance that he wasn't playing her. That the safety and peace she'd known in his embrace wasn't a dirty lie.

She closed her eyes, and leapt.

"There was this preacher," she whispered. "When I was a teenager. Mom was very religious, and this guy was the whole package, Lune, smarts and charisma and charm. He seduced her." She turned to lean back against the window, hugging herself. "I don't mean he slept with her. Nothing like that. He was too clever."

Reproach crawled in her throat like a scorpion, and she let it sting. "He *prayed* with her. Mom never knew my dad, and she only worked as an office temp. We had it tough, and when this preacher told Mom she'd get her reward in the next life, I guess . . . well, when you're washed up at thirty-two with a sixteen-year-old kid and a shitty job, it sounds pretty good, doesn't it?"

Luniel nodded, just once. Didn't speak. Didn't judge.

Morgan sighed. "She started spending all her spare time at church. Started giving them our things, what there was of them. I remember one day she gave away my clothes, this green cloth jacket I'd saved for. I was so mad at her, I . . . I said some really mean things. Sometimes he came to our apartment, and he was so nice to me. He helped with my homework, for God's sake." She swallowed, bitter. "I should've smelled something rotten. But I was too wrapped up in high school and boys and getting smashed, and if she was with him, I could do anything I wanted. She was trying to be a good mom and I . . ."

Luniel watched, dark and silent.

Tears blurred, and she shook them away. She deserved to hurt. "I let him take her. I was too damned selfish to care. And then one day I . . . I came home from school, and she'd blown the top of her head off with a shotgun. She had such short arms, you see, she couldn't quite . . ."

She swallowed bile. "She'd given everything we owned to the cult. All her savings. My college fund. Insurance I never knew she had. She'd even pawned stuff, and borrowed money to give to *him*. She owed a small fortune to loan sharks. And his e-mails were on her computer, telling her to kill herself. He'd convinced her to sign everything over to him, and then he told her that Jesus was coming and she had to make ready. Kill herself now while her soul was prepared."

Luniel's eyes burned scarlet. "Did anyone ever . . ."

"No, he was long gone. She had almost nothing and he'd taken it all. And she wasn't the only one. They'd conned people all over. I was so mad, you know? At him for lying. At her for believing him. But mostly, I was mad at God." The old rotten sickness and blind anger swamped her, and she clenched shaking hands. She wanted to scream, wail, hit something.

But Luniel just gazed back, as blue as the twilight ocean but tainted deep with sorrow. "Believe me, I know that feeling."

Tears choked her, boiling inside. He'd suffered at God's hands, too, and he hadn't lost faith. But that only made it hurt more. "She was a good woman, Lune. She believed in Jesus, or God, or whoever. She loved Him so much. More than she loved me," Morgan admitted, her throat tight. "And He let her blow her fucking face off and die for a con man's stupid lies. Would He care if I starved to death?" She sniffled, wiping her nose. "So I said, screw Him. And I didn't ask anyone for a damn thing. I, uh . . . did some ugly things to pay Mom's debts. And then I worked my way through college and med school."

"Must have been tough."

She managed a teary smile. "Yeah. I mean, boohoo, right? I'm not the only penniless student ever to grace this earth. But I've never forgotten what she taught me. If it looks too good to be true, it's rotten to the core. And no matter what the preachers say, God doesn't give a shit."

Luniel didn't speak. Just stared at her, wild and shadowed with thunder in his eyes.

She wiped her face, squirming. Why did she tell him all that? He'd only use it against her. Make up some lie. Insist that one rotten berry doesn't spoil the pie.

But he just tucked his hands behind his back, looming dark and intense like a storm about to break. "Then I guess . . . asking you to have faith in me now would be too much."

Not a question. A fact. Like he understood.

She shrugged, helpless. "Faith is for fools."

"Maybe. But I am not my faith, Morgan. Forget what I am, where I come from. You don't have to trust in heaven. Just trust *me*." He touched her chin, a light caress, but it made her look into his eyes, and the dark promise there ripped her heart raw. "I'll always fight for you. I'll never lie to hurt you. Please. Let me . . . let me be what you need."

"What I need?" Sick laughter cracked her voice. "I don't even know what I *want*. I thought I had you pegged, see? I thought I knew you for what you were. But everything you've said has come true, and I . . . I really want to trust you, Lune. I can't believe you're lying to me, even though . . ."

"Even though you know I must be?" Shadows swirled over his face, and he let his hand drop.

She caught it, desperate. She longed for his understanding, so badly she ached. She couldn't let her courage fail her now. "Even though you're too astonishing to be real," she forced out. "It's like . . . I'm getting a chance I don't deserve. Why me? Every other poor sucker has to stumble on in the dark. Why am I the one who gets the proof?"

His fingers tightened on hers. "Is that all I am for you, Dr. Sterling? More data?"

"I thought so! I wanted you to be. And then I saw you kissing Iria, and I . . . oh, fuck." She tugged her hand back and turned away, her cheeks flaming. *Shit. Now I've done it.*

He gripped her shoulder, stopping her. "I wasn't kissing Iria."

Her senses lurched. His stormy presence threatened her, his dark-sweet scent a dangerous temptation. She tried a smile, but it broke. "It doesn't matter. I'm an idiot—"

"Shut up and listen, human," he insisted, fire in his eyes. "That wasn't a kiss. If I wanted to kiss her, I'd have done it like this." And he cupped the back of her head and swept her mouth to his.

CHAPTER 22

She gasped. Sparkling, so tender, his lips soft yet strong, his flavor a dark allure. Such a haunted kiss, burning with sorrow and need. Her eyes fluttered closed, her defenses melting away in a flush of unreason. She wanted, so hard it hurt. Wanted to feel him, touch him, take him away from the death and the pain and be with him forever.

Trembling, she slid her arm around his neck, drawing him closer. His feathers brushed her wrist, and sparks showered in reaction. He deepened the kiss, growling softly, quivering with restraint as he wrapped his arms around her. Such a wild, animal sound, hunger that wouldn't be denied. She locked her wrists around his neck, yearning for his naked body on hers, the maddening delight of his touch.

He pulled back a fraction, his hot blue eyes burning. His lips shone from kissing her, and his night-black feathers stood on end, crackling with desire. So beautiful. So brutally male. "Don't challenge me," he whispered against her lips. "You make me reckless, and you don't want to go there. Escape now, before I forget my manners and can't stop."

Her heart dropped a beat, dizzying. She didn't want to escape. Her beautiful angel had trapped her, helpless against his rage and desire, and she didn't want to be free.

She licked her lips, tasting him, and leaned forward, defiant. "No."

His eyes flashed scarlet, sinful with desire. And he yanked her against his chest, and let his passion explode.

His mouth assaulted hers, the intensity of the contact sucking her breath away. He kissed her hard and hungry, bruising, so hot and so loaded with passion that she gasped, inhaling him, aching deep inside. His tongue hunted hers and tortured her until she melted into hot dizziness. He tasted so raw, so real. Like her first impression of him, seemingly a hundred years ago last night: a man, fragrant flesh and hot blood and desire, but *more*. Much, much more.

"Morgan," he murmured into her mouth, "I can't help it. Be with me. Belong to me." His hot golden glitter showered over her, tingling all the way inside. He dived his fingers into her hair, capturing her, and kissed her harder, deeper, more fiercely. He didn't let her breathe. He didn't let her think. He just took her, wild and irresistible, and in seconds, everything that seemed so important melted in a heady rush of desire.

Oh, God. The pleasure stabbed deep, the warm safety of his embrace, his hot sweet taste, the insane delight of his mouth on hers. Her body ached against his, and she pressed closer, wanting to feel him, his hot metal armor on her breasts, his hard thigh muscles, the steely heat of his cock through smooth leather. She wrapped her fingers in his crisp silken hair, tugging him down to her, and he gripped her ass and lifted her so she could fold her legs around him.

Mmm. So big and solid, his body between her thighs, the hot pressure of his erection against her secret crevices. She wanted him naked. Wanted to lie beneath him and be possessed, let him love her to oblivion and fight the pain away. "Yes. Take me."

With a powerful thrust of wings, he slammed her back against the wall in his embrace. His big body crushed her, his strength so arousing, she groaned and shuddered. She'd never longed to be dominated like this. Never wanted to lose control. But this man made her burn for the rich delirium of surrender. She wanted him to possess her utterly.

She sucked hard on his tongue, wanting him inside her any way she could get him. He nipped her bottom lip, tugging it between his teeth with a possessive snarl. "Witch," he growled, rough with desire. "I've resisted every earthly woman for eight hundred years. But not you. You take me apart."

He scorched kisses onto her throat, tasting, licking the hard throb of her pulse. When he bit her softly, she moaned, her fists clenching in his hair. He felt so good. He kissed her collarbone, and lifted her higher so he could bite her jutting nipples through her shirt.

"Oh, yes." Pleasure stabbed all the way down, like a hot wire wrenching tight inside her. Hot slickness coaxed from her body, making her ready for him.

He groaned, sliding his hands over her ass and up between her thighs. "You smell so fresh. I love it. I want to taste you."

His words inflamed her. Her secret flesh throbbed. She wanted his fingers there, his tongue, his cock. Wanted him to finish what he'd started last night.

White light flashed, and he was on his knees at her feet, tugging her jeans open. Her knife clunked on the floorboards. He pulled off her boots and stockings, pulling her jeans over her hips and whisking them away.

Cool air caressed her naked thighs, but his body heat burned her. She flushed, stinging. She was so wet and aching, the evidence of her desire must be clear.

But Luniel's eyes gleamed, hungry. "Sweet heaven, you're beautiful." And he licked a fiery trail up her thigh. Grazed her with his teeth, coaxed out shivers and moans. Nipped at the soft flesh on the inside, and she groaned in frustration and parted her legs, wanting more. He teased his thumb along the crease of her hip, under her panties, and ripped them off her.

She gasped, the violence of his passion making her ache. She didn't want gentleness. She wanted delirium, and it frightened her. What he was doing was too intimate, too arousing. She might forget herself. "No. Not that. I can't take it. Please. Just . . ."

He nipped her, a delicate reprimand that made her gasp and shiver. "Don't be afraid. Don't fight it. Just let me show you." And he eased his hot tongue between her folds.

Her palms smacked into the wall, her legs melting to water. So deliciously hot. He licked her in long smooth strokes, flicking her sensitive peak. Her hard little bud flowered in his mouth, swelling tight, and he groaned against her as he stroked it. She didn't remember the last time a man had touched her like this, and the intimacy made her want to weep. She cried out in delight, pressing closer.

"Nuh-uh." He laughed, his breath a hot tease. "Don't make me tie you up, Morgan. You're not in control. Just be."

And he nuzzled her delicately, licking so softly, teasing just the very tip of her until she squirmed uncontrollably, her nerves stretched tight. Every muscle quivered, her wits fogged over with pleasure.

At last, he relented, suckling her, softly then harder, and she shuddered, the tension unbearable. It felt so good. Too good. "Oh, lord. Stop. It's too much. I can't!"

But he wouldn't. Wouldn't let her go. Just bent her to his will, parting her flesh with his fingers and licking and sucking until she reeled, feverish, the pleasure straining hard to new heights. Fuck, he was good at this. Giving up control to him made her shiver. When he finally let her come, she was going to explode.

"So beautiful," he whispered against her flesh. "Now let yourself go, love."

"Oh, yes." She clenched her fists in his hair, dragging him closer, drowning in his touch and his hot male scent. Her nipples ached, her flesh tingling deep. So close. "More. Harder. Please, I want you in me—oh!"

He pushed two slick fingers into her, hard, glorious, and she gasped, and broke apart. Hot breathless release, sparkles erupting in her belly and shooting all the way to her fingertips. So good. She clutched him, panting, and he curled his fingers inside her and stroked that sensitive spot deep in her flesh, so raw and perfect that she wound up tight and exploded all over again, harder. Insane, screaming pleasure, her body afire, wild sensation that rippled on and on.

He kissed her there, delicious, like he couldn't taste her enough. Her mind boggled, dim with insane delight. Twice, she'd come twice and he'd barely started with her. She still had half her clothes on. No man had ever done that to her. And still she longed for more, yearned for the smooth thrust of his hardness inside her, his deliciously brutal body on hers, velvety wings wrapped around her, the scent of his hair, his tongue in her mouth. Taste him, suckle him, let him take her any way and any place he wanted. "Oh God, Lune," she gasped, disbelieving as shocks tore her nerves to glittering shreds, "I'm yours."

And her midnight-winged angel gave an agonized groan, and tore himself away.

Luniel clawed the floor, ripping his nails red. His body twisted, cramping, a mess of desire and frustration. She was still panting from his touch, her dusky scent an agonizing temptation.

Fuck, she was the sexiest thing he'd ever laid eyes on. Spread her legs, feel her hot wet flesh, push himself inside her tight channel, make her come again, louder, harder, kiss her and bury himself deep in her and groan his pleasure into her mouth . . .

Fuck. Fuck fuck fuck. His cock was so hard, it throbbed, the hot blood hurting him. He could still feel her tight bud between his lips, the way she moaned when he sucked on it and the pulsing explosion as she came and heaven's holy grace, how he wanted her.

His torn fingernails healed, and he slammed his fist into the floor, timber cracking. He knew he shouldn't have put his mouth on her. Shouldn't have tasted her there, licked her, sucked her sweet flesh between his lips. But he couldn't help it. Couldn't resist her tempting woman scent or her stirring gaze or the flooding emotion in his heart.

And then she said it—*I'm yours*—and his deceit kicked him full in the guts like a hellspawn's poisoned curse.

Lies. Selfishness. Cruel insanity. To pretend he could ever make her his. To imagine he had even an icicle's chance in hellfire of deserving her.

He was weak. Unworthy. Twice already, minor skanky hellshits had hurt her, and he hadn't stopped it. Against this Prince of Poison . . . Lune shuddered, sick. The best of intentions didn't mean shit. He'd tried with Eleanor, and he'd failed. He couldn't keep Morgan safe.

Lune wanted to scream. Hurt himself. Set himself on fire, let heaven's curse burn the sordid truth from his flesh. He'd let Morgan think he could take care of her. Let her trust him enough to kiss him, touch him, offer him her precious body.

It was all bullshit.

"Lune?" Her voice, breathless.

Don't look at her. Just . . . don't. "I'm sorry." His throat parched, and he had to repeat himself. "I'm sorry. Just . . . don't touch me."

A rustle as she knelt behind him, the tiny waft of Morgan-scented air across his feathers a sweet agony as she reached out and hesitated. "Lune, I don't get it. Am I not . . . ?" A swallow. "You don't want to."

His heart wailed at her pain, but he smacked it down. "I can't give you what you need. I'm no good for you. Just go away."

"Don't be ridiculous." Quiet, but cool. He'd hurt her. A lot.

But better now than later. He risked a glance around, still on his knees, and her honey-brown eyes glistened with tears that shredded his nerves. He wanted to kiss those tears away. "I'm no good for you," he repeated stubbornly. "I'll only hurt you."

"What do you call this?" Her chin trembled. "Don't tease me. Either you want to be with me, or you don't. Sorry, but you don't get to do this by halves—"

"The demons will kill you, Morgan!" He swept around to face her. "They'll damn your soul just to piss me off. What part of that don't you get?"

"Look, I know I've been stubborn about believing you. But you've kept your word to the letter. I . . ." She flushed, but didn't look down. Took a deep breath. "I do trust you, Lune. I can't help it. I feel safe with you."

"Well, you shouldn't," he said cruelly, but his treacherous heart did a giddy somersault. Heaven, she deserved so much more for that admission.

But he couldn't give it. Not now. Not ever.

"Why not?" She waved her hands, frustrated. "We've done okay so far. I thought we fought pretty well together. Why are you so convinced you'll get me killed?"

"Because that's what happened last time!" Helpless fury brewed hot in his guts. "Okay? I loved her and the demon prince stole her soul, and I should've saved her but I didn't. She's screaming in hell forever because I was weak. You want that to happen to you?" Frustrated glitter burst from his wings, and he yanked them back, harsh. "Jesus. I should never have let you come with me. I should never have touched you."

"A bit fucking late for that now." Her gaze flashed dark, her mouth hardening.

"I said I was sorry." Fuck, what a useless little word.

"Yeah. Well, I'm sorry, too." She stumbled to retrieve her jeans, pulling them back on. A tear slipped down her nose and dripped on the floor. Lune wanted to howl with stupid loss.

But he made himself watch her. He deserved it.

He swooped to his feet, adjusting his armor with sharp yanks that nearly tore the buckles free. "I told you before. We need Quuzaat to tell us who he's working for. I can't jeopardize my mission to help you. You should go back to work, forget about everything—"

"The hell I will." She rounded on him, cheeks flushing. "You just gave up the right to tell me what to do. 'Until the last star burns out,' you said. Well, this virus is *my* mission, and damn if I'll give it up because you've lost your nerve. God, I can't believe I said *trust*. I must have lost my mind."

"Morgan—"

"Shut up. You know what your problem is? You're scared. Of this Prince of Poison. Of me. Of anything that makes you vulnerable."

His blood stung, mortified. "You have no fucking idea what you're speaking of."

"Don't I?" Her eyes glinted. "News flash for you, angel. *We're all scared.* But some of us don't let it paralyze us. You want to bet against yourself before the game even starts? Fine. But you dragged me into this, and you can damn well help me finish it."

Her defiance itched like a wasp sting. But it also made him want her all over again. He clashed his teeth, on edge. "Don't be foolish. You can't do th—"

"You can't stop me," she warned, her chin high. "I know where you're going—the Prince of Poison's party, right? That housing project, where that guy showed us? If you won't take me with you, I'll just get there by myself." She smacked a dramatic hand to her forehead. "Alone? Oh, gosh! I'll be demon bait!"

His wings twitched to smack sense into her. "Are you fucking insane?"

"No! I'm being realistic!" She propped a belligerent hand on her hip. "Don't get an ego swell, flyboy, but you are the quickest, strongest, fittest, meanest, dirtiest badass killer I've ever met. And even if you weren't, the column in my contacts headed

'Guys I know who can slaughter plague demons' only has one name on it." She shrugged, cold. "Sorry, but tonight, you're my date, and you're not weaseling out of it by pretending you don't want me."

"It's not that simple!"

"Isn't it? Then tell me, tough guy: why did you really stop touching me?" Her gaze drilled him, relentless. "Are you afraid of this demon prince? Or afraid you might give a shit?"

Her icy tone stung, but her words burned, deep into the empty black void where his soul used to be. With a stinging crackle, dark resolve he thought he'd lost forever caught fire.

Electric heat burst from his feathers, fury and desolation and eight hundred years of guilt flaring up like tinder, starting a darker, purer blaze in his heart.

Keep it frosty, angel. Michael, long ago, some dusty battlefield before Lune fell. *Don't get involved. Monkeys come and monkeys go, but heaven has a very long memory.*

Longer than Lune's. Stronger than painful memories of Eleanor. And rich with higher purpose than his selfish obsession with Morgan.

He swooped up to her, closer than he dared, and leaned in, tasting her scent on his tongue, enjoying the dilation of her pupils, her breath's tiny quickening, the dusky feminine whiff of her body reacting to him.

It didn't matter.

Frosty fire poured into his veins. Stupid, to think his feelings were important. He was just a tool, and he'd do the job he was made for. Even if it scarred his heart for eternity.

Because eternity didn't care. Raging against the pain was useless. It was all just a game.

"Do I *give* a shit?" He laughed, and it sparkled dark with ancient menace he barely remembered. "Morgan, I am so far beyond just giving a shit."

She lifted her chin, so close he could taste her boldness. "Then what's wrong with you?"

"I'll tell you what's wrong with me." He brushed his lips across her ear, whispering. "I want to possess you, make you mine forever. I want to listen to you laugh and watch you smile. I want to make love to you until you weep with pleasure. I want to fuck you and make you come so hard and deep and hot, you won't remember your name." He inhaled, tasting her delicious shudder. "And when the Prince of Poison eats your soul? I'm gonna scream my heart out for a thousand years."

He eased back a little. Her mouth trembled, and she bit her lip, defiant. Determined. So beautiful, he ached.

But fuck the pain. Love was supposed to hurt. And fate was fate. It couldn't be changed. Not by one heartsick angel.

So bring it on, you sick motherfucker. Let's play.

Lune flashed his most chilling smile, and held out his arm for her to take. "But you know what? *None of it matters.* Heaven doesn't care. So come on, Doctor. Let's hunt the soul-thirsty bastard down together. If that's really the way you want it."

Their gazes met, and the air stretched between them, taut with words unspoken, feelings unshared. *I'm lost without you. Don't fucking die on me.*

But he didn't say any of it.

She just folded her arms, and tilted that crooked grin that sped his pulse. "Wager's on, flyboy. But give me a minute to change. If I'm dying tonight, I'm doing it with underwear on."

CHAPTER 23

Silvery light flashed, and Morgan blinked, the grubby East Harlem street corner flickering into view along with the salty smell of fried rice and pepperoni. A buzzing neon sign spelled "HAPPY WOK" in green above a greasy sidewalk café. A deli and grocery, a pizza store called "Muchos," a fried chicken place with an animated crowing rooster.

Warm twilight licked her skin clammy. On the corner, the burned-out project loomed, broken brick walls casting threatening shadows. Some of the buildings still stood, blackened shells. More were only jagged black wall fragments and piles of twisted rubble. Beyond, traffic sped along FDR Drive, and the shore of Wards Island glittered, searchlights sweeping over the fenced hospital compound.

She shrugged out of Lune's embrace, awkward. He still felt good. She didn't want to think about it.

Didn't want to think about what he'd said. That he'd abandon her to munching zombie death if he had to. That the demon prince would eat her soul, and there was nothing she could do about it. Before, it hadn't seemed real. But now she was eerily certain he meant it.

He'd touched her. Loved her, so intimately, his passion's rich intensity a fading glimmer deep in her body.

Now, his gaze fell on her, distant, cold as the ocean. She shivered, hot and chilly at the same time. He was so remote. So detached. So . . . empty.

Lune dragged his sword from empty air in a swathe of laser-blue light, and pointed it towards the burned buildings. "That way," he said, icy. "Kill everything you see. Don't hesitate. The Prince of Poison is the prize. And Morgan?"

She kept her gaze steady. "Yeah?"

His expression defrosted, a tiny gleam of warmth. "Stay close to me. I'll fight for you. You know I will."

Sorrow leached from her heart, but she staunched it. "Until it gets too hard, you mean?" she retorted coolly, flipping out her knife. "Sure. Thanks so much. Just watch your own back, angel. It's a bigger target than mine."

And she stalked forward, crouching, letting her hungry knife guide the way.

Inside the estate, darkness thickened. Her boots crunched on pebbles and broken bricks. A trio of rotting zombies jumped them from a dusty doorway, sick-gleaming eyes and clawing hands. They soon crumpled, stinking under steel and light flash. Black rubber-skinned bonecrushers cackled, hurtling out from behind a burned wall. Morgan hurled her knife, spitting skull bones deep. Lune's blade scythed blue, and heads rolled.

Starvewraiths struck, screeching, talons ripping her hair. She dived, chin slamming the dirt. The spelled knife went spinning through the air to carve a hole in the monster's belly. Black blood showered, and Lune backflipped and tore the thing's head from its neck. The other one plummeted, headfirst like a ballistic missile, its cruel beak gnashing. Morgan rolled. Its face drilled the concrete six inches deep, and Lune sliced off its head.

"Jeez, they're everywhere." Morgan crawled to her feet, heart pounding. The knife slapped back into her palm, and it felt good there. Exhilaration ached her muscles, her breath laced with unholy excitement. The warmth of spattered blood on her face was an ugly pleasure. Was this how Lune felt when he killed? This horrid-sweet delight?

Lune gave her a feral grin. He breathed hard, hot sparks tumbling from his wings. "Having fun?"

She didn't want to like it. Didn't want to feel what he felt. "Screw you."

"I'd love to, but didn't we work past that already?" He backed along a wall, and peered around the corner, sword in hand. "Here it is, I'd say. Poison HQ. Charming."

She ducked under his wing to take a peek, feathers tingling against her cheek.

Desolation. Scorched ruins of apartment blocks, bricks and steel girders tangled, only one or two stories left of ten or twelve. The leftovers of gang shenanigans, the damage too big for a suicide bomb. More likely arson. Tar puddled, and melted glass coated the ground, hardened to slippery shapes. Rubble still littered the wrecks. It stank of death and flesh, and somewhere horrid music grated, death metal, howling lyrics and guitars like nails on glass.

Zombies shambled everywhere. Mostly muties, odd-faced, their bodies deformed. Fighting, screaming, attacking each other with rocks and blades and bared teeth. Some climbed the ruined buildings, or muttered together in groups, kicking things and flailing their rotting limbs. Beside a burned-out playground, a pile of corpses ten feet high rotted in a mess of flies and rats, and the zombies dived in, munching, screaming with foul hunger.

Morgan gulped, sick sweat trickling from her hair. Hundreds of them. Even if she and Lune found this Prince of Poison, what then? How would they escape? And if even one of those infected monsters scratched her . . .

Luniel flickered his sword away, sliding on his human guise with a faint shimmer. "Color me inconspicuous," he whispered. "What's the plan?"

"You're asking me?" She struggled to keep her voice low.

"You're the one with the most to lose. I'm all for 'dive in and kill every last stinking one of 'em,' but I don't think that's strategically sound from your viewpoint."

"Then how do we find this Quuzaat? What's he look like?"

"A demon prince? He can look like whatever he wants, within reason. But in human disguise they're generally handsome, sniveling little smart-asses with beady red eyes. I'll see his aura before I see him. But they like to gloat. I'm betting he'll be the one with the big shit-eating grin on his face."

She eyed the laughing zombies. "Well, that sure narrows it down."

A dark laugh. "We do have one other option."

"And that is?"

"Let him find us."

"How, exactly?"

"Make a spectacle of ourselves. I can flash a little glory. Ring his cosmic doorbell, so to speak." Lune's eyes glinted, wicked. "Or, we could just raise a little hell. How many of those jars we got left?"

She counted. "Ten."

"Good. Ten too many for these assholes, then." He hesitated. "Look, we can wait for Dash and the others, if you want. Until they're done with the Prince of Blood."

Morgan shook her head, determined. "And let Quuzaat poison even more people? No way."

"Was hoping you'd say that." He flashed his wings back in, deadly silent. "Grab on."

"Huh? What for? The water doesn't work when I throw it, remember?"

"I'm not leaving you here alone," he said stonily. "Grab on."

Stiffly, she moved closer.

He wrapped his bulging arm around her waist, and she slid her wrists around his neck, trying to ignore the tingling warmth inside her. Wrapping her legs would be nice, too, but she didn't.

He caressed gentle feathers across her cheek. "You still feel good."

"And you're still a gutless shit, so don't think you can sweet-talk me."

"Don't worry, Doctor. I've talked enough. Hold tight."

She held on tighter and, stealthy as a black-winged ghost, he drifted them into the air.

Silently, he floated on warm breeze, just a flick of wings to keep them aloft. He trimmed with twitching feathers, and they wheeled slowly, out above the horrible ruins at a few hundred feet. Below them, zombies wandered and scrapped, clambering over broken steel frames, stumbling into deep holes, crashing blindly into walls.

Past the playground, a huge, roofless cage had been cobbled together from rusted iron and wood and wire, and inside, a mass of people tangled. Hundreds of them, men, women and children, naked, the air torn with their screams. Zombies screeched and flung themselves at the cage from outside, desperate to break through and feast, and the people wailed and huddled together. A few stabbed through the cage with scrap metal or wire, trying to fend the zombies off. One lost his arm, a zombie grabbing it with virus-mad strength and sinking in his teeth, ripping flesh and sinew until the limb tore free.

Morgan's guts squirmed, and she remembered the guy they'd killed, his story of mass infection. Victims for the sacrifice. She shuddered. Truly, this Prince of Poison was a monster.

Luniel gripped her tightly, his heartbeat resonating swift and strong inside her chest. "Peace, Morgan. If we can save them, we will. Hold tight. I need to let you go with one hand."

Resolute, she curled one leg around his, and locked her wrists together.

Carefully, he reached over her shoulder left-handed and unzipped her rucksack. Took out jars, resting them in the crevice between her breasts and his body.

He took the last one in his hand. He whispered a charm, and the sigil on his palm glowed blue. "Come on out, Quuzaat, you ugly bastard," he murmured, and hurled.

One after the other, his throws deadly swift and accurate. The jars flew in shimmering white arcs. They hit the ground and shattered, afire with holy fury, and showered the zombies with steaming death.

Howls rent the air, the stink of burning meat. Here and there, zombies caught fire, flailing around like napalm victims. Others just fell, clawing at their hissing flesh, angry flames eating their clothing.

Morgan gulped, guts slick with salt. She wanted to hide her face. It was horrible.

Luniel crackled his wings alive in a firework of golden sparks. "Wait for it," he whispered.

And an invisible black hand wrapped them like a stifling wet blanket, and dragged them to earth.

Morgan hit the dirt, tumbling from his arms. Lune thumped beside her, wings smacking in the dust. Around them, zombies milled and gobbled, burning. And a cruel laugh crawled over her skin, cold and dark like midnight sleet. "Well, well. Look what the demon dragged in."

She shivered at the evil timbre of that voice. Empty. Black. Bereft of heart. Her nerves quailed. She didn't want to look.

But she had to. Had to look him in the eye. Needed to see her enemy face-to-face.

Choking in crisp dust, she dragged her head up.

Tall, supple, dressed in black. White silken hair flowing over slim shoulders. Cold narrow face, sharp chin, red lips curling in an evil smile. Eyes the color of hellfire, with black pupils that glittered under the moon.

And crouching beside her, Luniel stared, ashen.

The Prince of Poison chuckled, icy. "Luniel, you dumb fuck piece of heaventrash. How nice to see you again. I'm afraid Quuzaat isn't here right now. Will I do, instead?"

CHAPTER 24

Lune stared, sick, and the bottom dropped out of his guts.

Vorvian. The Prince of Poison was Vorvian.

His mind crashed dead like a truck into bricks. *The hellshit knew we were coming. And I've led her straight into his trap.*

Toxic hatred burned his blood, and he grabbed blindly for his sword.

But Vorvian leapt for him, and crunched hell-strong fingers around his skull. The contact burned, and swift like a striking wasp, Vorvian slammed Lune's head into the ground.

Stars swirled, dizzy. Vorvian crushed a cold boot into his wrist. Bones cracked, and the sword bounced from his hand into the dust.

One second, maybe two, he'd had to react. And he'd wasted them.

"Lune!" Beside him, Morgan struggled to rise, but Vorvian's twin snarling minions hauled her down, ripping her angel-spelled knife away. Painsuckers, pale and wiry, pointy faces split by leering razor-toothed grins. High-level demon vassals, tricksy and hard to kill, second only to the prince.

Lune's memory reeled, a sick horror film. The same sadistic hellshits who'd tortured Eleanor.

Morgan's cry shredded his heart. He wanted to howl. He'd lost her. It was only a matter of time.

Vorvian laughed, serpentine, his eyes afire with cruel delight. "Oh, this is priceless. You assumed it had to be Quuzaat, didn't you? Because of the plague? Well, guess what? I swapped with him when I heard this was going down. Ha-ha! It's a corporate thing, you know. Broadening my skill set. It's promote or perish these days."

Lune's shattered wrist bones knitted, a raw spike of agony. "Congratulations."

"Why, thanks! Q. was pissed, let me tell you, but I hear he's happy with the way it's turning out. Now he gets to slaughter your Tainted friends. And I get to . . . well, I get to wallow in this!" Vorvian raised his arms and whirled, long snowy hair flying. His laughter echoed from blackened brick walls. "Isn't it glorious? All this screaming warms my foul little heart—but you already knew that, didn't you?" He skidded to his knees, landing inches away, and his whisper scorched Lune's cheek like hellfire. "The way your little medieval girlfriend wailed when I fucked her. Hell, I loved that. Almost as much as I got off on swallowing her soul."

Luniel's vision misted, black lust for revenge blotting out sense. Eleanor burned forever for this monster's fun. Evil temptation clawed him, furious. *Kill the son of Satan! Screw stopping the end of the world. It's over anyway. Just rip the fucker's guts out, for Eleanor. And for Morgan.*

Snarling, he flashed his sword into his hand, and thrust for the demon's heart.

Vorvian chuckled, and dissolved to ashen rain. Lune's blade sliced empty air. He stumbled, and in a flash Vorvian reappeared, stabbing his scarlet-flaming hellsword at Luniel's throat.

Lune jerked to a halt on taut wings, nearly skewering himself. The filthy hellflame seared his skin. He struggled to slow his breathing. *Calm it, Lune. Can't fight him angry . . .*

Morgan yelled and struggled in the painsuckers' grip. One licked his greasy tongue up her cheek, and Lune's heart overspilled with helpless rage.

Vorvian smiled, devilish. "Watch it, godscum. We've played this game before, and I won." He poked at Lune with his blade, razor-hot metal hissing, and waved his hand at Morgan. "But look, you've brought me another one! You are *so* thoughtful. Really, I don't know what to say."

"Get away from her." Luniel parried the demon's sword aside, and the metals clashed, fire spitting blue and scarlet.

Vorvian laughed, taunting him. "Actually, I do know what to say, don't I? Your Eleanor thought so. She was so eager for me, it made me think she'd been missing something. Did you ever satisfy her, angel? Ever get her off?"

"Go fuck yourself." Eleanor was dead and damned. Nothing could change that. But the demon's crude words still stung like poison.

"Didn't think so." Vorvian smirked. "She came so hard on my cock, sweet Satan, I honestly thought I'd broken something. And she believed me so easily when I said you were tricking her. In fact . . ." He frowned, and scratched his head, theatrical. "She gave in so fast, I wonder if she loved you at all! Ha-ha! I bet *that's* gotta hurt."

Lune's heart stung, eight hundred years of fury and lust for retribution, and he knew Vorvian was playing him but he couldn't stop. He sprang, striking for the demon's heart.

Vorvian blocked, sparks screeching from the steel, and staggered back. But he laughed as he stumbled. "Temper, shithead. Insecure much?" His eyes gleamed orange with delight. "What say you, my lovely? Does he do it for you?" And he vanished again in stinking smoke, and flashed in on his knees in front of Morgan with a foul crack like thunder.

"Get away from me, you disgusting little rat." Morgan spat at him, furious, but Vorvian's minions dragged her back. One wrapped his skinny white arm around her ribs, and laughed as he squeezed her breasts, his sharp tongue circling her ear.

Vorvian clicked his tongue, scolding. "Now, now, don't be rude. My friends here won't stand for it." He waved his arm, scattering stinking magical ash, and at his hell-spelled call, zombies groaned and milled closer, surrounding them.

Lune swiped a few back. One shambled up to Morgan, his rotted face oozing. He rubbed his groin against her back, and grinned, skull-like. "Mmbl. Shhsmm. Fkkkk!"

She couldn't shrink away, not with the zombie behind her. Not with the painsuckers clawing her like lust-hungry beasts. Vorvian giggled, and tickled his sword tip in Morgan's hair. "You know, that's not a bad idea."

Kill them all. Lune's vision blurred, and he struggled for sense, but passion cried alive in his veins. He shouldn't kill Vorvian, not before the hellshit told him everything. But Lune's heart—fiery, insubordinate, burning for justice—didn't care.

He spun his sword, flame spilling. "Leave the lady out of it, devilslime. You afraid to face me? C'mon. Have at me, and let's get this over with."

Vorvian scratched his chin. "Hmm. Nice offer. Let's see . . . how about . . . are you fucking kidding me?" He kicked up his feet in a delighted little dance. "Ha-ha! This is far too perfect, Lune, old buddy. Watch me and weep." And he beckoned to his twin minions, who grinned and slavered in unison, and pointed one slender finger at Lune. "Sick 'em."

And the painsuckers let Morgan go, and sprinted on pointy bare feet straight at him.

Lune whirled and struck, crouching low to slice at knee level. One howled and fell, clutching its leg. The other tumbled aside unharmed. More zombies stumbled in, crowding him, hiding the painsuckers from view. Lune shoved them aside, his blood pumping hard and urgent. He had to get to Morgan. But they piled in heavier, their rotting limbs stinking, eyes rolling with sick hunger. He chopped and stabbed, dispatching dead things left and right. The painsucker wormed through the throng and struck, and his venomous teeth sank deep into Lune's forearm.

Teeth grated on bone, and horror howled up his arm. The pain was intense, unbelievable, like raw hellfire shredding his every nerve, the painsucker's foul appetite for agony making it a hundred times worse. Dizzy, Lune snarled and head butted him. He didn't let go. Desperate, Lune flashed the sword to his left hand and slashed. The edge slammed into the thing's head, splintering bone.

Acid demon blood gushed. The painsucker screamed, and tore free. Angelflesh hung in strips from his teeth. Lune didn't care. He yanked his blade away and faced up, spinning his sword left-handed. "Come get it, helldirt."

The painsucker snarled, his shattered skull oozing. His friend hobbled up, and with a hiss of stinking demonsmoke, the leg Lune had severed regenerated. Together, the twins flexed razor talons, and advanced.

Lune crouched, wings flared, and sprang.

CHAPTER 25

The Prince of Poison smiled at Morgan, and her spine chilled deep.

She shivered, disgusted. His black leather armor shone in the moonlight, cruel spikes of iron glinting on shoulder guard and dog collar. His pale, wiry arms gleamed, tight and feral, splashed with blood and dirt like his long snowy hair. He twirled a scarlet-fired hellsword that spat charcoal sparks. He looked like a crazy fetish boy, slender and handsome and totally insane.

Vorvian. The white-haired demon prince who'd tortured Lune. And now he'd infected Babylon with sickness. Ending the world for some filthy demon master.

Bile frothed in Morgan's throat. Hatred spiked her skin tight. The bruises those horrid creatures had made ached like fever, and behind her, the amorous zombie still gurgled and groaned, rubbing his wet skin against her clothes. "Crawl back to hell, you nasty little slime," she hissed. "You don't scare me."

Vorvian laughed, delighted. "Why, of course not! I'm not your enemy. Let's be friends, Dr. Morgan Sterling, MD."

Surprise must have shown on her face, because he cackled and jiggled about, a mad happy dance. "Yes, Morgan, I know who you are. And I can smell the stink of angel on you, darling, so don't go pretending you and glory boy over there haven't been doing the deed . . . oh, dear." He shook his head, feigning distress. "Someone's in trouble."

Morgan's heart crunched tight, and she tried not to look, but it was useless. One of Vorvian's minions was chewing at Lune's arm, blood splashing everywhere. She struggled to her feet, fearful.

"No, no, no. Stay put." Vorvian shoved her back down. Just one finger on her shoulder, but her knees hit the concrete with a jarring thud. The bastard was strong.

He squatted before her, jabbing his sword tip into the dirt and leaning on the hilt two-handed. His face loomed uncomfortably close, and his ashen scent made her gag . . . but it was nice, too, musky and old, like sweet memory of things longed for.

Morgan pulled back, disgusted, but behind, that zombie just kept dry humping her. It squelched. Ugh. She couldn't move.

Vorvian smiled, handsome. "So how shall we amuse you, darling?" he murmured, and some vile hellspell in his voice licked her skin, warm and intimate. "Shall I let this rotting monkey fuck you? Hmm? Would you like that? Seems like he's still got all the right parts. Better than angel cock, let me tell you. If you can even dignify that with the name."

"You're disgusting."

He looked pained. "Now that's not fair. I only aim to please. A lot of you dirty apes enjoy my poison!" He waved his arm at the famished zombies milling around, cackling and chewing and pounding each other over the head. "They look like they're having fun, don't they?"

Morgan's heart burned black. The dark depths of her fury surprised her. She wanted to tear this fucker's eyeballs out for what he'd done. "Don't you dare rationalize to me, you evil son of a bitch."

"Wouldn't dream of it, darling. Live in fear, or die laughing. Some think that's a good deal." Vorvian leaned closer, and waved the eager zombie away. The creature moaned and obeyed, wandering off. "But I rather think I'll keep you for myself. Kiss me, pretty. Let's taste what you're made of."

Morgan scrambled backwards, but he grabbed her wrist in a flash, still leaning on his sword with the other hand. His grip was like tempered glass, light but unbreakable. That tempting ashen scent hit her again, insidious. It crept down her nose like a smoky incubus, wheedling, searching for a home. She wanted to vomit. She wanted to inhale, swallow, keep him inside her.

She spat at him, defiant. "I'd rather die."

"Than kiss me? Don't believe you." Amusement glinted green in his eyes. "You don't believe in hell or heaven, Morgan. You die, it's forever, right? You really want to flicker out for the sake of one kiss?"

Her heart faltered. Science made her meaningless. Short-lived meat. Just one more animal screaming to a careless sky. She'd always liked it that way, until she met an angel who did strange, improbable things to her heart. Lune's world was filled with pain and anger and cruel eternity, but at least it meant she mattered. "That's my problem, not yours."

Vorvian laughed, velvet and fire. "Are you sure? One kiss and we'll see. Would it really be so bad? You might like it."

"Don't count on it." Involuntarily, she recalled Luniel's kiss, rich and breathless with passion, the way she sprang alive inside when he touched her. Kissing another man after that would be tame in comparison. Kissing this . . . monster would be an aberration. Sacrilege.

She squirmed in Vorvian's grip. His fingers felt smooth, warm, alive around her wrist. So human. Not unearthly, like her angel. Fascination gripped her, hot and horrid. He was tricking her. He had to be.

"No?" Vorvian dragged her closer. His hair fell on her shoulder, crisp and hot, and his whisper seared her cheek like poisoned fire. "Let me rephrase. Kiss me, Morgan. Or I'll crush your angel's bones under my boots until you do."

Behind Vorvian, Luniel still fought the demon's minions. He killed one, stabbing it straight through its cursed heart, but staggered as the other crunched sharp teeth into his calf.

Morgan's heart lurched. But Vorvian's devil-spelled scent overpowered her, weakening her will. She fought, blindly, struggling to keep her head. "Not a chance. You can't beat him."

"You don't think so? I beat him once already. Didn't he tell you? And now I've got a thousand hungry zombies, and he's got . . ." Vorvian smiled, slick. "Well, he's got no one. Not even you." And he tossed back his snowy head and howled.

Her blood curdled. An awful, keen, shrieking howl that shivered her bones and dragged unwilling need to obey from deep inside. All around the blackened crater, zombies staggered in their tracks, and stumbled towards them.

Towards Lune. They flailed and gibbered, leaping at him, falling under his sword and boots but swamping him by sheer weight of numbers. He fought, swift and deadly. The second demon minion fell dead. Zombie body parts rolled, and flesh burned in screaming blue flame, but they kept coming.

Morgan's heart wailed, lost, and she sucked in a deep breath to scream his name.

Glittering red dust tickled her nose. She sneezed. And Vorvian laughed, sharp and cruel like an icicle piercing her soul.

Ash. He'd thrown hell-spelled ash. And like an idiot, she'd breathed it right in.

Demon mind poison. Acid horror slid into her veins as she remembered Iria's words. They'd already invaded her dreams. But this time she was awake.

"Morgan!" Lune yelled over the din, and his despair hurt her, deep inside.

Because the spell already had her aching for the demon's touch. His charcoal scent dried her mouth. Hot shivers racked her, from his light grip on her wrist deep into her body. Resistance flared, but it couldn't compete with the rising flame in her belly, tempting her to awful sin.

"Morgan." Vorvian's whisper caressed straight to her bruised soul. "Forget your angel's lies. Truth is, there's no fate but what you make. You can control your destiny, Morgan. I can give you what you desire. Kiss me. You know you want to."

It sounded so right. So true. Her throat stoppered, and she couldn't speak. Couldn't voice the denial that stole up her throat and shriveled dead.

Vorvian released her wrist. She didn't pull away. Not even when he touched her hair, the light of his fiery hellsword glinting wickedly in his eyes. Her evil dream soaked into her mind, thick with sultry caresses and sighs, and her blood burned. It was Vorvian in her dream. She wanted to be close to him again. Wanted to kiss him, suck his demon tongue into her mouth, feel his sleek caress again on her body, his flesh moving inside her.

Wanted to tear his lying devil's heart out and eat it.

But she couldn't move.

Tears ran down her cheeks. Furiously, Luniel fought the gnashing zombies. "Morgan," he panted, "don't! He'll curse you. For the love of heaven . . ."

But too late. Vorvian already cupped her chin. Before, the demon's palm felt cool. Now, his touch burned. And with a devilish laugh that iced her spine and inflamed her belly with sick desire, he swept her lips to his.

Ashen fire made her gasp. His mouth burned her, his tongue slipping inside. He tasted of charcoal and burned meat and sickness, disgusting but somehow delicious. Ash clogged her lashes, sealing them shut. His fingers tightened on her chin, and he kissed her deeper, forcing her mouth open wide. And something hot and thick crawled down her throat like a greasy worm.

She gagged, spitting, her eyes flicking open in shock. But his lips sealed over hers, his grip immovable on her chin. She couldn't breathe. Couldn't choke. Could only gulp in panic as the diseased thing slithered down into her guts. It coiled and muttered, like a poisonous snake waiting to strike. Her stomach heaved, desperate to empty itself, but nothing came up.

Vorvian dragged her up with him, his mouth still crushing hers. Dimly, she heard Luniel yell, ripped raw with anguish. Vorvian's teeth stung her lip, breaking the skin. She cried out, but the sound dissolved in his mouth like salt. He bit his own lip, a soft crunch, and she couldn't stop his blood trickling over her tongue. It burned, bitter and sweet, tasting of meat and sulfur.

"There," he whispered, kissing her, smearing their mingled blood over her lips. "That wasn't so bad, was it?"

At last, Morgan heaved in a lungful of demon-scented air. And dirty fever shivered over her, settling in a sick wash of heat.

Sweat broke on her skin, trickled down her neck, welled between her breasts to soak her shirt. Her pulse raced. The glands in her throat swelled rapidly, pain stabbing. She coughed, and it hurt, deep in her lungs where wetness festered thick. Her skin shuddered and crawled. Her bones ached. Her eyes stung hot and swollen. And her belly hollowed with the first stirrings of evil, ravenous hunger.

She gulped, famished. Already the blood in her mouth tasted good. She wanted more. Hungrily, she licked her bleeding lips. Mmm.

Dread iced her nerves like cold wire. A scream galloped up her throat, and she opened her mouth, but only a dumb choking sound came out.

Vorvian smiled his beautiful devil's smile, and raked a possessive thumb over her lips. "There's a good girl."

CHAPTER 26

Morgan fell to her knees, her head whirling sick. The virus. He'd infected her with the virus. And now she'd die, ravenous and rotting, spreading the demon's filth wherever she stumbled.

She heaved in another poisoned breath, and screamed.

Vorvian giggled like a naughty little fetish boy, and skipped away, humming.

Her throat rattled raw. Acid tears slashed her face, and she struggled to crawl up, run. But already, hunger cramped her guts tight like leaden weights, burning, demanding, whipping her to munch, kill, eat until she died.

Greedy saliva spilled down her chin. Her head ached with fever and dehydration and the stark, angry horror of what the demon had done.

Lune yelled, bright blue steel crunching bone as he fought. Her heart stung, the rich memory of his embrace tormenting her. The warm dark safety, the darker passion, his feathers' hot midnight scent, the liquid sunlight streaming through her veins when he kissed her. But he couldn't help her.

Wouldn't help her. He'd said as much. He'd kill her. She was already dead to him. Damned. A creature of hell, beyond redemption.

Sickly, she pushed the thoughts away. Let Lune save the

world, if he wanted to. She'd be dead. Rotting. In hell forever for what she'd done.

She could still feel Vorvian's lips mashing hers, temptation's hot caress deep in her flesh. She'd wanted him, wanted to believe him. It had seemed so right. Now, her weakness sickened her. He'd gotten to her so easily, such a simple spell. She'd always considered herself strong willed. Now, she knew how feeble she really was.

Hot damp hands pulled her up by the wrists. She dragged her head up, gagging on putrid fleshstink. Zombies. Oozing grins, raw flesh decomposing on their faces and hands. Dirty clothing, ripped, ruined with blood and shit and who knew what else.

She yelled and fought, dizzy with fever. But they didn't attack her. Didn't eat her. Just grinned, and pummeled her with their fists, bonking her over the head with crazy zombie affection. Their decaying sweat smeared over her skin.

Disgust wilted her hungry stomach sick. They recognized her. Accepted her. Loved her, for what she'd become.

One slurped his tongue up her cheek, gurgling. Horror squirmed hot snakes in her guts, and she recognized her amorous friend, the dry humper. "Mmmn," he said, his blue eyes gleaming dully with decay. "Fnnsm blll. Fkkk."

Another zombie clunked his skull against hers, a clumsy caress, and the blue-eyed one snarled around rancid teeth and ripped the guy's arm off. Flesh squelched, and the armless zombie howled as her possessive new friend beat him over the head with his own bleeding limb until he stumbled away. And then Blue-Eyes turned back to her, sniffing greedily at her cheek.

Oh, sweet Jesus. His decomposing breath made her retch. And—heaven help her—he had a hard-on, strong and burning against her thigh. But still this vile hunger gnawed her stomach hollow.

Unwilled, she licked bloody lips. Her gaze slid over the zombie's decay-blackened skin. So smooth and slick. So tasty. Her head swam, famished. Images flashed, sinking her teeth into flesh, skin tearing, bone popping, infected saliva running deep . . .

Blue-Eyes groaned with glee, and smeared his rotting lips over hers. Her stomach heaved, and she threw up. Sour and stinging. Right in his face.

Her body shuddered, repulsed and compelled at the same time. Hunger made her drool, longing for warm raw flesh. Her teeth ached to bite. This was so vile. She couldn't take it. *Oh, God, please just let me die.*

But more zombies grabbed her, dragging her to the ground. She struggled. Her skull clanged against the concrete. She needed to pee. Blue-Eyes climbed onto her, sliding greasy hands under her t-shirt.

She punched him, but he liked it. He nipped her belly with a happy little grunt, not quite piercing the skin, like he was teasing himself. He slobbered, wetting her. Her guts watered sick. She kicked, but the others held her down, sniggering.

Blue-Eyes just moaned and slurped his lumpy tongue over her skin, fumbling with spongy fingers to undo her buttons and peel her jeans down. He crawled up her body, sweaty with fever, and his fruity breath crawled over her tongue and down her throat.

Horror pierced her cold like a poisoned blade. And her mind went away, drifting through smoke-tainted air on the shrill currents of her screams, and she watched, detached, while below her, her body shuddered and yearned and bled . . . and ate.

CHAPTER 27

Morgan screamed, and Luniel's lost soul stripped raw.

He staggered on limp wings, shuddering in protest at the sound of her pain. Zombies gnawed at him. Blindly, he slapped them aside. He couldn't look. Couldn't see her, cursed and broken, at the mercy of hungry hell-things that snapped and tore at her precious skin.

Vorvian had taken her. The curse was upon her. She'd kissed the vile demon, hot and hungry, and just like Eleanor, nothing Lune could do or say would bring her back to him.

Clarity zinged his mind electric. He should have taken her away from here. Chanced his gutless heart for once and told her the truth. *Morgan, I've only known you for one day but my heart is yours. I want you to be mine. Come away with me before I get you killed, and together we'll watch the world burn around us.*

And now he'd never get the chance. She was cursed, lost to sense and reason. He'd failed her.

Pain tore his heart afresh, and deep inside, an evil little voice cackled bright. *Shoulda known better, angel. You can't change fate. Shoulda killed her at the beginning, while she was still going to heaven. She'll burn forever because of you. How'd you like that?*

But he couldn't let her go. Not yet. He gripped his sword, numb, and hurled himself towards her.

Serpent swift, Vorvian sprang into his path, and they hit the ground together.

His skull rattled, ashen demonstink making him retch. Vorvian grabbed his hair and slammed his head into the dirt again, and dizzily he clawed for the demon's smug red eyes. Slimy fucker was strong. Too strong. Always had been. Vorvian ripped out a fistful of feathers, splurting blood in Lune's eyes. Crimson blinded him, and Vorvian pinned his shoulders down with pointy knees, and jammed his sword blade crosswise, a hair from Lune's throat.

Lune fought, flinging out a desperate plea to glory. He had to get up. Had to get those monsters off Morgan, let her die in peace. But hellflame rippled red over Vorvian's skin, and his devilmagic glued Lune to the ground, invisible magnetism that smoked and stank like brimstone. Lune's feathers plastered to the concrete. His hair yanked tight like it was stuck in glue. He strained aching muscles, useless. He could barely move.

"Well, I've gotta say, this hasn't been as much fun as I thought." Vorvian twisted his wrist, and sizzling steel stung Lune's throat. "You're far too easy to torment. Still," he added with a wicked grin, "your girlfriend tastes pretty good, hey what?"

He bent closer, and Lune snapped at him, rage lighting his feathers blue, but the demon dodged, and fastened his teeth on Lune's ear. The bite sizzled, and Vorvian dragged Lune's head around with teeth and fist to make him look.

Morgan, spread on the ground, zombies holding her down while one peeled her clothes off. She kicked and yelled, but ever more weakly, her eyes glazed with terror and disgust and ripe hunger that longed to be satisfied.

Helplessly Lune fought the demon's spell. "Morgan," he panted, "hold on. Don't let go. Please."

Her gaze met his. Bloodshot. Fevered. Empty. The zombie atop her smeared his lips over her cheek. The amber light in her eyes faded. And she stretched her fever-hungry jaws open, and bit.

Lune choked on anguish. He wanted to squeeze his eyes shut, turn away. But he couldn't stop watching. Couldn't stop seeing his beautiful lady made into a monster. Tearing skin, popping muscle, blood . . .

Vorvian squirmed with a pleasured groan. "Ooh, lookie. Morgan's hungry. Do you think she'll like being fucked by a rotting psychopath? She'll be lucid for a while. Shouldn't be surprised if it tips her over the edge. And then she'll be mine, Lune. To do with as I please."

"Don't count on it, asshole. She'll die before she submits to you." Lune bared his teeth, feral, but inside his nerves screamed. He couldn't make himself believe it. She was lost.

"Oh, I don't think so, pet." Vorvian dropped a cheeky kiss on Lune's nose. "Making them hate you is almost as good as fucking them. Is her cunt as tight and smooth as Eleanor's? Probably not, eh? These modern girls screw like rabbits. But still, it'll feel good to know my cock's inside your woman. Again."

Rage flowered hot, a fresh wash of strength, and Lune aimed a head butt at Vorvian's chin. His hair ripped free of the spell, and he connected with a satisfying crunch.

Vorvian grunted, his crushed chin reforming with an angry flash of hellfire. "Hey, that hurt!"

"Good. Is making me suffer all you care about? You petty little shitwad."

"Actually, yeah. Pretty much. Are we having fun yet?"

"Curse you, hellspawn." Glory tingled, and Lune spat a sizzling heavencurse into Vorvian's eye.

Vorvian yowled and swore, batting the burning fluid away. His right eyeball glazed over, half-healed, and he leapt backwards, landing with his blade poised. "Rat-fucking godscum. Look what you've done! Gone and pissed me off again." He screwed his eye shut, straining, and it finally healed in a stinking puff of smoke. "So I'll be off now. Got errands to run. Plagues to spread, zombies to rule, that sort of thing. All this is only the start of my work."

Lune jumped up on bleeding wings, the spell finally broken. Behind him, Morgan splashed in blood. "Monologue away, hellshit. I'll chew your fucking entrails out."

The demon howled laughter. "Ha-ha! You're so funny! Aren't you forgetting something?"

Lune speared a wish, and his sword smacked into his sweaty palm. Blue flame dripped electric with the force of his fury.

"Yeah, actually. How long will it take for you to bleed to death, again?"

A mock shiver. "Ooh. I'm so scared. I was thinking more along the lines of . . . you can't be in two places at once?" Vorvian grinned, and ducked closer over his sword to whisper. "It's just like old times! You can kill me. You can save your tasty little bitch. But"—he made a sad face, poking his bottom lip out—"I'm not so sure you can do both, Lune. I'm so sorry. But hell, it's your choice!" He cackled, cruel sparks spitting scarlet, and gave a cheeky wave. "Enjoy the show, now. See ya. Bye."

CHAPTER 28

Blood thudded hot in Lune's skull, his muscles afire with lust for vengeance. But Vorvian already danced away into the howling crowd. Free to wreak fresh havoc. More zombies. More disease. More death.

Desperation sliced his nerves ragged. *Can't let Vorvian get away. Not again.* The monster deserved a horrid death. And if Lune let him escape again, it wouldn't only be Vorvian who tumbled screaming into the fire. He'd already used up his chance. If he spurned heaven's mission for a woman a second time, they'd cast him into hell without a blink.

He leapt aloft, chasing Vorvian's vile stench. There he was, skipping between shambling zombies. Angry glory struck Lune's veins afire, and he swept back burning wings to strike.

But Morgan's shrill scream dragged him to a halt.

The thing in Morgan's body lay shrieking, her near-naked skin smeared in zombie filth. But in her eyes, a tiny light of life glimmered, terrified and alone. And it seared a hole in Lune's frozen heart.

Somewhere in there, she still lived. Somewhere, his lovely Morgan wailed in horror at what was happening to her.

And the thought of leaving her there scarred Lune's heart afresh.

Kill Vorvian. Save Morgan. The fucking demon was right. He couldn't do both. And the twin hooks of duty and heartache jabbed deep into his lost soulflesh and tore it in two.

He slumped to his knees, his glory draining away in a glimmering blue flood. His wings dragged in the dust. He lifted his face to heaven, and squeezed stinging eyes shut, his anguish screaming out like an accusation. *I can't do this! I can't let her die. Sweet heaven, why do you hate me so much? Why give me a heart and then curse me for loving her?*

No stars. No warmth. No glory.

Only silence.

Despair ripped him raw. Every second he wasted, Vorvian slipped further from his grasp. He didn't care. He blinked away moonlight's shimmering glare. *You win, okay? I'm already in hell. Just tell me this is right. Please. Tell me what to do.*

But the cold breeze of holy displeasure slapped damp hair from his cheeks, and the fire in his sword sputtered and dimmed.

Because he'd already decided what to do.

And if it meant his soul was damned, then fuck them all and so be it. He'd accept his fate. They might own his soul, but they couldn't own his heart. He'd already given it to Morgan. And what good was his soul, without his heart?

Cold resolve sparked his nerves taut, and he vaulted to his feet and dived for her.

The blue-eyed zombie squealed and fell when Lune crashed into it. Its skull smacked the concrete, brains bleeding out, and it thrashed like a beached fish. The other zombies snarled and snapped, but Lune flung them off in a hail of blood and scooped Morgan into his arms.

His dull iron sword hit the dirt as he cradled her against his chest. Her t-shirt was torn away, her feet bare, her jeans peeled down to her knees. Her panties were gone. He tried to pull her jeans up, to cover her, but his hands shook. She was so vulnerable. So fragile. And he'd let Vorvian have her. Heaven, he'd practically given her to the demon himself.

A scream welled up, and deep inside in the dark empty space where his frosty angelic soul once lived, some twisted creature spat black sparks of shame and vengeance. Screw heaven. He didn't need their blessing. If he accomplished only one thing

before the world burned, he'd track Vorvian down and rip the
evil scumsucker's skin from his body. But not now. Not while
Morgan suffered.

"Morgan. Love. Talk to me. Please." Bite marks pierced her
skin, deep in her upper arms where the flesh was soft. Filth
smeared her throat, her belly, between her thighs, and Lune's
stomach clenched. Fuck, if that rotting thing had . . .

She thrashed, senseless, sweat pouring. She was burning up.
He wiped stained hair from her cheek, and the touch hissed,
threatening, stinging his fingertips.

His guts clenched. Already, the demon's curse made her
reject his touch. A few minutes more, and he'd have burned her
to the bone.

The zombies advanced, decaying lips twisted in anger. Lune
warded them off with a snarled curse, setting their hair alight.
At least that still worked. "Morgan. Wake up." He kissed her
burning forehead. She tasted salty, of sweat and dead filth. He
didn't care. He kissed her bloody lips, searching, desperate for
that spark of life.

"Mmmn." The cursed part of Morgan murmured, licking her
lips hungrily. But still her body struggled to be free.

He wrapped his wings around her, begging her silently to
wake. "Morgan. It's me, Lune. Can you talk?"

Her eyes flickered open. Scarlet horror swirled, and she
clutched him weakly with bleeding fingers. "Lune? Oh, God.
Help me. I can't . . . uhh . . ." And her eyes rolled back, syllables
blurring into senseless animal noises as Vorvian's curse dragged
her under again.

Lune choked on a howl. She was still there. Barely holding
on. Rage and sorrow flamed his feathers with lust for revenge,
but somehow an anguished cry to heaven still screamed from
his heart.

*Please, if you're still listening. Help me. Don't let her leave
me now.*

Silence rang, cold and empty. And still Morgan muttered,
feverish, tossing her head from side to side.

So be it.

Lune wrapped his wings tight, his cheek resting on top of her
head, and flashed out.

* * *

Strong arms wrapped Morgan's body in the hot scent of angel feathers, and as if climbing from the depths of a dark, stinking pit, she fought awake.

Soft light stung her eyes raw. Hardwood floor, pale walls, gleaming glass. Soft cushions crushed beneath her. She heaved in a fire-spiked breath. God, it was so hot. She was burning up. The air scorched her throat, sandpapered her eyes, drained her muscles to water. Her pulse thudded in her skull, too rapid, and she tasted blood. Her stomach cramped with nausea, and something hot and slimy coiled there like a hungry worm. She needed to throw up, pee, cry her heart out.

"Morgan, stay with me." His voice echoed, from a distance, like her ears were stuffed with water. But the soulful vibration stroked her with gladness. Lune. Her angel. This was his apartment, where they'd . . . almost made love. It seemed so long ago. But he'd come for her. Hadn't let her die. Hadn't let the demon steal her soul, and secret sunlight shone on her heart.

She ripped her sticky lips apart, trying to tell him everything was okay. His delightful scent drifted into her mouth, washing away the grime. Her fevered body heated more. He always smelled so nice. So . . . tasty.

Hunger whispered hot seduction in her belly. She licked her lips, inhaling again. Mmm. So delicious. His skin's warm clean flavor, hot blood pulsing beneath. She wanted to lick him, tongue his fragrant essence into her mouth and swallow.

Her mouth watered, drooling. How good that skin would feel in her mouth. Between her teeth, crushing, the thin membrane popping and his salty hot flavor bursting down her throat . . .

Her body shuddered with lust. Her stomach cramped, aching to be sated. Fuck, she was so hungry, she was getting turned on. Lune stroked her hair, and his strong wrist brushed her cheek. She could see the veins, blue and pulsing, and desire burned deep in her belly. Crunch her teeth into that taut skin, tear a slow chunk of flesh free and swallow, the blood pouring . . .

Something inside her wailed dimly in horror and disgust. Noisy thing. She kicked at it. *Be silent, thing. I'm hungry.*

And a dark and sultry whisper caressed her ear, tainted

bright with a hell-spelled smile. *That's a good girl. Yummy angelflesh, munch crunch slurp. You eat.*

Why, I think I shall. Her eyes slitted, crafty. Tasty angel, so virtuous. Wouldn't even take her when she'd asked him to. A splurt of hellcurse in his blood would do him good. He liked her. Wanted her. She knew that. His tongue between her legs had felt so good. And she longed for sensation, taste, smell, touch, anything to slake this raging hunger. Mouth full of meat. Body filled with his hard flesh. Eat. Fuck. Both.

She sighed, and curled against him in the cushions, arching her back to press her breasts against his armored chest. Her nipples tweaked hard, and she shivered, feverheat sliding over her like the hot licks of a lover. Mmm. He'd taste so good.

"Luniel," she murmured, the demon's spell cutting a seductive edge to her voice. "Touch me."

CHAPTER 29

Morgan's whisper scorched Lune's shoulder, ripe with hell-curse. He smoothed her hair, his heart racing. "No, Morgan, you're sick. I have to make you well."

And how the fuck would he do that? He had nothing. Heaven had deserted him. He was probably already damned . . .

She pressed her half-naked body against him on the sofa cushions, murmuring darkly with pleasure and devil-warped desire. "Mmm. You feel good. Touch me. I'm so hot, Lune, I'm burning up. I need to feel you."

His flesh ached. Even in sickness, she was so beautiful, he burned. Her naked skin was so soft, so inviting, the dark lace of her bra so thin. He wanted to tear his armor off and crush her breasts against his bare chest, feel those taut little nipples rise against his skin . . .

Blood rushed to all the wrong places, and his mind stumbled, blind. All wrong. She didn't mean it. She was sick. He couldn't . . .

His mouth dried. "Hush, love. You're fine."

"No." She gathered her hair above her head, arching into full view. Her jeans were undone, offering a tantalizing glimpse of creamy belly, the fine dark blush where hair grew. She slid her hands down her thighs and pushed the denim downwards.

Underneath, she was naked, and moisture slicked silvery between her legs. "No, Luniel. I need you inside me. Touch me. I know you want to. I'm aching for you. Make me well."

His wing light sprang alive, spilling treacherous lust. The warm female scent of her desire inflamed him. He wanted to grab those smooth hips and pull her onto him, feel her hot wet flesh enfolding him. Inhale her demon-scented breath, and die in her embrace.

She laughed, low and seductive, and his feathers shivered, hot and taut. She rid herself of her jeans, and crawled towards him. Her dark curls tumbled invitingly. "Shy, my handsome angel? Don't be. I know what I want."

He scrambled back from her, thoughts racing as hard as his pulse. He had to help her. Make her stop. Did he have any holy water left? It might still work, he still believed, after all, even if they didn't believe in him and sweet fucking heaven, he was hard for her, she was so damned beautiful and he wanted to pin her under him and push her thighs apart and fill her, fuck her, own her . . . "Morgan, stop it. Let me . . . oh, shit."

She pushed him onto his back and climbed on. She locked her thighs around his hips, and rubbed herself against his aching cock with a sultry sigh. Her lace-clad breasts crushed against his armor as she bent to whisper, her lips an inch from his. "I want you to fuck me, lover. So deep and hard, I can't breathe. I want you to sit me on your lap and bite my nipples while you fuck me and make me come. I want to slide your cock into my mouth and suck you until you explode. Wouldn't that feel good?"

Fuck, it'd feel so good he'd probably die. "Wait. Don't do that. Stop it . . ."

But she'd already slid her hands to his hips, unbuckling his bloodstained leather beneath her. Her burning hands found his straining cock, and at the first expert stroke of her nails he groaned and pressed up against her, his balls clenching tight. His body tingled all over, weak. Heaven, he was so sensitive. So hard.

Morgan laughed, her wicked hands doing things to him he'd only ever dreamed of. She leaned over him, her lovely breasts hovering in thin lace, and he couldn't help reaching for her, caressing them, sliding his hands behind her to unclip her bra and get her naked.

She crooned in satisfaction, rubbing her breasts into his palms. Her dark pink nipples jutted. Hellfire, he wanted to suck on them, make her moan. They were smeared with blood. He didn't care. He just wanted to . . . *holy fucking Jesus.* She slid the head of his cock against her slick wetness, and he nearly howled in frustration. He could feel the dimple of her entrance, rubbing on him, so firm and tight. And so deliciously hot. Her fever made her flesh burn. Fuck, how amazing that'd feel, wrapped around his cock as he pushed inside her to the hilt . . .

No. Lune gripped her hips and levered her off him.

"Come on, sweet angel. Take me." She writhed, luscious, breasts and limbs and dusky woman scent and, Christ, how he'd ever stopped was beyond him.

But he had to. This wasn't her. Not his beautiful Morgan. Just the hungry virus, a fevered dream. And screwed if he'd have her like this.

He fought her into his arms, ignoring her kicks and struggles, and dived for his cool white bathroom. His spelled knife still lay on the sink where he'd left it, and the vanity mirror glared at him, accusing. He laid her in the bathtub and held her down by one shoulder. She struggled, whimpering, her pretty lips trembling. "Please. I want it. You have to. I need it so badly. I'm so fucking hungry for you, I'll die. Please."

He dropped the plug and flipped the water on cold. It rinsed off blood and dirt, and she squealed, the fever fighting back. She slid her hand over his hip into his pants, trying to undress him, and licked her swelling rosy lips. "Mmm, let me taste you. I want you in my mouth. Give it to me, Lune."

He jerked away, yanking his buckles tight before he could give in. A hot ache stabbed. He barely fit, he was so hard. He stuffed his hand in the pocket—ouch—and yanked out his last blessed jar.

The water glimmered in his grip, angry blue. For all he knew, it'd burn him as well as her. But he didn't have time to care. He popped the lid with his thumb and emptied it into the bath.

The water splashed. Glittered. Faded.

A sob clutched Lune's throat. He couldn't save her. Couldn't scare Vorvian's curse from her body. And this glorious, maddening, intoxicating woman would die, eaten up by fever and hunger and cruel demon vengeance.

What a fucking waste.

He gripped the bathtub, shaking, and banged his forehead against it. His grief, his guilt, the anguish of losing her seemed so weak and selfish. Pointless. But his heart still screamed, a lost howl of reckless fury, and it was all for her.

Morgan crushed hungry fists in his hair, drooling, trying to tug him closer. The metal bath crunched in his fists. Her brilliant love for life, cut so short. That fire in her eyes as they argued, her bright animation as she talked of science and medicine and wanting to help people. Eternal torment was hideous, sure. But life on this earth was the brief sunlit flash that made it all worthwhile, and now hers was gone.

He loved her. It wasn't a question anymore. She'd stolen his heart, and he wanted her at his side forever. But what he wanted didn't matter a damn to him now.

Tears dripped onto the floor, the first he'd shed in eight hundred long years of shame and denial, and his shattered heart cried out to heaven.

Don't let her die. Do what you want with me, I don't care. Just don't let her blink out like this. Let her have her life. It's worth so much more than mine.

Glare blinded him, and glory whispered hot over his feathers.

He blinked, clearing his eyes. A faint golden shimmer surrounded him, heaven's light, the warm glow he'd thought was lost.

His heart skipped. Was it a sign, that golden shimmer? So long since he'd felt the gentle touch of heaven, anything other than a grudging flash of glory to keep him alive.

But this felt kind, enlightening. Almost . . . tender.

Morgan thrashed in the running water, gnawing for him. Her teeth grazed his knuckles. They stung and sizzled, holy on unholy, and in a wild flash of inspiration, Lune knew what he had to do.

Swiftly, he fumbled behind him on the sink. The cool spell-silver of his knife licked his fingertips, and he grabbed it and jammed the stinging point against the hollow of his throat.

His pulse jerked, desperate, trying to escape. But he steadied his hand with a deep breath. *My blood for hers. My life for hers. My soul for hers. All that I am, all that I have. Sweet heaven, just let her live.*

CHAPTER 30

Luniel closed his eyes, and drove the blade deep into his throat.

Pain stabbed to his core. Blood splashed red into the water, down his armor, onto Morgan's fevered skin. She howled, sizzling. Lune choked, but jammed the blade harder, twisting with the last shred of his strength, and then crimson sheeted everywhere and he couldn't hold the knife anymore.

Dizzy, he fell forwards against the bathtub. His ears screamed deaf. His limbs slackened, nerves imploding. He couldn't breathe. Couldn't think. Could only feel the blood, throbbing against his skin as it forced out under pressure. It spilled over Morgan, washing her in hissing crimson as the demon's curse fought back.

She struggled and choked, steam curling from her burning flesh. Blue sparks of glory ignited, and sank glittering under her skin. Her pretty mouth stretched in agony. Her body convulsed, and retched, and from her mouth spilled bile and chewed flesh and . . . a slithering black devilworm that hissed and gnashed jagged teeth.

Lune gasped, but no air went in. Scarlet mist flooded his eyes, and he barely saw the horrid curse-thing drop thrashing into the red-stained water. It shrieked, thwarted, and dissolved in a blue flash and a twist of ashen smoke.

Morgan sucked in a shuddering breath. Her mouth opened, a stop-motion scream, and then Lune's vision died.

Satisfaction made him smile inside. He'd given her the best of him. He'd never made love to her. Never told her how he really felt. But that didn't matter. He didn't matter. Only Morgan.

He crumpled, his strength drained. He couldn't feel his limbs. The knife ripped out and hit the water, a distant slow-motion splash. God, he was so cold, here in the dark. Her scent shimmered, and drifted out of reach. His flesh cooled, and in his ears, his pulse faded. Slowed. Stopped.

Silent. Black. Empty. The first eternal second of forever. He drifted, dim, waiting for the flash of hellfire.

A dull ache spread through Morgan's limbs from the blackness, as if she woke from a tense and ugly sleep. She groaned, and forced her sticky eyelids open.

Pale tiles greeted her. Her head clunked on lacquered steel. Warm clear water splashed. She looked down, dazed. In the bath. Naked.

She fought to sit up, slipping. Her whole body ached like she'd worked out for hours, and her muscles shriveled, weak. She coughed, raw, and gripped the side of the tub to rise.

Luniel lay on the white floor, silver armor shining, enveloped in a soft blue glow. His black wings sprawled limp. Beside him, fallen from his hand, his silver-steel knife gleamed.

"Lune?" A dry croak. "Lune, are you okay?"

He didn't move. Wasn't breathing. And in a cruel flash, Morgan remembered everything.

Kissing that foul demon, the vile worm creature that slithered down her throat. Fever, wracking her body with agony and insane hunger. The crunch of flesh between her teeth and . . . *oh, God. No.*

She'd eaten. Swallowed human flesh. Let that cursed zombie touch her, lick her, grope its loathsome fingers over her, smear her in filth and rotten skin . . .

Her face burned, and she dry retched, painful, her guts desperate to be cleansed. But nothing came up.

She wiped her eyes, coughing, and grabbed a towel to wrap

herself in before scrambling to her knees at his side. His warm blue light flowed over her, soothing, but it couldn't burn away her self-disgust. She'd touched him, while the sickness twisted her wits. Kissed him. Tried to seduce him, so she could eat. All in the grip of the horrid virus, sure, but she'd said and done things that made her skin burn and her guts cramp with shame.

And then he'd killed himself. Bled himself dry with his silver-spelled blade. For her.

"Lune, wake up." Her whisper choked her, sick. She smoothed his hair, tugging it away from his face. He was so warm, she thought distantly. So fragrant and fresh. No blood. No wound. Healed. But he didn't move. She pressed two fingers for his pulse. Nothing.

Tears spilled out, scorching. She ached, deep inside where she'd sworn she'd never let him close, never let him deceive her.

Well, he hadn't deceived her.

He'd given everything for her. He'd let the demon escape. Drained out his life. Thrown away his soul. And now she'd be without him forever.

She buried her face in his warm feathers, inhaled his sparkling scent, twisted her fingers in his rough-silk hair. The hot blue glitter of mercy stung her skin, harsh and unforgiving. She didn't deserve mercy.

Her tears slicked hot. "I'm so sorry," she whispered against his lips. "I should have believed in you. You earned it. I called you a liar, Lune, but the truth is"—she swallowed tears, the confession too late, a dying shot of starlight in her soul—"I'm the liar. I . . . I care for you. I was just too scared to let you care for me. And now you'll never know. I'm so sorry—oh!"

White light cracked like thunder, burning away the blue.

Her ears rang. And Luniel sucked in a shuddering breath.

She jumped to her knees, cradling his face in her hands. "Lune?"

"What the . . . ?" His eyes fluttered open, heavenblue, and focused on her. He scrambled his hands beneath him, and stared, his breath short. "Morgan. You're alive."

Sunshine flooded her heart. Shaking, she touched his face. "I'm here. Shh. It's all right. You okay?"

He pulled her into his arms, crushing her against his armored chest. His heartbeat thudded against her, strong and steady like it had always been, and his glory's warm glow surrounded her. He kissed her hair. "I am now. Thank you, Morgan."

She clutched him closer, dazed. "You're thanking me? You're the one who stabbed yourself in the throat. What the hell happened?"

Lune laughed, shaky, like he didn't trust his luck. "I think . . . I think I always had the answer. I just didn't ask the right questions until now. I was selfish, but you made me forget that. You can thank heaven for saving you, Morgan. I just . . . I just asked. For you. That's all."

She closed her eyes, melting into his embrace, his scent dizzying. "And they said yes? Does that mean you're saved, too?"

His beautiful laugh tingled through her again. He uncurled his left hand, the crossed lightning sigil still shining from his palm. "No such mercy. I skipped hell this time. But I'm still Tainted, if that's what you care about." His arms tensed around her. "Is that what you care about?"

"What do you mean?" She pushed back to look into his face.

He gave a sheepish shrug. "About me being Tainted. If you thought I was . . . y'know. Redeemed. When you said . . . what you said just now."

Morgan's skin heated. "You heard that, huh."

"Afraid so." His ultrablue gaze trapped her, so unguarded and vulnerable, it burned. "Did you mean it?"

All her old fear and self-doubt clamored, an evil discordant symphony in her head. *Don't go there. Don't trust him. It's all a lie, Morgan. Why would he want you? Why would anyone want you?*

But she ignored it. Her voice cracked, overcome. "Yes. I meant it."

She held her breath, but the sky didn't fall. Lightning didn't strike—at least, not again. Luniel just stroked her damp hair back, caressed her cheekbone, touched gentle fingertips to her lips.

She closed her eyes on fresh tears, and he eased her down beside him into the rich soft cushion of his feathers. "Well, Morgan Sterling," he whispered, brushing his mouth over her tears to catch them, "you've just scared the hell out of me." And he captured her for a kiss.

CHAPTER 31

His lips were so deft, so tender. One kiss, then another, hesitant, like he didn't know what she wanted, or whether she wanted at all. She responded, tasting him, hot and delicious, all the sweeter now that she let herself *feel*.

She climbed onto him, kissing him harder. He wrapped one wing over her, so warm and velvety, spilling that gorgeous toffee scent, and when his tongue found hers at last she gave a soft little moan of delight. Her breasts ached against his warm silver. Only her towel came between them, and the metal's hard smoothness inside his delicate feathery cocoon made her shiver with fearful desire. Such a strong, unyielding, frightening creature. His touch delighted and terrified her at the same time.

He kissed her deeper, rougher, a growl rising in his throat, and rolled her beneath him, pulling her thigh up around his.

Feeling his hard body atop her, between her thighs, made her dizzy with need. He was so big. So male. Already she ached for him, afire. She was naked under the towel. How good he would feel next to her, searing skin on skin . . .

She slid her arms around his neck and lost herself in his brain-melting kisses. His tongue claimed hers, stroking her to sweet fever, and when he slipped his hand beneath her towel to cup her ass, she groaned and pressed into him. His fingertips teased her, delving deeper towards her secret places but never quite touching, and her wetness ached and flowered, longing for him.

At last, he pulled back, with a groan of protest. He was breathing hard. So was she. His eyes flamed dark with desire, and passion-drunk sparks danced like fireflies from his wings. "Do you trust me?"

Her nerves spiked in warning, and she struggled for breath, her pulse racing. His scent bewitched her. His kisses intoxicated her with longing. If he touched her any more, she'd lose control. "Umm. Lune. I . . ."

"It's okay." He kissed her again, tender, so hot, drawing desire from deep inside. Not a threat. Just a tease, a sultry promise of delirium. "We don't have to . . . y'know. If you don't want to."

Right. Like any woman could not want to right now. Her laugh turned to a soft moan as he licked burning kisses down to her collarbone. "No, I . . . it's just . . ." She swallowed, trembling. The fear in her heart wasn't rational or right. But it paralyzed her, made her want and shiver and cringe at the same time. "I'm afraid, Lune."

He trailed his hair over her shoulder, closing his eyes on a sigh. "Don't be. Just . . . let me love you." And he did, teasing her skin aflame with openmouthed kisses. He tasted her throat, her shoulder, inside her elbow. Heat tingled deep inside her, stroking her to fresh desire. He was so tender, she ached. And when he nuzzled her towel aside, baring her breast to his mouth, she gasped and arched her back, the wicked promise of his kiss blinding her.

"Heaven, I love your breasts. They're so soft. So hot." At last his tongue found her nipple, the nub so hard and sensitive she groaned. He suckled her, softly, then harder, the tension winding tight all the way down to her sex, and then he bit her gently and she sobbed, it felt so good.

But her treacherous nerves shrieked foul, clenching cold on the swelling knot of need in her belly. Everything about her feelings for him screamed of lies and cruel seduction. He couldn't be this true, this good, this passionate and desirable and mad for her. She wasn't that special. This golden sunshine on her heart couldn't be real . . .

The ugly fear that coiled deep in her soul sniggered in scaly black delight. *What did you think, Morgan? Of course it isn't real. Are you mad, trusting your feelings like that? He's using you. Just wants to fuck you. And when you wake from this lust-drunk dream, he'll laugh and betray you . . .*

She fought back, determined. *No, demon. You're lying. This is real. Dive back into the stinking pit you crawled from, and leave me be.*

"Morgan?" Lune's whisper tingled her skin, his lips brushing her breast. "You okay?"

She sighed, triumphant. "Lune, I am so much better than okay. Love me."

She crushed his silky black hair in her fists, pulling him onto her, her blood afire for him. He took her other nipple, torturing her until she whimpered with pleasure. Her flesh ached, damp and hot. Every touch of his lips and tongue made tension crush tight inside her, and she groaned in amazed delight. The way he made her feel, so strong and beautiful, like nothing could ever hurt her again.

It couldn't be a lie.

She gasped and shuddered, and gave herself up to his glory. "Yes, Lune, more."

But with a final teasing suckle, he let her go, and claimed another dark and glittering kiss that stole her breath. White light flashed, and in a dizzy instant she was on her back beneath him in the soft dark cushions of his loft. Moonlight spilled over them, and his wings shone. His blue eyes glowed with desire. His hot scent dizzied her. He fluttered to his knees, and started to unbuckle his armor.

Morgan swallowed, dry. "Don't."

He halted, shuddering. "Shit. Sorry. Am I going too fast? I didn't mean—"

"It's okay." She inhaled deeply, letting her courage breathe. She'd made her decision. Surrendered to this powerful heat. And she wouldn't just let it happen to her like a scared little girl. She didn't just want a taste of this new freedom. She wanted to drown in it. Drown in him. "Just . . . let me."

His gaze smoldered indigo, and he gently guided her hands to his buckles. The silver slid smoothly under her fingertips, warm with his body heat. The soft leather straps slipped easily from the buckles, two on each side, and he dragged the armor off over his head, mussing his damp hair. Underneath he wore his light undershirt, pale and perfect, all the sweat and demon-slime burned away by that cleansing flash of glory.

For a moment, her stubborn mind jumbled. *Heaven's light. Angel. Wild. Crazy. Unbelievable.*

But for these few precious moments, she was crazy, too. It didn't hurt, or shame her. It was wonderful. Dizzying, like a glowing rainbow in her heart.

She swallowed, nervous, and slipped her hands under the thin pale cloth. Smooth, hot male skin over hard-packed muscle and bone. She traced the elegant lines of his stomach muscles, caressing the ridges leading to his hips, tracing the hard curves under his tight leather pants. His breath grew ragged at her touch, and he caught her hands, kissing them like fever. "Behave, sweetie, or this'll be over way too soon."

She tugged his shirt upwards, and he stretched and vanished his wings, letting her slide it off. When he shimmered back to reality in a wash of hot breeze, her throat stoppered. The moonlight loved him, pouring over his luminous skin, shadowing his muscles, glowing on his sparking feathers and dissolving into the silky blackness of his hair. God, he was beautiful. Perfect. Frightening.

He gave a flashburn smile at her scrutiny. "Like what you see?"

She laughed, breathless. "Cocky much, angel?"

"I want to hear you say it."

"Oh, yes. I like it very much."

His shoulder muscles flexed, like he wanted to grab her. But he just knelt astride her, and glided his fingertips over the towel that still wrapped her waist. "Do you want to, or shall I?"

Muscles deep inside her clenched, aroused. She was naked underneath. He'd already seen her, of course. Too much of her. But she still flushed at the dark desire in his eyes as she tugged the towel aside.

At the sight of her, golden flame licked his feathers. He growled, and raked hungry teeth over his lip. Heat scorched up from her belly to the top of her head, embarrassment and desire warring a hot battle in her veins. "Like what *you* see?"

"Let me show you how much." He climbed up her, letting her feel every hard-muscled inch of his body, and began to kiss her. First her mouth, deep and slow and soulful, his tongue wrapping hers, exploring, claiming her. His dark-sweet flavor enticed her, and she sucked on his tongue, trying to get more of him inside her. His fingers wrapped her wrists, pressing them into the cushions, and he eased himself against her lightly, stroking, full body contact. She shivered, her desire igniting. His power over her sparkled hot longing deep inside her. So safe and warm and strong.

He trailed burning kisses along her jaw, under her chin, down her neck where her pulse beat hot. He lingered, tasting her skin, licking the sensitive spot beneath her ear. He nipped her earlobe, and she gasped, a hot sting of pleasure.

He kissed her shoulder, seared his tongue along her collarbone, nuzzled between her breasts until they ached for his mouth. God, was it hot in here? She was weak, dizzy, wet and sore between her legs. His touch, his scent, the tightness of his grip made her burn.

He lifted her wrists above her head, and held them there, his weight pressing her down. The new tension in her muscles drove her wild. She twisted, arching her back, begging for his lips on her.

"You like that?" A secret smile against her lips.

Oh, God. She did like it. Liked him holding her down, making her his own. "Uh-huh."

Lightly, carefully, he wrapped her hands with his shirt and knotted them to the bedpost over her head.

Her pulse shot wild, warping her desire into fear. Trapped. Vulnerable. "Lune—"

"Shh. Trust me. If you don't like it, say so." And he tortured her body with caresses, trailing lips and fingers and silken feathers over her shoulders, her hips, the curve of her belly, the soft insides of her thighs, all the way down to her toes and back again.

By the time he finished, she trembled uncontrollably, her skin aflame with every whisper, the fiery ache between her legs a torment. Tears swelled her eyes. It wasn't supposed to be like this. She'd wanted to keep in control. But this was beyond control. He made her ache and burn and thirst for things she hadn't allowed herself to want since . . . since forever.

Things like love. Affection. Surrender. The other half of herself she'd always denied.

He sucked one nipple in deep, and she cried out. His tongue felt so good, her nipple so fat and hard in his mouth. Tension built rapidly inside her, and the bindings only intensified the pleasure. And when he nudged her legs apart and caressed one light finger over her, sultry storm light flashed through her veins and she shuddered and cried and let the pleasure take her.

After what seemed like minutes, the shocks subsided, and she gasped for breath, her flesh tingling. Her heart ached, too, and she tried to brush it aside. *Don't be stupid. It's just sex. The man brings you to one orgasm and you think it means he gives a shit.*

But the warmth deep in her soul couldn't be denied.

He licked his way down her body, tasting her, and pushed her legs up to bite into the backs of her thighs, growling as he did so. She gasped, aroused again by his passion.

And he coaxed her legs apart and kissed her there, just a feather-light brush of his lips. He stroked her with his tongue, teasing her sensitive bud out of hiding and tormenting it until she moaned. And then, when she thought she couldn't take any more, he circled her entrance with a fingertip and slid his big finger in deep.

She writhed, pleasure breathless, wanting to feel him everywhere. She was so wet, his finger slid right in. To have any part of him inside her felt so damn good, and to have him do it while she was tied up and helpless was the sexiest thing she'd ever experienced. His tongue teased her straining nub, and he added a second finger, pushing them in and out. Preparing her. She gasped as he stretched her. She recalled his big heavy cock, straining hot in her hands, and shivered in delightful anticipation. She wanted him to open her, claim her, make her tight hot spaces his forever . . .

Oh, shit. His fingertips brushed the sensitive spot deep inside her, and she gasped in forbidden pleasure that threatened to undo her. "Lune. I'm going to come. Make love to me. Please."

She felt him smile, and he eased his fingers from her, a caress that made her flesh throb, frustrated. She wanted him to fill her now. He stood over her, dark and massive, and deliberately undressed, showing off for her, peeling the dark leather from his neat hips and hard ass and long muscular thighs until he was naked in silvery moonlight. He sparkled, desire glimmering over his skin. His cock jutted, a drop of moisture already shining. Her eyes ached. He was magnificent.

Slowly, he climbed up her body on all fours, hot sparks shedding from his wings to caress her. She trembled, deeply aware of his heat-blue gaze raking over her, the flush sweeping her skin.

He nudged his hips between her thighs, and trailed his glittering hair over her flank. "Shall I untie you, beauty?" he whispered. "Or should I take you like this?"

Her breath hitched. "Would you untie me, if I asked?"

He shifted his hips so his hot silky cock slid along her wet flesh. When she groaned and pressed against him, his wicked little grin weakened her will. "You'll just have to trust me, Morgan. Do you want me to untie you?"

Crimson desire misted her vision, but fear spiked cold. *Yes. Please, God, just let me out of here before I crumble . . .* But she clamped tight on her panicked nerves. "No. Don't. I don't want to be afraid. I want you like this."

Lune took her mouth in a heated kiss that dizzied her. "I want you any way I can have you," he growled, and he found her entrance with a swift nudge and pushed inside.

She shuddered, her flesh clenching around him. Hot, perfect. And so hard, like satin-coated iron. His sultry flavor filled her mouth, his fiery kiss tortured her lips. She fought to relax, to let him take her deeper. But it wasn't just his flesh becoming part of her. She felt him in her deepest secret places. In her soul, where for so long she'd been cold and alone.

Her heart ripped raw, vulnerable. "I can't. I want to, but I can't . . ."

"You can." His blue eyes burned dark, but he didn't move inside her. He just caressed her hair and kissed her, hot, rich with angelscent, so tender that her heart broke open all over again.

Tears lit flames in her eyes. Her angel was far bolder than she. He didn't shrink away from the edge. He just jumped, and trusted he wouldn't hit the ground.

Her heart teetered, and fell. And she sighed, and kissed him deeper, and wrapped her thigh around his hips, welcoming him.

He shuddered, pushing deeper inside her, muscles clenching in restraint in his arms and thighs. When she moaned in hot delight, he slid his hand under her bottom and pulled her to him, seating himself fully at last.

So hot. So full. She strained against her bonds, her body lit aflame. And then he moved, and the smooth friction exploded inside her like fireworks. Her flesh ached, so deep that she cried out, shuddering. Nothing had ever felt so good.

He groaned, moving a little further with each stroke. "Heaven, Morgan. You're perfect."

She arched her back, falling into him. God, he felt so good inside her. Her breasts rubbed his chest. His sparks tingled over her skin. His hair tumbled in her face, across her lips, hot and sweet and silky like the part of him that was inside her. Her tied fists clenched, frantic. She wanted to touch him, grab his feathers, rub her palms over his straining muscles as he pleasured her. But she wanted to stay like this, too, and let him love her until she died.

He wrapped one arm around her waist, pulling her to him on a flick of wings. Her muscles clenched in fiery delight, drawing him on, pulsing around him. He bent to take her nipple in his mouth, and she cried out as tension pulled a hot wire from her aching breast straight to her core. He sucked, drawing her tighter, hotter, harder. The angle made his cock rub against that secret spot in her flesh, grinding rich pleasure deep inside her with every thrust, and when he growled and bit her nipple hungrily, her muscles spasmed and she broke apart.

Lightning struck her center and speared outwards, rich neon light along her nerves. Harder than before, hotter, until stars flashed in her eyes and she panted, dizzy with insane pleasure.

Lune rode it with her, sweat sliding between them, holding her body tightly to feel her every clench and shudder, and his cock swelled ever harder inside her as he drank in her pleasure and swallowed it with a growl. His lips burned hers, hungry. "Morgan. You're beautiful."

When the shocks faded, she struggled for breath, her blood afire. His kiss made her drunk and dizzy, and her flesh sparked electric, wanting more. She wasn't done. She still wanted him. Wanted total surrender. "More of you, Lune. Make me come again. I need you."

He laughed, breathless. "You ask too much, woman. I can't do this much longer." His damp hair caressed her face, delicious with his golden scent. He slid his hand between them to stroke her. Her little bud swelled under his caress, torturing her. He groaned into her mouth at the feel of her. "I love that. You're so hard there. So eager for me."

She couldn't talk, only moan helplessly. He kissed her mouth urgently, flexing to fuck her ever deeper and harder and hotter. Another orgasm hit her, shattering, and this time he groaned her name and came after her, a sizzling burst of heat, his flesh shuddering and pulsing so deep inside her she couldn't breathe.

Heat glimmered over them, heavenblue. He crushed his mouth to hers, swallowing the last of her cries with his own, and while she was still dizzy with pleasure, he untied her hands with a smoking flash of glory and crushed her to him like he'd never let go.

She murmured against his chest, dazed. His heart beat swift and hard against her cheek. His cock still slicked hot inside her, his hair falling over her face, his dark wings shimmering under the moon, and she never wanted him to move.

But he would, of course. And then she'd be alone again. Unless . . .

She sucked in a breath, trying to find her lost voice. "Lune . . ."

CHAPTER 32

"Mmm." Lune tried to breathe, but air wouldn't come. His pulse still raced. His flesh still tingled deep. His wings still flamed, ablaze in sweet delight, and that weak, dizzying heat that swallowed his limbs and wouldn't let go was surely blood, streaming from his savaged heart.

At last, he gulped a lungful of Morgan-scented air, and it floored him all over again. Heaven, she was amazing. So far above everything he'd dreamed. Her kiss made his veins sing like glory, her delicate skin against his a fragrant miracle, her soft wet flesh surrounding his the most insane pleasure he'd felt in three thousand years. And when she came on him . . . His cock twitched in hungry memory. He'd nearly lost it right then.

Hell, he'd nearly lost it the moment he'd slid inside her. Her eyes aglow, that lovely hair loose, the moonlight caressing her beautiful curves . . . And holding her in his arms like this, still inside her, her limbs lazy with pleasure and their mingled scents coating her skin like warm honey, made him want her again.

His throat swelled. Heaven had gifted her to him, and that miracle of mercy still rocked him giddy. But her gift to him was so much greater.

He didn't deserve it. Didn't deserve her. But now she was his, and he'd never leave her. Never let her out of his sight. Spend the rest of eternity proving he was worthy.

"Lune." She pressed her cheek to his chest, damp.

His pulse jumped. Shit. Tears? Had he hurt her? He wanted to smack his stupid head into the wall. Already he'd fucked up. He was used to leaving before he had the chance. How was he supposed to fix this?

She tilted her chin up, her eyes still glazed bright with their love but shadowed deep inside. "Did . . . did you like me?"

"Huh?" His pleasure-addled brain couldn't make sense of it.

"You know. Was it . . ." She flushed. "I know I'm not very—"

He stopped her with a kiss. "Silence," he growled, nipping at her lip. "You *are* very. Any more *very* and I'd be dead."

She laughed, guarded. "You're sweet. But you don't have to say things you don't mean."

Anger fired his nerves, a burning echo of their pleasure. Not at her, but at the ungrateful, careless assholes—lovers? shit— who'd made her feel that way. "Things I don't mean? Heaven, Morgan, I've dreamed about you every minute since I saw you, and you know what? Compared to the real thing, my imagination sucks."

Her eyes glowed, smoky. "Really?"

"Yes, really." His wings twitched, hungry. She was so sexy, her hair spread on his chest, her luscious breasts pressed against him in sweat. Her scent grabbed him by the balls and wouldn't let go, and he growled and rolled onto his back with her atop him. His dick hardened, still inside her. It hurt, but he didn't care. Her trembling slickness slid on him as he swelled, a deep pleasure that made him groan. "Shall I prove it to you?"

She gasped, and giggled. "Whoa. That was fast. Some weird angel mojo?"

He gritted his teeth. "No. You're just the sexiest woman alive . . . oh, fuck." Damn, it was hard to talk with his cock inside her. He wanted to crush her, wrap that gorgeous hair in his fist, hold her down and tease her mercilessly, pleasure her with mouth, fingers, feathers, until she begged him to fuck her or she'd die.

But not now. Not yet. Sweat prickled his skin, the effort of holding back. She needed affection, safety, reassurance that he wouldn't leave her now. Not the raw and bleeding edge of his desire.

But she was so tight and smooth and hot . . . he just had to move. He thrust upwards, into her warm depths, and already his balls stung hard for release. She moaned, that sexy little sound that turned him on. God, he loved this. Loved the sounds she made, the way her nipples jutted, the dark flush in her skin as her pleasure rose . . .

He swooped to his knees, settling her astride his lap, and impaled her with a powerful thrust, all the way in. "Ride me."

Her head fell back, her rose pink lips parting, a sigh of pleasure. He gripped her sweet ass as she moved, and tasted her breasts, those swollen pink nipples hard and springy on his tongue. She gasped, clutched his hair, dragged him close. Her flesh squeezed him, that pulsing rhythm he strove for. "Oh, God, Lune," she gasped. "I'm coming again!"

Dimly he registered her surprise. Like she wasn't used to four orgasms in one session. He reminded himself to hunt down her former lovers and beat the losers senseless for neglecting her, and then all rational thoughts flashburned to hot desire as she moved faster and harder and her cries rose to a scream as she let herself go.

Heaven's bleeding grace, she's beautiful.

Heat exploded in his balls, and his muscles jerked and he spent himself as deep inside her as he could go, the aftershocks of her orgasm still clenching his rock-hard cock. He gasped, rocked to the core, his vision blurring as the pleasure wrung him dry.

Her hair spilled in a fragrant wash on his shoulder as she collapsed against him, and he held her, dazed. How in heaven had he ever held it together the first time she came on him? She was too much. Too wonderful. Too perfect.

He crushed her to him, kissing her hair, and words swelled in his throat, so compelling and terrifying, he gulped. Insane, beautiful words like *love* and *forever.* The kind of words that would frighten her away if he said them too soon.

He took a steadying breath. "Morgan—"

Above him, glass shattered.

His raw-cut nerves jerked, and on pure screaming reflex, he dragged his wings back and dived.

He hit the loft's wooden floor, rolling with Morgan in his arms, and half of hell poured down on the bed.

Broken glass rained from the skylight. A gaggle of furywraiths screeched, their leathery skin afire. They slashed hungry claws at the cushions, straining for skin and flesh. Six of them, each as big as a man, deformed necks curling birdlike, arms and legs blackened like burned toast and wiry with muscle. Sticky black batlike wings sprouted from their shoulders, flapping in ashen stink.

The furywraiths spread out, menacing, their beady red eyes shining with malice. Acid splashed from their gnashing beaks, setting the bed alight in the blessed patch where Lune and Morgan had lain.

Were they Vorvian's hellscum? Lune could smell greedy demon breath on the wraiths' skin. It didn't smell like Vorvian. But their hellspelled wrath spilled unholy fire into his blood. He should never have brought her back here.

Then again, he hadn't expected her to survive the curse.

Lune leapt up, dragging Morgan behind him. She yelled, teetering over the loft's edge, but he held her arm fast, wings astretch to hold their balance.

"Let me go!" She fought, the wraiths' spellfury staining her eyes black, and she curled a cruel lip and sank her teeth into his wrist. He held on. The furywraiths' stink was making her angry, irrational. When he killed the skanky fuckers, she'd be free.

Lune wished his sword into his free hand—the wrong hand—and the creatures hissed and fell back, shielding their eyes from the dazzling blue flame. His mind raced, calculating distances, trajectories, the force he'd need to drop them. One ducked its ugly head and struck for Morgan's belly, and Lune slashed its legs off in a hail of stinking black blood. "Get away from her, hellshit."

But danger stung his feathers hot. Fuck. Fighting left-handed—and naked—wasn't ideal. But he couldn't let go of her. It was twelve feet to the floor. If he dropped her, she'd break.

The crippled wraith scratched for his face, its yellow talons dripping with neon-green wrathpoison. Its five friends cackled and closed in. Three dived for Morgan at once, and Lune leapt backwards, landing on the edge on his toes. Morgan shrieked and dangled. He cursed, muscles jerking. He could flash out.

They'd only chase him. He couldn't face six at once with a sword, not in such a small space, not with Morgan to protect. But he had to kill them all.

The hellspawn tilted crafty eyes at each other. They grinned. And all six of them leapt into the air, the razor-beaked points of a six-pointed star, and dived for Morgan at once.

CHAPTER 33

Demon-spelled fury fogged Lune's mind scarlet, blotting out reason and syllables until he could only think one thing. *No. Must protect. Must keep safe.*

He flung Morgan over his head, sending her flying onto the cushions. The furywraiths squealed, trying to change trajectory to avoid his scything blade. One fell, headless. Another exploded in burning flesh as he stabbed it through the heart. He somersaulted and flung his sword at a third, slicing its twisting body in two mid-air. And then he landed in a fighting crouch on the hardwood loft floor, and flung his palms out with a frantic prayer to heaven, the first angelspell that flew to his mind.

Grace. Keep them away from her. Bring them to me. Now.

Blue light flashed from his sigil, welling brighter, a blessed flash of euphoria. Ash sizzled like acid rain, and fell, the wraiths' wrathspells dissolving. And the three cackling creatures poised to strike over Morgan's huddled form halted, and curled their long birdlike necks towards Lune, infatuation gleaming on their gnarled black faces.

* * *

On the bed, Morgan screamed in alien fury, and curled her arms over her head, waiting for the hell-things to rip their beaks into her flesh.

They didn't. And suddenly her anger evaporated, the spell washing from her body like hot storm water.

Her heart thumping, she let her hands drop.

Lune crouched, blue light welling from his outstretched palms, a sweet crooning sound low in his throat that raised goose bumps on her arms. The three demon-things muttered and writhed their skinny necks, their shiny red gazes fixed on him.

"Here, pet. Come to Lune." Lune beckoned, midnight wings stretching in invitation. The creatures warbled, affectionate, and hopped towards him, all their fury drained away.

Morgan shivered, strange euphoria like a hot shower over her skin. She felt relaxed. Calm. Her head clear, her mind lucid. She rubbed her cheek in the cushions, so wonderfully warm and comforting, and yawned, delightfully sleepy. She wanted to take a nap right here. Curl up in Lune's arms and doze off with him kissing her hair . . .

The creatures sidled up to him, rubbing their heads against his wrists like big leathery cats. He stroked one, slipping loving fingers around its neck, and crunched his hissing fist tight.

Snap. The thing's neck broke, and it crumpled and sighed and died.

Morgan smiled, lazy. Mmm. Such a sweet lover. She'd never felt anything like it. Maybe if she crawled over there, he'd touch her, too.

The remaining two wraiths didn't even blink. They purred and nestled into his night-dark feathers. Lune petted them, running his palms over their sleek heads before he jammed his thumbs into their eyeballs and broke their necks.

The mesmerizing blue glow faded. Lune flung the broken bodies aside with a curse and a hiss of burning flesh, and glided to his feet.

Morgan jumped to her knees, stung. Her wits slammed back into her head like a horrid back draft, sucking the breath from her lungs and setting it afire.

He'd loved those monsters to death. Seduced them to murder

with warm caresses. They'd believed he'd do them no harm, and he'd lured them to him and finished them off.

Lune landed on his knees in the cushions and pulled her into his embrace. "You okay? Did they touch you?"

He kissed her hair, and his heartbeat thudded against her naked breasts. The malicious memory of her desire struck her cold, and she shivered and pushed him away.

His blue eyes burned. "Sorry, I didn't . . . what is it?"

Her voice dried to a croak. Her nerves screamed, betrayed, slicing her newfound peace to shreds. She had to know. "Lune . . . how did you do that?"

Lune stared. "What?"

"That thing. That spell." Her gaze stabbed him like demonblades.

His mind blotted, confused. "That? It's just a compulsion. A calming spell. There were too many, I couldn't fight them all."

She hugged a cushion, like a shield. "I felt it. It was horrible. I wanted to . . ." Her pretty lips trembled. "I wanted to crawl over to you and die."

Broken glass jeweled her hair. He wanted to brush it away, but she looked so . . . distant. Unforgiving. Scared, all over again. "I'm sorry. I didn't mean it for you, love. They're just hellspawn. What does it matter?"

"It matters!" Her voice ripped, tense. "I thought we were real, Lune. I thought what I felt was real!"

His blood spiked cold. "What? Of course it's real! I don't get it."

"Oh, God." Her face paled, and she clutched her cushion tightly, bending over as though her stomach cramped. "Oh, dear God. Lune, tell me you didn't do that to me. Tell me you didn't use that spell on me to make me fall for you. I couldn't bear it. Please. For heaven's sake."

"Of course I never . . ." Lune's voice withered. His heart teetered over a long, cold cliff, and fell. "Oh, shit."

And Morgan's beautiful amber eyes drained to empty gray.

CHAPTER 34

Lune's guts twisted, burning like hellfire, and his heart screamed. God, he wanted to lie. He'd never wanted any sin harder.

But he couldn't. Not to Morgan. She deserved the undiluted truth, even if she hated him forever.

"When?" Her voice scraped, mechanical, a dull echo of the golden tones that had hypnotized him.

His throat constricted, trying to keep the words inside, but he forced them out. "The first time we met, in the morgue. I spelled you to stop you shooting me again. To calm you down so you'd talk to me. That's all."

"That's all?" Her gaze lasered sharp. "How the fuck is that all, Lune? You *held* me. We *kissed*." She scrambled backwards off the bed, clutching the cushion in both arms to hide herself. "You tricked me. You made me want you! How could you do that?"

"I didn't mean it that way!" Heaven, what a shitty excuse. "It's just a euphoria spell. People are afraid of us, it's how we get them to listen. I didn't know it would do that!" Guilt seared his bones like brimstone. No, he hadn't known for sure. But he'd let her kiss him. Let her melt into his arms. Enjoyed it.

"And what about after that? You touched me. God, I let you . . . Everything we've done was a lie!"

"No!" His guts crawled, salty, and he nearly retched. He scrambled to the floor at her feet, and the disappointment in her eyes stabbed him cold. "Look at me. Look into my eyes and tell me I'm lying now. I love you, Morgan. I'll always love you."

His throat swelled tight, but satisfaction thrilled him. There. Let the fucking sky fall. He didn't care. Surely she'd understand.

But despair shone pale on her face. "I don't believe you."

A cruel fist of agony crushed his heart. Words were useless. Petty. Meaningless.

Morgan blinked helpless tears. "How can I believe you? How can I ever trust you now?"

"Because it's the truth!" Desperation roughened his voice. Lousy fucking reason. But he'd no better one. He longed to kiss her hands, beg her to forgive him for all the stupid things he'd said and done. But it'd only make it worse.

Her ugly laugh hacked his nerves ragged. "Right. Sure. God, I'm such an *idiot*." She grabbed his shirt and scrabbled it over her head. It reached to mid-thigh, and she tugged it viciously around her hips. She yanked her glorious hair back, defiant, and her blazing gaze hit him head-on with all the force of her rage and disgust. "You're a hundred times worse than Vorvian, you know that? At least he's got the class to admit it when he's caught in a lie."

"Morgan—"

"I don't want to hear it!" Her voice rose to a shriek. With an effort, she calmed herself, breathing deep, and when she spoke again, her tone licked frosty. "Don't say anything else, okay? Just let me down, please."

Woodenly, he took her hand. She flinched at his touch, and it slashed him raw. He lighted her down to the apartment floor. His wings ached, and he longed to pull her into his arms, but he just set her gently on her feet and stepped away, bereft.

"Thanks." She stalked to the couch and tugged her jeans on, her mouth set tight. She wouldn't look at him. Tears glimmered, but she didn't let them fall.

She was so broken. So heart sore. He'd hurt her more than he'd ever imagined he could. "Morgan, please—"

"I'm leaving now." Her disdain bit his heart like poison. "I don't want you to follow me. Don't come to my place. Don't call me. I don't want to see you again. Your little game is over, angel. I hope you had fun."

She strode to the door and let herself out, and deep inside him, something wild and heartsick screamed in agony.

But all he could do was watch her walk away.

CHAPTER 35

In the bright-lit lobby, Morgan stumbled, tears blinding her.

Her throat ached to scream. Her stomach twisted like barbed wire, and she stabbed her thumb at the elevator button, desperate. *Don't let him follow me. Don't let him see me.* Her legs shook, weak. Thank God this wasn't a walk-up, or she'd never make it to the bottom.

Shame and loss jabbed her heart like a scorpion's sting. She'd been so stupid. She'd trusted him—trusted an angel, for fuck's sake—and it had brought her only pain. To think she'd believed it was real, the way she felt, the connection they'd forged over blood and heartache, the shivering delight of his touch, the glory in her soul when he looked at her.

Something so good could never be real.

Her mind stumbled and fell, tumbling over and over until it hit bottom, a cold midnight lake of truth and bitterness. Her heart was false, weak, not to be trusted. Trust brought only pain. Better to stay in the dark, where she couldn't be hurt.

To think she'd believed that for a few sweet moments, she'd turned her face to the light.

The elevator slid open, and she walked unsteadily in. Her reflection glared at her from the gleaming metal wall, muddled and distorted. Her eyes burned. The shirt she wore still smelled

of him, his angel-fire scent an accusation. Frantically she wiped
at her skin, her face, her arms, her belly. She wanted to rake her
nails over it, strip naked, get him off her.

The elevator lurched to a halt, and she banged her head back
against the wall, trying to clear her head, inject some rationality.
*Don't overreact. He was just some guy. He was gorgeous and
charming, and the sex was great, but you made a mistake. So
live with it. Forget him, and go back to your normal life. You're
a big girl.*

But the irrational part of her mind screamed and beat its fists
like a toddler throwing a tantrum, refusing to be silent. *Not just
some guy. Not just sex. We made love.*

She sniffled, and wiped her hair back, swallowing. Yeah.
Sure. In a spell-drunk haze. The bastard lied, and she'd fallen
for it. *That'll teach me to lose the plot. Next time some hot guy
tells you a story about needing you to save the world? Tell him
he's full of shit and walk away.*

She walked out into the lobby, fighting unsteady legs. Crumbling plaster walls loomed, threatening, spray painted with ugly
tags. A red New Anarchy symbol splashed like a bloodstain.
The warm floor slipped under her bare feet. In the corner, a
hobo sprawled insensible in a dirty black duster, whiskey-
stained drool trickling from his unshaven chin.

Outside, through the barred window, the street flashed with
neon rainbows, dark and dangerous. The park loomed, a threatening dark tangle, backlit by hellish bonfires that danced and
spat shadows. A gunshot cracked, glass shattered, people
shouted.

She shivered, tugging Lune's shirt closer and tucking it into
her jeans. Four in the morning in lawless Harlem. Sick freak
happy hour. She licked parched lips, still swollen from kissing.
Fatigue tore at her, and a deep ache still burned in her muscles.
She'd wrapped her legs around him, strained her arms trying to
touch him, clenched her inner muscles to soreness around his
hot flesh as he loved her . . .

She shivered, fire and ice, and pushed the images away. Back
to normal. Which meant, back to the lab. Manhattan virus was
real. She'd seen it for herself, demon or no demon. People were
dying. She'd no time for self-pity.

But she was alone. She didn't have her knife, or even her

capsicum spray. She wasn't even wearing shoes. On the subway at 4:00 a.m., she'd be fair game for any tweaked-out loser who took a fancy to her. Girls died screaming that way.

Determination forged icy steel in her spine. She was tough. She'd killed zombies and hellspawn. Resisted a demon. Conquered a lying angel's spells. No way would she let some limp-dick gangsters spoil her night.

She edged over to the hobo, who snored and muttered, his dark hair lank and greasy. Still paralytic. Swiftly, she tugged his coat aside and felt for a weapon. No ankle holster. Nothing on his flanks. No . . . wait. Her fingertips brushed metal at the back of his belt. She wrapped her fingers around the grip and yanked it out.

Nine millimeter, laser sights, spring-locked trigger. With trembling fingers, she ejected the round and popped the magazine. Hollow points, only a couple of shots missing. She sighted, the laser buzzing to life, and a quivering green spot drilled the wall. She breathed, steadying her aim. Squeezed the trigger experimentally.

Click. Hair-trigger. Ugly. *Stupid thing to be stuffing down your pants, friend. Lucky you didn't blow your own drug-sick ass off.*

She reloaded, cocked and flicked the safety on, and with the weapon steady in her hand, her courage polished bright. She had no intention of stuffing it down her pants. She'd carry it in her hand, and if any dumb-ass god-sick gangboy with a hard-on decided she was his lucky night, he'd learn the hard way what it meant to mess with her. And if demons attacked her again . . . well, she'd just have to deal.

Because she'd learned her lesson. *Trust no one but yourself.* And Morgan Sterling, MD, wouldn't pray for deliverance. Not from an angel. Not from anyone.

Morgan flexed tense fingers around the pistol's grip, and strode out into the street.

Lune's muscles shuddered, and he bit back a scream. Moonlight slashed in the broken skylight, accusing him, and glory scorched living warning through his veins. *Keep it real. Keep it frosty. What's done is done. Don't let her get to you.*

But it didn't soothe. Didn't heal. Didn't fix what he'd done.

Stiffly, he swooped to his loft. Fuck, the place still smelled of her, that honeyed woman scent he adored. The burned cushions still dipped from her weight, and a curling strand of her hair glimmered dark. He tugged his pants on, roughly, almost tearing the leather. He left the breastplate where it was. No point going after her. She'd only run from him.

The irony was fucking laughable. He'd finally proven to himself he could keep her safe, and now she wouldn't let him. He loved her, and he'd made her hate him.

Nice work, Lune. Well thought out. You fucking idiot.

He dived down and landed with a thump in front of the dresser. Whiskey. Now. It took a lot of alcohol to feel anything. He'd drunk himself a little crazy that night with Jadzia. How far away that seemed. How . . . insignificant.

He poured a glass of Glenlivet, his fingers slipping on the bottle, and drank it down straight up. The harsh liquid burned his already stinging throat. No matter. No more than he deserved.

He downed another, his stomach slimy with self-hatred that squirmed and bit like a serpent. *Vorvian was right, shithead. Eleanor didn't love you. How could she, when you couldn't give her a life? And Morgan, holy Jesus, as if a glorious fire goddess like Morgan would ever want anything you've got.*

He slumped against the wall, his wings crushing, and slammed his skull into the wood, twice. Heaven, he wanted oblivion. The ache in his heart to smother. The stupid hateful voices in his head to die in brutal silence. The torment of her accusing eyes to fade away, just for a few moments.

The hateworm in his guts sniggered. *But it'll never fade, will it? You broke her. It's your fault. She'll never stop haunting you.*

Lune gritted his teeth. He'd see her always, seared into his heart like he'd looked too long into the sun and blinded himself.

Fuck the glass. He swigged from the bottle, draining half of it. His vision wobbled. At last, a reaction. He chugged the rest, whiskey trickling on his chin, and flung the bottle away to smash on the floor. His balance blurred, and in dark satisfaction he fumbled on the dresser for another bottle.

In his pocket, his phone rang.

He ignored it, ripping the wrapper from the screw top and twisting it open. Another bottle should do it. Getting drunk was vile. But he felt vile. Worse than flesh. Dirt. He'd drink himself to darkness, and then tomorrow, he'd wake up and deal.

Tomorrow.

The phone rang out. A second later, it rang again.

Persistent motherfucker. Lune took a swallow, and fumbled the phone out. Dash was calling. That was nice. "Dash, what the fuck . . ." He laughed, and stifled it with another mouthful. *Fuck her and get it over with,* Dash said. Wow. That worked so well.

"Lune? What the hell's wrong with you?" A scuffle in the background, shouts, the silky song of sirens.

"Nothing, man." Lune smothered another laugh. "Really. It's all good. Never been better."

"Whatever. Look, I've been meaning to tell y— motherfucker!" Steel clashed, a splat of bodies. "Shit. Sorry. Look, I've been trying to tell you. The Prince of Poison. It's—"

"Vorvian. Yeah, I know. I saw him." Lune's voice echoed in his own ears, dull. Whiskey burned his mouth sour. "He . . . Fuck. It doesn't matter."

"Is everything okay?" Soft, sharp with concern.

"No. Yes. I mean . . ."

"Talk to me, Lune. Is Morgan—"

"She's gone, Dash." Lune's eyes burned. "Vorvian got away. I fucked it. She's gone."

Dash sucked in a breath. "Jesus. Okay. Look, don't sweat it, dude. Once this is over we'll track the skanky hellshit down together and rip his guts out. Right?"

"Sure. Whatever."

"I mean it, kid. It's not your fault and I'll tell 'em so. If we go down, we all go down together."

Lune bit down a scream. He didn't want forgiveness, or sympathy. Just pain, guilt, oblivion. "It's really not—"

"Listen, I appreciate you're preoccupied, but we could really use you down here. This bloodfest is getting hairy. Ugly hell-spawn crawling down our throats. You up?"

Lune tilted his head back to chug more whiskey, and his guts wriggled, protesting the misuse. Fatigue ached his limbs. His fingers shook, weak. His blood burned sluggish. The alcohol sloshed in his wits, blurring dreams with cold reality, and glory sparked weakly along his nerves, shedding no warmth. He'd never felt less like fighting.

So fuck it, then. Go down screaming. Why wait? What's left to live for?

Crazy laughter rocked him, and he emptied the bottle and dropped it to smash at his feet. "Sure, Dash. What the hell. Save some of those sick motherfuckers for me."

He ended, and stuffed the phone into his pocket. Dived unsteadily for his loft, dug out a fresh shirt and buckled on his silver. His fingers fumbled, drunk and thick on the leather.

Honey scent seduced his nostrils, and the bittersweet memory of Morgan tortured him. Coaxing his buckles open, her fingertips gliding over his chest . . .

His skin burned, desire and loss. She was gone. Alone. She'd never trust him to protect her. And without protection, she'd die alone.

Better start living with it.

Ruthless, Lune yanked the last strap tight, and flashed out.

Crouched in shadow beside the gleaming glass wall of a corporate lobby, Dashiel cursed, raw. Lune sounded all fucked up. If Vorvian had taken Morgan . . .

Shit. Lune was a good kid with rotten luck, and Morgan seemed like a decent woman. Life sucked.

But bigger fish to batter right now.

He adjusted his sword grip, sweaty hair sticking to his neck. The traffic barriers cast moonlit shadows on the concrete sidewalk, and heat shimmered thick with the stink of gore. The Prince of Blood's fucked-up sacrifice party was somewhere near, and the place streamed with sniggering hellspawn, hungry for a bite.

Speaking of which . . . A shuffle from behind a shuttered-up newsstand pricked his ears sharp. Two fat imps hunkered, banging their knuckles like red-skinned apes. Their sharp teeth flashed under scything helicopter searchlights from above, and they swung spiked chains in circles, threatening.

Hot breeze dragged Dash's hair back, the thud of the blades pumping his pulse harder. He flung himself horizontal, a stinging flash of glory dazzling from his palm. The red apes shrieked, blood spilling from their eyes. He hacked them apart with twin slices of his sword and a blistering curse.

He landed, flaring his wings to a halt beside the glass lobby wall as the helicopter banked away. Glory fired his blood, a crimson seduction he couldn't resist. It licked his throat with delicious thirst for slaughter, and his muscles exulted, quivering.

Heaven help him, but he loved it. Better than sex, or any weak human drug. All the mad-sweet impulses of fight and fuck and die, sprinting in his veins, pumping through his flesh, hot and glorious. His senses flashed bright, sharpened to raw predator's instinct. He sniffed the air, hungry, as he unlocked the revolving door with a silvery flash of magic and stole through in search of prey. Only more death could release him. Only slaughter filled the screaming hole where his soul once lay . . .

A faint rustle stung his hypersensitive ears, and he whirled and struck.

Japheth parried, two-handed, steel clashing crosswise. *Fuck.* Dash checked his counterattack, inches from the kill. "Jesus," he panted, struggling for control. "Watch who you creep up on."

But Japheth just grinned, savage, and flung Dash backwards, his blade point driving unerringly for Dash's throat.

Japheth held his sword steady, determination icing his veins. Holy steel could kill an angel, just as easily as a demon's blade. One flick of his wrist, and it'd be done.

Dash backed up against the shiny steel wall, his feathers flaming darkly. "Watch it, kid—"

"Shut up." Japheth steadied his sword arm, a cold flash of control, but the hot darkness clogged his feathers, crept inside his armor, licked him like a hungry demon lover. He wanted to hide, curl up in cold comforting denial and pretend this wasn't happening.

Just like he pretended hunger and lust and desire didn't happen. It was easier that way. Chilly. Unaffected. Remote.

But the guilt swelling inside him wasn't chilly. It scorched like acid, melting through his ice-walled facade until it reached his heart and gorged itself, and he wanted to scream his culpability to heaven.

But heaven already knew.

Dash glared, poisonous, but didn't strike back. "What the fuck are you doing?"

"I can't do this anymore." Japheth's hand trembled. "I can't stay here. It's killing me. I have to get home."

"What the fuck's that got to do with—" Dash's face darkened. "Fuck me raw. Michael put you up to this, didn't he? I told you to stay the hell away from him."

Japheth flushed, bitter. Like resisting had made any difference. "I'm sorry, Dash. I have to do this."

"Why?" Dash demanded. He vanished his sword, a snap of angry blue sparks. He could have flashed out. He didn't. "Because he said so? Kill me and get redeemed? What's wrong with this picture, Jae?"

"You're wasting your breath."

"Yeah, maybe I am. You've got a big fat blind spot, kid, and it's shaped like a wiseass archangel who can't keep his dick in his pants. Can't you see how he plays you? Since when did slaughter win redemption?"

Japheth laughed, acidic. "That's just beautiful, coming from you."

"That's different." Dash's tone was even. Calm. At ease with his addiction.

"The hell it is!" Japheth's sword twitched, slicing an angry crimson line along Dash's neck. "We all kill demons, don't we? For heaven's glory? How is this any worse?"

"Demons are evil. They deserve to die."

"Do they?" Japheth wristed sweaty hair from his forehead, shaking. "What does *evil* mean anyway? We kill them, they kill us. What's the difference?"

"The difference is that we give a fuck whether it's right or wrong! Redemption is in the heart, Jae. Not in a list of rules."

Japheth stared up into Dash's burning eyes, and the last safe lick of frost over his heart melted.

Rage lit like magnesium. He slammed Dash hard against the wall, jabbing the blade point under his chin. "You think so, huh? After you've spent the last two thousand years acting like a bloodthirsty whore? Forgive me if I don't believe you."

"I know it's so." Dash gritted his teeth, the blade slicing

sharp. "Wanna go back upstairs? You've gotta forgive yourself for what you've done."

"Right. That easy, is it?"

"No one said it w—"

"Screw you, okay?" Sweat trickled from Jae's hair, and he shook it away angrily. "If it's so damned simple, why don't you just flit back off to heaven whenever you f—"

"Because I'll never forgive myself!"

Japheth's breath drained cold.

"Okay?" Dash's dark eyes flamed scarlet with shame. "I can't forgive the things I've done, or the way I feel. I've drowned my soul in blood and screams, and it felt so fucking good that I deserve to burn in hell. Forever."

Guilt and sorrow scorched Japheth's heart, a raging fire he couldn't quench. He tried to pray, but the acid pain of a lie clawed his lungs, and the words dissolved into bitter ash in his throat.

Dash didn't give him the mercy of looking away. "I'll never be redeemed. I know that. I'm too far gone."

Jae's eyes ached. God, he wanted to stab, bleed, get this over with. He wanted to spring to wings and flee. "Dash—"

"But you aren't." Dash gazed down at him, inches away like a lover but infinitely more powerful. "You made a mistake, and Michael smacked you down for it. But you've got a good heart, Jae. Don't let him spoil it. Don't fall so far you can't ever climb back." His wings flashed a gold-glittered challenge. "Now. Either kill me, and get it over with. Or get your glory on, golden boy. We've got demons to hunt."

Japheth clamped cruel teeth, an agony of decision. Holy fire tingled sweet seduction in his blood, and his fingers tightened on his sword.

CHAPTER 36

Morgan blinked, and shook herself from a treacherous doze.

Whoa. She teetered on her stool, the laboratory desk banging into her elbows. The digitally enhanced microscope image came into focus, and she scrabbled to stop her glass eyedropper slipping from her hand.

Shit. How long had she been drifting? The wall clock said *too long*. Nearly six in the morning, the fluorescent lights glaring gritty in her eyes. She'd been here for an hour, testing, making up slides, observing cellular mutations and deaths. The yellow infectious wastebin on her desk was packed with discarded samples, and a hot ache stabbed behind her eyes with ferocious vengeance she felt sure had only begun.

Nothing yet. But she had to keep trying.

She took a few deep breaths, trying to wake up. A concave glass sample dish still sat in the viewing slot, an infected skin sample. She dipped a clean dropper in her solution, the digital measuring scanner sucking up a precise quantity, and she bent to the stereoscopic viewer and delicately slotted the dropper's point under the view screen.

Her tired hand spasmed, and the dropper broke with a crack.

Glass stabbed. She yelped, yanking her stinging hand back.

Blood sprayed from the cut. A tiny drop landed on the dish, and almost imperceptibly, it glowed.

Morgan gaped. Smoke wisped from the glass, so tiny she could barely see.

Holy shit on toast. She peered at the screen, her throat tight. The blood had barely touched the edge of the cellular growth. But the infected cells were disintegrating . . .

No. She gulped. They were *healing.* Regenerating. The corruption was reversing, the angry scarlet skin cells reverting to their original, pale, lenticular shape.

Her blood was killing the virus.

Her mind raced. How? She'd been sick, and now she was cured. Could her blood now contain antibodies that attacked the virus? Nothing showed on the slide. Virus cells themselves were too small. But the skin cells were springing back to life, like . . .

Like magic.

Like it's a curse, and you're heaven-spelled. You're still blessed, Morgan. From what Luniel did to you. From loving him.

Her eyes burned, and she shook it off, determined. *Don't think of him. Don't even think his name. Just test it and see. You're a doctor, not a charlatan.*

She leapt up to scrabble in the drawers, coming up with a needle and a screw-in plastic sample tube. New gloves, snip snap, the used ones in the bin. Her fingers trembled as she swabbed inside her elbow with alcohol and pushed in the needle. She screwed the tube on firmly. Bright blood welled, agonizingly slow, and she gritted her teeth on impatience waiting for the tube to fill.

At last. She unscrewed the tube, eased the needle out. She slapped on a Band-Aid, careless, and ran to the fridge for a fresh, unrelated sample.

People were dying, right now. She didn't have time for controls or full testing regimes. But desperate hope flowed in her heart, suspiciously like a prayer. *Just let it work. Let this be real.*

The sample was already prepared and fixed, thanks to Suhail. She scrambled to slide the dish into the view slot. Grabbed a fresh dropper. Dipped it into the blood, her hands shaking. Refreshed the image. There they were, skin cells, engorged and angry with the virus. Her throat swelled, a hot lump of anticipation. Carefully, she squirted in a drop of blood.

A tiny flash of blue lit the dish. On the screen, the red blood cells spread, flowing like a rain of bubbles, surrounding the skin cells. And then the bubbles dissolved, and the skin cells swelled and shuddered and . . . *transformed*.

Yes.

Her stomach clenched in triumph. Score. No time to waste. She had to test it in the wild. And what better place than Vorvian's horrid lair? Her thoughts raced ahead, planning. *No way to replicate my blood so soon. Even if it's possible. Have to use the real thing. And soon. Now. Before . . . well, before whatever it is wears off.*

She jumped up and stuffed the tube into her pocket, stumbling in her haste. She'd need equipment. Something to subdue a victim, capsicum spray or nerve agent in a can. Syringes, gloves. More blood. She raided the drawers, stuffing what she needed into her coat pockets. She closed her eyes for a second, calming herself, and turned to leave.

The guy sitting behind her grinned.

She jumped backwards, hands flying to her chest. Black t-shirt, wiry brown arms, ripped jeans so tight they creaked. She gulped, sweat and crisp hashish, trying to catch her breath. "Jesus, Suhail. You scared the crap out of me."

But at the sight of him, relief flooded her, cool and calming. Another human spirit in a night filled with monsters.

"Gotcha. Tee hee." Suhail's dark eyes shone, amused. Today, he wore a piratical golden earring and a red bandanna, and his t-shirt said I'M OUT OF BED AND DRESSED—WHAT MORE DO YOU WANT? "Wasn't expecting anyone to be here. You sick yesterday?"

"Uh. Yeah. What are you doing here so early?"

"Catch-up. Same old." Suhail eyed her strangely, scratching his belly. "You look like shit, Dr. M. Big night?"

"You wouldn't believe me if I told you." But the memory of Lune's cheeky smile cut her like a blade.

"Try me." Suhail tugged his shirt down, but not before she saw the glint of weapons. Gun down the back of his jeans. Switchblade stuffed into his belt. A gas canister's lumpy shape in his pocket.

Her thoughts sharpened. Suhail was tough. Streetwise. Smart. And he had a gang of take-no-shit friends.

The kind of guys who could get her back to Vorvian's housing project alive.

Assuming Suhail didn't laugh in her face. And assuming Vorvian was still there. But she'd deal with that later.

Laughter broke in her chest. Surely, there was something wrong with her life, when the only person she could trust was a crazy gangboy. But she had little choice. Suhail had always stood up for her when it counted. And at least he wouldn't trick her with magic.

Her lip trembled. No, Suhail wouldn't enchant her with his bewitching smile. Wouldn't deceive her into hungering for his touch, the fiery glint of heavenblue eyes, his mind-melting kisses, the burning ecstasy of his hardness inside her . . .

Her wits clogged like wet wool. This was ridiculous. Luniel was just a guy. Why couldn't she let him go?

Just some guy. Yeah, right. The cruel voice inside her head taunted her, unrelenting. *He gets you, Morgan. He fell from grace, and picked himself right up and fought on. He sees you, and he doesn't shrink away. You'll never have that again. Sure, run. Hide your face from your reflection. It's what you're good at.*

She eyed Suhail, nervous. "Wanna walk with me? I, uh, need some air."

"Sure." He shrugged, and they headed out, down the corridor and into the lobby. "So," he added as they pushed through the dark-glass security door and outside, where the rising sun slanted a bright wake-up call onto the tree-lined sidewalk, "are you gonna tell me what's going on, or do I have to guess?"

Morgan squinted in the sun, flushing. "Am I that obvious?"

"C'mon, Dr. M. We're friends, right? What's on your mind?"

She swallowed. "You know what you said the other night, about the Manhattan virus? God's plan, and all that?"

"Uh-huh." Suhail slung his wiry arm around her shoulder, easy. "Thought you didn't believe in God."

Doubt pierced her chest like a sob, and she swallowed before it broke. "Yeah. Well, have I got a story for you."

CHAPTER 37

Morgan finished talking as they walked out onto Park Avenue, and Suhail stared at her, his dark eyes shining. "Fuck me with a glow stick. You've changed your mind!"

She shrugged, hot under the heightening sun. The street was crowding already, commuters and loiterers, cafés and food stands opening. The greasy smell of hot dogs made her stomach growl. "So sue me. When porridge hits you in the face, you've gotta believe in oatmeal."

Suhail grinned, and slapped her shoulder. He dug in his pocket for a twenty and bought two dogs, layering on the tabouli and chili, and handed one to her. "Welcome to the club, Dr. M. Pity you're on the wrong team, but, hey, I can make allowances."

"Who said I'm on any team? All I know is, this end of the world thing is real."

"Everyone's on a team these days. And somehow I don't see you praying six times a day and covering your hair. But then again, neither do I. Look, pork! And I'm still here." He took a huge bite of his hot dog. "So," he managed with his mouth stuffed full, "this angel of yours. Is he hot? Can I meet him?"

"Not your type." She ate, savoring the delicious flavor of oily meat and chili. She'd left out the part about sleeping with Luniel. She didn't want Suhail to know she'd been conned so easily.

"Surely you jest. Everyone's my type. They just don't always know it yet." A sly glint crept into his smile. "So . . . this Prince of Poison dude. You said he's throwing his little munch party up by the Wards Island Bridge, right?"

"Yeah." She shivered, remembering Vorvian's slimy, poisoned kiss. Suddenly her appetite wasn't so good. "It was horrible. Like a war zone. Bodies and blood and . . . and all those poor people . . ."

"So let's kick his ass."

"Huh?"

"Lock 'em and load 'em, and let's whip some butt for God."

"You mean it?"

"Hey, I'm a believer. If an angel came to me, I'd be saying 'yes, sir, whatever you say, sir, go ahead and magic my blood, that's fine with me.' What is it you folks say? 'God works in mysterious ways'?" He offered her a high five, his fingers stained with mustard. "Who the hell am I to say no?"

She connected, excitement twisting her stomach. "Thanks. I could really use a friend right now."

"Screw this demon, right? This is our island." He popped the last of his hot dog into his mouth and chewed, his words indistinct. "This cure of yours, it really works?"

"It did when I tested it." She pulled the blood tube from her pocket. "This is all I've got."

"You got plenty more in you, right?" He grinned, infectious.

"Uh-huh." She forced herself to take another bite. She needed the food. "You got something in mind?"

"All in good time. How far do you reckon we can dilute it?"

She shrugged, sweaty hair sticking. "Who knows? I've never tried magic before. A bit, I guess."

Suhail touched the SIM implant behind his ear to activate it. "Call Tariq," he instructed, and winked at her as the call connected. "T., it's So-so. Yeah, you, too . . . Listen, you know those gas grenades we ripped off from the National Guard? Yeah, the bio-bombs? I got a use for 'em. That thing we talked about . . . uh-huh. I got it right here. Can you be at 105th and First by"—he checked his watch—"zero-eight? Sure, I know the Kings won't like it. You care? Bring the boys, it'll be a blast . . . Heh. Thanks, I'm here all week. Kiss ya."

He disconnected. "Dr. M., we have ourselves a plan."

Morgan grinned. It felt good to have a friend who didn't want anything from her, or ask difficult questions. She offered him the rest of her hot dog. "You want this?"

"You sure?"

"Yeah. I'm not hungry."

"Thanks." He took it, and polished it off.

She shoved hands in her pockets as they walked. "Question. What's a bio-bomb?"

"It's a disease weapon. A shell that disperses ionized cell-rich carrier particles. They stick to whatever they touch. Like the nerve gas in bug spray, only it's not nerve gas, just vapor. You have to add the pathogen, or in this case, the cure."

"My blood?"

"Yeah. At least we won't have to worry about infecting ourselves." He grimaced at her expression. "Listen, we didn't start the Manhattan virus, okay? A bio-bomb is usually an artillery weapon. For an outbreak this big? You'd have heard the explosion in Queens."

"Okay." Morgan swallowed. She knew where the virus had come from, and it wasn't a bio-bomb.

"But these ones aren't shells, see? They're modified tear gas grenades. Made for chemical agents, but we can pack 'em with biologicals just as easy. The idea is, you inoculate yourself against whatever it is, and then you fire it from an underslung grenade launcher. Of which good So-so just happens to have a cache." They stopped at traffic lights, and Suhail peered out into the thickening stream of cabs and couriers. "So. We meet Tariq, inject the grenades with your blood. Find your demon and his zombie freaks. Brass 'em up, and watch the evil bastards burn in hell." His face glowed with zeal that wasn't entirely likeable, and he mimed firing a grenade, whistling as the imaginary ballistic fell to earth.

Morgan pursed determined lips. No, not likeable. Suhail might be fun to hang out with, but at heart he was a crazy-ass messenger of destruction. Anyone who thought it'd be cool to fire a biological agent at short range was either suicidal or insane, probably both. Maybe he thought God would protect him. Still, his fervor matched her own. Vorvian had destroyed lives. The sooner he was wiped from the earth, the better. And if that meant she had to go a little crazy-ass herself . . .

A cab zoomed past, and Suhail eyed the sun, already beating down hot. "It's kinda far, huh."

"Yeah." She fumbled in her pocket automatically, and stopped. "No cash for a cab. Sorry. Subway?"

Suhail pulled his pistol from under his t-shirt. No one took notice. He cocked it, gunmetal gleaming in the sun, and stepped out onto Park Avenue with a two-handed grip, the barrel aimed skywards. "Nah. Let's drive."

Japheth cursed, blistering his fingers, and wrenched his shuddering sword point away.

Dash just stared at him, and it drilled right into Japheth's unguarded heart like a demon's hell-spelled blade.

He whirled away, fury sparking from his fingers, uncontrollable emotion spilling out. For centuries, he'd kept icy control, and now that was shattered. Surely, Michael was just testing him. This wasn't the answer. What was the point of redemption, if he'd hate himself for eternity?

He hurled his sword away, and it crashed into the opposite wall, leaving a fiery trail. An acid-ripped scream clogged his lungs, and his rage exploded, an inferno of unreason he couldn't quench.

Glass shattered, and wind howled. Orange flames licked his skin. His feathers singed. The walls shuddered and cracked. His skin was alight. His nerves shredded raw. He couldn't contain it. Couldn't fight his rage, his envy, his spitfire lust to gorge or fuck or kill.

Dimly, Japheth felt Dash's knuckles crack into his jaw.

The punch flung him off his feet, and he collided with the wall and hit the ground with a bone-jarring crunch.

Dash grabbed his wind-whipped hair, yanking his chin upwards. "Enough, Jae. Wrap it."

Japheth sucked in a burning breath. Centuries of bottled-up injustice stung his bones, and lightning crackled from his fingers to set the ceiling alight.

Plaster rained, a rumble of thunder. Dash shook him harder. "C'mon, pull your icy shit. Don't fucking flake on me now. I need you frosty. You want your redemption? Help me stop the end of the world."

Dash needed him. Purpose. Focus. He smacked his own skull back into the wall, hard, and the ugly hateclaws with a death grip on his mind loosened.

He panted, grasping for his lost control. Flames licked his fingers, and he snuffed them out with clenched fists. The fire around him shuddered, and flickered low. Gradually, the room refocused, the cool waters of habit flowing over his ragged heart. *Deny. Ignore. Club baby seals. Think about something else, before you do something you'll regret.*

Japheth scrambled to unsteady feet, dizzy. His burned flesh healed with a sickening squelch. His veins still seared like hellfire, the remnants of his sinful rage floating like evil ashclouds.

Dash grunted in satisfaction, and cuffed him over the head, hard enough to flash stars. "You deserved that, you little shit."

Japheth gulped. Apology was inadequate. Would be forever inadequate. "Dashiel, I—"

"Shut up." Dash eyed him, empty. "No time. You with the program, or do I have to kick your feathered ass?"

His skin stung with shame. Dash would just push this aside? Forget it? Pretend it never happened?

Fine. He swallowed, cold, and frost settled over his heart. "Sure. Let's do it." He retrieved his sword, bracing for backlash, but the steel just glowed, blue and bright like it always had. He twitched his wings, steeling himself, and shouldered Dash aside.

"Jae." Dash's whisper pierced his skin like a hot needle.

Japheth halted, shaking.

Dash lighted beside him, his own blade flashing into his hand. "I get you, man. I really do. But point that sword at me again? I'll chew your fucked-up little heart out and eat it. Okay?"

CHAPTER 38

Suhail drove the stolen cab like a juiced-up maniac, and sooner than Morgan had thought possible, they screeched to a halt by the burned-out housing project, where the grade school's high security fence glinted in sunlight.

Morgan climbed out and clunked the door shut, her pulse alive. The hot air hung rich with death's rotten stink. No breeze lifted her hair. She itched to move, run, fight. She'd discarded the white coat, and felt in her jeans pockets for the blood-testing kit. "You wanna take some more—"

"Not just now." Suhail held up a finger for silence, and like hungry ghosts, his gang oozed from the broken building.

Three of them, dressed in jeans and ripped t-shirts, guns and knives spiking silver in the sun. One wore his long hair coiled in a black scarf atop his head, the ends sprayed with blue fluoro paint. He carried a black zipped sports bag over his shoulder, and his jeans were held together with safety pins.

Suhail sauntered up and smacked fists with him twice, a gang salute. "Tariq, meet Morgan Sterling. She's got some zombie-kickin' blood for us."

Tariq surveyed her, his kohl-lined eyes shadowed. "She's a white chick, man. Probably a freaking Jesus lover."

"So? Fuck you, T. Did God give you the monopoly on zombie hate?"

"You sound like an unbeliever."

Suhail shrugged, impervious. "Hell, I like unbelievers. They have cool phones and shit. It's getting my neighborhood bombed to matchsticks by neo-Nazi assholes that pisses me off, and guess what? I didn't see Morgan there. Grow up, man."

Tariq jerked his chin, a denial, and his friends lined up behind him, menacing.

Morgan smiled, nervous. "I'm not any religion. I'm a doctor. I just want to help."

Tariq scratched his blue-sprayed hair with a sigh, and tension dispersed like mist on a breeze. "Shit. White girl too pretty for you, So-so."

"And you're not?" Suhail grabbed his crotch, lewd. "Bite me, princess."

"You should be so lucky. You sure you wanna do this?"

"Hell, yeah." Suhail nudged her.

These guys were creepy. Zealots. Fanatics. But it took extremes to defeat extremes. She steeled herself, and nodded. "I'm up for it."

"Okay." Tariq unzipped his bag, and tossed a heavy gun to each. Black assault weapons, metal burnished dull, laser sights and an underslung tube for grenades.

"Sweet." Suhail handled his expertly, unseating and reseating the magazine, clearing the grenade launcher. "Courtesy of the United States Army. Thank you, Mr. President. Kiss my skinny anarchist ass."

Tariq glanced at Morgan. "You ever fire one of these?"

"No." The weapon made her blanch. She didn't care. She wanted to see those people cured, watch the light fade from Vorvian's haughty eyes.

Tariq showed her, glancing up with warm painted eyes as he demonstrated. "Safety. Empty mag warning. Grenade launcher, takes four shots. You load here, twist this, snap it shut. Slam and you jam, so be careful. Squeeze, don't pull." He dipped his wire-pierced lips to her ear. He smelled like Suhail, hash and sweat. "And don't shut those lovely eyes when you fire."

Her heart thumped as she took the weapon, but amusement

curled her lips. "Why, Tariq. Are you flirting with a Jesus-loving white girl?"

"You tell me. Am I?"

She eyed him, defiant. "I believe in justice. That's all you need to know."

Tariq's eyebrow arched, and he dipped her a graceful salaam. "You've got guts, lady. God be with you."

"Thanks, I guess."

Suhail was already messing with the grenades, little silver cylinders about three inches long, popping the reservoirs open and injecting the blood with a dropper. He tossed her a handful one by one, and she caught them and loaded like Tariq showed her. Her fingers slipped on the hot metal. The weapon was heavy in her hands. *Please, let this work. Let this not be a stupid dream.*

Tariq finished loading, and kicked the bag aside. "Okay, ladies. Let's roll."

Vorvian's estate still crawled with zombies.

Morgan wrinkled her nose at the stench. Horrid memory caterpillared over her skin. The demon's dark kiss, his hands on her body, the way his influence wormed under her skin and into her, a sick lover's caress . . .

The brick wall itched her sweaty back. She dragged wet hair from her forehead. Beside her, Suhail whistled an inaudible tune between his teeth, and closest to the corner, Tariq ducked his blue-sprayed head around the edge and whisked it back again. "I heard this was going down, but shit, this is *epic*. There are thousands of the meatsuckers."

Suhail scratched his ear, listening. "What's that garbage he's spouting?"

Morgan strained to hear, and her blood trickled cold. She'd know Vorvian's supercilious voice anywhere. Sounded like he was giving a speech. ". . . my rotting friends, it's time to get truly pissed at these living monsters who think they're better than you. We are a swarm of insects. We are a great plague, my friends! And we will cover every inch of this stinking island like locusts and eat our way to oblivion!"

Suhail chuckled. "Zombie people power. Who does the fucker think he is, Gandhi?"

Raucous cheers, grunts and hungry moans rose, a sickening wave. Morgan shuddered in memory. She wanted to block her ears, drown out the sound of the horrible disease that had poisoned her.

Tariq spat on the ground with a curse, and crept around the corner.

Blindly, Morgan followed. *Squeeze, don't pull.* Ahead, a blackened brick wall stuck broken from the ground, and around it, zombies wandered and punched each other, moaning. She pulled the weapon in tight to her shoulder, and fired.

The shot rammed back into her collarbone. The grenade popped, whistling in a sun-flashed arc. It exploded amid the flailing bunch of zombies, scattering its bloody vapor onto their skin.

They spat, and yammered, clutching their abused ears. One howled, her arm blown off. But the blood didn't burn her. It didn't catch fire or sizzle or light with holy vengeance.

It didn't do anything.

Morgan crouched, stunned. Maybe it was used up. Maybe she'd waited too long, the heavenspell dissipated by time. Maybe, she just didn't believe in it enough.

Now, the confused zombies muttered and shambled and fixed their roving eyes on her. And Tariq's fingers fastened around her arm, and he dragged her to her feet.

"Huh?" She stumbled. "What are you doing?"

"Suhail, give us a hand, will you?" Tariq knocked the weapon from her hands, and jabbed his knee into her kidney. She grunted in pain, and expertly he bent one arm up behind her back.

Now she needed to pee. Her shoulder ached, and she tried to shake him off. "Let me go. It's not my fault. I thought it'd work!"

"Then you're as dumb as I thought." Tariq twisted her wrist hard, making her yelp, and jammed his gun barrel into her side. "Shut up. It's not like you didn't know we'd screw you over. White chick like you, trusting us? Shame on you."

She struggled, sweating cold. She'd heard evil stories about what gangboy fanatics like him did to people like her. "I don't care about any of that! Let me go!"

"I don't give a fuck what you care about, lady. Vorvian will love himself a slice of white-girl-doctor pie."

"What? Suhail, tell him. Make him let go!"

But Suhail just bit his lip, and didn't move. "I'm sorry, Dr. M. I can't."

Oh, shit. Frantic, she stared at Suhail's young face. His eyes, brown and cold. His skin, dark but unflushed. He wasn't infected, she was sure of it. Neither was Tariq. *What the hell?*

Desperation attacked her voice. "What are you doing? Suhail, please!"

Suhail shrugged, hard. "The prince promised us victory if we gave you up. He'll help us crush our enemies, give us the edge over those Aryan Brotherhood assholes—"

"You've got to be kidding!" She fought, useless. She'd done it again. Trusted him because she thought he was like her, and he'd screwed her over. She'd never learn.

"Afraid not. We're God's people, and we're getting squeezed out of our own place. We can't kill this prince, and our own guys are getting the virus and turning on us. What choice do we have?"

"God's people? Are you serious? Didn't you listen to anything I told you? The world's ending! We're all in this together."

Tariq wrenched her wrist harder. "Tell that to the Brotherhood."

"But Vorvian's a demon!" She gasped, all the air sucking out of her lungs to bleed and die. "He's evil. You can't seriously be going to team up with him!"

"Martyrs go to heaven." Suhail prodded her with his rifle barrel. "Even if they break a few rules."

"You son of a bitch." She struggled, tight with futile rage. Religion poisoned everything, no matter what its flavor. "I thought we were friends!"

"Sure. I like you, Dr. M. I'm sorry. But this is for God. Did you really think sharing a few hot dogs would top that?" His brown eyes didn't falter. Not an ounce of shame or remorse. "I know you don't believe. You probably don't understand. I'm sorry for you."

"Don't you dare feel sorry for me, you twisted little prick." Morgan gritted her teeth, and kicked for his face.

Suhail ducked. Tariq wrenched her elbow apart, hard. Pain exploded, and her vision clotted black.

By the time she focused, they were dragging her across broken concrete, slobbering zombies watching on. Morning light angled through the broken buildings, and atop a mound of rubble, Vorvian whirled in golden sunshine, sparks trailing from his fingertips.

His white hair flew, his arms outstretched. And when he saw her, he tumbled to a stop, laughing like a drug-fucked banshee, his thin handsome face aflush with delight. "Dr. Morgan Sterling," he cackled, wiping tears from his scarlet eyes. "How the fuck are you, sweetheart?"

CHAPTER 39

Lune flashed into the Prince of Blood's sabbat, or as close as he could figure with his wits afloat in whiskey. His head swam, and his feet hit wet concrete with a graceless thud.

The stink of dead flesh punched his guts, and his feet slipped. He caught himself, hands sliding in muck. Blood. The floor was covered in blood. His oversensitive ears grated, screams, rending flesh, humans howling like ghouls in pain.

His guts heaved, single malt and bile. Heaven's grace, he didn't know if he could do this.

He dragged his sword blindly from the air and forced his stinging eyes open. A screeching hellsnipe thrust sharp talons into his face. He tore it apart on pure instinct. Bones cracked. He tossed it aside, staggering, and the full gory vision of the Prince of Blood's death-wish party slapped him in the face.

A vast basement, tainted with smoke, blood dripping down the firelit walls. In the center, a huge steel vat, crimson gore spilling over the sides. Corpses piled around it, throats slashed, their skin pale and drained. The air hung foul with screams and acid fear, the bitter stink of cursed souls that glowed sick scarlet in his angelsight. More humans thrashed in makeshift cages built from wire and broken steel. And everywhere, creatures of hell swarmed and feasted, hungry eyes, sharp claws, tongues drooling blood.

In the corner, a rotting starvewraith tore at a child, crimson staining his beak. There, a gang of rubber-skinned bonecrushers raped a screaming girl, two holding her down while another had his way with her, munching on her throat at the same time. Lune glimpsed Trillium, a furious flash of steel and reddish feathers, and Iria, exploding imps with her crossbow, her dark iridescent wings aflutter.

Beside Lune, a gang of scaly monsters giggled and gnashed their teeth like evil children. Pale angel wings flashed, and he glimpsed Jadzia, her blond hair flying, fighting them off with a whirling blade.

Lune gripped his sword tighter, and dived in unsteadily to help. Fever sweat and alcohol made his grip slippery, but in swift seconds the hellkids lay dead. He eyed them dully. Dead flesh. Blood. It meant nothing.

Jadzia flung him a ghostly smile. "Hey, Lune," she gasped, and spun to fight a fresh onslaught.

He whirled with her, and they fought a pair of sniggering green envywraiths, their wiry bodies whippy like rubber as they flipped and twisted. Green jealousy fogged the air on their breath, and Lune spat it out, tart like poison. He hurled his sword at one, slicing it neatly in two on the backspin, and when the other charged him with a hateful wail, he grabbed it, one fist around each arm, and tore it in half.

Flesh ripped. Blood hissed on his face, and he scorched it off with a toxic heavencurse that set the dead envywraith's hair alight. He hurled the burning meat aside, and his sword grip smacked back into his hand in a flash of holy flame.

It didn't feel good. He didn't feel anything. The meaninglessness of it all hit him like a smothering wave, and he staggered, choking, his breath sucked away.

The next minutes or hours blurred, a hot stinking cloud of bleeding and dying. He fought to keep his feet. Angelfire dazzled him. He blinked the glare away. Dash and Japheth, by the vat, where some higher-level demon in human shape slashed throats with a long razor, his scarlet hair splattered with gore. The demon's pointy face gleamed, black eyes alight with wicked golden glee. He held the kicking victims, emptying their blood into the vat and then tossing the corpses aside for his fawning minions to gobble.

Bile frothed in Lune's throat. But that demon's rotting stink was all wrong. He wasn't Quuzaat, the Prince of Blood. Just some lower-level minion, twisted cruel with rage and ambition. "Jaz, let's . . ."

But Jaz was gone, whirled away into the fight. Distantly, he hoped she was okay.

He somersaulted, unrolling taut feathers with a crack beside Dash. "Am I too late?"

"Hell, no. I saved some for you, as instructed." Dash flashed him a glory-wild glance. "Jesus, you stink like a distillery. Are you fucked up?"

"Ah. Yeah. Pretty much."

Japheth greeted him with a frosty grin. "Sinner."

"Fuck you." Lune whirled his blade and slashed in, and the air split with hellish death screams.

The red-haired demon yowled and flung his latest victim aside. He wore stained black leather, and hellfire hissed from his fingers. "Come get it, angelfilth—well, fuck me with a pitchfork!" His face lit up with unrestrained glee. "It's the Tainted shitwits. So glad you could drop by. Especially you, Lune. I've been dying to meet you all week. Pity your lovely lady friend couldn't make it. Did you enjoy the imps I set on you? 'Cause I did!"

"Motherfucker," growled Lune, real ire igniting at last. "*You're* the asshole who sent those wraiths to my place tonight?" He didn't know this turd from a cowpat. It didn't make sense. He didn't care. "You scared my girl, you stinky little shit. Come to Lune, and get what's coming."

"That's more like it." The red-haired demon giggled. "Great to see you guys again so soon, too. Two brushes with celebrity in as many days! Dashiel, the junkie angel of death. Carved up enough flesh today? Maybe we can do a deal, I enjoy a good thrashing before I win."

Dashiel snapped cruel teeth. "You talk too much."

The demon slurped blood from his razor, lickerish. "Mmm. And the golden girl. Japheth, right? D'you know I fucked your boyfriend? Hell, darlin', *everyone's* fucked your boyfriend. But I guess you knew that."

Dash's wings jerked in surprise, and Japheth's face drained pale. "You're Michael's pet? That skanky black thing in the cage?"

The demon cackled in delight, waving his blade. "That's Zuul to you, pretty boy. We can have a chat about *skanky* once I've peeled your skin off—"

"How the hell did you get out?" Dashiel advanced, sword poised.

"Oh, dear." Zuul's smile turned cruel. "For a dirty sinner, you're so naïve. How the fuck do you think I got out?"

Fresh sickness splashed in Lune's stomach, and his nerves screeched in denial.

Michael had sent Zuul to chase him. Attack him. Stop him from finding Ithiel's killer.

Ice-winged son of a bitch. But why?

Zuul's scarlet hair sprayed blood as he danced a happy little jig. "Ha! Lune's figured it out. But it doesn't matter, y'know. I'm just holding the fort for Prince Quuzaat. Soon he'll be here, and you can kiss your feathered asses good-bye."

Japheth hissed sparks and attacked, blue flame leaping cold from his blade. "Just shut up and die."

Zuul darted backwards, an ashen blur. "Listen, Lune, I've got a message for you. I was hanging out at Vorvian's party just now? And your girl dropped by. She and V. were getting on real nice, I gotta say. V.'s a real charmer. Figures out just what a girl wants. She said to say . . ." He frowned, mocking. "What was it again? Oh, yeah. That was it. *'Fuck you, angel.'*"

Lune staggered, dizzy, and he barely dodged the demon's scything razor.

It wasn't true. Demons lied. Not Morgan, in Vorvian's clutches. Surely, she'd stayed away. Hadn't tried to challenge Vorvian's power.

Curse her brave, stubborn hide. What was she thinking? Why didn't she just go home and get back to her life? No matter her courage, she was human, fragile like soulglass, and Vorvian was an immortal monster with power beyond the stars to make her hurt.

But Lune's empty heart still glowed with admiration, burning away the sickness and the whiskey. She hadn't given up. And neither would he.

He couldn't leave her to her fate. Even if she despised him forever, he couldn't fail her now. He'd died for his honey-bright lady once. He'd do it again.

And again. As many times as it took. And before he went, he'd rip Vorvian's cruel lying heart from his ribs, and swallow it whole.

For Eleanor. For Morgan. For me.

Golden fire licked his veins, and to the sound of Zuul's slick laughter, he flashed out.

An iron-strong hand wrapped Jadzia's wrist, and dragged her from the melee.

She stumbled, drunk on the scent of thunder. A wall thudded into her side, blocking the fight from view, and she gazed up into hot scarlet eyes.

"Jadzia." Shax's breath seared her cheek. "Don't be afraid."

Her pulse darted like prey. The demon was inches away. His black hair tumbled silken on her shoulder, and his hellish warmth taunted and burned.

But the music he made of her name sparkled deep inside her, dangerous. Her sword quivered, angry sparks snapping from the blade. Glory and killing rage still sprang hot in her blood. This was stupid. Why didn't she strike? Finish him off?

But deep in the bruised crevices of her heart, she knew.

Sweet heaven, help me.

She swallowed, parched. "What do you want?"

"I had to warn you." He spidered hot fingers over her hair, and it tingled. "I don't have much time. The Prince of Blood is coming. He's going to summon Azaroth. You have to stop him."

"Azaroth? Who's that?" Her wits fluttered, useless like broken wings. Her pulse burned. He smelled wonderful. She wanted to lean forward, sink into his embrace. If he was tempting her with hellspells, it was working. Oh, boy, was it.

"The Demon King. Lord of Emptiness and Despair. Vassal to Satan, the Lord of Lies, whose return Azaroth intends to ensure. Are you listening, lady?"

"Uh. Yeah. I—"

"You have to stop Quuzaat summoning him!" Shax's eyes glittered. "Quuzaat has the holy vial. If he drinks the vat's cursed blood from it, Azaroth will ascend. Right here. Tonight. Believe me, you don't want that."

Fascination gripped her, horrid and delicious. "Why are you telling me this?"

"I think you know." He yanked her wrist tighter, pulling her in, and their lips collided.

Oh, lord. His kiss tasted of thunder and storms and blood. So hot, a forbidden fire she'd never known. He bruised her mouth with his, delicious, finding her tongue and ravishing her. His body molded to hers, hungry, his desire hot and hard for a few precious seconds before she yanked away, dizzy with need.

Her chest heaved, air suddenly insufficient. She'd kissed a demon. Let this hellspawn put his tongue in her mouth. And it hadn't felt evil or wrong.

But it sure felt sinful. Sinfully, deliciously good.

"I can't stop thinking about you, Jadzia." He trapped her against the wall, unrelenting, his beautiful lips still gleaming from her kiss. "You haunt me wherever I go. I can't let Quuzaat get his way, not tonight."

His ashen heat intoxicated her. His desire for her made her shiver. God, it felt real. He actually wanted *her.* Not just release or oblivion. "But—"

"Make Quuzaat drink his own blood from that holy vial, and see what happens." Shax's hungry lips burned her ear. "I want to see you again. Say you will."

Her nerves screeched. *Kill him. Now. Before you do something you'll regret.*

But she exhaled in a rush, and it spilled out. "Yes."

He laughed, warm and thrilling. "My princess," he whispered, and dissolved to glittering black ash.

Compelled, Jadzia inhaled, and his scent sparkled, all the way down.

A shout behind her made her jump and whirl, the real world thudding in like falling bricks. Shit. If she'd been seen . . .

In the room's center, Dash and Japheth fought, splattered in gore and aflame with glory. The vat overflowed, blood spilling like crimson rivers, and a thin red-headed demon capered and cackled with glee, waving a bloodstained razor. "Here he comes! All hail the prince!"

The air tore, ripe like rotting fruit, and with an evil shimmer and a fat belch that stank of vomit, the Prince of Blood squelched in.

CHAPTER 40

Morgan stared up at Vorvian on the pile of rubble, and hatred scorched acid in her heart.

Tariq and Suhail still held her fast. She struggled, her need to revenge all those undeserving dead a burning fog that ate away at her reason. *Kill him. Bite his evil skin until his blood gushes bright. Tear his hair out, crush his skull, claw his eyes until they pop.*

Vorvian cracked up with laughter. He'd been eating. Gore smeared his mouth, and he licked it off with a pointed red tongue and held out his arms in a mocking embrace. "Thank you, boys. Very kind. I knew I could rely on you. Off you go now." He leapt down, landing like a cat in a graceful crouch.

"You promised to help us, demon. Don't fuck with us, or you'll be sorry." Suhail's voice rang strong, and grudging admiration soured Morgan's tongue. Brave little shit.

Vorvian waved a negligent hand. "Your scum-shit enemies are already dying. Run along, now. Play your silly games. Uncle Vorvian's finished with you."

They let her go, and she jerked away, defiant. "I'm sorry," Suhail whispered. "I have to."

"Screw you." Morgan flexed her aching shoulders. Behind her, the two gangboys' footsteps retreated. No point in her running. Zombies would floor her before she got ten feet. And if she'd learned anything last time, it was that getting naked with a zombie wasn't something she cared to repeat.

Vorvian slinked closer. "No need for rudeness. It was a fucking stupid idea, Morgan. As if your blood could ever harm me! You've ditched your angel, remember? Heaven doesn't give a shit about you."

He lifted her chin with one finger, and she gagged on his stink, ash and vomit and rotting flesh. And underneath, that ineffable sweetness, longing and wishes lost . . .

She spat, furious. "Get your greasy hands off me. You know nothing about heaven!"

"Oh, but I do." His hair sparked, angry gold, and he grabbed her chin to make her stare into his face. "Heaven's cursed me every day since I was made."

"Boohoo. I'm so *sorry* for you."

"You should be. It's your turn next, human. They just don't call it a curse. They call it *destiny*. Stupid, ugly fate you can't avoid, just because some faceless *thing* in the sky *says* so."

Her nerves quailed. She'd always longed to control her own destiny. But she struggled, tearing her gaze free. "Not listening, demon. Your lies stink."

"Do they? Look around you, Doctor." He pulled her with him to his knees. She fought, but his grip was like ice, unbreakable. "Tell you what: I'll trade you. One wish. One heart's desire. That's all I ask."

She shrank back, as far as she dared. But she knew she had no choice. *Play his games, or die.* "And what do I get?"

"Why, you get lives, of course. Isn't that what you came for?" He pointed with her finger at the milling zombies. "Tell me what you desire, Morgan, and I'll let them go free."

Her wits stumbled. "Huh?"

"Cured. Human again. The more truthful you are, the more lives you'll save. Fun, eh?"

"No." Morgan shook her head. "No, it's a trick."

"Of course it's a trick! But what choice do you have?" His eyes gleamed, delighted. "Unless you'd prefer another dose of the screaming hungries. I rather enjoyed giving it to you—"

"Okay!" She shuddered, defeated. Not that. Never again. Her skin still crawled with the memory, hot bleeding flesh crunching between her teeth, the salty delight as it slid down her throat. The rabid desire, the hunger, the way she'd teased Luniel, touched him . . .

Wildly, she fought to remember every silly story she'd ever heard about dealing with demons. *Read the fine print. Don't take anything for granted.* "Okay, you filthy scumbag. I'll play. But only if you play fair. I'll tell you one wish. Just one."

"Your *deepest* wish," insisted Vorvian happily. "And I'll know, so don't even think about lying."

"And I get all these people, cured and alive. They get to leave safely. No changing the rules after we start."

A pained scowl. "You wound me, Morgan. Truly."

"After last time, you want trust? Screw you."

"We can include that if you—"

"Not in this universe, pretty boy." She cut him off, impatient. "Let's get on with it."

"Fabulous!" Vorvian leapt up, and smoothed his hair with a two-handed flourish, like a stage magician preparing for his biggest trick. "This is gonna be awesome! Ready?"

She scrambled up, relieved to be free of his grip. She took a deep breath, steeling her wits. One false word, and she'd be helltoast. "Yes, I'm r—"

"Good." And swift as a striking cobra, Vorvian whiplashed in a curl of stinking black smoke, and slammed his palm into her forehead.

Hellfire flared, and her vision drowned in blood.

Vorvian's cold-rich chuckle caressed her. She struggled, but couldn't move. Her bones spiked cold. No air. No light. Just her pulse, thudding in her skull like a zealous drum, and the cruel sound of Vorvian's delight. "Did you think I'd let you choose? No, silly! Your thoughts are mine now. I'll dig out what you want most. I'm the guy who can get you things, Morgan. For a price. I think you'll find me generous."

She tried to scream, but he plucked the sound up like a wet sock and tore it away.

"Now," he murmured, "what have we here?" And ghostly fingers of demonic compulsion forced into her mind.

Memories swirled, like drowning flotsam. Hot gunmetal in her hands. Broken glass stinging her finger, her blood splashing onto a dish. Raw anguish, the inevitable crushing truth of an angel's lie. Luniel's hot midnight feathers brushing her face, his heat-scented hair, his body's scorching caress on hers . . .

"No, that's not it." Impatiently, Vorvian tore the images away. "I want your *deepest* wish. Nice, but no cigar. Hoity-toity little Morgan, doesn't need a man, blah blah. But . . . oh!" His excitement drove her pulse harder, horrid. "What's this?"

Her mind spiraled, a black vortex of despair, and down she hurtled into bleeding memory.

Brains, splattered on the wall like red paint. Mom's body, limp. Fingers still curled in the trigger guard. Dark brown hair, so like Morgan's own, riddled with bone fragments. Her pretty lips cold and pale. Morgan had tried to kiss them. Tried to put Mom's face back together. But the blood only smeared, the flesh torn beyond help.

Morgan yelled, struggling in Vorvian's grip. *No. Not that. Anything but that . . .*

But years of bitter guilt swamped her, cold and thick like floodwater, swirling over her, clogging her throat and dragging her down to the icy depths of certainty.

Her fault. Just like she'd told Lune. If she and Mom hadn't fought, if she'd listened, given Mom the time of day instead of weaving home drunk and smoking herself sick and giving herself to every sly-eyed boy who wanted a piece, just to get some attention . . .

Vorvian laughed, devilish. "Mommy's love? That's it? Satan's balls, I'm puking over here. That's pathetic, Morgan. Truly. Let me tell you a secret: *Mommy's dead and in hell.* She'll never love you! Ha ha!"

Anguish ripped her nerves raw. Hell had never been real. Just a story to frighten children. But now, she believed it. Torment, never ending, on and on, beyond world's end and forever. And it made her want to scream her heart out.

"Oh, come, it's not that serious. Breaking eggs for omelettes, all that. At least I'll get to have some fun! Some things are worth giving your soul for, aren't they?"

Hot temptation licked her, and she moaned, tossing in her fugue. "No," she managed, her mouth full of cotton. *No surrender. Not until the last star burns out.*

"You think not? How about . . ." Vorvian's evil inspiration

pierced her skin, a thousand stinging needles. "How about *this*?"

And his vision rained over her, a handful of ash, glittering like a crystal-bright dream.

She saw herself, white coat and gloves, working in the lab. Tissue samples, assays, a team of assistants, human subjects in a barrage of trials, the sick hunger fading from their eyes. Meetings in a drug company's sleek offices, talks with government officials in the laser-lit shadow of the Capitol. A new medicine, safe and easy and free for all.

She'd found a cure for the virus. A medical cure, no lies or trappings of faith. Just a drug. Just a disease.

Temptation flowered in Morgan's belly like desire.

Living in a new apartment, fresh and modern. She was rich. Desired. Respected, a prize-winning virologist. A new boyfriend, clever and handsome, his own money and career but devoted to her. She'd never heard of angels or heaven or the end of the world. Luniel wasn't even a memory.

And Mom . . . Mom wasn't dead. No guilt. No bad memories. Just a middle-aged lady, face lined but still beautiful, and she prayed and went to church and it made her happy. No one tricked her or lied to her, and sometimes, they spent weekends together.

Morgan choked on hot tears.

Vorvian stroked her mind gently, coiling around her desires like a sleek serpent lover. "Mmm. Now that's nice, huh? You'd like that."

"No . . ." Morgan shook her head, wild, but her denial shattered and blew away like storm glass. She'd never wanted anything harder in her life.

For it all to go away. For everything Luniel said to be a lie. No heaven. No God. No fate.

And no soul-rotting memories of love lost. No screaming hole in her heart when she thought of her magnificent angel. No crushing fear of betrayal.

"A cure for the curse," Vorvian crooned. "Think of the lives you'll save. Millions of people will live because of you. And you'll be happy. Don't you deserve to be happy, Morgan?" His seductive ashen scent enfolded her, and his voice in her ear wrapped rich temptation around her flesh and wouldn't let go. "All you have to do is give me your soul."

Her tongue swelled, throttling her voice. Flashes of Luniel, his doomed lady, how she'd given up her soul and torn the beating heart from his chest. He'd loved that girl, and she'd thrown it back at him for a demon's falsehood.

But Luniel didn't love Morgan. It was all a lie. And she could keep those people alive. The Manhattan virus gone, an end to all that suffering.

"Forget your angel," whispered Vorvian. "He's not here to protect you now. And forget faith. Heaven's only hurt you, hasn't it? I'll give you everything you ever wanted. You're a scientist, you've no use for your soul. Why not give it to me?"

An end to their suffering, yes.

But also an end to hers. Live in the real world. Deny eternity. No lies. Only harsh, icy truth.

Her bruised heart wailed, lost. *Luniel told you the truth, Morgan. You were just too scared to believe him.*

But the demon's cruel whispers wreathed her mind in despairing black smoke, and she shuddered and thrashed and gave in.

Deep in the steamy sabbat, Jadzia stared in disgust at Quuzaat, Prince of Blood.

Fat, ugly bastard. Tall, but muscle running to fat, his greasy jowls wobbling under lank pond-slime hair. His pudgy butt swelled in tight leather pants, and his gut squeezed into a bulging vest that barely contained it. He lifted his arms, coalescing from hell in a shimmer of stinking ash.

Around him, the fight died down, as hellcreatures fawned and gibbered for his attention, genuflecting and scraping their faces into the ground.

Dash and Japheth still fought, whiplashing on taut wings, but the legion of creatures forced them backwards, towards the stinking vat of blood.

At Quuzaat's feet, sniggering green imps dragged forward a struggling woman and gnawed her throat open. Blood fountained, and Quuzaat rinsed his face in the splash, licking his chops like a hungry dog. The woman's soul struggled, a smoky red cloud in Jadzia's angelsight, but Quuzaat slurped the air hungrily, and the soul sucked up his nose like a wriggling red ghost and disappeared.

Jadzia's guts squirmed. Quuzaat just belched, and rubbed his fat stomach, grinning. The green imps licked his boots clean, and he waved them away grandly.

"Hello, friends." Quuzaat's voice slid like a greased knife, cold and sticky as he addressed the crowd. He wiped blood back into his hair and licked his fingers with a slobbering flourish. Quite the showman, his sloppy grin wide. He brandished a gleaming golden bottle, wide at the bottom and narrowing to a long thin neck. It smoked in his hand, angry at the touch of demonflesh. "Are you ready for a party?"

Creatures screeched and wailed. Jaz swallowed, hot. The holy vial. The one he'd stolen and emptied, turning the ocean to blood.

Shax's words chilled in her memory. *If he drinks cursed blood from it, Azaroth will ascend.*

That didn't sound good.

"Are you ready for something *wild*?" Quuzaat jigged about, his belly wobbling as he soaked up the cheers. He grabbed one of the homicidal green imps, and flung it into the vat. It splashed, and surfaced, gulping and glutting itself with glee.

Quuzaat waved flabby arms, encompassing the room. "You might have noticed," he called, "that there's a bad smell in here tonight. A *feathery* smell! A nectar-licking, toffee-sucking, god-fucking *stink*!" More excited roars from his audience. "Well, have I got a treat for you, my friends. We're in for a visit from the Demon King himself! And I wouldn't be surprised if he lets the best of you rip those shitty heavenfreaks limb from limb!"

A cacophonous cheer. "So let's finish this, friends. Give me your rage, your hunger, your bloodlust. Show me what you've got. And when our lord Azaroth arrives, we'll see who's won his favor." Quuzaat waddled to the makeshift cage beside the vat, grabbed a human by the legs and ripped him in half, brandishing the dripping pieces like a crazy-ass caveman. "Let the slaughter continue!"

The noise broke to deafening levels, and the fight exploded.

Something slashed Jaz's leg with cold burning teeth. She struck at it blindly, heard flesh rip. Tore her sword free, crushed a skull under her boot, grabbed a thing's wing in her teeth and ripped it off. She spat, disgusted, burned lips and a bad taste in her mouth.

But her mind sprinted in crazy circles as she fought. Shax's touch hadn't burned her. *Make Quuzaat drink his own blood and see what happens,* he'd said. But was Shax tricking her? Tempting her? Leading her to chaos and misfortune?

Or did he truly mean to help her?

The dizzying pleasure of Shax's kiss sneered in her memory. *Traitor. You kissed a demon. You wanted him, like a sin-sick slut. What'll you do next? Betray your friends to hell?*

She steeled herself, jumping over a slithering black snake-thing and crushing its spine with her boot. It wasn't like that. Shax had felt for her. Connected with her. What they had was . . . sweet. Not evil.

Never trust a demon, Jadzia of the Tainted. Michael's chilly advice echoed through the decades. *It'll only get you killed.*

But if Azaroth ascended, they'd *all* be killed. Worse. They'd get tortured, then killed, after a very long time. If she died trying to stop Quuzaat—lost her soul to hell, even—it was worth it, to let her friends live on. To atone for the wrong she'd done, in that hellish cavern so long ago.

Already, Quuzaat leaned over the vat's edge, hunger firing his beady red eyes. He dipped his face in and blew scarlet bubbles, laughing. Crimson gore gleamed on his fat face, and he gulped it down, gorging himself. "Ah. Very nice. Almost worth giving up the plague for." And he jammed his hand inside his shirt, and came up with the golden vial. "Time for a royal visit, eh lads?"

Jaz spun her sword to loosen her wrist, and dived for the vat.

Already, Dashiel and Japheth fought with their backs jammed against the scarlet-dripped iron, and sleek black-winged Iria slashed her way towards them, firing her crossbow one-handed. Trillium darted and screeched like a red-green vulture above, slashing off heads with abandon.

Bloodstink made Jaz gag. She hit the ground and rolled, her wings smearing in filth. Her head clunked into the vat, dizzying her. Dash and Jae sparred with a skinny red-headed demon, and as Jaz shook herself, Dash sent the thing's sword flying with a chilling crash of steel and flung him to the ground on a feral heavencurse. Coldly, Japheth crushed the skinny demon's skull with a stamp of his boot.

Jaz yelled, straining over the din. "Guys! Help me cut the prince!"

Iria dragged her up one-handed, skewering a three-armed hellspawn with the other. "What?" she shouted back, hoarse.

Already, Quuzaat filled the vial with blood, admiring the light gloating on the surface. Jaz jammed her lips against Iria's ear. "That's the vial in his hand! We have to cut him! Make him drink his own blood from it!"

Iria's gaze flashed over her, sizing her up. Jaz flushed, but held her ground. "Okay," Iria yelled at last. "Best plan I've heard so far. You grab, I'll slash."

"Okay!"

And together, they dived for the demon prince.

Iria's head slammed into Quuzaat's flabby side, and Jaz grabbed his legs and yanked hard.

He staggered, and the liquid spilled from the vial, missing his open mouth by inches. "Fucking angelscum!" he roared, and kicked at Iria's face, landing a crunching blow.

But Jaz held on, and launched for his outstretched hand. Grabbed the vial. Tore it from his fingers on a rich heavencurse, reigniting the gold with a blue flash of holy rage. And Iria whip-lashed, and fired her silver crossbow into Quuzaat's throat from two feet away.

The shining bolt slammed home. Quuzaat roared and gurgled. Black blood splashed smoking into the vial Jadzia held, and ignited with shimmering blue fire. And she dragged Quuzaat's head back by his lank slime-green hair, and emptied the vial into his mouth. "Swallow this, devildirt."

Quuzaat choked, his eyes wide. Blue flame whistled from his mouth, his nose, his ears. He retched, trying to get rid of the heavencurse, but his newly toxic blood kept burning. His eyeballs melted and ran down his cheeks. He let out a hell-spiked howl that disappeared in a roar of holy flame, spurting from his mouth as he burned to death from the inside. His husk of a body crumpled, and fell to ash.

The flames hit Jadzia in the face, setting her hair alight with glory. It sizzled, delightful, energizing her muscles with fresh power. Around her, hellcreatures howled spitting fury at the death of their prince. Some flashed to ash and disappeared. Others fought on, shouting defiance, and still others dived for the trapped humans, determined to slaughter as many as they could before the angels finished them off.

Jaz staggered, relief washing her like rain. It worked. Heaven hadn't discarded her in disgust for kissing a demon.

Her mind speared to Shax, and her heart beat faster. He hadn't lied. Where was he? Did he escape, or fight on?

Angrily, she dragged her thoughts away. She should join the others, end this, set the prisoners free. But glory rush and fatigue weakened her limbs to rubber, and she fell, everything flashing to white.

CHAPTER 41

Lune's feet hit charred concrete in the stink of rotting zombie flesh. Vorvian's housing project, blackened walls and broken bricks. He dragged his wings upwards, flinging himself into sunlit air. He had to find Morgan.

The mid-morning sun flashed on the jagged skyline. He ducked one wing, wheeling on uplifting breeze. Below, zombies milled, yelling and waving their machetes at him. In his angel-sight, the demon's curse hovered around them all like a sour green aura.

No sympathy cooled his burning blood. If they'd hurt her, he'd burn them all to ash, even if it took every last drop of heaven's favor . . .

There. In a stinking green mist of hellish lies. Snow-white hair. Fetish-clad Vorvian, crouched on the ground, holding a body . . .

Lune pulled his wings back and dived. The ground hurtled close, and he landed in a handspring, bones jarring. Flexed, glory sizzling blue. Smashed his boot into Vorvian's face, and came up spitting fire.

Vorvian hurtled backwards, slamming into the pile of rubble. His bones splintered, an evil crunch. And Lune skidded to his knees in the dirt and gathered Morgan in his arms.

"Morgan. Wake up. Fight. Don't let him . . . sweet heaven, no." His sword clattered down, forgotten. She thrashed and moaned, eyes rolling in the grip of some horrid hellspell he couldn't grasp. He touched her forehead, and glory flashed violet, a rich dark heavencurse to fight the evil.

But her skin only blistered like demonflesh under his palm. And Vorvian spluttered laughter and hauled himself from the rubble, his bones knitting in a puff of stinking black smoke.

"You're too late, Lune! She's already mine." Vorvian's smashed jawbone smoothed over and healed, and he waved his arms delightedly. "Wow, is this déjà vu, or what?"

Molten fury lit Lune's muscles. He wanted to chew the fucker's eyeballs out. But it didn't matter. "Morgan, wake up." He kissed her lips, and it burned. Delirious, she snapped at him, her teeth sinking into his lip. His blood scorched her, and she screamed, smoke bubbling from her tongue.

Lune shuddered, lost. He wanted to howl, thrash his wings to the sky, scream out his agony to heaven and curse them forever.

Vorvian giggled. "She's under, angel. She can't hear you. And even if she could, do you think she'd choose you over her heart's desire? Happiness? A cure for the virus? I think not."

"She's just one woman. One soul! You don't care about her! Let her go. Please. I'm begging you."

Vorvian crouched, laying a slim hand on his shoulder. It singed, glory on hellspell. "I'd love to accommodate you, old friend. Truly I would. But that'd be treason, wouldn't it? Azaroth would kick my ass. I mean, really? Giving souls away for free? The Apocalypse isn't a charity event."

The demon's ashen stink made him retch. But Morgan squirmed in his arms, moaning with hunger, her eyes rolling back to whites.

Lune clutched her tighter, savagely blinking his eyes clear. He wouldn't let her go. Wouldn't let her touch the monster. "No. Stay away. You'll have to kill me first."

Vorvian laughed, but his gaze was grave. "You're a bit slow, Lune, old buddy. Do you really think it's just your *death* I want?"

Oh, shit.

Heavensense dazzled him, a screaming warning from above not to go there, and the glory in his blood shuddered, squirming, trying to escape its fate.

But his nerves fired hot with eight hundred years of rage and disobedience, and his love for this amazing woman forged his heart bright like fresh steel.

He looked up, straight into the demon prince's eyes, and the blazing glare of his conviction singed Vorvian's snowy hair black. "I can't give you my soul. Heaven took it from me. It's not mine anymore."

Vorvian pursed his lips, ready to curse or laugh or deny.

Lune let his smile glow, one last glory-rich seduction, and feral promise edged his tone sharp. "But I can make them give it to you."

CHAPTER 42

Vorvian licked sharp teeth in anticipation, and Lune's guts stabbed cold with the looming wrath of heaven.

But he ignored it, defiant. *This is mine. It's all I've got left to give her. Back the fuck off.*

And the glory sizzled, and vanished, leaving only a chilly void.

Vorvian sighed, and drooled, spit shining on his chin. "Oh, my. Now, my friend, you're talking business. Let's do it."

Shaking, Lune planted one last kiss on Morgan's bruised lips. The touch didn't burn. Already, hellfire threatened in his bones. *I love you, Morgan. Forgive me.*

And he laid her down, smoothing her hair, and knelt in the dirt at Vorvian's feet.

"I—" His voice shook, but he forced it calm, placed his hand over his heart for steadiness. "I give you everything that I am. Your master is my master. I will slaughter your enemies. I will aid your friends. I will curse heaven's children wherever I find them, and every soul I meet, I will lead to your door. I will spend my eternity as an angel of hell, and when the Lord of Lies returns to reign over the earth, I will worship him."

Above, the swirling breeze stilled, and clouds drifted in

front of the sun. On the ground, Lune's discarded sword glimmered, one last flash of heavenblue fire, and its light died.

Vorvian drew in a ragged breath, sweating with desire, triumph afire on his face. "Say it, Luniel. Say the last bit. I'm waiting."

Lune's throat parched, his voice cracking dry. "I surrender, hellscum. Now let her go."

Through a hot black fog of despair, Luniel's words soaked into Morgan's ears, and some tiny speck of sense left inside her screamed and shuddered in brute denial.

He'd already killed himself for her. But this was worse. Oblivion was one thing. Eternity as a demon's slave . . .

Well, that just wasn't worth it.

Vorvian's temptation kissed her like a lover's sweet lips, tormenting all her secret places with promises of fulfillment, release, pleasure. His slimy-hot parasite munched cruel teeth into her soul, and dragged it out like a skewered oyster from its shell.

She squirmed, but couldn't break free. *Never mind your angel. He doesn't love you. Heaven doesn't love you. Only I love you. Only I'm willing to give you what you want, what you deserve. Doesn't that prove it?*

But Lune's sacrifice overflowed her heart, and shame and sorrow stung her lungs like poison. Her flesh cried out in denial, her skin aflame with all the horrid things she'd said to him.

Faith is for fools, she'd said. But Lune hadn't lied. Hadn't tricked her. Hell and heaven were real. He was real. He'd meant every blessed word he said.

Including *I love you.*

She couldn't let him crush his soul to ash for her. He was too precious, too desperately human. His words flowed back to her, drenched with pain and desperate empathy she'd been too afraid to embrace. *I'll always fight for you. I'll never lie to hurt you. Let me be what you need.*

Heaven was a weird and wonderful thing. She didn't understand it, and she still wasn't sure she trusted it. But she didn't have to believe in heaven to believe in *him.*

Lune, don't give up on me. Let me be what you need.

Fresh ferocity ignited in her veins, a shimmering reflection of heaven's glory, and she spat and cursed and fought harder. *Let me go, demon. Take your lies and be gone. I don't believe in them, and I don't believe you.*

Vorvian's greasy parasite wailed and gnashed its teeth, thwarted. She grabbed it, and twisted.

Bone snapped. Agony ripped through her, a burning flash of hell-streaked lightning. And dazzling heavenlight poured over her, filling the cold empty wounds in her soul.

She strained towards the light with all her strength, and with a discordant crash Vorvian's spell broke, and she tumbled back into the real world.

She blinked, and scrambled up on scorched legs. Lune was on his knees, wings stretched back in supplication. His sword tumbled dull in the dirt. He bowed his head, and wet black hair hid his face.

Before him stood Vorvian, gloating. "Well, angeldirt, that's quite an offer. I especially like the part about *surrender*. Can you say that part ag—"

"Accept or no, demon." Lune's voice rang harsh, empty. "I haven't got all day."

Vorvian smiled, satanic, and licked his lips to answer.

CHAPTER 43

No. Morgan's flesh crept cold in denial. *He's mine. You can't have him. Not when we've just begun.*

And she sprinted, her thighs aching with fatigue, and dived for Lune's sword.

The iron stung cold in her hands. She fell, and the blade sliced her cheek, grit grinding into her shoulder. She didn't care. She scrabbled to her feet, grabbing the worn steel grip. *He doesn't deserve this dark eternity. Not because of me. Heaven, help me save your child.*

Ozone stung her nose fresh. Energy struck her from above, like uncanny lightning through her veins, and she whirled and stabbed for Vorvian's heart.

Flesh sliced, the magic-sharp blade sinking deep, effortless. Blood bubbled black.

Vorvian's eyes flashed glassy white. He grabbed the blade in two hands and twisted it, yanking her closer, and laughed, spitting stinking ash. "You can't kill me, Doctor. Not with this. You don't believe in heaven, remember?"

Her teeth gritted tight with the effort, and she drove the blade in harder, up to the hilt. "Maybe not. But I believe in *him*."

And the blade dazzled with angry blue light, and with a

crack of thunder that split the sky, Vorvian's body exploded in flame.

His dirty white hair caught fire. His flesh seared away to bone. His eyeballs melted, and he screamed, a horrible curse-laden hellshriek that ripped her ears raw. His body fell, disintegrating around the blazing sword, and crumbled to ash.

The shock wave shook the earth, knocking Morgan to her knees. The sword tore from her grip. Wind stung her eyes, swirling her hair. Around her, zombies howled and fell in the thousands, moaning and thrashing in a mass seizure of death.

Lune yelled her name. Blindly she crawled towards the sound. Her limbs ached, energy leaking, the strange flame in her veins sputtering out. The wind flapped, and died, and the shrieks faded to eerie silence.

She struggled to her feet, blinking. The place was littered with bodies. Unmoving. Silent. Already, the stink of decomposition soured the air. All dead, the life sucked out of them by Vorvian's dying curse.

Morgan's throat swelled. But she couldn't turn away. The bodies were everywhere. The city would have to incinerate them, she noted clinically. Far too many to bury. And all that rotting flesh would only harbor more disease . . .

Luniel touched her shoulder, warm. "Morgan. Don't."

The sight of him alive, luminous, his black wings coated in dust, misted her eyes with tears. "They're all dead. I could have . . ." Her voice crumpled like tinfoil. "They could have lived. He promised me. If I'd just . . ."

If I'd only given you up for lost.

But even as she spoke, she knew it wasn't true.

"No, they couldn't." Lune's gaze shone steadfast. "Demons lie. His promises were false and twisted. And these people were far gone, Morgan. You saw them. Their bodies were wrecked. There's no cure for that."

Morgan's lip trembled as she remembered how close she'd come to accepting Vorvian's offer. "Is he dead?"

Lune nodded, pointing at the ground. A ragged black hole rotted the concrete, where the demon's essence had been. "Ashes scattered. You won't see him again."

"And what about you? Did you . . . I mean, was I . . ." Her

mouth was caked with dirt. She couldn't finish the sentence. *Was I too late? Are you damned?*

Lune flexed his fingers, and with a brilliant flash, his sword blazed in his hand. Fresh. Bright. Heavenblue.

Just like his eyes. God, she couldn't take it when he looked at her like that. So warm, so precious, like he wanted to keep her safe forever. It made her melt. It made her want to run into his embrace . . . or from it. "Does that mean you're forgiven?"

He watched the light ripple along the blade, and his little laugh sparkled her skin. "Forgiven? Not likely. Given another chance? For the moment." His gaze lighted on hers again, warm and certain. "I'd do it again. In an instant. Just so you know."

She couldn't speak. Her heart was too full.

He flashed the sword away, and licked his lips, uneasy. "Look, Morgan . . ."

"It's okay." Her stomach crinkled tight. "I know I said horrible things. I'm sorry. I don't expect you to forgive me."

"Forgive you? I should have been honest with you." He ruffled dust from his feathers, a nervous twitch in glittering sunlight. "So I'm being honest now. Apart from healing your wounds, I only ever spelled you that one time. And I never intended it to go anywhere. But you kissed me, and I . . . well, I kinda stopped thinking. Everything else . . ." He flushed. "Well, everything else was just me not knowing what to say. I'm kind of a hands-on thinker. But I never spelled you to touch me, or to feel anything for me. I hope you can believe that."

"But you can't prove it." Morgan twisted her hands, nervous.

"No, I can't. I'm sorry." His gaze shadowed, but didn't drop. Didn't falter. Didn't give her a moment's respite.

Her heart quailed, and her belly filled with the cold-sick cocktail of doubt and fear that had ruled her life for so long. But she swallowed it down, firm, and her heart teetered.

Don't look down, Morgan. Just jump, and trust you'll be caught.

She sucked in a deep breath, and dived over the edge. "I believe you."

Surprise lit his eyes silver. "You do?"

"I should never have doubted you. You've done so much to

prove yourself to me, and I threw it back at you because I was afraid." Her throat cramped, and tears sprang. She wiped them away. "God, I've acted like such a princess. I'm not special, Lune. I'm just . . . me. You shouldn't have to prove anything to me."

"Yes, I should." He drifted closer with that silent, uncanny grace. "I love you, and I'll spend your life proving it to you. If you'll let me."

A warm inner smile lightened her heart. "Could I stop you, angel?"

"Probably not. I'm kinda persistent like that." He wiped dirty hair from her cheek.

"So I've noticed." Her skin tingled, his touch more compelling than any spell. His wings folded around her, warm and fragrant with his wonderful fresh scent, and she tilted her mouth and closed her eyes and the kiss he planted on her burned with desire and relief and honest passion.

In a second, she was trembling, overcome. His lips caressed hers, thirsty, like he needed to drink from her or die, and she wrapped her wrists around his neck and opened up to him, letting all the doubt and fear and thoughtless untruths drain away. He cupped her butt and lifted her, and she gave a little hop that launched her into the strong cradle of his arms.

White light flashed, and in a dizzy instant she was on her back in soft quilts beneath him. She gasped, laughing into their kiss. "Where are we?"

"Your place." He nudged her chin up, kissing her throat until she moaned and arched against him in the sultry shadow of his midnight wings. "I thought you could use a shower and a rest. Unless you'd rather do something else."

She wrapped her fingers in his hair, luxuriating in the rough silkiness. "No way. If I take a shower, angel, you're taking it with me."

"Mmm. Behind you, by choice. I heard somewhere that you like that. Promise?" Already he undid her buttons, tugging her dirty jeans off.

She flushed, remembering her fantasy, but it made her hot, too. "Oh, yes."

"Good. That way I get you twice. Don't think you're getting away." He peeled her shirt—his shirt—over her head and tossed it away.

Underneath, her breasts were bare, and he pulled her onto his lap and kissed them, teasing her nipples with his tongue and sucking them into his mouth until she gasped and shuddered, on edge. "Stop it. How come I'm naked and you're still dressed again? No fair."

"Be my guest." A smile of pure vanity that melted her heart. He was so beautiful, her angel. So splendid, in heart and body, and still he wondered why she wanted him.

Desire consumed her, and she fumbled with his buckles, desperate to touch him. He helped her, that sparkling blue spell that vanished his wings, and the silver fell away. His shirt peeled off in her hands, and she gloried in his smooth skin, the feral play of muscles beneath her hands and lips and tongue. His delicious flavor tingled her mouth, sweet yet raw, tantalizing, the shivers spearing all the way to her sex. He tangled his fingers in her hair, tugging her closer, and she moaned as wetness flowered hotter between her legs. She had to taste him more.

"Naked, angel. Now." She pushed him onto his back and fell on him, tugging off boots and tight leather. In the dim light, his muscles shone, luminous, a ghostly dark glow like black neon, and his feathers flamed golden. God, he was magnificent. She needed him now. Needed to prove this wasn't a dream, soak herself in his scent, drown in his caress until the feeling never went away.

She straddled his thighs and took him in her mouth, relishing his hot satiny flesh against her tongue, between her lips. His flavor was stronger, richer, more edgy, just as she'd imagined. His hands fisted in her hair as she stroked him, licked him, and the deep sound of pleasure he made vibrated deep in her core. She took him deeper, sucking, and he groaned. "Enough, witch."

She didn't stop. Didn't want to. Wanted the feel of his pleasure, the taste of him filling her . . .

He pulled her off him, and flipped her onto her back under him with a swift sweep of wings. He pinned her wrists on either side of her head. "I said, enough," he growled, and with a powerful thrust he filled her completely.

Oh, God. The sensation dizzied her, so hot and full, and this time he wasn't slow or gentle. He drove into her hard, deep, taking her and making her his own. He slid his arm beneath her, lifting her hips to his thrusts, watching her body's reactions, finding the places she liked and torturing them. She clutched his hair, crying out in delight. He was so deep inside her. So hard. So good. Pleasure wrapped around her, tightening, so intense she might shatter, and finally she erupted, nerves melting from the inside out, her muscles clenching hard on his cock until he dived for her mouth and drowned his own climax in a deep, breathless kiss.

She panted, coming down only slowly. He inhaled her, drinking her scent with a soft groan, his cock still buried deep in her body. "You're amazing."

She traced her finger along his sweat-smooth flank, enjoying the feel of his muscles twitching, and reached for his dark-shining feathers. So soft, silken on her fingertips. Such a miracle. She laughed, still catching her breath. "No, I'm ordinary. *You* are amazing."

"Not where I come from." He moved inside her, easing gently in and out, still enjoying the friction. "Runt of the litter, that's me. You'll brush me off in an instant when you get to know the rest of 'em."

She gasped, dazed with pleasure, shocks still zinging through her. He felt so good, and it wasn't just because he was an amazing lover. Maybe what they said about fucking versus making love was true. The thought brought a smile, swiftly followed by a blush that she'd neglected something important. "Why, Luniel of the Tainted, are you fishing for compliments?"

A sexy grin that melted her heart. "Maybe."

God, she adored that smile. She stretched up for a kiss, loving the warmth of his lips, his tongue loving hers, the little groan deep in his chest as he enjoyed her. "I'm in love with you, Lune," she whispered against his lips. "And I want more of you."

Warm sparks tingled over her, and the passion in his kiss answered her better than any words. He rolled onto his back, pulling her with him, and his fresh hardness inside her made her gasp and shiver. His heavenblue eyes glowed deep. "That'll do it."

She sat up, and he grunted in pleasure and gripped her hips, settling her on him.

She gazed down at him, absorbed. Such a beautiful angel, and all hers. He'd never hurt her. Never lie to her. Always be at her side.

More than she deserved. Everything she'd ever wanted without knowing it.

She wriggled off him and up, teasing him with a hot stroke of her fingertips. "Race you to the shower." And she skipped away, giggling in fragrant wingbreeze as he cursed—most terribly unangelic—and dived after her.

CHAPTER 44

Jadzia groaned, and blinked her eyes open.

Blinding sunlight. She squinted, lifting her arm to block it out. Rocks jabbed into her back. She pushed up to sitting, her vision clearing. A glass-smashed office building, rubbish in the street, the foul stink of fleshsmoke from a fire. In the gutter sat Japheth, shirtless, golden feathers dragging in the dust as he resolutely pressed dents from his armor, his jewel-green eyes frosty. Dashiel paced, rolling his shoulders, coffee-dark wings afire with glory. Trillium leaned against a teetering streetlight post, smoking a cigarette, the ashflare glinting in his eyes.

Iria knelt beside Jaz in the street. Her wings and armor were still splashed with blood. "Welcome back."

Jaz wiped stinging eyes. "What happened?"

"We killed the prince." Iria smiled, exhausted but still dazzling. "After that, it didn't take long to get rid of the rest of them. Look, about that—"

Dashiel swooped over to raise her to her feet. "You okay, darlin'?"

His hand shook, wired, and she clutched it and kissed him fondly on the cheek. "Yeah. You?"

"Never been better." He eyed her darkly, and she swallowed, dreading his questions. His good opinion meant everything to her. If Dash found out she'd kissed a demon . . . "Nice plan of yours," he said mildly. "Did you—"

"Awesome, wasn't it?" Iria cut in smoothly. "We thought it up together. Maybe there was some of heaven's wrath left in that vial, we thought. Had to be worth a try."

"Sure." Dash's gaze flicked from Jaz to Iria and back again, but he let it slide. "Nice work. I'll give the vial back to Mike next time I see him."

Jaz swallowed cool relief. "So does that mean we're done? I mean, it is over?"

"No such luck, darlin'. Those first two plagues are out there. Damage done. We still haven't stopped the chain of signs. But for now, drinks are on me. You up?"

From the gutter, Japheth snorted. "It's eight in the morning, Dash."

"Not in Hawaii, it isn't. Jaz?"

"You got it."

Iria grinned. "Oh, yes. Take me to the men, baby."

"I'll be in that." Trillium tossed his cigarette away and joined them, sweat gleaming on his tattooed arms. "Japheth? You can have iced water if you want. Vinegar, if you're feeling penitent. I promise my sinful ways won't rub off on you."

Iria guffawed. "No, they'll just rub off on the fifty people you hit on."

"Jealous?" Trill flashed a handsome grin.

"Not in this lifetime, funboy. Japheth? Just this once?"

Japheth buckled his armor back on, and shook his head, eyes clouded dark.

"Come on, kid." Dash nudged him, but his gaze stormed. "Take your mind off things."

"No." Japheth edged away, frosty. "I've got somewhere to be. Maybe I'll see you later." And he finished the last buckle and flashed out.

Trillium shrugged, orange hair glistening. "Whatever. Somebody call Lune, if he's not shacked up with that nice lady friend of his."

"Someone say my name?" Lune flashed in, the pretty doctor in his arms. His black wings shed golden sparks, and Jaz swallowed a laugh. Obvious what they'd been doing. It made her think of Shax, and secretly she flushed.

Trill snorted. "Always late to the fight, Lune. Keep it in your pants."

"Screw you," said Lune cheerfully, and planted a soulful kiss on Morgan. She gasped, laughing, and Jaz swallowed a pang of envy. Lune was nice. But he wasn't for her, and that was okay.

"Jesus," grumbled Dash, shielding his eyes. "Get a room, you two."

"Already did." Lune grinned, practically bursting with pride. "Did I mention Morgan killed the Prince of Poison? Oh, yeah. Fucking brilliant, my friends. My girlfriend kicks *ass*."

Jaz cheered, and kissed him, her heart light. Morgan grinned at her, and Jaz grinned back. Iria and Trill whooped, and Dash clapped Lune on the shoulder. "Excellent work, ladies and gents. You'll be needing a drink, then."

Lune lifted an eyebrow at Morgan. She nodded, and he slung his arm around her shoulder, affectionate. "Wouldn't miss it."

Trillium shoved him. "Hey, can I dirty dance with your new missus?"

"No," Lune growled.

But Morgan winked. "If you think you can keep up."

"Lady, you are *on*. Gotta go home, put my face on. Ten minutes, Waikiki?"

"You got it." Dash claimed Trill's high five, and they all turned to go.

Jaz gave a tired smile, her heart warm. A crazy, fucked-up bunch, but she wouldn't trade them for anything.

Even Shax? A cold whisper in her heart begged a question she didn't want to answer. *What if you could have him? Would you trade your friends for that?*

A hand touched Jaz's shoulder. She whirled, her heart skipping.

Iria's dark green eyes were cool. "I covered for you with Dash. Now level with me. What's going on? How did you know that vial thing would work?"

Jaz swallowed. "I . . . I overheard. Some hellspawn talking, that is. They said something about the vial and Azaroth, I . . . I thought it'd be worth a try."

Silently, Iria plucked out a long dark hair caught in the hinge of Jaz's armor. The hair caught fire, singeing Iria's fingers, and hissed to a smoky wisp.

Jadzia stared, her lip trembling.

Iria smiled, secretly. "It's okay. I won't tell. A little rebellion tastes sweet, eh?"

"Um . . . well, I—"

"You have a good time, honey. Just be careful, and make sure it's not you who's being used, okay?" Iria kissed Jaz's cheek, and vanished.

And Jaz stood, shivering and solitary. Her thoughts somer-saulted, wild. She should go. She'd be missed. But . . .

Her heart ached, warm and swollen, a sorrowful echo of all those years she'd spent alone. She didn't want to be alone.

"Shax." His name stung her throat, poison or elixir. "Are you there?"

Silence, and a warm wind that caressed her cheek like a kiss.

She slid her fingers over the spot in wonder, and a smile lightened her heart. "Thank you," she whispered, and flashed out.

Japheth flashed into Michael's courtyard, his fingers aflame with fury.

Hot evening breeze ruffled his hair, lifting ripples on the clear blue swimming pool. Gore still plastered his hair, his gilded wings clotted and wet. Michael's disciples lounged by the water, and shrank back as Japheth stalked across the terra-cotta tiles.

He flung the glass door aside so hard, it cracked. The white-suited minion squealed and jumped aside. The living room was empty, and Japheth dived for the bedroom and kicked the door open.

In front of the mirror, Michael dressed to go out, his ice-blue wings glittering as he buttoned his white silken shirt. He flicked a glacial glance, that glory-bright smile. "Jae, sweetie. Tough day?"

He looked magnificent. Japheth didn't care. His veins stung sharp with sinful rage, and he strode up and hit Michael full force in the jaw.

Crunch. Japheth's knuckles broke. Michael staggered, flar-ing clumsy wings for balance. *Weren't expecting that, huh.*

Michael didn't fight. Didn't light the sky with wrath. He just wiped glowing blood from his lip, intense with shock or admiration. "Babe, if you want to talk this over—"

"Shut up." Japheth steadied his voice, a fresh level of calm he hadn't known he possessed. He flexed his damaged knuckles, and they healed with a swift ache that couldn't match the burning pain in his heart. *Say it. Just say it. Heaven, give me strength.*

"I loved you, Misha." Rage and loss shook him to the core, but he didn't falter. "Heaven have mercy, part of me will always love you. But we're no longer friends. Don't call me. Don't visit me. Talk to Dash if you need me. And if you ever—" He gritted cold teeth. "If you *ever* turn me against my friends again, I swear to God, I'll carve your eyeballs out and feed them to Satan myself."

And he flashed out to his empty Babylon apartment, and stumbled into the shower, where he stood under cold water in the dark, his cheek pressed to the tiles, until the fire in his blood glimmered out and ice sealed frigid around his heart.

In the blood party's ruins, where scorched corpses littered the floor and makeshift metal cages hung open and empty now, Zuul groaned in intoxicated delight, and dragged his crushed head from the floor.

Sweet fucking Satan, that had hurt. His balls still ached, excruciating. The exquisite splinter of his bones, the swelling brain tissue, the blood pouring from his mangled face . . . The Tainted angels had nearly destroyed him, and he'd had a fucking good time doing it.

But only *nearly* destroyed. Zuul was stronger than he looked. An angel's sword through the heart might do it. Crushed bones were just a pleasant nuisance. Still, next time he saw Japheth, there'd be payback. No uppity golden-feathered maggot stomped on Zuul's head and got away with it.

His cheekbones knitted, the pain blurring his vision black, and he curled into a shuddering ball, spasms wracking him with passion-sweet agony.

A cold hand brushed his forehead, a fresh sting. "Zuul."

That frigid voice spiked terror down his spine, and he wet himself. His bruised brain gibbered. *Azaroth's here. Embodied. In person. Satan save me.*

He scrambled up, still blind, trying to stand straight with his skull only half-healed. "M-my king. Forgive me. How did you . . . ?"

"Foolish child. Do you really think I need some petty ritual to summon me?" Azaroth's breath smelled cold, of ancient ice and emptiness.

"Forgive me, my king," Zuul begged, desperate. "Prince Quuzaat, he . . . I couldn't save him."

"No matter, Zuul." Azaroth stroked Zuul's warped cheek, a teasing stab of pain. "His death was not your doing. Your efforts with the Tainted Host are noted. You have done well."

"Thank you, my king." Zuul's breath calmed, relieved, but his thoughts tumbled faster. Azaroth's vengeance was usually swift and terrible. How had Zuul lucked out? "But . . . the vials . . ."

"The sea is still blood, Zuul. The disease still festers and spreads. My plans are unaffected. The Tainted angels have won no victory." Azaroth's tone frosted the air with disdain.

Zuul's feet slipped on fresh ice, and he waved his arms to keep upright. Bones wrenched in his skull, healing. He still couldn't see. "Th-then what now, my king?"

"Now, we watch, and wait. The first two plagues have driven Babylon insane with fear. I anticipate quite a lovely frenzy of violence, Zuul. Let them hide and fight and kill each other. The time will soon be ripe."

"For the next plague, my king?" Zuul dared, thrilled. He wanted part of it. The rewards were beyond his dreams, if he could only earn them.

"Of course. Even now, the third vial is within my reach." An icy kiss burned Zuul's forehead, a delicious agonyspike that drove straight to his balls and exploded, making him gasp and shudder all over again. "Five more plagues, Zuul. Five more princes. Do my bidding well, and maybe you can be one of them."

Wind whooshed, rushing to fill the void, and Azaroth was gone.

Zuul slumped to his knees, panting, and his bleeding lips cracked into a smile.

CHAPTER 45

Morgan stretched, yawning, the lights of the Babylon County morgue gleaming on her keyboard. She signed her autopsy report digitally, and closed the file with a sigh.

So many bodies, so much death in the last two weeks since they'd killed Vorvian. The havoc Quuzaat and Vorvian had wrought still crippled the city with fear, drumming up a frenzy of violence. The plague and the bloody ocean had driven some already tense people over the edge, and Morgan's dead were the gunshots and stab wounds, the fear killings and lynchings and opportunity victims. She'd seen enough plague bodies to suit her, thanks very much.

The Prince of Poison was dead, but his disease lived on. The city had incinerated the bodies from the bombsite, too many to bury. And zombies still roamed the streets, terrorizing neighborhoods and infecting mutie gangs with lust for meat.

Morgan shuddered, and headed for the refrigeration room. She was working hard on impressing the boss. Maybe, if she kept at it, she'd get that senior assistant ME job.

The fridges shone, spotless, and she checked the notes, which no longer bore Suhail's signature. He'd never come back to work, and she wondered uneasily if Vorvian had made good on his promise to Tariq and his gang. She doubted it.

Just another couple of bodies to check over, and she could ride a cab home and call Lune. The thought made her smile. He always made her smile, even though the Tainted were constantly alert, on edge, waiting for the next catastrophe to hit.

Sometimes, they gathered at Lune's place, sparring or just hanging out, and Morgan saw tension between them that hadn't been there before. Dashiel was dark and taciturn, and gilded Japheth barely said a word, his handsome green eyes cold. Even Jadzia was tense and jittery.

As for the seventh of their number—Ariel—he still hadn't returned from his search for the third holy vial. Morgan had looked the Bible verse up. Something about the fresh water turning to blood, just as the ocean had, and people drinking it. The end of the world still wasn't over.

But in the meantime, she wasn't giving up. People still had lives to lead. Except, of course, the corpses in her morgue.

Morgan sighed, and reached for the fridge.

White light flashed, and her angel tugged her back into his embrace, wrapping her in dark-feathered wings. "You're late, Dr. Sterling."

She smiled, snuggling. She was getting used to him appearing from nowhere. "For what?"

"This." He tilted her head up to taste her neck, and she murmured in pleasure and turned to kiss him, already warm with desire. Kissing him was like breathing. She never tired of it, and the longer she went without, the more she longed for it.

He growled with satisfaction, and started undoing her white coat. "Miss me?"

"Of course." She wriggled, laughing. "I'm working, Lune. What exactly is it you do all day?"

"Besides letting Dashiel kick my ass, and thinking about you? Nothing." He nuzzled her collarbone, nipping at her blouse. "This seems to be in the way."

She pressed against him despite herself, already breathless. "But I have to work."

"No, you don't." He kissed her chin, her lips, her cheek. "The work'll still be there tomorrow."

"But . . ."

"But come home with me, Morgan." He cupped her face. "It's late. Take some time for yourself. For us. Just because the world's ending doesn't mean you shouldn't live."

She sighed, and relented, teasing her fingers through his crisp silken feathers. "Well, I guess if we've only got a few minutes left . . ."

"Screw 'minutes,'" he growled, crushing her close. "It'll take more than a few minutes for what I've got in mind for you."

"Mmm. Promises. Like, how long?"

Her beautiful angel folded her in his glimmering black wings, and his luscious scent and the desperate passion in his kiss took her breath away. "Forever," he whispered. "I never cared for eternity before. But it's only been two weeks, and already I want them all."

His words poured sweet sunshine on Morgan's heart. She'd never considered herself sentimental, but Lune brought out the dreamer in her. She hadn't realized she missed it, until now. "Can we really save the world, Lune? Do you believe it?"

"I believe our fate is what we make it." He kissed her again, hot and slow, drawing her on until she shuddered and yearned. "So let's make it good while it lasts."

"Until the last star burns out?"

Lune's eyes shone, heavenblue. "You better believe it."

And Morgan wrapped her arms around her angel, and let him flash her away.

Turn the page for a preview of
the next Novel of the Seven Signs

REDEMPTION

Coming soon from Berkley Sensation!

CHAPTER 1

And the third angel poured out his vial upon the rivers and
fountains of waters, and they became blood . . .

—REVELATION 16:4

Japheth gazed into the hot moonlit sky, and prayed. *Lord, let me
kill every last vampire in Babylon.*

Starting with this lot.

Six of them, creeping from steamy shadows. Streetlamps
flickered, burning their crazed eyes crimson. They snarled with
their long sickle teeth, and clawed the air with bitten hands. One
had dreadlocks. Another wore a cheap suit. One had pink-dyed
hair and pierced eyebrows. They stank of spoiled meat and
sweat. And they were soaked in blood.

"Charming." Dashiel flashed his blue-flaming sword, two-
handed, and flared his dark wings for balance. His silver armor
glowed, angry. "It's *Night of the Living Junkies*. Did you bring
popcorn?"

"If they kill us, we'll be just as dead." Japheth's golden feathers prickled, a warrior's instinct. His spell-sharpened gaze
snapped left and right, senses itching for scents, alive for the
tiniest rustle. Distances, heights, relative strength. Trajectory
plotted, bing-badda-boom.

Amen.

He conjured his sword and dived full-length. The sky-lit
blade burned cold in his hand. The creatures spat hell-stung
curses, slashing at him with ragged nails. Japheth somersaulted

over them, a flurry of gold. *Snick!* A head flew, spraying crimson. *Splat!* Another. He sprang a backflip, slicing a third creature apart at the waist.

He landed with a crunch on the bloody sidewalk, and surveyed the carnage with satisfaction. Very cool. Killing demonspawn was what he was made for. And every dead vampire took him one step closer to heaven.

Dashiel had already head-sliced two more. Their corpses leaked a gory puddle on the concrete. The last vampire screeched, insane with hunger, and hurtled for Japheth's throat.

Its teeth sliced his shoulder. Its breath stank of dead flesh. Japheth ignored the sting, the burning hellcurse. He flashed his sword away, grabbed the creature's neck in both hands and twisted.

Snap! Its head flopped, caustic gore spewing from its mouth. He tossed the corpse aside, and sizzled the blood from his breastplate with a hissing heavencurse. "Four for me, two for you. Getting slow, old man?"

"Bite me, baby face." Dashiel vanished his sword in a blue flash, and wiped blood from his eyes. "Jesus. Last month shambling corpses, this month hungry metrosexuals with bad teeth. What gives?"

"You know what." Japheth flexed scorched palms. Already the wounds were healing. Angelflesh on demon always burned. He didn't mind the pain. It meant he was doing heaven's work.

And since he'd been Tainted—since Michael tore his soul from his body and banished him to this dirty, decadent earth, neither damned nor saved—he couldn't afford to sin. Not if he ever wanted back into heaven.

"You really think these blood-munching idiots are another vial?" Dashiel laughed. "Isn't it meant to be rivers of blood this time? These days everything's a fucking sign. The wind blows the wrong way across Times Square and suddenly it's the end of the world—"

"*'They have shed the blood of saints and prophets, so you have given them blood to drink, for they deserve it,'*" quoted Japheth ironically. "It's in the Book, right next to the rivers of blood. You really should read more, Dash. It's kind of important."

"I must be the prophet, then." Dash grinned. "Because sure as hell's a shithole, I ain't no saint."

"Isn't that the truth." Japheth hoisted a severed head to the light. Even dead, the thing's hair still sizzled in his fist. The corrupted stink assaulted him, that unmistakable mix of charcoal, rotting meat and shit. Moonlight glinted a gleeful hellcurse in its empty eyes. *"Give me your soul, angel,"* it seemed to cackle silently. *"Die screaming. The world's ours now."*

Not on my watch, scumbreath. He poked a stinging finger into its mouth. Its jaw gaped, blood and broken teeth. Sure was crowded in there. Curved canines and incisors, unnaturally long, with sharp serrated points. This thing wasn't human, not anymore. "Look, it's a new variant. Three rows of teeth. Brutal."

Dash peered closer, wrinkling his nose. "Okay, that's ugly. The curse must be mutating. Spreading, too. There's more of 'em every week. Slimy shitballs are crawling from here to SoHo."

Japheth tossed the reeking head away. "Well, whatever it is, we can still kill 'em. I call that good news."

"You've got a one-track sense of fun, you know that?"

Japheth grinned, feral. "Whatever gets you through the night."

"Bloodthirsty bastard." Dashiel cracked his neck bones, tense, and flexed glittery brown wings. "Fucking hellspawn. There goes my quiet evening."

Japheth could hear Dash's heartbeat, strong and swift, sparkling with heaven's glory. Dash had issues with glory. Until he did something about it—likely, he'd find some willing woman and take it out on her—he'd have sweetfire poison pumping in his veins, a raging headache, the hard-on from hell.

Japheth preferred to fight himself into exhaustion. It was safer that way . . . but he suppressed a dark twinge of envy. "Yeah, right. When's the last time you spent the night alone?"

"When's the last time you didn't?"

Japheth smiled brightly. "Screw you."

"Tricky, with the size of the stick up your ass."

"Yet somehow you manage." Japheth wiggled his little finger, smirking.

Dash snorted, shaking his dark head. "You know, I get your whole sinless, warrior-for-god, let-me-back-into-heaven kick. But it wouldn't kill you to relax once in a while."

"You sure about that?" Lust was a sin, even for a Tainted angel. He'd never win redemption that way. And besides, all that meaningless carnal pleasure was . . . sordid. Self-indulgent. His heart wasn't in it. He had better outlets for heaven's holy wrath than getting hot and breathless with a beautiful stranger.

Like slaughtering hellspawn. Killing was a sin, too. That was in the Book. But not when the monsters had already sold their souls to hell. That was mercy, or heaven-sweet vengeance. Either way, it was good.

He flexed fervent wings. He didn't want to talk, or play heartless sex games. He just wanted to coat himself with demon-cursed blood, score a few more dead hellspawn for heaven. "Relax, yes. Sludge my wits with some dirty crap cooked up in a toilet bowl in Queens, and make a slut of myself with some woman I don't care about? I'll skip it, if it's all the same to you."

"Who said anything about sluts?" said Dash innocently. "Chicks dig that silent warrior vibe of yours. Lots of them are perfectly nice girls—"

"Which is why they're better off never knowing me."

Dash tilted his gaze skywards. "He's a killer, not a lover. I'm sorry, did I miss the chapter where it says 'thou shalt be a frosty-assed son of a bitch'?"

"Yeah. It's right under the part where it says 'go forth and screw yourself into damnation.' I think you stopped there."

"Okay, fine, I give up," Dash grumbled. "Your loss." He rolled tight shoulders, and the golden snakecharm around his neck glinted in evil red moonlight. "This vampire thing is getting worse. I'll run it by Mike, see what he wants to do."

Japheth sweated, like he always did when he thought of Michael, who alone had the power to return him to heaven. Once, he and the icy archangel were close. Now? Not so much. "Because that worked so well last time," he replied tightly. "We barely got out of the first two signs alive."

Dash shrugged. "Above my pay scale, brother. Stopping this Apocalypse is Mike's circus. Let him be ringmaster."

"You're gonna trust him? After he ordered me to kill you?" Sometimes, Michael tested him, to see how far he'd fallen. He still remembered how close he'd come, the fire licking his blade, the horrid compulsion to kill racing in his blood . . .

"Still alive, ain't I?" Dash waved a careless hand. "Spit it or swallow it, Mike still owns our soulless asses. Does it piss me off? Every damn day. But what am I gonna do, get another job?

Oh, wait, opportunities in the private sector for 'kick-ass angel of death with no soul' seem to have dried right up." He dragged his long dark hair from its iron-curled clip and refastened it. "So screw it," he announced happily. "Let's get drunk. You coming, or is that a daft question?"

"To a bar, with you and your hard-on? Let me think."

"Suit yourself." Dash clapped him on the shoulder, irritatingly. "Happy killing. Watch out for the Angel Slayer."

"Yeah. Right." Some jerk-off in the West Village was killing angels. Almost a dozen in the past few weeks. Stabbing them through the heart with a demonblade and pissing off into the night like a mincing coward.

Hungry lightning crackled around Japheth's sword grip. Bring it on. Just let the bastard try it. "The Angel Slayer better watch out for me."

"Atta boy." Dash winked, and flashed out.

Alone in the moonlight, Japheth ruffled clotted golden feathers. Thick summer heat slicked his skin. Flames flickered in an upstairs window. Shadows leapt. Smoke curled, gritty in his mouth. Gunfire cracked, and in the distance, a woman screamed.

He whispered an ancient prayer, and glory sparkled into his blood like frosty flames. His breath quickened as the rush hit him hard. His eyes watered. His muscles tightened, shuddered. Yeah. Pleasure, hunger, sweet desire—it was no contest. His heavenly gifts hadn't been taken from him, not in all these long years of being Tainted. But he knew the glory could desert him at any moment.

Better use it while it lasts.

He crouched, one hand braced on the pavement. His nerves glittered on a fighting edge, his senses razor sharp. No time to lose. Somewhere, demons plotted destruction. The Angel Slayer lurked in shadow. The street still reeked of hell-cursed vampire blood.

And Japheth of the Tainted was just in the mood for more.

CHAPTER 2

"Don't squeal, godscum. Just die."

Rose Harley twisted her demon-spelled knife deeper into the angel's heart. Hot blood gushed, painting her crimson to the wrists, and her skin blistered foul with holy wrath.

Fuck, she hated the self-righteous stench of heaven.

She drove the knife in harder. Angry red hellsparks crackled from her blade. The angel choked, his eyes blank, and stopped thrashing. Blood soaked his jeans, his shirt, his prissy white feathers.

Dead. Skewered on demonsteel. Meat for the rats.

Good fucking riddance.

Rose ripped her knife free, satisfied. The fourth she'd lured to his end this week. Stupid thing wasn't even smart enough to come to the Village in full armor.

The angel's corpse slumped to the pavement, face first, a pile of limbs and bloody feathers. At the smell of his cooling flesh, Rose's guts rumbled. Her wicked fangs pressed hungrily at her lips. She hadn't fed in too long. But angel's blood was poison to a vampire. She'd have to wait.

She yanked a bloodstained white feather from his wing and jabbed it into her braid with the others. Her hair singed in protest, but only weakly. The dead angel's glory was already fading. Idiot flyboys. Always so superior, with their false tales of salvation.

But the Apocalypse was happening. The End was now. It was too damn late to be saved.

Rose jammed her knife away in its thigh holster, spat on the corpse with a blistering curse and stalked away into the dark.

The street glittered like evil rubies in her vampire night-sight. Dark doorways, glinting barred windows, neon signs flashing, broken. A fragrant vine brushed her damp face as she turned the corner. Deserted, shadows dancing like ghosts. Fire-light flickered, crackling an eerie melody, and heat hung thick and gritty. Like half of the West Village, this place was burning.

Good riddance to that, too.

Her sturdy bootheels clunked on the broken sidewalk. She didn't bother to mask the sound. Sure, she was being hunted. She'd refused allegiance to the West Village vampire coven master—what a whack-job he was, with his barbed-wire piercings and sadistic pleasure games—which made her fair game for his most devoted minions. But the night was hers now, humming in her blood, licking her muscles to tingling strength.

Bad luck for any dumb-ass creature who tried to jump her.

She wiped bloody hands on her jeans, wincing as the burns scraped raw. Angel on demonspawn always burned. No matter. It'd heal overnight, slowly, but still faster than a human. Hell possessed vast power, and now it was at her fingertips. All you had to do was surrender to the dark.

She flexed her strong thighs, and grinned. All those hard years of dance rehearsal—in her previous life, and how long ago that seemed—had made her flexible, agile, stronger than she looked. Now, she was lethal. She was Chosen, the first rank of vampires, made not by fleeting infection from another vam-pire, but by the demon Prince of Thirst himself.

It felt damn good to be powerful.

But the hour grew late. Again her belly growled, reminding her what she needed. Demon-haunted moonlight cast reddish shadows from quiet brick apartments. Smoke drifted, the crackle of flames from an upstairs window. A cat scampered across her path, twitching its black tail.

She searched the sky warily for dawn's pale tinge. Nothing

yet. Sunlight didn't burn her, or any Count Dracula shit like that. But it itched, deep inside where the demon's curse coiled and muttered like a hungry slug. Morning stung her eyes, made her achy and weak, like a flu. And it'd only get worse, the longer she lived with the curse.

On Greenwich Avenue, lamps cast bright halos over empty shops and cafes. Village Square lay deserted, eerie, lit orange by a burning pile of garbage. She crossed over to Ninth Street. No sensible human walked abroad at night in the West Village, not since the vampires moved in. But the neighborhood rustled and murmured, unseen, every sound distinct in Rose's preternatural ears. Late-night traffic from Sixth Avenue, thumping car stereos, a siren's distant wail. Whispers from locked apartments, sobbing, sighs of despair or pleasure. Stinging sweat, pain's bright static, the hot poison tang of a kiss.

Terrifying, when first she'd been made, the cacophony of human existence. Now, her rich senses exhilarated her.

Sweat trickled in her hair, and she swiped it away. Sultry summer closed in around her, the sickly stench of blood and angel sweat still strong . . . and her stomach still grumbled, demanding. She needed to feed.

Her throat tightened, reluctant. Killing angels was one thing, those princes of bullshit and false promises. They deserved it.

Feeding on people was another thing entirely. She'd have to crunch her jagged teeth on flesh, feel the liquid fire splashing into her mouth, down her throat, the rich salty tang of human terror . . .

She shivered. The first time she'd fed, weeks ago, she'd gagged it right back up, disgusted and turned on at the same time. She was clumsy, newly made, and the guy had died, of course. Just a skinny kid wearing eyeliner and bruises, desperate for cash. He hadn't deserved the dumb lonely death of prey . . .

But it wasn't the boy's tears that sickened her the most. Not even her guilty flush of pleasure.

It was the banality. So easy, to drain him dry. Life was such a stupid, fleeting thing. Fire had thundered in her veins, triumph, exultation. Her first kill.

Actually, no. Her second . . .

Horrid images raped her, stark and flash-lit like crime-scene tableaux. The night she was made, a ravenous fever-drenched nightmare. Twisted wet sheets on the bed, a gore-streaked teddy bear, a wet blond hank torn out by the roots . . .

Rose swallowed, sweating. That night, the demon prince's curse had made her a monster. She'd screamed aloud to heaven, begging for absolution. Just one mistake. One little mistake, and now Bridie was gone forever. Brown-eyed Bridie, six years old, who liked applecakes and hide-and-seek. Who called her Auntie Rosie, and had mostly (but not altogether) stopped asking when Mommy was coming home.

But silence had greeted Rose's prayer.

Silence, and dark eternity as a demon's slave. Never be free. Never enjoy the sun. Never sate this terrible thirst . . .

Defiance burned like poison in Rose's hell-cursed heart. Praying was useless. There were no second chances. Heaven had abandoned her. And she'd spend the rest of her days seeking retribution.

"Angel Slayer," they called her on the online news feeds. Her tally had reached twelve. She wore the bloodstained feathers in her hair to prove it. And she'd keep right on slaying till the slaying was done . . .

Her ears pricked.

Footsteps. Just around the corner. Sure and almost silent.

She paused, beyond the streetlamp's dim halo. Listened harder. Light breathing, the spritz of male sweat . . . and blood.

Fresh, coppery, delicious, disgusting blood.

Her mouth watered. Prey. A human, abroad late at night in the Village, alone . . .

The dry stink of altar smoke made her gag. Ew. How had she missed it? Feathers zapping electric, bright steel like salt, the ozone tang of heavenspells.

Angel.

She laughed quietly. *Must be my lucky night.*

But this one smelled different. She inhaled deeper. Mmm. Sweeter, somehow. Fresher, the reek of heaven worn thin. Almost . . . human.

Her fangs crunched out, famished. She snarled, and forced them back in. Drinking angel blood was like swallowing acid. She'd tried it in ignorance, when she first slew an angel, and it blistered her mouth raw. A demon's curse and an angel's filthy glory didn't mix.

But *this* angel's glory sure smelled good.

The footsteps whispered closer. Rose murmured a poisoned wish, and around her, the darkness thickened. Warm shadows wrapped her body, caressing her. She crouched, thighs tingling. Two in one night. All the better. She'd stab this prince of bullshit through his lying heart and watch him die.

And tomorrow, she'd hunt down another. And another. And more, until her thirst for retribution was satisfied—and she knew with hell-black certainty that no matter how many she killed, it'd never be enough.

Before the curse, like any ignorant beast, she'd pondered the meaning of life. Whether she had a higher purpose. If there really was a god.

Now, she knew.

Her sins would never be forgiven. Her life meant less than nothing. And her purpose was to kill every lying, self-righteous asshole of an angel she could find.

Because God was real, all right. And He loathed her.

Japeth paused, feathers twitching.

There it was again. The faint reek of demon corruption . . . but with the added coppery stench of stale human blood.

Vampires. Maybe the Angel Slayer.

Cold satisfaction tingled his tongue. The shadowy vigilante had killed eleven, that they knew of, and Michael was pissed. Everyone was pissed, even the Tainted Host. The word was that the Slayer must be a higher-level demon, maybe even a new prince.

Japeth wiped sweat from his eyes. Demon, hell. Sure, the Slayer was inhumanly strong. But it wasn't a demon's style. Demons were like terrorists. They gloated. Wanted everyone to know who was responsible for their dirty deeds. They valued infamy over life, a twisted breed of courage.

This craven Slayer just stabbed you in the heart and flitted off into the dark. Japeth's mouth soured. A killer with no principles, just random malice. Worse: A coward.

Yeah, the Angel Slayer was definitely on Japeth's list.

But a few more vampires? They'd do sweetly.

He inhaled, relishing the power flooding his body. Since he'd been cast to earth, black rage frosted inside him, a monster who hungered to devour every hot, sweet, aching thing it couldn't have . . . and only the blood of the damned could satisfy it.

Only killing hellspawn sprang the glory alive. A hot, sweet rush, better than sex or uneasy chemical oblivion. It reminded him there was a heaven, and that one day he'd go back there.

Keep it frosty, angel. Michael's advice, from some ancient battlefield before Japheth fell. *Save your hard-on for the enemy. They're sure as shit saving theirs for us.*

But it was more than that. Japheth was Tainted, banished to earth with his soul held to ransom. Just one stumble away from hell. If he screwed up again, he'd never be redeemed.

And unlike Dashiel, Japheth hadn't given up on redemption. To bask in heaven's liquid golden sunlight again, away from the ugly temptation of earthly things . . .

Japheth sniffed, tasting rich summer air. The dirty scent was thickening. Silently, he lighted upwards and drifted around the corner.

Leafy, fragrant branches brushed his face. Red neon letters crackled, casting a hellish electric glow. Sweat slicked his golden hair. He floated into the shadows, searching with his magical angelsight for the telltale auras of living souls . . . and then his nerves wrenched at the sound of a woman sobbing.

There. His sharp gaze locked on her. Crouched against the wall, hugging her knees tight. Bloodstained jeans, tangled dark hair in a braid. He couldn't see her face, but she was long-legged, lithe, a glimpse of smooth skin showing where her t-shirt rode up over her hip.

Japheth stared, his heartbeat quickening. So . . . delicate. Vulnerable. And covered in blood, both vampire and human. Had she been attacked? Live or die, it was lose-lose. A blood-sucker's bite drove them mad, boiled their minds in screaming nightmares until they starved or bled to death from self-inflicted wounds . . . or until they mastered the curse, and lived on as vampires.

He should kill her now, while she was still herself.

"Get away!" The woman scrambled back, hugging those long legs tighter in an effort to make herself small. She was sniffling. Trying not to cry.

Japheth bit back a bad word. He'd seen countless humans suffer at demon hands over the centuries. His indignation was blunted, the sorrow dulled. But the idea of some sniggering hellshit wiping its foul sticky fingers on this woman . . .

Cold rage made his head ache. He had a job to do. Flash his knife, and slit her pretty throat . . .

The vampire behind him chuckled.

He whirled, and grabbed the slavering monster by the throat. *Crunch!* He held the thing at arm's length, fingers digging in. Just a young man, tiny fangs dripping, mad, demon-spelled hunger lighting his eyes.

Close call. He'd lost concentration. Curse her.

The boy squirmed. "Don't kill me, I didn't do nothin' . . ."

Japheth's palm sizzled, stinking. He squeezed harder. He liked pain. Pain was manageable. It reminded him what was important. "Tell me something I don't know about the Angel Slayer. You've got five seconds."

"Don't know nothin'!" Blood trickled down the boy's chin. Only a few days made, still mad with hunger. *Three . . . Four . . .* "I ain't never seen—ugh!"

Five. Japheth flashed his sword left-handed, and stabbed the vampire through the heart. Blue flames exploded, and the body withered to stinking ash.

He was a man of his word, after all. Lying was a sin. And he didn't remember it written anywhere that a promise to hell-spawn didn't count.

He vanished the sword, and his burned hand healed with a swift blue sparkle. Since Michael cast him down—the memory still stung raw, deep in his empty heart—that was the story of his life: *Better safe than screwed.*

Speaking of which . . .

That female still huddled against the wall. He could smell her terror, bitter-sharp like lemon. It bristled his feathers. What was she thinking, hanging around the West Village at night? Everyone knew the vampire coven was nearby. And now she was doomed.

But his fingers clenched tight, unwilling to strike. So delicate and innocent. Damnation was a b . . . well, it was unfair, when it wasn't your fault. When you caught it like a disease. Unlike the Chosen—who'd all submitted gleefully to the demon prince's tricks; how else did you swallow a demon's blood from the source?—she likely didn't deserve the place she was going.

He sighed, resigned. He didn't know for sure she was infected. And he couldn't just leave her here, covered in blood like shark bait. "I'll take you home," he offered coldly. "It isn't safe here."

She just sobbed, hiding her face.

He crouched, impatient, wings flaring. "Don't be afraid. I won't hurt you . . ."

The woman looked up, and Japheth's voice died, strangled by the sudden hitch in his throat.

Heaven's sweet grace, she was lovely.

He swallowed, painfully. Hot dark eyes, bottomless, framed in long, curling lashes. Exquisite heart-shaped face, bruised with bloody tears. A pretty dark spot graced her left cheek. And that mouth . . . He'd be haunted tonight by visions of those full, cherry-ripe lips. He wanted to taste them, drink the soft honeyed heat of her kiss . . .

He coughed. Yeah, well, he wanted a lot of things. Wanting and doing weren't the same. Like he'd remember how to kiss a woman in the first place.

But his skin tingled, hot and glittery, and blood rushed to all the awkward places. He shifted, aching. Lord, he was flushing. She'd see what he was thinking, laugh at him for it. "Umm . . . are you okay? You've got blood . . ."

"Yeah." Low voice, a husky promise of pleasure. She wiped her face, and laughed shakily. "They attacked me, but I ran away . . . God, I'm so embarrassed. I don't usually lose my cool like this. You must think I'm such a flake." She licked her bloody bottom lip, and turned her haunting gaze up to him.

Japheth stared, transfixed. The tip of her soft pink tongue was the most hypnotic thing he'd ever laid eyes on. *Hell, no. Don't go there* . . . but too late. He'd already imagined her warm dark flavor, the softness inside her mouth, that naughty tongue teasing his. Those swelling cherry lips, sliding over his cock, drowning him in her sweet heat . . .

He clenched shaking fists, willing this ugly desire to fade. He didn't know her. She was wounded, bleeding, frightened. Thinking about . . . those things with her was very uncool. *Heaven, forgive me . . .*

She inhaled, and the tiny catch in her breath quivered his feathers hard and hot.

And for the first time in centuries, his ice-walled resolve melted.

In a flash—*how did it happen?*—he was on his knees. The wall at her back grazed his palms. Her breasts swelled against his metal-clad chest. She gasped, rich with excitement, and hot blood pounded in his head and he wrapped his fingers in that sinful dark hair and gave himself up to her kiss.

Oh, Lord. She tasted of flames and blood, so good he groaned. For one precious, shocking moment, her lips molded to his, delicious, alive . . .

And then his mouth caught fire.

Pain flashed, accusing. Burnt skin soured his tongue. Her hair sizzled his fingers with telltale wrath. And a hot demon-spelled blade pressed sweet agony against the thudding pulse in his throat.

Vampire!

Ash rained like snow, the broken remnants of demon magic. Too late, hellcurse's foul stink sickened him. He'd been holding his breath, he realized distantly. Hadn't smelled it. Too fixated on sinful pleasures to see the evil glimmer in her eyes. But now, her scent was unmistakable.

No accidental vampire, this scheming seductress.

She was Chosen. Hell's whore. The demon's willing slave.

She laughed, and cruel, sharp fangs crunched out. "Bleeding Christ. You're all so fucking *stupid.*"

Japheth's mind stumbled, dizzy. His heart still pounded, his blood still screaming with toxic need. Should've known his irrational lust for her wasn't real. She'd spelled him with her evil magic, and he'd fallen for it spectacularly.

But that didn't change the ugly truth. The beautiful bitch was hellspawn. And he'd kissed her.

CHAPTER 3

Rose laughed, evil pleasure licking deep. Sweet fucking Satan. The dumb shock in this angel's eyes was better than sex. She could still taste him, coffee and chili and delicious *what-the-fuck-just-happened?* She licked scorched lips. Mmm. So innocent, this golden-winged altar boy.

Different from the others, who'd taken what she offered with sly, furtive delight. She smirked. Angels had the morals of rats, only worse, because they lied about it. But this one had kissed her wildly, his passion uncontrollable. Almost like he'd never kissed a woman before . . .

Whatever. His innocence only made her revenge on heaven sweeter. She gritted her teeth, and thrust her knife in for the kill.

But her steel met empty air.

He'd already swept up on golden wings. Coffee-scented breeze staggered her. She sprang to the balls of her feet, snarling, brandishing her knife.

Fuck. Too slow. She'd gloated too long, and now he'd gotten away.

The angel crouched, glittering wings backswept. One hand outstretched for balance, the other leveling his sky-fire sword at her, horizontal before his eyes. He wore dark leather pants and a silver angel's cuirass that sparked with electric blue rage.

Blood spotted his feathers, slicked in his sweaty golden hair. A dark and angry warrior, primed for battle. His gaze stabbed her, poisoned with malice, frigid and greener than hatred.

"Angel Slayer," he hissed. Barely audible, quivering . . . but not the passionate, reckless head rush of thirty seconds ago. Lethal rage, frosty, calculated to the last inch for the kill.

Jesus. Rose thought *she* had issues.

But her pulse raced, lacing her blood with heady fight-or-flight. She'd lost the surprise advantage that had helped her make her previous kills. And the bastard was strong, agile. Big, too, those glistening muscles packed with power. She'd need all her wiles to win . . .

"Very good," she mocked, circling to get a better range. "What's the matter, angel? Can't fight properly with a hard-on?"

"I always fight with a hard-on, whore." An ice-spiked laugh. His accent was elusive, mixed. "Maybe slitting your throat will get me off. Whaddaya say?"

"Have at me, then, sucker. You're cutting into my feeding time—umph!"

Blue fire scythed past her nose, sizzling. She swayed, dizzy. She'd ducked his blade by an inch. Fuck, he was fast.

But so was she. She dived into a handspring, and rolled to her feet, still threatening with her knife. He was already there, and kicked her legs from under her.

Excitement tingled in her flesh. Fighting was dancing, but with sharp objects. She whiplashed and jumped, aiming a back-handed slash at his face. He thrust up a wing, blocking her strike, and grabbed her wrist to fling her off her feet.

Her skull cracked the pavement. Groggy, she fought, but he straddled her, pinning her shoulders with his knees.

Wildly, Rose kicked, but connected only with a cushion of feathers. He slammed her wrist into the concrete. Skin sizzled on skin. Her knife dropped from numb fingers, and smoothly he aimed his burning blue sword point at her throat. "Don't talk and fight. It makes you careless."

Fuck! She wanted to scream in frustration. That was way too easy. He was good, she'd give him that. He was breathing hard, and she couldn't help noticing the bastard filled out his silver chest plate admirably. Blood stained his golden hair, and the big muscles in his arms gleamed with sweat. His shining feathers quivered taut with rage. His thighs strained inches from her nose—strong, hard-packed thighs, not one wasted curve—and as her gaze traveled upwards, treacherous heat rose in her belly. He hadn't been bullshitting about the hard-on. She could smell him, heady, more chili espresso than angelstink, with a musky lash of hot male flesh. An impressive hunk of powerful masculine beauty.

What a pity he was an arrogant waste of space with dogshit for honor.

And what a *stupid* fucking thing to be dwelling on, when he was about to send her screaming to hell.

Rose thrashed, and spat curses that blistered his fingers. She threw a spell, hellsmoke stinging, but he deflected it easily now that he was on his guard, and ash exploded, raining harmlessly. His blade singed her neck. Her wrist sizzled where he crushed it. She didn't care. "Spare me your preaching, godscum. I don't want to be saved."

"Oh, I won't preach to you, bloodsucker." His gaze glittered, icy. Impossibly green, this angel's eyes. "I wouldn't waste my time. You're already damned."

For a moment, she quailed. She didn't want it to be true. She'd made a mistake, let herself be seduced. What happened to Bridie was an accident. She didn't deserve this stinking, disgusting life. The blood, the slaughter, a demon prince's dirty urges, the endless threat of eternity in hell if she didn't comply . . .

But too late. She'd crossed that bridge. Bridie was dead. No going back.

And this angel's precious heaven didn't give a shit.

"Fine," she snapped. "Then fuck your god, and fuck you." And she spat, right into the angel's face.

It hit his bloodstained cheek, and sizzled to steam, and she waited for the burning thrust of steel into her throat.

But he just stared, his handsome mouth trembling, and in a sweet-smelling blue flash, he vanished.